C000008976

IN THE
LOST BOYHOOD
OF JUDAS

CHRIS HASLAM

- for

Matthew - and
Deborah.

Great to have, made
contact again -

ASHRIDGE PRESS

Keep well.
Every best wish, Chris

Published by Ashridge Press
A subsidiary of Country Books
Courtyard Cottage, Little Longstone, Bakewell, Derbyshire DE45 1NN
Tel/Fax: 01629 640670
e-mail: dickrichardson@country-books.co.uk

ISBN 1 901214 32 X

© 2005 Chris Haslam
Cover design © 2005 Liam Mills

The rights of Chris Haslam as author of this work have
been asserted by him in accordance with the
Copyright, Designs and Patents Act 1993.

All rights reserved. No part of this publication may be reproduced,
stored in a retrieval system, or transmitted, in any way or form, or by
any means, electronic, mechanical, photocopying, or otherwise,
without the prior permission of the author and publisher.

British Library Cataloguing in Publication Data.
A catalogue record for this book is available from the British Library.

Proceeds from this novel will go to
The Injured Jockeys Fund.

Printed and bound by:
Antony Rowe Ltd.

ACKNOWLEDGEMENTS

In July 2000 my research for the majority of this novel was stolen from the boot of my car at a local beauty-spot outside Cheltenham. There was nothing for it but to return to Australia, where I had done the research during a sabbatical from Cheltenham College, and start afresh. Everyone I asked in Oz was helpful, but I would particularly like to thank... Tony Abbott; Richard and Emma Allen; Cath Allen; Vonnie Black; Nigel Curtis; Libby Lyle and Chris Dixon; David Ernest; Hamish and Jodie Farrow and girls; Deirdre Frappell; James and Cath Freemantle; John and Vicki Haslam and boys; John and Elizabeth Isles; Paul and Monica La Cava; Peter McBride and Kir; Sally and John McKenzie and family; Steve and Kate Norris and girls; Val and Peter Norton; Marnie O'Bryan; Vicky and Andrew Rouse; Bridget Scott; John Sevior, Rebecca Gorman and Marcus; Richard and Lisa Smithers, and Barb and Brian Stacey...

Nearer home I have been encouraged by... Ros and Brian Art; Chris and Philippa Atkinson; Rich and Jo Bond; Kate Boorman; Martin and Jenny Bowden; Richard Brown; Kate Chamberlain; Gillian and Steve Collins; David and Kate Evans; Neil and Trish Folland; Steve and Fiona Gray; Sara and Damian Griffiths; Judy Grill; Sally Grindley and her twins, Chris and Sam; Sean Hamill; Jean, Bob and Anne Harper; Tal Haslam; Tim and Joanne Hastie-Smith; Will Hayes; Markus and Jon Hebbourn; Caroline and Sue Howe; Ken and Jasmine Hoyle; Robert, Eleanor and Edward Kirby; Mary-Lou Johnston; Ian and Sarah Keith; Richard,

Margaret, Vicky and Rachel Morgan; Mike and Lucy Muller; Ian and Cheryl McCluskey; Gary McIlvenny; Charles and Juliane Montgomery; Paul Montgomery; Will Nelson; Jean, Charles, Tim, Lynda, Robert and Graham Parker; Rowena Pratt; John and Anne Pritchard; Tim Saunders; David Shapton; Townley, Mary, Jane, Tim, Pauline, Abbie and Sarah Shenton; Ted and Barbara Sutton; Mark Tennyson; Nathan Thickett-Menghini; Nin and Loris Tinacci; Chris and Melanie Townsend; Peter and Beth Trythall; Vicky and Paddy Tuck; Wendy Tyler; Suzanne Villiers; John Watson, and Topsy Wood.

On the professional side I am indebted to Jane Bailey (my mentor); Karen Hayes, Joanne Harris, and the Arvon Foundation, where I met Gerry Hill-Male, Frank Hopkinson, Avril Leigh and Jill Shaw, all of whom have been stalwarts...

On the equine side I was much helped by John Francome, Edward Gillespie; Michael Henriques; Richard Pitman, and the Scudamore family: Michael, Peter, Maz, Tom and Michael junior...

On the technical side: Owen McNeir, Paula Watson, Vicky Lewis and Ed Robinson...

...and by no means least I am grateful for the encouragement from my English classes at Cheltenham College and Dean Close.

DEDICATION

This book is dedicated to my godchildren: Catherine Tolman, Chris Gale, Robert Burnell, James Hoyle, 'J.J.' Grill, Hannah Bond, Katie Watson, Kit Grill, Barnaby Reekes, Rebecca Muller, William Grill, Olivia Norris and Emily Farrow... a motley baker's dozen...

...and to my nephews: Myles, Bryce, Lloyd and Alfie, four horsemen of the new apocalypse...

'In the lost boyhood of Judas
Christ was betrayed'

George William Russell
('AE')
'Germinal'

CHAPTER ONE

Accidents happen on ordinary days. Lachlan Stacey was descending from the top of the Sydney Harbour Bridge, both hands on the walkway, when he looked down onto Hickson Road far below. A car pulled away fast from the wharf and knocked over a woman crossing the street towards Pier One. It was odd seeing the accident from above, like watching toys in sudden confusion. But no hand came from the heavens to stand the toys up again. His gull's-eye view saw the driver climb out and stand still, the woman under his car.

Then a policeman dropped his rucksack and ran to the stricken figure. Two women beat him to it, but moved away at his approach. A nun stood by the traffic lights, unexpected witness to the event. A coach was filling up its cargo, unaware. Everything was in slow motion.

Kerryn caught up with Lachlan and looked down.

"What happened?"

"The car just hit her. She was a sitting duck. From here it looked planned; it was so quick."

"Always is. Come on, Lach, keep going."

For a moment, he stood firm. The other climbers had not noticed the accident; still admiring the view on one of Sydney's crystal days, they pressed on along the gantry, harnesses clicking beside them. On Hickson Road a clump of onlookers milled round the car, which had reversed, but there seemed to be no panic. Lachlan was eleventh in the line of climbers, Kerryn behind him, bringing up the rear of their group. He was aware of the gap between himself and the ten people ahead of him. Looking round, he saw the next group was closing on him. Someone shouted and there was a ripple of laughter. In his headphone the commentary sparked back to life; he was more interested in the motionless woman two hundred feet under his gaze. But the other climbers were waiting for him, mystified; then they started to negotiate a steep staircase down to the right. The accident disappeared from view.

Robbie's accident, two weeks earlier, had caught Lachlan off guard. Twelve thousand miles away, in England, he had returned from visiting his errant brother in prison, to a quiet evening with friends in the Lake District. The calm had been shattered, first by a fox, then by a phone call. He thought back to his muddled reaction and swift return to the boy's bedside in the Intensive Care Unit of a Melbourne hospital. Fourteen-year old Robbie had severe head injuries and was battling for his life. The day after Lachlan reached him, his estranged wife, Kathy, had arrived from Vancouver, unannounced, together with her new partner, a rising Canadian politician. She had moved to Canada over a year before to further her legal career. Suddenly back in the maternal rôle she had relinquished, she was demanding that both boys returned to Canada with her. They would thrive there. Lachlan was accused of neglect: he had been on the other side of the world when the accident happened. Visiting a criminal close relative. Lachlan had come to Sydney for twenty-four hours to see things in sharper perspective.

Robbie was still fighting for his life. If he survived, Lachlan stood to lose the boy to his mother, who remained at the hospital, caring for her son in a way she had reneged for over a year. The boy lived on machines, unconscious fodder for a tug-of-war.

Lachlan felt Kerryn nestle into him, and turned. She was not convinced by his smile. He could no longer see into

Hickson Road, and the girl in front of him, an Italian, had gone down the steep iron ladder. Kerryn put her hand on his.

"Robbie?"

He looked beyond her.

"Phone as soon as we get down."

His eyes sought the apex of the Bridge from which they had descended. The next group was almost upon them, grey tracksuits speeding along like a caterpillar with an urgent message. He turned round and, backwards, began to climb down.

Having survived the walkways, they were back under the bulwark of the Bridge. Cold rocks sweated around them. Another group stood ready for their ascent, each climber adorned with a miner's lamp.

"Why are they wearing those?" he wondered aloud.

"It'll be dark when they come down," said Kerryn.

Time held no sway on the Bridge, so neither had any idea how long they'd been on the climb. Lachlan felt a distant sense of achievement, though the journey was so well monitored it was hardly perilous. Since Robbie's accident there was a numbness in him, a torpor that made excitement heavy. On the Bridge that numbness fled. And there had been a welcome moment of fear. His first step out of the shadow of the Rocks onto the Bridge itself had come without warning. They were high above a road. Gripped with weightlessness, as brain and knees swapped places, he gazed below. Small holes in the gantry impaled him. Dizziness took over. He stood still. It was easier being over water, he reasoned. His harness reminded him he could not turn back. But some people, overcome by vertigo, must have had to. The guide would be prepared for it, despite surprise from other climbers in the group. As a boy he had steeled himself to ride the big wheel at funfairs, but he could not brave modern monsters that threw you into space, then catapulted backwards, taunting gravity's control. He

3

swallowed, gripping the sides with white knuckles. His younger son ribbed him; at nine, Merrick was fearless, leaping from one dizzy height to the next, a modern-day Blondel on his Niagaran tightrope. Lachlan wanted the boy with him. He wanted both boys, Robbie walking, thoughtful, as Merrick chattered on.

When he and Kerryn moved into their cubicle to take off the grey tracksuits, he was reluctant to remove his. Anonymity had aided him.

"Do you think the woman survived?"

"Woman?"

"The one who was knocked down on Hickson Road."

"No idea."

Her nonchalance bit into him.

As soon as he was out of the building, he rang the Newcombes in Melbourne, with whom Merrick, and Kathy, were staying. He hoped the boy would answer, dreading his mother reaching the phone first. Instead, he got the ansaphone, which irked. Had Robbie relapsed? He dialled the number again for the same response and left a banal message to say he'd call back soon.

"I shouldn't have come," he fired at Kerryn, accusing. "Too much of a risk."

Kerryn said nothing. Self-flagellation was Lachlan's constant companion; already it was bursting into guilt.

Now he was earthbound again, he felt the numbness waiting to throw its cloak over him, but slowly. No torture was ever rushed.

The sun was still warm over the harbour as they walked down to Circular Quay: it wasn't 'circular', if anything it was rectangular. Rectangular Quay had no ring. Green and yellow ferries edged in and out among the congestion, the usual commuter rush hour.

"Drink?" Kerryn swung her hair in the breeze.

4

Lachlan nodded. They strolled along the concourse, past cafés, bars and entrances to jetties, where people headed without that look of despair captured by T.S. Eliot, the look that shows in eyes the world over at the end of a working day. Occasionally someone ran, dodging through crowds until he heard the clang of a metal grill as it shot closed. Kerryn was chatting about the climb.

"Great safety record," she affirmed. "No accidents there."

Lachlan's mind raced back to the woman who'd been knocked over. He needed to know what had happened. To prevent anything untoward happening on the Bridge, they'd donned the grey tracksuits, taken off watches and been allowed no cameras. Even handkerchiefs were banned, each climber having one attached to the wrist by an elastic-band. Nothing could fall, least of all a person chained to the Bridge by a foolproof iron latch that followed at his side throughout.

"Don't you think it's ironic?"

"What?"

He was impatient now. "That accident. For all our protection on the Bridge, we still see something happen in its shadow."

"The woman's probably at home now, absolutely fine," said Kerryn, pressing on towards the Opera House.

"She could, of course, be dead."

"Always the dramatist."

"Well, she could…easily. I don't know how you can dismiss the prospect."

Kerryn ignored him. His impatience grew…

"You only need something to happen once," he started, feeling a wave of sadness engulf him. He'd read articles on the man who'd fought for the Harbour Bridge franchise for years, determined to secure the rights to climb it. That endeavour had not been wasted. He had come through, against the odds.

Not everyone goes behind the Opera House, to the seaward side. In the full gaze of the Bridge they sat at a table with shrubs nestling against a sheet of glass, and ordered a bottle of Chardonnay. On the harbour, traffic was plentiful: a large cruiser eased past, its tannoy audible. Spacious yachts bore down on smaller craft hardly moving on the sparkling water. A plane droned over the northern beaches. Tourists who ventured this side of the Opera House walked with purpose, conscious of being out of bounds. Occasional umbrellas denied some tables their sun.

A few bars of song rang out to their left, then died. Lachlan wanted them to continue, unsure at first if they were from a passing vessel or the mighty building above them, its pointed triangles unusual from this angle. Lachlan wondered again if the story that the Opera House was designed by a Dutchman who had never seen his winning creation was apocryphal.

Kerryn was reaching for her glass when there was a thud next to their table and a cloud of dust. A lump of pinky-brown earth lay on the concrete beside them. They shot eyes up to the harsh glass above, seeing reflections of people passing inside the building, but there were no clues as to the lump of earth. Underneath the white sail directly over their table, two lights shone, helpless, in the sun. Lachlan could see concrete that was dirty, but not crumbling. Two joggers had stopped, seeking the source of the mystery. A waiter ambled out, unperturbed.

"This happen often?" asked Lachlan as the man passed, tray balanced on two fingers. The waiter paused, holding on to his tray, looked up cursorily, then moved inside without answering their question.

"Obviously," said Kerryn bending to finger the earth, which disintegrated on contact with flesh. "No such thing as a perfect evening," she laughed, red nails clasped round her glass. The couple at the next table was oblivious to the earth-fall; the woman pressed jewelled hands into her man's arm, despite a lack of interest on his part.

"Relax, Lachie. It's not going to happen."

"I'm not so sure," came his reply.

They moved slowly back towards the quay, Lachlan dialled the number in Melbourne again. Same lack of response.

"Ferry or jetcat?"

He mused. The light was just starting to fade for their journey across the harbour.

"Jetcat."

A statue stood on stilts by the jetty, covered in silver paint. But it did not remain a statue for long: every time a passer-by threw cash into a tin box open at its feet, it abandoned stillness for calasthenics to reward generosity with a silver windmill, or a silver lollipop. People flattered the statue's ability. But her reaction spoilt the illusion; she was not a statue, more an automated joke. Lachlan was reminded of the acrobat he and the boys had seen in Chester.

"Don't be so serious," said Kerryn, catching up with him. He said nothing. They walked away, pausing by a manhole cover in the pink and grey tarmac. There were several covers commemorating writers with a link to Australia. A quotation sat in the centre of the studded plaque with a potted biography of its author at the base. No one else was reading the inscriptions. Purple and lime green flags alternated along the edge of the wharf, proclaiming the up-coming Writers' Festival. A piper in full Scottish dress struck up ahead of them; the noise reminded Lachlan of reels at faraway Hogmanays. Kerryn saw his expression and commented on his mass of contradictions.

"Isn't everyone the same?" he shot back testily.

"Not everyone." She pursed her lips. Anticipating what game he would play was losing its lustre; he was not easy company at the best of times. She felt pressured.

A cruise liner had swanned up the harbour, dwarfing all

7

except the Bridge. The tops of white-vested figures scurried about on different levels as the vessel sought its berth. Against the white of the ship's mass the Opera House's sandy brickwork looked suddenly tired.

"Where's Moldavia?" asked Lachlan, seeing black letters on the ship's hull.

"Not where you'd think."

"How do you know where I think?"

"Go on then."

"It's near Poland, a new east-European state. Didn't Sherlock Holmes pursue his deadly enemy to some water-fall there?"

"Moriarty."

"That's him. Good name for a villain." Lachlan did not smile.

"I've a feeling it's the West Coast of Africa. But your answer's more fun."

She took his arm. The liner had blocked out all the green and yellow ferries zipping in from Manly, Neutral Bay, Parramatta and Taronga Zoo.

A woman with a bag boasting 'Liz Davenport, New Bond Street, London' breezed into Kerryn as she stood gazing at the next plaque. The woman muttered a brief apology, and moved on, heels increasing their hectic pace as Kerryn concentrated on Joseph Conrad's affectionate words for Sydney Harbour. When had the Pole been to Australia, Lachlan wondered, looking up beyond the busy railway station to monogrammed office blocks, pencils stark against the sky.

One of the ship's crew dropped off a small gangplank, and landed silently a few metres ahead of them. He looked at Kerryn and smiled, a swarthy hand ruffling jet-black hair.

"Moriarty?"

"No such luck. Friendly fellows the Moravians," said Lachlan. "Of all east-Europeans they are the most amenable." Kerryn's eyes welcomed the bait.

Aboard the jetcat, Lachlan's eyes roamed the harbour. Dusk was almost non-existent in Australia but it was darkening now. When he'd first landed in Australia the light had captivated him. There was so much sky, stretching down to touch the horizon whichever way he looked. He'd seen the light captured in the paintings of Frederick McCubbin, whose tawny landscape 'Down on his Luck' hung over Lachlan's Melbourne fireplace. Visitors found it depressing; he savoured its captive mood.

The jetcat belched and was soon cutting a swathe across the bay, as if mocking the cruise-liner, already deserted. They sped past Rushcutters' Bay, Point Piper, Rose Bay, heading on towards Vaucluse. The beaches sprinted by. At the entrance to the harbour, where they were veering left, a destroyer forged through the Heads. Wind-surfers played duck and dive with the jetcat as they passed in open water. Eyes played tricks in the light. It was a fascinating seascape. Shadows cut into yachts, whose crew hung out into space, tipping and slanting in the feisty breeze. The declining sun lent them a macabre touch. Kerryn was trying to read, feet up on the railing, watched by a lone seagull, preened for gazing. A water-tower topped houses stacked at all angles for a harbour view.

As they came into Manly, Lachlan saw the fairground, its wheel motionless, coloured baskets like abandoned fruit gums against the fading blue sky. Red roofs predominated around the bay; a yellow water-taxi breasted the jetcat's swell. Straight ahead a tall building peered out from behind Norfolk pine trees, challenging the sunset, where streaks of muslin cloud spread out, starting to tinge with colour. To their left 'SHARKS' stood out on the aquarium and Lachlan realised he had never taken the boys there. Wind-surfers still dipped nearer to the shoreline. A lone crane looked like a giant hair-slide propped up against the horizon. Moored

9

boats all pointed the same way.

As soon as the gangway slid into place, passengers gorged onto the ramp, and down into the road. The luxury of a taxi was too good for Kerryn to miss, and they roared up the hill to Balgowlah. Lachlan rang the hospital the moment they were home. There was no change but he left a message for Robbie to say he'd be back next day, and put the phone down feeling as he had with that first step on the Bridge. The meal Kerryn produced had little taste.

He knew he would dream. But the severity of his brain's nocturnal activity surprised him, again. He was on top of the Harbour Bridge and, as he leaned over, he dislodged a piece of metal. The iron fell slowly towards the water just as a passenger ship was passing underneath. Lachlan saw catastrophe coming. His dream slowed down, prolonging the moment. The iron sought its target with care, selecting a young boy playing quoits on deck. He was knocked to the floor, then down through several layers into the dark engine room, where he landed, skewered on a rusty anchor. Lachlan did not wake at once. The dream allowed his gaze to zoom back from the stricken child until he flew upwards to the top of the Bridge, like an eagle, preening non-existent feathers.

"You look cheerful," taunted Kerry at breakfast before suggesting a swim, which Lachlan declined. He was tense.

"You've time in hand," she ventured, passing over the Vegemite. "We could nip down to Shelly beach on the way to the airport."

He looked at her, fighting the notion of congesting traffic. Kerryn stood up, pushing the last piece of toast in his direction. "Build yourself up."

"I'll get my swimmers. Just in case."

They swam. At an early hour the beach was not quiet, businessmen opting to taste the Pacific en route to work, or jog from Manly Beach, Dee Why, even Curl Curl. Lachlan was amused by Aussie names. He'd once stayed on a farm in the north of the state for a friend's wedding and enjoyed dropping his thank-you card to 'Touchwood, Tumba Rumba Road, Book Book, Wagga Wagga, New South Wales'.

A Sydney winter's morning resembles high summer in European countries, as Lachlan's recent visit to the U.K. had reminded him. There he had plucked up courage to swim in the ocean twice in Devon, where by mid-afternoon the sun had warmed the water as much as it could. But still they froze, he and the boys. An arrowhead of memory struck him as he saw Robbie dive into the water on a long stretch of beach where American soldiers held an ill-fated rehearsal for the D-Day landings in World War Two. He remembered the tank recently winched ashore and Merrick's joy on inspecting it at close quarters. Less than three weeks ago. His mind telescoped: time eluded the brain, so that big events seemed both recent and part of bygone history. Merrick's gaze at the tank was fierce, causing Robbie to catch their father's eye before moving on.

The number of men who had drowned when the practice landings went wrong was hard to assimilate. Cold black water in endless high waves coming from all angles made visibility impossible, heightening panic, pumping the pulse in ears straining for the call of another human voice. He thought, again, of the woman knocked down on Hickson Road.

Ahead of him, Kerryn was far out in the bay, head bobbing under a lime-green cap. Lachlan trod water as he watched her, envying the fact she was at ease.

Towelling down, he saw she was still some way from shore. A glance at his watch confirmed it was not as late as he'd thought, but there was no time to linger. He dressed quickly, then crossed to the cafeteria for two coffees. There was a queue; he affected nonchalance, though jerky movements gave him away. Kerryn ran up and put a wet hand on his forehead from behind. He pressed back anger;

the smile did not materialise.

"What did Henry Mackinnon write? 'Mankind is destined to live on the edge of perpetual disaster.' He was right."

"On the edge of. Not permanently entangled in. Don't be such a fatalist."

Lachlan saw a man pick a leaf off one of the trees, twirling it in his finger for a moment, till he let it fall, its existence not registered in the unfolding of his day. 'As flies to wanton boys,' muttered Lachlan.

"Where's that from?"

"'King Lear'," he replied, surprised she'd heard. "One of my favourite lines."

"Sounds punishing. Typical you."

"Meaning?"

"You know what I mean. I bet you're still wondering about that woman yesterday. Did you want to ring a few hospitals?"

He looked at her. "That's a bit close to the knuckle."

She stood, biting her nether lip.

"Sorry. But it is wearing."

"What is?"

"You being so pessimistic."

"I'm not pessimistic."

"No?"

Impatience crossed the border into anger.

"You care too much," she ventured, echoing a line Brodie had thrown at him during 'Macbeth' rehearsals.

"Is that a fault?"

"You tell me."

Looking up, he saw a helicopter hovering over Watson's Bay. Nearer to them, a plane was etching its message in the firmament. 'Happy 21 Bir. Lachlan stood and watched the aviatic scribe. The 't' was proving tricky.

The café had a garden fringed with palm trees; bougainvillaea blazed, even in July. They wanted to stay, but turned their backs on the place, concentrating on the coffee in its tacky polystyrene beakers. Lachlan looked up to his left. The city was never where he expected it to be, so it took a moment to locate the top of the Bridge like a criss-crossed rope over a deep line of trees. They passed a young Australian wooing an excitable Japanese girl on a low wall, beside the pathway. The girl was paper-clip thin. Lachlan's stride was checked; fears had fights inside him, wrapped in endless layers like pass-the-parcel, desperate to be pulled apart. They walked on towards Kerryn's car.

There is something about the smell of Sydney. Its harsh cosmopolitan make-up and fickle weather make it the subject of banter among Melburnians. Yet still Sydney has a lure Victoria's capital cannot match. People think Melbourne English and old-fashioned, quaint criticism of a country born in 1788. But Lachlan felt there was more going on in Melbourne: dance, music, sport and theatre in venues cross-wording the city. He'd seen plays in closed-down churches, car showrooms, gardens, garages, gymnasia, even the jail. Sydney is racier, glitzy, American, her jewels displayed on loan to the world; Melbourne guards hers. Sydney for a holiday; Melbourne for a life.

On the drive to the airport he was tense; he knew there would be roadworks. And the Spit Bridge chose to open at an unheralded time, causing more tight nerves in his head.

"There are planes every half hour," said Kerryn, eyes ahead.

"That's not the point. I said I'd be on the 11.25."

"Said to who?" Kerry murmured to herself.

"Bridge or tunnel?" she queried as they bounced through Mosman, past a Mexican restaurant where he'd once burnt his thumb, ending up at the Medical Centre late in the evening. A female Asian doctor had looked after him with unexpected joviality.

"Bridge, of course." He hated tunnels, and lifts.

Flashing under the parapet they'd conquered not twenty-

13

four hours previously, Lachlan looked across at the Opera House. Its roofs were more magnolia than white, a mushroom shade favoured by the English, not common in Australia. Above them he saw specks of people advancing like Lego men in their uniforms. Until yesterday he'd thought climbing the Bridge reduced its mystery. Now he knew different.

At the airport he was numb again. Kerryn's sunglasses were twirled round her fingers from habit as she kissed him on the cheek. He hugged her, glad of the warmth. She was not sporting her usual bracelets, making her arms look bare and pale. He was reluctant to let her go.

"I thought you were in a hurry?"

He still held her, eyes shut.

"My love to the boys." She hadn't met them often. "I'm sure Robs will pull through. But we don't want him going off to be a Mountie."

He nodded, though attempts to conceal emotion failed.

"I'll be in touch."

After check-in, he rang the Newcombes. Jo said that Merrick had gone off to soccer. Kathy was at the hospital.

"I'll go straight there," he said.

On his way to buy a paper he was unable to shake off a memory of some years before. Kathy and the boys had taken him to the airport for a Teachers' Conference in Brisbane. As he turned from the monitor telling him his gate number (she had been unable to linger), he watched her back view disappearing, holding hands with both boys. Merrick was jumping in the air, still holding her hand as Robbie plodded down the concourse exuding purpose. He told himself it was a celluloid scene from a film, not a life, but the memory was with him, out of his control.

He made straight for a copy of 'The Sydney Morning Herald' and even before paying was scouring the paper for news of the accident on Hickson Road. He found nothing, then sat down in the lounge, certain a more thorough search would reward him. But there was still nothing. He had to know what had happened, how the victim was. Calmness was beyond his grip; he saw a student sitting opposite. Lachlan needed to make contact with the accident, as people had with his. Infinite strands of a web spun by strangers reached out to him; he wanted to mull over the fact that, like him, they'd had no warning. No warning over a breakfast, perhaps snatched with a husband detailing his meetings that day while the victim stayed silent, anticipating her hours to come. It wasn't just about death; it was about the jolt to routine, to life as it had been, as it promised to be, still. Teasing us into feeling safe, making plans, enjoying responsibility, looking forward.

He wondered if there'd been a newspaper report on Robbie's accident. No one had said. The student was staring at him. There was an announcement: a slight delay. Lachlan was unmoved.

"Have you the right time?" the student asked, having plucked up courage.

"11.10."

"My watch is fast," came the reply. As he altered his watch, Lachlan asked himself why he couldn't wind back time to the day the boys landed back in Melbourne. Mockery of the gods, again.

By the time he boarded, he was aching with fatigue. The break had exacerbated, not alleviated his trauma. He felt no strength for fighting Kathy, or helping Rob pull through.

The plane gathered momentum. Engines roared, his head was blazing. He saw Botany Bay beneath the wing, and pounded his neck into the cushion. The woman behind said something; it sounded like Kathy's voice.

"I've taken the boys. Both of them."

CHAPTER TWO

As Lachlan left the theatre the Melbourne evening was still warm. He opened his shoulders, seeing a tram coming from the city towards his stop. It was noiseless, for a moment, then a high-pitched squeal rang out as it lurched on. He jogged across the road and jumped on to the running board, waiting for a moment as a smart woman took her time to alight. She smiled at Lachlan, and too late he responded with a lame crinkling of the lips.

The tram was far from full, despite it being the first day of the Australian Open Tennis, an event Lachlan's boys were eagerly anticipating. He'd earmarked Saturday for it. Stifling a yawn, he reflected on his day; directing 'Macbeth' was always fraught. He'd never taken much notice of the superstition, though he enjoyed referring to the play as 'Harry Lauder', and he relished the scope the tragedy promised. Brodie, his co-director, had been pleased with the actress playing Lady Macbeth; female psychology was a feature of the production. Lachlan was happy with that; it gave him room for male psychology and this particular Macbeth, a man of no great experience but much potential, had already shown himself keen to experiment in the scenes with Lady Macbeth. For three days each director had worked alone with the protagonists; tomorrow would see if the two co-alesced.

The man in front shifted his paper and Lachlan caught the headline, predictably on tennis. As a kid he'd always copied out the draw for Grand Slam tournaments, first at Wimbledon and now here in Australia, something the boys no longer needed to do now computers gave all the information at a touch. Lachlan was not a computer man, to his sons' amusement. "You're so out of it, Dad," said Merrick, often, as he continued to punch the stone grey buttons with unrelenting chubby fingers. Lachlan usually smiled, or tried to. Computers couldn't yet tell Shakespearean actors where to stand, how to speak lines, or what to feel. His more technical mates told Lachlan with glee that the day was not far off, a prospect that made him shudder.

He yawned again, and smiled at the speed with which lines from the play shot into his mind. Rehearsing was exhausting, but he was used to it. It went with the territory. On the rare occasions when he directed lighter plays, Lachlan had to admit he felt less taxed but also less fulfilled. It was said that comedy was hardest of all to direct, but he wasn't sure. The plays that had given him most joy had been serious, if not without a vein of humour he worked hard to highlight.

Having grabbed pasta and salad from the nearby shops, Lachlan turned into Harrison Street. The boys would be hungry now. No sooner had he put his key in the lock than there was an explosion of noise and two fair-haired lads raced to the door, competing as always.

"I'm ravenous, Dad," said Merrick as his fingers probed the bag of food in Lachlan's hand.

"Sampras has just won the second set," asserted Robbie, speeding back to the screen. "That's him two sets up and going for the record." Sporting records intrigued Robbie, and he reached for his baseball cap. The cap was almost colourless now; Lachlan had brought it back from New Zealand, and it became Robbie's talisman.

"Are we still going to the tennis on Saturday?" asked Merrick, quietly, as if afraid there'd been a change of plan.

Lachlan smiled. "I think so," he replied, dropping the pasta into now boiling water, his eye falling on a letter from England that lay waiting on the table. It was from Rebecca

17

and, as always, she had adorned the airmail envelope with colourful stamps for Robbie's collection. The stamps were striking: four butterflies spread across the right-hand corner. Lachlan studied them for a minute: Grizzled Skipper, Brimstone, Painted Lady and Dark Green Fritillary. The Grizzled Skipper was the most imposing. He remembered the Ulysses butterflies he'd seen in the Queensland rainforest, a piercing aquamarine.

"Can I have those stamps, Dad?" piped Robbie, holding them up, his thumb leaving a mark on the pale blue envelope.

"Yes, when I've read Beck's letter," came the reply and the lad was gone, back to his tennis.

When the boys had gone to bed Lachlan was able to relax with his sister's words. Before opening the letter he gazed at it. Letters were life-blood to him, writing and receiving them; through his life they'd been stepping stones glinting in the sun, a never-ending reflection of his odyssey. He hoarded letters and diaries, rarely reading them again but knowing they were there and enjoying that knowledge, a touchstone that energised. Sometimes he would leave a letter unopened for days, anticipating its contents, revering it; he was seldom disappointed and hoped his own letters had a similar effect on their recipients.

Air mail letters were especially precious; in his year off after school, travelling in Europe, he'd gone with excitement to the poste restante of cities in France, Spain, Switzerland, Austria, Germany and Greece. Bilbao had been a treasure trove for letters: seven of them waiting for collection, and rationed over the coming days like favourite chocolates kept out of the sun. He'd not expected letters at every call, but Geneva, Munich and Athens still had a black mark, yielding no correspondence. Now friends urged him with a sort of ruthlessness to communicate by e-mail: so much easier, quicker, facilitating the instant reply, but

Lachlan was not convinced: with letters he was in control.

He slit open Rebecca's missive with the letter-opener given him by his godmother for his 21st birthday, carved in the shape of a quill: he'd lost it once for more than a month, and guarded it after that, knowing where it lay, using it always. The letter was incident-packed; his sister was a rigorous correspondent. Writing as she spoke, Rebecca was able to create atmosphere out of the tiniest happening. Today's letter was full of her plans to convert a room in the house she and her partner shared in Chester into her physiotherapist's surgery; it would be a squeeze, but they could do it. Lachlan smiled to think of Saul's reaction to the plan. Saul was full of schemes, always on the move, just like Rebecca. They carried others with them in their energy, including her elder brother, when he was in their company.

In addition to creating the practice room Beck was painting the house. Two years ago, when she and Saul had come out to Australia not long after Kathy's impromptu departure, they had stayed in the city one weekend when Lachlan took the boys on a fishing trip, and he had returned to find the dining-room a new shade of apricot. On entering the room, he had laughed out loud, much to the relief of Saul, on his knees at that moment finishing the beading that served as a skirting-board, a quaint English term that made Lachlan smile.

"It's different," quipped Rebecca as she walked into the room with a bottle of white wine and three glasses.

"Certainly," replied her brother, "and in time, I might even get used to it."

"Zany," muttered Robbie on passing through to the garden, and Merrick had simply raised his eyes heavenward. Two years later the apricot seemed subdued. No doubt the Chester neighbours would soon be treated to supper in a vermilion' dining-room. Lachlan was not the only one obsessed with colour.

Beck and Saul had been to the races at Haydock Park, she wrote. Gloriously crisp day, azure sky, good fields and Saul had found three winners. He was a shrewd punter, who said little when making selections, but always allowed for the possibility of returning to the bookies' satchel to relieve them of its weight. They'd all been racing in Melbourne when Saul and Rebecca were over, but Lachlan remembered Dame Fortune had toyed with them cruelly that day, as she had on other days, under more serious circumstances than when they put a few dollars 'on the nose'.

The end of Beck's letter was more weighty. She had been trying to arrange a prison visit to see their brother, Iain, Lachlan's twin, but her letters had fallen on stony ground; she had received no reply. Although Iain did not share her predilection for writing, it was unlike him not to reply. Iain and Beck got on well, both having decided at their respective times, and for different reasons to return from Australia to England, or Scotland in Iain's case, and they had seen each other frequently, until the incident. That had truncated things, as it had between Lachie and Iain, though Lachlan was determined this would prove only a temporary blip. No, 'blip' was too casual; 'hitch' was more appropriate. 'Rub,' Hamlet would have chosen, crisp and close to the quick.

Lachlan read the letter again. What was his sister saying between the lines? Having taught English for years, Lachlan was alive to nuance. A colleague at his last school, one of several private institutions in the city, had played the cynic. "What are words after all? Only sounds in sequence, totally unintelligible to half the world's population?"

Lachlan had revelled in the counter-argument, taking up a sabre conflict with this devil's advocate. Too few colleagues had been vital enough to debate, even at lunch with the hour's freedom it ensured, so it was left to the senior students to offer colourful variance to Lachlan's views. As a director, he now enjoyed different arguments, where words could be conveyed to release the meaning they underpinned; the most convincing actors to work with were those who developed their own ideas in rehearsal, much of which was spent travelling beneath the words, turning different sides to the light.

As he put the letter down in front of him, he became aware of a form curling awkwardly round the door like a drunken question mark.

"Can't sleep, Dad."

Lachlan got up and pulled the boy to his side. "What are you thinking about?"

"Not a lot."

"Really?"

"It's Mum's birthday tomorrow." There was the trace of a sob, stifled.

Lachlan knelt down, his face close to Robbie.

"So it is, mate. I'd forgotten."

"You shouldn't."

"No, maybe I shouldn't"

"No 'maybe', Dad! You shouldn't."

"You like a hot chocolate?" said Lachlan.

The boy nodded, rubbing his eyes with a forearm. "Are you having one?"

"Why not?"

Any age was bad when your mother deserted and when it happened Robbie had just turned eleven. Whereas Merrick had been presented with the fait accompli of his mother's sudden departure, Robbie had sensed the lacuna growing. He'd internalised it, producing school work of sobering depth, which had not escaped his English teacher. At the parent/teacher interviews this woman, a New Zealander, sensed she was on tricky ground confronted with both parents in the nominal five-minute slot. Kathy gave a strong performance as the encouraging mother and exposed no chinks. Lachlan's eyes could have given it away; when he saw the teacher again some weeks later he'd wanted to ask if she had read his eyes that day, but desisted: talk of the boy was more important.

Over the ensuing two years Robbie had come to speak of Kathy more frequently, aware that his father had no answers, asking questions like was there a theatre on Vancouver Island, were there whales off shore, how long did letters take to arrive? Despite his youth, he was aware of Lachlan's pain in these conversations, breaking off abruptly if there was even a flicker of uncertainty in the response. He'd be a good teacher, Lachlan thought, though at the moment Robbie claimed he was going in for the law.

It was past eleven when the boy padded out of the room, his faded surfing shirt askew on brown shoulders. Lachlan sat on: so many of the boy's questions were still his as well. He traced the lines of one particular enquiry the boy had made of him, something it had taken guts to ask. 'Gutless' was one of the charges with which Kathy had pole-axed him, and he found it hard to fathom. He tried to apply reason as to why their marriage had wrinkled away, but made no headway now, as then.

He reached for Rebecca's letter and read it again. She had written in her turquoise ink, which cheered him. It was six years since he had last gone back to England, when he was still teaching. When they were still a quartet. They'd stayed with Rebecca, who had not yet met Saul, crowding into her small flat on the outskirts of Manchester, which gave him an excuse to take the boys to a soccer match. Back in his Aberdeen childhood, Saturday afternoons at three o'clock had been hallowed times, their father escorting his twins to the match whenever possible, one of the rare occasions when he'd removed his dog-collar. Once, they'd seen a fight, when a young supporter of the opposing team hit an old man with a bottle; Lachlan was surprised at the ease with

22

which the bottle broke, green shards splintering around him with splashes he hoped were red wine, but knew were not. The old man crumbling in front of him in slow motion had never left him, explaining his fear of violence, even when directing fight scenes in his plays. He had a good sword-master for 'Macbeth', a Scotsman, aptly, whose painstaking fight plots had intrigued Merrick. The young boy had booked himself into a rehearsal, watching wide-eyed throughout.

Lachlan's mind raced into the rehearsal schedules: after this production there was Timberlake Wertenbaker's play, 'Our Country's Good', then the controversial 'Wolf' and lastly Gogol's comedy, 'The Government Inspector'. That took him up to mid-July. He could go to England in late June. The boys might have to miss a few days school before their mid-year holiday, but they would survive.

He was amazed at the speed of his decision. They would spend time with Rebecca and Saul, aim to see Iain, and have a holiday. He'd not been to Devon and Cornwall; perhaps now was the time. And those friends of Kerryn in the Lake District had always said he was welcome. He could take almost three weeks.

Decision made, he stood up quickly, letting the letter fall onto a coffee table. The boys would be chuffed. He switched the kettle on for a last cup of tea and went back to the dining-area surrounded by books. Something new was what he needed now. His fingers flicked along one of the shelves, most of whose inhabitants he'd read, at least once. There was a great deal of Lawrence whom he'd studied at University. That was a complicated man. Yet much of his writing hit the spot: his essays had been a fascination of Lachlan's, not least the one in which he advocated the need for two lives: one to learn our mistakes, the second to profit by them. Such ideas often sprang to Lachlan's mind. A Frenchman, La Rochefoucauld, had struck a chord with him; he remembered particularly the notion that in the misfortunes of our best friends we find something that is not unpleasing. That still made him feel bad, twenty years later, because it was true.

Robbie had recently studied one of Lawrence's poems, about a snake coming to the poet's water-trough in the shade of Mount Etna. Lachlan showed Robbie other poems; the boy liked 'Humming-Bird' best and had taken it to his room. Now Lachlan plucked out an orange-spined paperback which David Newcombe had given to him last birthday.

He read the first two chapters in bed, having looked in on Robbie. Tomorrow held its usual fist of challenges; Lachlan noticed the clock said 12.34. It was often that time when he reached for the light-switch. Into his head came one of the lines from 'Macbeth' they'd been working on that day, sleep knitting up the 'ravell'd sleeve of care.' Gentle image in that savage play. He turned over, conscious there was too much space just for him, and waited for sleep to come.

CHAPTER THREE

Lachlan was standing in the middle of a maze five feet high; a red kettle squatted on a stone plinth, beside which was a carved fox, sitting upright. The fox winked at him just as the kettle boiled. He noticed a playing card in the grass and bent down to pick it up. It turned into a toy helicopter. The fox jumped off the seat and trotted stealthily away into the maze.

Without a pause he was in a small cabin inching up a forbidding mountain. Someone else sat opposite him, but had covered her face. Below, two kangaroos hopped out from under the trees onto the icy run. A race was in progress, and the slalom posts were all vicars holding a loaf of bread. When the next skier came hurtling down, the two kangaroos tried to bar his route; he took evasive action and soared into the sky, turning into a giant butterfly with writing on one wing. Lachlan was on the floor of the cabin trying hard to read the writing. His companion showed neither interest nor surprise at his antics. The butterfly began to float towards them, but at that moment the ski-lift shuddered to a stop. Lachlan felt pain and realised his left knee was bleeding. There had been a broken bottle on the floor of the cabin that he'd failed to see.

And then he was laughing, loud, gutsy laughter, sharing it liberally with a band of nuns in an Italian square. A dalmatian eyed them solemnly. Just then a farm girl in red and white shorts started to collect eggs. For every egg she took she left a small pizza. The nuns laughed on as a car, one of the old Gestapo-like vehicles, swept into the square, bearing Mussolini and a beautiful woman. She threw

25

crocuses out of the car, which stopped by the nuns. One of them, smiling, ventured forth with her arms outstretched. There were firm, generous hugs as a small boy ran up to the nun and began tugging at her habit. She took no notice. He jumped into the car from which Mussolini had vanished, and was driven away, waving blue and yellow flags.

When Lachlan woke up, he'd had other dreams, he knew, none of them lasting as long as the feature-length ones; this was not unusual. Some nights he had six dreams and wrote them down while they lingered. Once or twice lately he'd had a rich variety of dreams, but other cares intervened in the moment before wakefulness, driving his colourful pictures away.

It came as a surprise when friends said they had no dreams. Not that they couldn't remember them, but that dreams simply didn't come. He wasn't sure if he envied these mates or not: the thought of uninhibited sleep both drew and repelled. With him, dreams came to stay.

A friend at the theatre was good on dreams. Often Lachlan thought he had explained a dream, at least for himself, only for his friend to come at the dream from exactly the opposite angle. They dabbled in Jung and his theory of synchronicity. Lachlan had always seen that as coincidence, things happening in close succession, knowing something before it was said. Now he was not sure there was such a thing as coincidence. Déjà vu fascinated him, as he began to realise that images didn't have to go into the subconscious before the dream. Not long ago he'd dreamed of a well-shaped skull, and two days later he noticed a stone in a derelict house that was a perfect skull, so smooth. His friend threw the name Yorrick at Lachlan, the starting point to thoughts. Lachlan felt a kinship with Hamlet, and thoughts emerged about Yorrick before he became a skull.

Yorrick was the first death in Hamlet's life. Since the bushfire Lachlan felt close to death.

His daydreams were reassuring because he was more in control. Night dreams were less manoeuvrable, though sometimes he'd been successful in setting up a dream, then enjoying it. Those dreams left him feeling different when he woke. But he still wrote them down.

That day's rehearsals did not go well; by lunch he knew there would be no squash game in the early evening as planned with Dave. They were entrenched in the banquet scene, Macbeth taking time with his lines, Lady Macbeth archly keen to try out the psychology she'd worked on with Brodie. Banquo was bored. It was his scene, Lachlan had told him. They could have dispensed with the actor, fielding instead some mechanical presence, or state of the art shaft of light. But this production was full-blooded: Banquo was there, alive, with his gory locks. Most actors would relish the scene. Lachlan had directed the play at school, and he remembered Banquo's over-zealous enjoyment of the coagulate. Not so now. He felt his irritation rise. It was hot, a January Wednesday in Melbourne, the temperatures expected to rise up to 38°, and the public preview of 'Macbeth' was in ten days' time. Ross was wheezing apologetically, Angus a blaze of sweat, only Lennox gave his all for what was to be his début. Brodie was in brittle form, her clipboard barking out disdain for all but Lady Macbeth. Had Brodie ever played the rôle, Lachlan wondered? She'd spoken the lines not long ago when Lady Macbeth was 'indisposed', keen to exhibit that female psychology crucial to her understanding.

Macbeth yawned, catching Lachlan's eye. He was used to seeing ghosts. Lennox kept smiling throughout. Ross ceased to wheeze. Banquo disappeared and they ran the scene without him. Brodie's clipboard made less noise until Macbeth was wading in his sea of blood, which she cut short. Banquo sidled back, chewing, looking at his luminous watch, a gesture more attributable to Fleance. He sneezed; Lennox blessed him.

Ghost scenes were notorious. Shakespeare. Ibsen. Much easier for an Elizabethan audience, Lachlan said. But were 16th Century denizens so used to the supernatural they accepted it unwhimpering? In Sydney one of Kerryn's mates had asked who'd seen a ghost, and Lachlan had been surprised at the lack of response. He'd trotted out his own experience, again.

It had been a warm day in late spring, what the English used to call Whitsuntide. These days Lachlan's understanding of Whit Sunday was a golden island off the coast of Queensland; then, it had been a week off school, a grey granite building not far from the sea in Aberdeen. The sea was just as grey, a favourite author called it 'gunmetal', but in the spring it always held the promise of sunlight speckling across it, endless ripples of a lighter grey that, if watched for long enough, might turn blue. Rarely had Lachlan seen that blue, but it was possible. By contrast, the sallow cement of school could never lose its shell of slate; all days away from it were treasured.

His parents couldn't afford the full week's holiday, they could never leave till Monday with his father's strict Sunday régime, so day-trips were decided upon, and on this day they had gone to Findlater castle, the only castle he remembered with a view of the sea. This castle held instant promise, and on their arrival instinct triggered 'hide and seek.' Lachlan hid first; he was found within minutes, a beaming Iain already intent on his chance of escaping his brother's eye. He ran off with glee. Whilst waiting for the statutory seconds, a time he wittingly cut short, as he knew Iain did, Lachlan gazed down from the ruined battlements. His parents were sitting on a seat not far from the entrance to the castle, a gateway emboldened by the rusting teeth of its impressive portcullis. Rebecca read to their mother on the seat. A girl in a wheelchair was being pushed up the slope by a large man two steps in front of a smaller woman. Behind the woman, a boy trounced along, hands in pockets, kicking stones. Lachlan felt a sudden bond with the boy, part of him wanting to run down, arms outstretched like a Spitfire and enlist the boy's help in finding Iain. His father looked up and waved. Lachlan did not respond; he was all of eight now, fiercely independent, on a mission of discovery.

It was hot. Their mother had cautiously put the twins into identical yellow sweaters she had knitted; they both wore grey shorts and ankle socks in unstriking fawn. The usual echoes of symmetry. They had different colour tooth-brushes, but that was all.

Lachlan yelled 'Coming!' to an unheeding silence and sped off in search of his brother. It was getting warmer. He sought Iain briskly, confident of success, though conscious he need not linger; competition between them was strong. Minutes later he stopped in the ruins of what a notice informed him had originally been the kitchen. It made him hungry. But he had work to do, and time was sidling by. He looked up chimneys, down dark stone staircases, into child-size crenellations reaching out over the sea that today was blue. Iain was nowhere to be found.

Back where he started, he looked down towards the gate-way. His father waved again, then returned to his paper. Rebecca was chasing seagulls; he could hear her squeals; his mother was crouched behind the girl, hands reaching for her legs like a wicket-keeper, watching.

A moment of cold air surprised him; he was getting anxious now. The castle had been combed. How could a boy escape detection? Running down towards the keep, he saw a cleaning lady with a headscarf and overalls. She smiled at him as he bulleted past. Stopping, he spun round; there were no rules now, he could ask.

"Excuse me?"

She looked up and smiled again.

"Have you seen a boy dressed just like me? Anywhere?"

29

In his memory she leaned on a broom. She was gentle, not as old as he'd supposed. And she told him. Lachlan ran back through the kitchen to the wine cellar. No one. In the corner was a recess, but he'd looked in there. He edged nearer, now inexplicably tense. He had looked inside, but he had not looked inside and above. There, three feet above him, in a recess expertly made for the purpose of hiding, he saw a pale fawn sock, and grabbed it.

Jumping down, Iain was both exultant at the long time his brother had taken, and angry that he had been discovered at all.

"You had some help," he accused.

Lachlan said nothing. Even without speaking, the cleaning lady would give the game away when they passed her in the corridor.

"All right. So how did you know?" pressurised Iain.

This would go on all day. It was simpler to give in.

"The cleaning lady told me."

"Cleaning lady?"

Iain's face was a picture. For once he was silent, thinking. "But they don't have cleaners in castles."

And he was right. They spent half an hour excavating the castle, but she was gone into the ether. Lachlan even asked his father, still sitting on the seat with his paper.

"Did you see a cleaning lady go past here, Dad?"

The vicar was surprised; even allowing for the boy's fecund imagination, it was an unusual question.

"No, Lachlan. Why?"

"Nothing," was the reply. He glanced at Iain whose face registered triumph.

'I win," he said smugly.

Humour was the Newcombes' hallmark. David was a dentist in the city, Jo a counsellor for Years 11 and 12, at one of the private schools. Both had been at university with Lachlan. Jo, a year older, moved in many circles. She was the serious companion of men, which explained her softer side: not for her the strident Aussie female assertiveness, she was of gentler, milder mould, yet more than able to assert. For that reason she had got on well with Kathy, meeting her often for coffee, as well as in their foursome. Lachlan was aware that Jo and Kathy were still in touch, but the former avoided mention unless there was something to impart concerning the boys, which she handled with minimum fuss and, at times, a little humour. She was the go-between.

Dave and Lachlan had long been mates in the full Australian sense. After a casual introduction the first Sunday at a cocktail party after church, their paths had crossed often on the sports field, where Lachlan was impressed by Dave's generous nature in defeat. The budding teacher even went to a few dentistry lectures, earning himself the tag 'mascot' in an attempt to understand how his friend would endure life probing the cavities of strangers. The attempt had failed, to Dave's amusement, an amusement increased when, years later, Lachlan asked him to be his dentist. At that moment, at the country wedding outside Wagga, Dave had thrown back his head roaring with laughter, a roar that was his trademark. His laugh revealed David's sturdy teeth, and one still uncapped crown, about which he was careless.

The dentist supported Lachlan's thespian career in his amateur days, during which time Lachlan, as assistant stage manager, once swept up a pair of dentures that no one claimed, not even props. They now sat proud on a busy shelf in Dave's waiting room. The men were godfathers to each other's sons. 'Touching,' Kathy had observed when Lachlan told her Dave had agreed to be godfather to Robbie; in Christian life, unlike so many other matters, she appeared content to let Lachlan make the running. For months before leaving, she had chosen not to come to church with Lachlan and the boys.

Over dinner Lachlan told the Newcombes of his spot-decision to go to England later in the year.

"Can I come?" said Jo, dark eyes blazing with excitement.

"I'd expect no less," returned Lachlan, and Dave smiled. The Newcombes were always happy to look after the boys, great companions with their own children, Harry, fourteen, and Emily, twelve. For years the families had gone on holiday together, often in a couple of rented camper vans. Starting with a trip to Adelaide one Easter, when the kids were small, they had loved the Barossa Valley, enjoying the unexpected German flavour of the small towns there. One Easter Saturday they had a memorable time at Oakbank races watching the Von Doussa Steeplechase, prelude to the Monday's Great Eastern. Lachlan had taken a picture of the horses thundering up a gentle gradient towards the fallen oak tree, a picture he still had, and Dave, despite protests of luck never smiling on his gambling ventures, had napped the winning outsider, Gold Ramekin. Kathy had played safe with the favourite a, fast-finishing third. A fine drop of red had been taken that night.

Easter had proved a good time for holidays; the next year they ventured to Alice Springs and Ayers Rock. Far North Queensland was a hit and Port Douglas charmed them; they rode horses through rain forest onto the beach and, having unsaddled them, into the sea, an experience later featured on a holiday travel programme. One night they'd left the vans and camped on a beach, only for Dave to be admonished next morning by one of the locals; a croc. had been seen on the beach not four days earlier. Dave took his rebuke with dignity. Venturing further afield to New Zealand proved a trial, with rain every day bar one, but waterfalls had stayed in their memory, ebullient, insistent, gorging.

And when Kathy left, Jo and Dave sent Lachlan to the Top End, to the Territory. He'd spent a few days in Darwin years before, and looked in on the sights of Kakadu; this time he joined a Wilderness Walk for nine days, seeing only wild horses, the odd bird of prey and wonderful scenery. Walking with total strangers had proved a boon: he had nothing to live up to, no reliability to maintain, could show only the parts of himself he chose. The isolation was searing and soothing at once. He'd developed a rapport with the guide, a Tasmanian, and the other walkers had been affable; in different circumstances, two, at least, would have become friends. More than one night he'd lain awake on his rock bed looking at a moon that grew full, then burst into a sliver of banana in the silence of a heat-drenched day, a gentle conspiracy that went some way to calming his questions.

As always, the boys had been fine with David and Jo. Returning to Melbourne, Lachlan stayed on at the Newcombes' for several days, then faced the silence of Harrison Street. Sensing a change was vital, he left teaching within two months, starting at the small Melbourne theatre that had once lent one of its number to Lachlan's school as an actor-in-residence. It had been the presence of this actor that convinced Lachlan to move from the job he still loved, when allowed to do it and not bundled in the bureaucracy that had changed school-teaching forever. With Kathy gone, this move had seemed less of a risk, although Robbie was not convinced. Risk-taking was anathema to him.

There was no question the boys would come to England with him.

"You'll see Iain?" said Dave, refilling Lachlan's glass.

"I'll try."

Dave smiled. He'd never met his friend's twin, and understanding him from what he'd gleaned was not easy. Dave had an older brother on a property in Queensland, to whom he was close enough. There were no complications. Occasionally he wished there were, some gremlin to blitz that would bring them closer together. He tried to imagine the gremlins for Lachlan.

"Does that mean you won't make Easter?" Jo leant

forward. They had sketched in a week on the Great Ocean Road; now the kids were bigger, they needed to be occupied.

"Not sure, Jo," came the reply. "I'll try."

Robbie and Harry came in, with Merrick not far behind, stifling a yawn.

"We're off," said Lachlan, rising, "See you at the tennis on Saturday."

Harry nodded, keenly, punching Robbie in the ribs as he ducked out into the hall.

"Game Agassi," he baited.

"Game Sampras," came the swift rejoinder. For a moment Merrick looked lost.

"Who are you barracking for?" Jo asked him.

"Not sure – yet," he replied. "Tell you when I've seen them play."

"Just like his Dad," said Dave.

It was after 10.30 and they drove home in silence. No letters lurked in the mailbox, just a couple of 'flyers'. In the hall sat the publicity team's designs for 'Macbeth.'

"Something wicked this way comes," read Robbie. "Good poster, Dad. Who designed it?"

"I did."

A snort from Merrick showed denial was unnecessary. "Sad case, Rob. You'll probably go the same way."

But Robbie was already with his book.

CHAPTER FOUR

The theatre wasn't in Lachlan's blood. But it had become a passion. Tracing it back was something he'd found himself doing more and more as the frustrations with his teaching vocation had been first admitted, then probed. Over thirty years before, he'd gone one wintry night with a friend, Jonathan, and his parents to see, 'Wait Until Dark' in the gloomy Regency building that housed one of Aberdeen's two theatres. They sat upstairs on the front row and he was enthralled, following the play's twists and suspense with a kind of pleasure he hadn't felt before.

During the interval his friend's parents had spoken of other things, trivial and incongruous. He wanted only to follow shooting lines of thought fired by the plot; it held so much. His friend had not noticed Lachlan's discomfort; he was eyeing other members of the audience with interest, a severe disappointment to Lachlan. Back home, he told his parents every detail he remembered, knowing that he had created only a vestige of the suspense. His father had followed every detail, his mother soon buried herself in some chore. It had been a birthday treat for Jonathan. Lachlan felt it had been wasted.

Before his own birthday came around, in mid-summer, he had scoured the papers to see what would be playing that night. It was an old-fashioned, adult play his parents told him, not realising the depth of his urge to return to the theatre. He had gone to the cinema, the 'pictures' they called it then, and seen an epic on the Roman Empire that ended with a crucifixion. But it hadn't made up for the

35

immediacy of a live performance. Jonathan preferred the film to his own birthday event, which at first smarted with Lachlan, but quickly passed into a different feeling.

Soon after, they had left for Australia. Abandoning friends had not been easy, and the experience was exacerbated by the fact Jonathan had left Aberdeen only weeks before Lachlan. His departure had been sudden; he told Lachlan at Sunday School one week, and was gone by the Thursday. Lachlan was deeply saddened. He felt there was a mystery at work. He had been given Jonathan's address in a town in the north of England where the railway ran close to the sea, and had written, once, to Serpentine Road. Settled in Australia, Lachlan had written a fuller letter, in handwriting neater than any schoolbook had ever seen, expecting his friend to be eager to hear of a country across the other side of the world. But there had been no reply. He felt let down, remembering Jonathan fiercely. How could he check the address was right? Who would help him? His father had started to listen one evening on the verandah of the new bungalow they now had in Melbourne, but a parishioner had called him away and the thread was not taken up again. If Serpentine Road was still there, Lachlan could look him up when he went over in the Northern Hemisphere summer. But he didn't hold out much hope.

It had taken ages to go to a theatre in Australia, which was odd in that their city was festooned with them. His parents had been more than once before they yielded to his pleas. He'd seen a musical, glitzy, fast moving, with catchy tunes, but he hated the ending. It was sentimental and took the heart away from the rest of the show. The bubble broken, Lachlan deserted the theatre for a time, his interest only rekindled by a part in the school play in Year 11. That, too, was an American musical, 'Guys and Dolls', but it was vital, had its own life, boosted him during rehearsal as much as performance and the spark was back. It helped that he was enamoured of the girl, a year older, who played the leader of the Salvation Army, pumping her trombone with zest.

In Year 12, the school did a Shakespeare, 'Much Ado About Nothing'. To his surprise, after the auditions, the director asked him to consider taking the rôle of Benedick. He demurred, believing himself not up to it, letting the chance slip away, and accepting the rôle of Leonato instead. If he had the chance again, he'd have taken Borachio or Don John, indulging the sympathy for villains that had sometimes surprised his students in later years. He'd not yet directed Iago, but was moving in on it. 'Harry Lauder' would help. As a teenager, watching a competent but uninspiring Benedick had not made him envious; it gave him chance to look on as an outsider, see how direction was given, instructions absorbed. The seed had been fertilised.

With the arrival of the actor in-residence at his school, Lachlan knew the seed had burst open. The actor, a tall gangling man, had thrown himself into the school production that he had chosen, an unusual, demanding play, parts of which were staged with captivating skill. Lachlan stayed on after lessons for rehearsals, came in all day Sunday, and was able to back up the actor's professional skill with an enthusiasm he assumed had ebbed away.

His interest had led to many late chats with this mentor in Lachlan's lounge-room, to Kathy's growing annoyance, culminating in their application to co-direct a play at The Tinderbox Theatre, a small concern outside Melbourne city centre in an old granary warehouse. Together they staged a competent production that did something to restore the theatre's sagging fortunes. When the actor left for Perth, Lachlan had stayed on, at first part-time, then full-time, combating the unusual hours with energy that seeped back imperceptibly after Kathy's departure. The boys were always a live concern in his attempts to stick to rehearsal schedules; again the Newcombes had proved outstanding friends.

The company Lachlan and newly arrived Brodie had

gathered around them was set up along old-fashioned repertory lines. The year before they left for Australia, an actor in Aberdeen had come to the gaunt vicarage as a paying guest. The man provided essential extra income to the vicar's family but had been kept at arm's length, which surprised Lachlan, as his father's favourite scripture was, 'Practise hospitality'. In later years he saw this treatment of their paying guest as typical of the English reserve his parents had clung to rather sadly in Australia, a place that knew no such reserve and was altogether more accepting of people.

The paying guest worked hard; he was hardly ever at the vicarage. One week he would be performing in the evening; at the same time, he would be rehearsing during the day for the next play to be put on, whilst somehow finding the time to read a third play that was moving ever-nearer on the dramatic schedule. His father worked hard, having little time for the twins, or Rebecca, but the guest worked harder still. He had left the vicarage at the end of summer and it did not escape Lachlan's notice that the theatre was closed until the next spring. "Went dark," someone told him, a phrase that stayed in his thinking, awaiting a key.

In the city now plays came and went regularly, each one bringing a company that performed for a while, then moved on. Financially, The Tinderbox could not compete with major theatres: his actors stayed longer, were paid less and had to curb their wanderlust. Now that 'Macbeth' was close to opening, Lachlan and Brodie had to turn their attention to 'Our Country's Good.' He had no doubts about that play succeeding, but the piece after that, 'Wolf', was a worry. Brodie had said from the start that 'Wolf' would not work: the risk was too high, the play itself obtuse. Lachlan's determination was strengthened by his refusal to share her view, and he was prepared for a battle royal once rehearsals got under way. Meantime, he needed to flex his interpretation of the play.

It was avant-garde, though the presence of so much theatre in and around the city rendered that term almost archaic. Set in the Russian Steppes, with more than a hint of Chekhovian chill and no hint at all of Checkhovian warmth, the play told the story of an unmarried station-master, who turned his stultifying isolation into gruesome deeds of calumny, all the time retaining his apparent joie de vivre at the railway station and, in time-honoured fashion, avoiding detection until the dénouement. Savage attacks were carried out on simple peasants, ostensibly by a wolf, whose mind-set stopped short of killing, but had no qualms about inflicting serious physical damage on his victims. He waited hours before he pounced, letting intended victims catch a glimpse, then disappearing for hours, only to return and perpetrate his deed. The mental fear he aroused was more striking than the physical pain. At the end, predictably, he took one leap too many and was apprehended by two young station-workers in a small hut by the single railway line. It was a coup de théâtre in Lachlan's opinion. The incensed animal was howling in pain, only a lantern lit the dim scene, but as the wolf leaped on to a rickety table he froze, as did the two workers.

Lachlan had seen the play, just once, and its ending had made a deep impression. Slowly the creature had torn off his wolf mask and clawed at his naked body in a frenzy, sharp nails shredding the tough hair on his skin until his nails filled up with blood that he sucked, longingly. Lachlan had been on the front row close to the actor; a piercing orange light had meant he could see the finger nails as they filled up with blood. But his eye had been drawn to the legs of the table; they, too, were filling up with blood. The lantern had gone down on the shuddering naked corpse, and an eerie light came up, slowly, on the four table legs. Blood continued to flow down the legs. The body was still breathing from its exertions and the play had surely ended. But blood had now filled the table legs; they crashed to the floor, the corpse with them. The lights cut for a second, then a single spot leaped out above the carnage. On the floor sat a domestic cat, its lips trickling with blood. Rarely had Lachlan been so stunned. He was unable to move, or applaud, and had remained sitting on the front row until a stage-hand came out to pick up the debris. The cat had gone, but blood still remained. Lachlan touched it and his fingers stayed tacky for days. It made Lady Macbeth's sleepwalking scene rather less dramatic. One day he knew he would direct 'Wolf'.

"Ridiculous," snapped Brodie. "It'll never work. The story line's too thin, the effects gratuitous and who would play that rôle?" Lachlan had waited to find the right actor. The rôle was demanding, but he knew the actor would come along one day. He said nothing to Brodie during rehearsals for 'Macbeth,' but it had suddenly come to him, that day of 38° when the company had not been firing. Angus was his man. Soon he would break it to him, when the time was right.

One thing Brodie could do was a warm-up. She fired straight into her actors, be it first thing on a 40° northerly morning or midway through a lacklustre session. She would hurl herself into a series of physical and verbal gymnastics that left most of the company struggling. Having been an actress, of which Lachlan was made well aware, she was well versed in techniques for relaxation, exercises she termed 'theatre sports' and long sessions were enlivened by her infusion of energy. Lachlan joined in with the rest, often enjoying it more than he'd expected, always reminded of the rather clumsy warm-ups to which he'd been subjected at university, where practical aspects of the curriculum were less obviously valued than the cerebral. He had chosen English and Drama over straight Drama, a choice he did not regret. But Brodie had more experience, and she revelled in control.

This particular morning her régime had worked well: lips were sliding readily to all corners of the facial range, gargling had been effected and the batch of actors now hung loose-limbed, eyes fixed on the iron ring of a trapdoor which Brodie had convinced them was the last brain cell after Armageddon. Lachlan wondered how many of his actors saw a slant of devilment in her stentorian orders. Lady Macbeth did not; she stared in fascination at the ring, her mind inching round as she prepared to yank it up and embark upon the journey of that single cell. He noticed she was sweating, freely, her lips purple with concentration, the furrows well sculptured in her wide, low brow.

"And relax......Your call's in ten minutes. No dress. Full technical. Keep those mouths moist."

Lachlan's was far from moist; he was perhaps not alone in this. Brodie jostled through to him and they were soon under way.

It was an uneventful technical rehearsal. The cauldron proved too bulky and Macduff was too quick with the fight. But the large scenes went well, banners unfurling in the confines like obedient dragons happy with no fire. The trumpets were early in Act Five Scene Four, and kettledrums needed attention, but there was surprisingly little traffic through Brodie and Lachlan's headphones. To finish early was unusual. Ever-patient Norman, the stage manager, brought them a cup of tea and disappeared behind the well-worn mannequin that held Macbeth's armour, humming to himself as usual, neglecting his own thirst. The theatre cleared fast as actors made for their freedom. Notes would be given 9.30 next morning.

Lachlan did not leave with the rest and found himself sitting on the king's cumbersome throne staring into the black. After a show it did not take any theatre long to be deserted. Some patrons referred to The Tinderbox as a studio, others a workshop theatre; he never minded, as long as they turned up for the shows.

Sitting for some minutes he was thinking of the trip to England. The country would be buried in greyness now, that interminable grey to which any weather would be preferable, even rain. In summer, as he remembered, days could be crisp and blue, but these days were rare as hen's teeth: the grey would always be waiting to ambush them. It was hard to think of England at the end of an Australian January, but by June even Melbourne would sample greyness; he would be ready to go overseas then. Already he had thoughts that were nudging at him, thoughts a long way from being framed, which he hadn't experienced before. Iain was in their slipstream, but there was another sensation, chimeric, distant, not quite comfortable. Like the aftermath of an accident. Very faintly he'd been aware of it the day he decided to go, even in the speed of that decision, crisscrossing Devon, Chester and The Lakes. Was it edged with fear or just apprehension? He tried to confront the feeling, but like those cheering dreams, it eluded him, even in the darkness here. He had such odd thoughts, echoes of deaths that had not yet taken place. Echoes was not right: they came afterwards, not before. What was the opposite of an echo?

There were so many people at the tennis, and it was a muggy day. With four children to look after, Lachlan was keen to get there as early as possible, but even arriving on foot the quintet was held up by crowds. Already the children had run out of drink; long queues were inevitable and, with matches under way, progress towards food stalls proved frustrating. They saw the end of a Women's Singles that had gone to three sets and the loser brushed by them en-route to the locker room, Harriet's request for an autograph unheeded in the throng. Sampras was due to play in the Rod Laver arena in the evening session, but Agassi had an afternoon match later on. Waves of support rang out from where Philippoussis was duelling, while Lachlan and his charges saw the end of a tactical encounter between a Croatian and a Swede. One of Lachlan's ex-colleagues from school greeted him on the stone steps, and there was a moment of panic when Merrick took time to bring back five ice-creams, two of which were beyond redemption, having melted away.

"Women's Doubles next," said Robbie glumly, his disappointment shared by three other males. Harriet wisely decided to stay silent. Instead they fought for more drinks and watched the end of the Philippoussis match on a giant screen. Beyond it, cars screamed into Melbourne under the mid-afternoon heat haze and Lachlan was reminded of the humid New York ending to 'The Great Gatsby.'

"I said, when's Agasssi on, Dad?"

Lachlan turned to Robbie.

"You were miles away. Do you know when Agassi's playing?"

"There's not really a schedule, son. Depends on how long each match lasts."

"Well, roughly then?"

Lachlan looked at his watch. 'It's the last game of the afternoon session. Maybe four thirty. But we've only got two Laver arena tickets."

"Shall I relieve you of those? For me and Harry."

"Harry and me."

"Stickler." The boy's eyes gleamed, then clouded suddenly. "Mum used to correct me on that, you never did – then."

About to reply, Lachlan's gaze was taken by Merrick straying into the path of a large car bearing Philippoussis away from the stadium. The player raised his hand at Lachlan, then sank back into cushioning.

"Somebody might hand their ticket in," said Lachlan.

"That's really likely."

"But not impossible," countered his father.

And somebody had. Two tickets for the show court. Lachlan told Robbie and Harry they could see the second half of the match and urged Merrick to be chivalrous with Emily, whose eyes were now bulging.

'It means you'll have to look after her. We'll swap tickets with the boys after the end of the second set. Meet at the gate on the ticket, Gate 15.'

In the event, Lachlan saw much of Agassi's first two sets through a gap in the cement-work. Meeting Merrick and Emily, he saw his son holding up a third ticket he'd procured from a man about to leave the stadium. So he went in with the boys.

Agassi's lithe and tiny frame dispatched his Swiss adversary, all too quickly for the knowledgeable crowd.

"He's like a butcher," said Harry, in awe, as they threaded a slow way home.

At least we didn't have to see the Williams sisters," said a relieved Merrick.

"Didn't see Sampras either, which is more to the point," muttered Robbie, putting on his cap.

Assembling for notes next morning before the dress rehearsal at midday, Lachlan was aware at once there was someone missing. Angus smiled at him and Lachlan returned the greeting: the man looked him in the eye, little suspecting the challenge his director intended to give him. Must pave the way soon, mused Lachlan, as Brodie stepped onto the stage in her customary black.

"Lennox is crook," she announced, not without a hint of glee in Lachlan's view. Lady Macbeth muttered something predictable about the play's cursed history, Banquo looked a trifle smug.

"You'll have to do it, Lachlan." He smarted; standing in for an actor was never easy, and with their limitations, understudies were unaffordable. Yet the director needed an overview, needed to see how everything fitted, from different angles of the theatre. Lachlan enjoyed dress rehearsals for the freedom they gave him to move around. It was vital not to be a part of the play. Now Brodie was in control. The lines were not a problem, the inconvenience was. Brodie slipped into sole charge. Having originated from the Western suburbs in Sydney she knew how to fight. The tussle had left her lacking in gentleness, as her dominant will continued to exhibit. But she was a good actress in Lachlan's view. Watching her now, as she gave notes to Lady Macbeth, he realised how much she would have liked to play that character, how much thought she had given the wife who is present so strongly until the play is half over, then disappears until her 'perfumes of Arabia' scene. At university, one lecturer, a male, had presented stirring evidence of the mathematical way in which Shakespeare crafted his two protagonists in the Scottish tragedy: there was value in his conviction, but Lachlan liked to think of Shakespeare as less of an abacus man, more a random jotter.

He gave his notes, some of which tailored sweetly with Brodie's. They did not compare views at this stage; that would happen after the dress rehearsal. Sometimes Lachlan had been surprised how willing she was to be converted; in time the chinks in both their armours had come to be less fiercely guarded. As a production came together, it benefited from their different approaches, female inspiration, male constancy. Lachlan thought directing was like teaching in many ways; it became increasingly hard to shun the politics noose, but alone with actor or student he could do so; he was still fired by the scope no one could take from him. Some friends had seen his move from school-room to theatre as a risk; to him it was a continuation of the vocation he'd had since Year 11, once his absorption with law had started to recede.

The rehearsal began twenty minutes late, a fact Norman picked up by tapping his watch-face with a twinkle. Lachlan took this gesture as a reminder to remove his own watch when he went on. The play was set in modern dress, dark blue rather than black, with packing cases not a solid set. It wasn't minimalist, that concept had never appealed to him, in or out of the theatre, but there had been cuts, for both he

45

and Brodie had wanted a focused production with no fraying ends. Banquo started off with uncharacteristic conviction, which caught Macbeth off guard and smartened him up, to the amusement of Third Witch, whom Lachlan had touted strongly for Lady Macduff. Brodie thought Third Witch a better rôle; he felt now she was right.

Waiting for his first entrance, Lachlan was surprisingly nervous. This was one viewpoint from which he had not seen the production. He knew of its shortcomings, notably in King Duncan, an actor of years' experience who had never risen above attendant lord. Duncan was a pinnacle for this man, but he hadn't yet cracked it. He had a slight limp, which made Lachlan sympathetic in his handling of the actor, a fact Brodie had not missed.

"You care too much," she said, not choosing the best of times. He was the only man he knew who felt sorry for people on looking at them, people on the tram, strangers at church, passers-by at an outdoor café, old people opening a purse. And it went further; only Lachlan would mourn a pair of sunglasses. Brodie was right.

Lachlan survived. Angus threw him a brief compliment as he placed his sword on the props table, and Brodie concurred. But Lachlan felt he had missed out on his overview, and silently wished Lennox well for the next day. On tour with one of his school productions Lachlan had to go on and deliver a one-liner in an R.S.L. hall near Mallacoota; it had been the subject of mirth for some time afterwards. He'd been happy to step back into the director's rôle then, as he was now.

Throughout the run, he made notes, complacency, he'd once read, being the cancer of time. There was never a perfect performance; it was a matter of aspiring. But he saw every rehearsal and every performance; each scene had a moment when it was done to the best of his actors' ability and piecing those moments together in his head gave him the definitive show. There was a sense of pride as well as possessiveness; the best directors always struck him as private in their final analysis of work staged. That certainly applied to Brodie.

"Quick wine?" she offered, more tentative than usual.

"Sure," he replied. The play would open with a yell. And Lennox would be in rude health. 'Tomorrow...'

CHAPTER FIVE

When she stopped calling him by name, he knew. Inevitability had been growing, concealed from the boys, he hoped, but if he had to pinpoint a moment when he and Kathy were sundered, it was the day she failed to add, 'Lachie?' to her question.

'Do you still need this?' sounded stark, unfinished, immeasurably harsh. He looked at her, but she wasn't waiting for the grace of a reply. Her back as she went out of the room looked hard, as if protected by a metal corset. He gazed at the space through which she had passed; it rebounded off him and retreated, hurt. Years of living with a director had taught Kathy how to sustain a rôle, but she had skilfully changed that rôle over the years. His being out late at school plays, on duty, at Parent/Teacher interviews hadn't helped, but now he saw no purpose in analysing the faux pas that had led them to impasse. A man of instinct, too often raw, Lachlan knew things had ended between them, though part of him marvelled at the way she continued to act with the boys.

Jo had been aware; there was no fumbling pretence with her. But he had wanted to tell Dave, confident Jo would not have done so. Choosing the time proved difficult; after hoping for days that the opportunity would present itself, he had to engineer an hour over a beer one evening after a dull staff meeting had overrun, leaving him anxious and sweaty. Dave said little, nodding now and then, his hands, hairy and comforting, spread on a pockmarked table. Later he shared his thoughts with Lachlan, quiet thoughts, not entirely

48

surprised. Only once had Lachlan seen him lose his temper, an occasion that stayed with them both.

At church Lachlan had spoken to the vicar briefly, and to his curate in more detail. Church had been part of his life since Aberdeen, despite a lapse at university. At school, he burrowed into his work, creating, suggesting, hinting at other people's emotion through the literature he loved; that kept his own emotion at bay.

One person had noticed his anxiety. Hetty Redvers was no psychologist, but she was shrewd. Around the same age as his mother, she had a stimulating faith, and was a Christian who lent another layer of meaning to the word 'good' without trumpeting her conviction. Until two or three years ago she had run a Bed and Breakfast in Mount Macedon, an hour out of Melbourne, with her husband, Gideon, a doctor not long retired. Lachlan and Kathy had taken the boys up there one long weekend and stumbled across the property advertising 'Bed and Breakfast' in a disused railway carriage. The boys were intrigued, leaping from the car to inspect the place, and Merrick tumbled headlong into deep grass. A woman came out of the house to welcome them, after which they stayed two days in the carriage, striking up a firm friendship.

Not long afterwards Gideon had gone for an early morning run and come back feeling fine. He was a man who prided himself on his level of fitness and was a strong swimmer. After a shower, he had felt odd and sat down. Minutes later he was grey. The irony of ringing for a doctor had been with Hetty long before this fated morning. A young G.P. came, swiftly, but it was too late: Gideon had suffered a severe heart attack. The couple had one daughter in Perth, who flew home at once, then remained with her mother for several weeks. During those weeks they decided to sell up so Hetty could move into the city. She no longer felt inclined to offer bed and breakfast; Lachlan spotted an auction for a house round the corner from them and bid for it

49

successfully. The local church had become first Hetty's haven, then her stage.

Lachlan's godmother being still in Scotland, he had adopted Hetty as his own. She had no time for fuss; she did things briskly, always. She swam daily in the local pool, served on committees, read voraciously and loved children. The Sunday after Kathy's departure, it was no surprise that Lachlan and the boys found themselves at her table for a roast lunch after church. Dessert, a wild berry crumble with ice cream, had won her to the boys and when they sat down with a video on the Roman Empire, one of Gideon's abiding loves, Lachlan found himself talking openly to Hetty. She offered no saccharine comfort, in fact Lachlan thought her rather harsh on him, but she had a capacity for listening. She was also wise. In a short time their conversation moved into beckoning meadows from arid scrubland, dwelling awhile on literature, a mutual joy.

She was a fan of the nineteenth century novel, especially Dickens, Hardy and George Eliot, the last of whom she deified. Lachlan once asked how her Christian principles sat with the knowledge of Mary Ann Evans' marital status; her eyes, light green and nimble as a jaguar, had answered his question. She was good on motive, in both literature and life, arguing fiercely that nineteenth century novelists were the first psychologists: nowadays endless pages in the media seek to probe why humans act as we do. The great novelists simply told us. One of Hetty's favourite novels was 'Barchester Towers' and she chuckled on recounting the scene when Bishop Proudie had to give in to his wife and her henchman, Slope. The bishop went upstairs noiselessly and came down next morning a broken man. Lachlan enjoyed her expressions and turns of phrase; she was a wordsmith as well as a sage. Obituaries were her irritation: what was the value in assessing a life only when it had concluded? Written in his lifetime, and shown to a man, it would give him the chance to rectify faults paraded after his death and realise virtues perhaps unseen. Hetty and Will Ladislaw would have got on well.

The next evening Lachlan joined the boys at supper with Hetty, who'd taken them to the cinema as promised. Her cooking was still winning their hearts. She had a pet wallaby in the garden, vestige of her days with a view out to Hanging Rock, and Merrick enjoyed watching, sometimes baiting, the animal. Robbie stayed inside with Lachlan; the conversation was likely to hold a gem or two.

They had just sat down, Robbie savouring the leather armchair against his bare legs, when Merrick ran in.

"Hetty, is the wallaby all right?"

She smiled, then confessed that it might well still be in trauma. She'd had the pest man earlier in the week, and whilst spraying outside he'd disturbed the wallaby, who panicked and hurled itself through the garden into the house. The man had tried to capture the creature and succeeded, but only after a time, during which evidence of the wallaby's panic had been deposited in various parts of the house. Hetty found the incident amusing; Merrick was unsure. Curiosity sated, the boy went back outside. Hetty passed Robbie a plate of shortbread, urging him to take a couple of pieces.

"How's the new school year?" she asked.

He told her. Robbie was quick to like teachers, Merrick more circumspect. Robbie was not made for science, like his father, and would abandon those subjects at the first opportunity.

"English?"

"I think he's good," said Robbie, concentrating, "not sure about the texts though. 'Animal Farm' doesn't grab me. 'Of Mice and Men' I've read. We've to wait till Year 11 for 'Great Expectations'."

"You can still read it now. I'd be glad to discuss some of the issues." Hetty envisaged a kindly Miss Havisham, changed out of the crusty wedding dress, sitting by a log fire listening to Pip read. What did boys today make of Estella, she wondered?

Reading her thoughts, Lachlan asked, "Which ending do you prefer, Hetty?"

Robbie looked up, unaware he had a choice.

"The second one, of course," came her reply. Neither of them wanted to spoil the novel for Robbie, so the conversation passed on. Hetty was going to Perth in late May and much looking forward to it. She listened to Lachlan's plans for their trip.

"Don't forget those jump races," she said. She knew he would enjoy seeing small country tracks, not the endless bare ovals of Australian racecourses.

Hetty had been to 'The Old Dart' only once, with Gideon, spending most of the time in Scotland, travelling up the west coast, before coming back down to Edinburgh, which was crowded as the Festival was on. But they had taken in a few shows on the Fringe, and despite the granite buildings, she enjoyed the place. They then spent time with relations in Epping Forest, too tame for her. Her sadness had been their failure to reach Dorset with its rustic charms.

"I'm re-reading 'The Woodlanders'," she nodded. Robbie slipped off the leather chair to her bookcase, flicking through paperbacks till he came to a slim one. There were plenty of years left for Hardy's gloom. "The village names are wonderful, aren't they? Melchester, Winterborne Abbas, Sturminster Newton, Piddletrenthide. I'm never quite sure which are invented."

"Nor me," agreed Lachlan. Vistas of English green flicked through his head, a green he remembered. There were so many different shades. Australia's browns and yellows lacked the soothing quality of green grass. At school his V.C.E. exams had been printed on light green paper, allegedly easiest on the eye. It seemed a strange concession on the part of examiners whose aim had otherwise been to inflict maximum discomfort.

He had always seen Australia as a force of contradictions, starting with the land. Harsh, glaring and hostile, it was also surprisingly fragile, brittle even. What seemed benign could turn harmful in seconds, which was not the case in England. Gentler names reflected a gentler land. Soon after landing in Australia, nearly thirty years before, Lachlan had listened keenly to a people who drawled in lazy, grating vowels that took the shine off tinselled aboriginal names like Coonawarra, Coolangatta, Kunundra, and Warrnambool, which he'd seen on the map. Pronunciation in Australia was regular; there were no dialects, which was surprising to a man born in Scotland, reared on Highland and Glaswegian tongues. Some English dialects were related to class, an alien concept to Australians. Hetty had read in the paper that the U.K. was still obsessed with class, as typified in its mail system: no other country distinguished between first and second class letters. Robbie looked up from the bookcase to ask Hetty a question and Lachlan moved outside. Long since bored by the wallaby, Merrick was sitting on the grass hunched over his Gameboy? Lachlan walked over to the fence, but Merrick did not acknowledge him.

Lachlan stood, hands in his pockets, savouring the moment. What was Lennox up to now? Angus? Brodie, he knew was with her new partner, probably in one of the new restaurants at Southgate.

"C'mon, big fella," he said scooping up the lad in his arms. The Gameboy went silent, and the three drove home.

That night he dreamt again. He was on pest control, working in the garden of a house in the country. He was staring into a mixing jug of poisons. Where the liquid should have been transparent, it was murky, lines furrowing the surface like paint before it is stirred. A piece of wood was clasped in his left hand: in his right arm was the spray gun. Just as he dropped the gun into his bowl to fill the canister on his back, there was a sudden movement by a tree stump at his side. It was a black snake. He stood rock-still. The reptile had seen him, but was unafraid. As Lachlan watched, his head full of heat and the firm impression of Lawrence's snake under Mount Etna, it started to uncoil; it was making for the open French window. He was unable to stop it as it slithered into the narrow gap. He knew both boys were asleep inside the house. Lachlan lost precious seconds dropping the gun and the wood. Forgetting he was still helmeted, he knocked into the window and was repelled. He was losing more time.

In the house the snake was nowhere to be seen. Down the corridor he stared, brain fugged. It was not his house, so he was unsure where the boys slept. The first room was empty. In the second Robbie lay sleeping on an orange chaise-longue, hands clasped as in prayer. Lachlan entered the room opposite, knowing at once the snake was there. Merrick slept in a transparent blow-up chair dressed in his soccer kit, including boots. The snake had curled itself round a picture above his head, a picture of two railway carriages jack-knifed after a collision. As Lachlan crept forward, the snake uncoiled down the wall towards the boy. Lachlan stopped, so did the snake. He stepped backwards, the snake retreated towards the picture. Another move from him and the snake set off again. He had to act.

"Wake up, Merrick," he breathed.

No movement.

"Son, you've got to wake up."

If the child moved it would alarm the snake, which stared at him, leering, on the cusp of victory.

Suddenly Merrick woke, the snake stared down, and a hand reached over Lachlan's head, grabbing the snake. The hand was Robbie's. Merrick leaped out of the room, Lachlan turned, and in that moment the snake arced onto Robbie, embedding its evil, scaleless head into the boy's leg, just below the knee.

The carriages started to applaud, blood running down the

wall each time they made contact, a noise fanfared in Lachlan's head, as, through the window, burst a wallaby, smiling an undertaker's grin. The snake had gone. Robbie lay motionless. As Lachlan bent down, there was a scratching squeeze-like sound; the wallaby had punctured the chair; and was smiling even more. It had managed to get hold of the spray gun, and was pointing at the inert form on the carpet, a demented ringmaster, treading sawdust with blood ....

Moments later, Lachlan was a window-cleaner high up on a hotel overlooking a busy wharf. The window he was cleaning was a mirror, his reflection grimly distorted. Inside the room, a woman in tails was conducting a small orchestra with a knitting needle, her back to him. But he could see her lips were green. Down on the wharf a fisherman shouted up to him, and he turned to reply, catching the woman's eye ....

It was 5.25a.m. Preview Day. Lachlan lurched into the kitchen, flicking the kettle on. He was cold. Padding into the hall, he checked on the boys, both sleeping. He thought of Kathy, who'd never had time for his dreams. He thought of Lady Macbeth, whose dreams took over her life. She had mocked them in her husband. Dangling an English Breakfast tea bag over his well-chipped mug, he knew all he wanted was a clear head. His cup of tea was lacking in colour as he carried it to the table. By the time he drank it, the contents were stone cold.

Lennox was the first person he saw on arriving at the theatre. Lachlan tried to hide his relief, but he suspected the actor noticed it, for there was the hint of a gloat in his terse greeting. Brodie was unusually cheerful; the new partner must be coming up trumps. Even Lady Macbeth seemed in good humour. The day was cooler, with a welcome breeze. Norman was the only one not happy: one of the chalices for the banquet scene had a deep gash in it and the cauldron chain had mysteriously shed a few links. Hardly cause for concern, Lachlan told him, and the old man raised his eyebrows slightly. Not long before curtain-up Lachlan bumped into Angus in the corridor.

"Angus?"

The other man was wary.

"Had a chance to look at that script yet? The one I gave you the other day.

"I've flicked through."

"And ... ? ."

"Too wordy."

Lachlan waited.

"Like the ending, though." Angus' smile could be sensed in the half-light. "A challenge for someone."

Lachlan moved on. As an actor Angus was not over-ambitious. There was little chance he viewed himself in line for the rôle. But his response did not deter the director.

He edged into the seat next to Brodie, their clipboards hitting heads. She smiled at him, and was in seriously good fettle. A bonus. They'd discussed the possibility of not having an interval in Shakespeare's tragedy, before deciding one was necessary. Current trends veered away from intervals, even in full-length drama, but this play needed to be distilled. They hadn't delved deep into its psychology for fun.

The first half went with inevitable blips: Macbeth was flat, Duncan was overdoing it and the porter scene still wasn't right. Neither Lachlan nor Brodie was happy with it; it needed a lot of attention. But the Third Witch was on song. Gradually Macbeth gathered impetus, the Macduff child-slaying was better than ever, and the fight scene was convincing. Lachlan never knew what aspects of the play would go well, but there were always bits he looked forward to more than others. This fight scene was an example: often in Shakespeare the fights he'd seen were cursory, effete things, raced through too fast. Lachlan enjoyed them, gave them time, appreciating the way his swordmaster took away responsibility, and taught him things. This swordmaster had not at first impressed Lachlan. All swordmasters worked differently, but none could quite compare with a man he'd used at school in his production of 'Hamlet,' Lachlan's favourite play. This man, Cadger, had been charismatic, inspiring not only students but also his colleagues in the staffroom, whose well-preserved shell of cynicism he had punctured without trying. Some months after the play, Lachlan took his cast down to Geelong, where Cadger was working on a T.V. film and they'd had supper, an event the kids referred to later. When he joined The Tinderbox, Lachlan tried to contact Cadger again, but he proved untraceable. Jack, their swordmaster for this play, was uninspiring but competent.

Just after the fight scene Lachlan looked around; the audience was not large. Eight or nine pressmen sat lazily, some of them with their legs dangling over the seat in front, not all taking notes. Brodie's partner was there, apparently engrossed, and four or five people he could not recognise were dotted around the small theatre. Hetty had ducked in soon after the start of the second half, she waved gently at Lachlan and looked back to the stage. She did not offer her opinions, but he knew she would be frank if he asked them. Lachlan suddenly felt sorry he'd not asked Robbie to be there; the boy was of an age now and it was time to differentiate between him and Merrick. Often logistics decreed they must remain together, usually with Dave and Jo, but it would do Robbie good to see something other than a performance after the run had started. Next time, Lachlan decided.

The preview finished, he and Brodie were kept busy with detail. Hetty and the rest of their audience had not lingered, though Brodie's partner stayed and spoke words of warmth. Lachlan wondered why he was surprised. He usually gave everyone the benefit of any doubts. And, looking forward, if Brodie were happy it would do everyone good. The actors disappeared quickly, and Norman ended his day on a less anxious note.

"Bodes well," he said, unconcerned by superstition, 'I thought light thickened by the end."

Lachlan touched him on the arm and thanked him. There was no substitute for men of Norman's ilk. Looking at his watch, which he'd done far less than usual this evening, he saw it was not as late as he'd thought. There would be time for a quick whisky with Dave as he picked up the boys.

CHAPTER SIX

As he jogged up to the steps of the Newcombes' verandah, Lachlan saw Jo sitting by the window. She looked tense. Only the table lamp was on, so for a second he did not notice Dave sitting with his legs outstretched, hands joined, shoulders hunched towards her. Jo looked up as Lachlan entered the room and made a wan attempt to smile.

"The boys are in bed, Lachie. They were tired out."

Lachlan nodded, lips pursed, but, as he made to leave, Dave shook his head gently.

"Jo's a bit knocked up," he said with his customary calm. "A lad at school."

'Not just any lad," came Jo's quiet voice. "I was sure he was getting sorted. Just a bit of a blow, that's all."

Dave etched the scenario briefly. The boy, in Year 12, had that day been caught selling dexamphetomine in the school-yard. Jo had rung his father, who claimed he couldn't get away from work. The boy was a twin, at which Lachlan's eyelids flickered across to Dave; back in Year 9 he and his almost identical sister had been a cause for concern as they spoke only to each other, ignoring their peers. A teacher had insisted they were seen by Jo, who had rung the mother and eventually met her, after which things improved gradually: the twins made attempts at integration, which seemed to Jo relatively successful, but then the mother had been summoned interstate to care for an ailing father, and the twins' behaviour had regressed. The mother was away again at the moment. Jo had not seen the boy for some time. Now he was in serious trouble. Dexamphetomine, or ritalin, was

59

used to treat Attention Deficit Hyperactivity Disorder; this was not the first time a pupil had brought the drug to school in order to sell it.

Jo had been a senior student guidance officer for six years. After her science degree, where her only disappointment had been not being able to study the overpopulated forensic option, she had done Honours and a two-year Master's in Educational Psychology. Despite healthy qualifications it had not been easy to find work. For a while her counselling rôle was part-time in two local schools; she had made up her week with supply teaching. She knew full-time work was hard to come by, joking that she would see a colleague cough and follow him round, hoping he'd perish so she could jump into his shoes. A lot of time had been spent sticking on band-aids. Jo found counselling the staff more difficult: violent or vindictive husbands were not unknown, and she had once had to look after a teacher whose erstwhile student had killed a man in St. Kilda.

In her present school, one of the city's largest, where she had secured a permanent niche, she was in essence alone. Being in isolation made things harder, especially in a large school. The Year 9 and 10 counsellor worked on the other side of the school; he might as well have been on another campus. In some ways conditions had improved; she had requested, and after several months been given, a back stair-case to her office so students could call without the stigma of being seen, and for safety she had turned the furniture around so she was not seated between the student and the door. Seventeen year old boys could pose a threat, as Dave always said; they acted spontaneously, whereas girls took time, and thought, sticking in, then twisting the knife. In Jo's school there was a large ethnic mix, which at senior level made for difficulties that could be papered over in primary schools. Religious rituals were a risk, as had proved the case last year with a number of Hmong. Ousted from the hills of Laos because of the Vietnam War, they had caused several problems before moving to Queensland, en bloc.

Caucasians could be equally stirring; not least those with affluent parents who left open their drink cupboards in country shacks or down by the beach. Less obvious, but equally harmful, were those who left heart tablets or even morphine: mixed with liquor, these were a temptation to teenagers.

Lachlan had learned from his conversations with Jo over the years, and she had helped him in his own counselling ventures. Although unqualified, he was someone to whom students turned, and he often sought Jo's opinion. He had been keen to see her line on crisis-counselling, when the client, after trauma, would be encouraged to remember when life was ordinary. Jo would encourage them to use the word 'normal', a term Lachlan had found a bête noire in his English teaching. But Jo's charges were encouraged to delve back into their experience, to "It started like any normal day." "So when did it change?" she would ask. Victims had to recognise the concept of normality before it could return.

Whether normality would come again to the twin in Year 12 was not certain. For now she felt let down, angry and alone. Trust was important, and brittle. Its ramifications went far beyond the immediate protagonists. In the last few weeks had there been a case in the paper where a child claimed to have been abused by her father. The guidance officer had followed protocol, informing the school principal, who passed this on to the appropriate agency, and the claim was investigated. It proved unfounded, but the family lived in a small town, a close community; rumours arose and the father had taken his own life in shame. Lachlan remembered Jo telling him that bruises had to be measured to verify they qualified as abuse. A school outside Melbourne had recently dispensed with its guidance officer, substituting her with a doctor one day a week, a policeman another day, and a minister when he had the time, but they were laying themselves open to litigation, a risk, in her view.

Where counsellors were retained they often found teachers resentful, possessive; he had experienced this more than once. It was a tough world. Had maybe never been tougher.

It was after one by the time Lachlan left; Dave was still on the verandah, hand raised like Gatsby in farewell. He would drop the boys off at school in the morning, as he often did.

Driving home Lachlan thought hard about Jo. In his schooldays there had been no counsellors or guidance officers; you coped. If you were lucky, one teacher might show himself receptive, maybe a tutor, or one of the faculty members, but there were no guarantees. In his own teaching Lachlan had tried to change that, encountering opposition sometimes and well aware how much time counselling took up, as Kathy found time to remind him. Kids had tougher problems now, he was certain. So did adults; he should know. On a theatre excursion just before he finished teaching, he had apprehended a Year 12 boy slipping back into the bar for another pint. The boy was contrite, and they had enjoyed a long chat.

"Has it always been so hard to be eighteen?" the youth asked, sipping the juice that replaced his previous order. And Lachlan said, "No". Some colleagues disagreed strongly with his opinion, but Lachlan stood firm.

The house was quieter than ever as he went in under a twist of new moon. It was not going to be a night for sleep. Soon after Kathy had gone, Lachlan had been blistered with sleepless nights. For a while he had struggled with the demon, only making himself more awake, expending energy in his desperation to make sleep come. He knew better now. The foe was easier left uncombatted, the darkness less hostile than he'd thought. He made a pot of tea and repaired with it to the dining area. Two of Merrick's comics lay ruffled on the table, together with a handkerchief whose blazoned 'M' looked more warning than crest. Across from it, Robbie's flap-eared bookmark showed another novel almost finished. The elder son was a more voracious reader than his father had been at that age. Lachlan picked up the paperback, feeling a stab of loneliness.

Even when the boys were just up the road, Lachlan missed them. He had a capacity for missing people. As a kid this had shown itself in homesickness, even on short trips away from the grey Aberdeen vicarage, and it struck him as unthinking that people dismissed homesickness like an imagined toothache. With him it had been a physical pain, down under his left ribs, that stayed with him, a muted version of the sharp stab that reared at him in the car when his father, overtaking, was forced suddenly to speed up, or brake to avoid collision. Nor had it disappeared, as childhood was put away.

He missed his teaching. Not the extra hours of assessment, grades, predictions and criteria, words that devalued the profession as a glib politician devalues language, but the kids, the life force. In his early days of teaching at a boys' private school in Melbourne, the wife of a colleague had trumpeted her conviction that the boys would always let you down. Distance had to be kept. He thought she was wrong; perhaps in those early days he'd gone too far to prove it, if only to himself. It was something to do with teaching English. During his week's observation at a rough school in the suburbs, he'd seen a lesson on 'Wuthering Heights' one hot Monday afternoon straight after lunch. The teacher had been inspired. The students listened. And contributed. When they'd gone, the teacher spoke to Lachlan at length. Whereas in other disciplines, he'd said, the subject matter constituted a barrier, something to clamber over before it could be understood, in English that subject matter was the way through. It was that simple. And the man was right: all Lachlan's endeavours had endorsed this teacher's point. At times he'd tried too hard to prove the point. When each new class tested him out with questions whose relevance was not obvious, Lachlan answered with a smile. "There are no red herrings in English," was a favourite riposte.

And only a few lads had 'let him down', that smug, inflated phrase. Teaching was a paradox: apparently so public a profession, in truth it was a private one. Only the students knew how effective a teacher was. Teachers should watch each other more, he'd always believed. There was less chance of that now than ever, though school inspections he'd welcomed as a chance to be looked at in order to learn from the experience. His colleagues built around themselves a battery of paper so as not to be seen.

He'd been fortunate and taught many great students. Rebels appealed to him. He kept in touch with quite a few; it was the natural course of things. Occasionally he'd meet them to catch up, come across them in a bar, see them at the 'footy' or the races, some even came to The Tinderbox and would have a drink after the show. Kathy had found this at first unusual, then quaint, finally unhealthy. In the early days of marriage they had more than once entertained his Year 12 tutor group and she'd been keen to make them feel welcome. That had faded. "More time for them than me," had been a joke before it soured.

He looked at the clock. 3.17am. When his mind was awash with thought, getting to sleep remained an obstacle. He'd understood Macbeth's problem, a problem the Thane successfully transferred to his wife. In the bathroom he noticed the toothpaste tube was almost empty; grubby thumbmarks had pressed it close to extinction. He wasn't in the mood for shopping now, though sometimes he'd slipped out at a similar hour, always surprised he was not alone in the supermarket. With its shelves packed to the roof and only a few people around, he'd still felt claustrophobic; in Scotland, he remembered, the shelves did not reach so high. Once, shopping with his mother not long before they'd left, his primary school headmaster had spotted them over the aisle and a bout of banter had been exchanged over the

Branston pickle. That incident came back to him often. In bed, he glanced at the clock: 3.28. In Vancouver, the day would just be beginning.

Australia Day he savoured. Each year he ensured that it was a day for the three of them. This year it was windier than usual, but the trio decided to picnic down on the beach, near Brighton with its brightly-painted huts. Both boys had inherited Lachlan's love of the sea. The wind was keeping people away and the streets were noticeably quiet, even for a public holiday, as they drove through a tolerant mid-morning sun. Last year it had been 40° and scorching. No sooner had he parked than two bright figures ran through scrub down to the beach. Lachlan was not far behind. The ocean waited, not as blue as he'd expected, and no soft mirror as sometimes. Catching up with the lads as they breasted the sand dunes, he looked out to a distant freighter sliding slowly out of the docks. White horses sprang up at random in front of them, spouting for a couple of seconds then sinking into anonymity. It was not easy to guess where the next small crest would spring up.

Robbie was pointing away from the beach. A number of butterflies darted all around them. "Eleven", he counted as a tiny white rag danced just past his hand. For a second Lachlan was put in mind of the stamps on Rebecca's letter; Robbie's thoughts were on an identical path.

"Not as bright as the stamps," he ventured, hand up against the sun.

"Those were English butterflies," said Merrick, with certainty.

"I know." The tone of Robbie's reply was not assertive. For all their quarrels, the boys got on well, though recently Robbie had been aware his viewpoint was more often along Lachlan's line than his brother's.

The last stray dandelions rocked as the three started down to the beach. As he'd surmised, it was far from crowded.

"Straight in, then," said Lachlan half-question, half-statement, and they clattered into the sea, odd pebbles spraying in their wake.

The picnic met with approval, though it was nowhere near lunchtime. Merrick threw a crust out in the vague direction of marauding seagulls, and to his surprise one of them dive-bombed him to reach the sand-blown morsel. It landed a few feet away.

"Look! That seagull's only got one leg," said Robbie.

"Quite common," replied the younger boy.

"Is it?" asked Lachlan, intrigued by this unexpected ornithological tit-bit.

" 'Course, Dad," came the reply. "Fish bite their feet off, it often happens."

Robbie snorted with disbelief. But Merrick clung to his guns. Further questions would lead to statistics on the number of sharks to have perpetrated the crime. Robbie could cope without that. "Are we off then? It must be almost tea time by now." Lachlan picked up the rug, inching Merrick off the last corner. He rolled and was still.

"Fireman's lift, Dad?"

"No arms, son. Hard luck."

As they reached the green Laser, its rust resplendent in the harsh light, a voice rang out.

"Hi, Mr. Stacey ......Lachlan."

Their faces turned. Two boys were unloading surfboards from a psychedelic yellow panel van, boasting even more rust.

A fair-haired lad slipped forward, hand outstretched.

"How are you, mate?"

Lachlan returned the firm grip. "Kieren." He smiled, waiting till the second boy had pulled a recalcitrant rope through the roof-rack.

"Ben. Good to see you. Have you met Robbie and Merrick?"

More handshakes. Lachlan saw Robbie force back his

shoulders as he met the boys' gaze.

The teenagers had both been in the boarding house to which Lachlan was attached; in their last year, he had directed them in a house play. Ben was a novice and edged into a minor rôle by his mates; Kieren was a professional, who handled the lead part with skill. Now he was reading medicine at university, whilst Ben enjoyed a year out.

"How's Johnno?"

"Good," answered Kieren, "but working too hard." It had been a source of amusement that Kieren did not have to go all-out to achieve academically. Ben, who had needed to work hardest of the three in Year 12, grinned at this.

"Any good plays, Lachlan?" Ben looked people straight in the eye.

Lachlan told them about 'Macbeth', fully aware they had enjoyed an elegant sufficiency of Shakespeare at school. "Come to the next one," he said, 'Our Country's Good'."

Kieren's eyes registered he knew the play, then he told Lachlan of the medical revue he'd been part of. He'd helped write some of the sketches. "They're close to the knuckle, you know."

It was Lachlan's turn to be amused. He'd been duty master on Friday evenings in the school's remaining boarding house; Ben, Kieren and Johnno had been responsible for lacing those evenings with mirth. Lachlan claimed Kieren was no scientist, being far too artistic, and the lad had put up his defence. The badinage continued.

"See you then, 'Sir,'" quipped Kieren, and they picked up their boards.

"Who are they?" questioned Merrick before the tall figures were out of earshot. Lachlan told him, glad at the stirring of good moments. As he looked up, the boys were just disappearing down the dunes; a tug of wind pulled Kieren's cap off, and he gave chase. Ben saw Lachlan wave in farewell; a moment later Kieren waved too.

In the evening he took the boys to 'Macbeth'. The

production had settled down despite inevitable hitches. Duncan had tripped at home; he now walked with a pronounced limp that did nothing to detract from his performance, and Lady Macduff's son was unwell, but they had trained two juveniles for the part, to appear on alternate evenings, so Brodie had quickly contacted his counterpart. Such mishaps were not 'The Scottish Play's' curse; they would happen whenever.

Taking his place a few rows back, Lachlan sat between the boys, happy to be incognito. Seconds later the witches had blown thought from him, and he settled down to enjoy the play. Macbeth and Lady Macbeth rode their power see-saw with aplomb, goading, stretching, tantalising the other. Infected by this energy, Lennox was acting better than ever; Lachlan permitted himself a measure of content. Ross caught the eye, and the fight scenes began to flow. Merrick sprang forward whenever a sword was brandished. From Robbie, Lachlan could also sense excitement.

But suddenly there was a hitch. Having delivered, 'Tomorrow and tomorrow and tomorrow' with rueful solemnity, Macbeth swung into his armour for the final fight scenes instead of first lamenting the desertion of his thanes. Lachlan leant forward in his seat. This was not even an amateur's error; the man had panicked. Lachlan's fingers drummed into the back of the patron in front of him, who spun around with a hostile glare. Then came the pause.

"Come on!" muttered the director.

Robbie looked at him but said nothing.

"Is this supposed to happen?" whispered Merrick, audibly.

Lachlan ignored the question. He imagined Macduff in the wings, unsure whether to enter, and Lady Macbeth realising her, 'Out, damned spot,' scene had been advanced by minutes. A stentorian cry rang out as Macduff decided on action, and the uncertainty was gone.

"Stay here, boys," ordered Lachlan the moment applause

68

had died down. He sprang out of his row and went back-stage, sidling through retreating theatregoers, giving a curt nod as the odd person complimented his production.

"He's trying to ignore it," grumbled Norman as Lachlan flew past. The door to the dressing room was ajar, the actor removing his capacious beard.

"What was that about?"

"Sorry, Lach, I..."

"You blew it. You let your concentration wander. You broke the first rule."

"I've said sorr..."

"Don't try and gloss over the fact." Lachlan's temple was throbbing.

The actor turned away.

"It's a public holiday production, with a full audience, and you choose tonight to mess it up."

The actor kept his head turned.

"Will you look me in the eye?"

Macbeth sidled around, still wiping spirit gum off his jowls onto a towel that had seen better days.

"One more lapse of concentration like that..."

"...and you'll play the part, don't tell me. Or will you get a real actor to do it?"

Brodie stood in the doorway.

"Leave it, Lachlan."

"You leave it, Brodie. The man's an amateur."

"I think he's got the message."

Macbeth was reaching for his shirt. He was scowling.

Brodie's shape left the doorway clear. Lachlan clenched his right fist, aware he had gone too far. The actor brushed past him with the briefest nod. Alone in the dressing room, Lachlan saw his red face accentuated by the bulbs blazing round the mirror. It was not a sight to savour. He was throwing water on his face when Brodie came back.

"The boys are waiting."

Lachlan nodded guiltily, and turned off the glaring bulbs.

Rejoining the boys, he realised Brodie had gone. Only Norman waited.

"Did I overreact?"

The stage manager nodded. "I gather so."

"Sorry."

"It's not me needs the apology."

'No, I know."

The boys sensed their father had been stressed; silence accompanied them to the car.

"Favourite moment?" he asked them.

"Young Seyton," said Merrick, after a pause.

"Siward," Lachlan corrected him gently.

"That was the best fight," replied the lad. "You always knew Macduff would hack Macbeth to pieces."

Dead right, thought Lachlan, biting his lip.

Robbie was smiling; the hero had enjoyed a good death in his opinion.

"Rob?"

He thought even longer than Merrick.

"I liked the porter," he said finally. "Those words. What does 'equivocate' mean?"

Lachlan was surprised by his choice, but answered the question, the word needing more than a simple explanation. Robbie concentrated hard then nodded, not certain if he understood. "Does anyone use the word now, Dad?"

"Occasionally. Perhaps in court. You'll use it if you become a lawyer, I expect."

"Him? A lawyer? That'll be the day."

"Quick bite at McDonalds?" asked Lachlan. Two faces looked at him; it was unusual for their father to suggest a meal at this late hour when they had school next day.

"Why not?" said Robbie, trying not to register his surprise.

They ate quickly. Lachlan had a big day coming up, auditioning for his next play.

In no time they were home, the boys pelting up the

verandah, then waiting impatiently while Lachlan unlocked the front door. Closing it, still feeling a stab of guilt at his outburst in the theatre, he saw the moon had not grown.

CHAPTER SEVEN

Kathy's competitive nature had been evident before she studied Law and Commerce at Melbourne University. Only daughter of a quiet businessman, whose second home was the leather cosiness of the Melbourne Club, she'd been a hot-shot at one of the city's all-girl private schools, and saw university simply as the means of accelerating her ambitions. While others revelled in freedom and the social whirl of freshmen, Kathy was fired by legal process and criminal law. Head down, she soared into her second year's challenge of constitutional law and tort; she ignored all other activities on offer, and in her third year was devoured by contracts and property.

Then, unplanned, she met Lachlan at a church function. She had been wary of men, but his ebullience and energy she found alluring. They married seven months later at the start of Lachlan's September holidays and avoided staging their reception at the Melbourne Club, settling for a marquee on the lawn after a church service she had planned with care. A week's honeymoon in the Whitsundays was characterised by tropical rain, before she had resumed her university course with increased verve. Lachlan had not sensed how much her passions were divided. Looking back, he saw that restrictive trade practices and commercial law engulfed her. After graduating with double honours, Kathy took articles with a large firm in Melbourne, where successive stints in property, banking, finance, commercial law and litigation claimed her fierce attention. Her pregnancy, discovered at Christmas, came as a surprise, although Lachlan was overjoyed and, after Robbie was born one cold winter's evening, Kathy took three months out. She seemed suited to motherhood and Lachlan took pains to be at home from school earlier. But ambition was Kathy's hallmark, and, having found a crêche, she was back in the velvet office at crack of dawn, working unreasonable hours. There were flare-ups between them, but she fought to keep her weekends and those remained companionable as Robbie grew up.

Four years later she was offered an associateship and increased responsibility; she played the game. The arrival of Merrick during a warm Spring Carnival occasioned another 'time-out', after which she took up the legal reins promptly. After Saturdays had been eroded, Sundays remained sacrosanct, until her disappearance from Church. Lachlan was taken by surprise, but Kathy was resolute: the law was their bread and butter, she was the major bread-winner and they needed to eat.

Arguments happened more often, always about trivial things. He remembered coming home late from a parents' meeting one hot February night.

"Have you put the rubbish out?"

He looked at her. "No!"

"I just wondered. It's Tuesday evening. The men come tomorrow."

"Well, I'll put it out later then."

"So long as you remember."

"I'll remember."

"That's fine then."

"Fine." He waited a second. "You could have put it out."

"Your job."

"We used to share. Remember?" He wondered how she would counter now.

"There weren't, perhaps, so many jobs then."

"Weren't there?"

"Perhaps not."

73

"Perhaps. I think there were more jobs."

"Just do the rubbish!"

What had been amusing idiosyncracies became catalysts for a fight. She came to hate him hanging round the house in his socks.

"You know what you look like in those socks?"

The acerbity of her greeting hit him. He sighed. "What do I look like?"

"Rhetorical question…"

"…expecting the answer? Do you know what I loathe about your comments? They're all calculated to impress legal people."

"Legal people don't need impressing. They're…"

"…impressive enough? Do all your comments rely on a legal brain to complete the phrase?"

"At least at work I'm dealing with a brain."

"Out of order. M'Lud, I crave a recess!"

"You can't do that."

"Why not? I think I can."

"Your knowledge of the law is…"

"Come on, surprise me. Choose a new adjective."

"Puerile."

"Well done, Madam Prosecutor. Your choice of word is exquisite. I would have been more prosaic… 'non-existent', perhaps? Or 'sadly lacking'."

Kathy grimaced.

"Does the prosecution rest its case?"

The grimace turned into an acid smile as she rose from the table, calmly folded her paper napkin, and left the room.

"You walk like a duck-billed platypus," teased inside Lachlan's head. He drummed his fingers on the table. Not long before she had accused him of being mean. 'Mean as a beekeeper,' was the phrase used. Its ingenuity stung.

But so much of the time had been good. Lachlan remembered Sunday afternoons when Merrick was tiny, the four of them walking along St Kilda beach in the driving

August rain, making for the café on the end of the pier which did raspberry muffins. Once, an alsatian had turned on Robbie, biting his cheek, for which a small masculine woman made only brief apology, leaving both parents with the certainty the dog would strike again. Kathy had seemed content sitting at the table nearest to the sea, watching her boys. She said little on those winter afternoons, cupping both hands round a mug of tea held up against red cheeks.

Strolling home as the sky lost its purpose to night, she slipped her hand into Lachlan's pocket, feigning cold. Robbie saw the move and looked away. The evenings were spent amicably. Occasionally they watched television; more often they read the boys stories, then sat on the deck with a pizza. Dave Newcombe looked in sometimes, chewing the cud for an hour, then jogging home. Silence between the couple was not a token of hostility; they sat back into it, ignoring the growing cold.

There had been good weekends down the Great Ocean Road, in caravans, bed and breakfasts or shacks lent by friends. Kathy was a great walker, often setting off after breakfast to be met by Lachlan and the boys, who'd driven to a meeting-spot by the sea. Nothing had suggested Kathy would leave for longer, with no meeting-point planned.

She was a fine mother when the boys were little. Nothing was too much of an inconvenience; it was Lachlan who found himself complaining at having to drop one of them off at a party, then pick him up two hours later. Other parents copped out on their children's birthdays, hiring entertainers in coloured costume; Kathy learned magician's tricks and tried them out at Robbie's party more than once, earning the plaudits of other parents, though Robbie froze with embarrassment in case the tricks failed, as sometimes they did. But his mother's manner was a winning one; Lachlan admired her for it, going as far as to buy her a floppy top hat one year, a hat fit for a conjuror, black, with green and red stripes of material soft to the touch. She wore it to the

M.C.G. one day and it was Lachlan's turn to be embarrassed. But her smile won even mocking hearts, as Jo reminded Lachlan. He was proud of Kathy's charms.

Was he the one to blame? The word made him uncomfortable; society had become litigious; everyone was up for blame. But when he thought about it, he was not at home as often as he might have been. Apart from duty in the boarding house, play rehearsals, the productions themselves, which took out every evening for the two weeks prior to performance, and school functions, which were many, he also met his mates twice a week after school, sometimes heading off to a play in the city on the spur of the moment, as in his bachelor days. It wasn't indulgent, or even necessary, but he enjoyed it. The boys were in bed when he got home. If they woke in the night he let Kathy attend to them, unless she'd specifically complained of being tired, which was rare.

Her always being in a hurry had come later.

"Why are you so rushed?"

"So rushed?"

"Yes, you're always in a tearing hurry...You never used to be."

"I've got more to do now, obviously."

"Obviously." He couldn't keep the sarcasm out.

"You know what they say...if you want a job done, give it to a busy man."

"Are you implying I'm not busy?"

She looked at him, surprised. "No. You do take umbrage easily".

"What do you mean 'umbrage'?"

"Offence. You take it easily. Where it's not meant."

"And who are you to say...?"

"What?"

"That I take offence. Your comments are loaded these days. There's always an extra layer."

"Of?"

"Meaning. For me to pick up."

"That's ridic-"

"Is it? I think not."

"You're the one who's so tetchy."

"Tetchy?"

"That's what I said, Little Sir Echo... 'tetchy'."

He shook his head. "You've not answered my question."

"I think I have." She reached over the breakfast bar for her handbag and swirled out of the kitchen.

"Perhaps you've answered more than that question," he muttered, cutting a large slice of bread, mis-shaped, and forcing it into the toaster.

He tried hard not to let the boys witness these arguments, though they clearly sensed ongoing tension. Kathy began teasing Lachlan more, exploiting his foibles, like his loathing for fires, pools and matches, which she saw as 'excessive'.

But still the boys looked smart, smarter than before the rifts in the marriage, and nobody could accuse Kathy of not caring for them. She rustled up meals in no time, though increasingly meals were bought, rather than prepared by her. When Lachlan drew attention to this, she rounded on him.

"You can cook, too, Bard."

He hated that soubriquet. Time was not permitting him to write the poetry he had coursing round his head, and where-as once she encouraged his writings, reaching over to snatch a look long before completion, now to be called 'Bard' brought with it fierce irony.

He looked at her one Sunday night as they sat, silent, on the deck, Kathy's hands cupped round a mug of coffee, more concerned to keep a drink warm than a marriage. She had been ambitious for him once; now, that ambition applied only to her. The law had toughened her.

As the evening drew on, Kathy went inside and came back with a dry-as-a-bone over her shoulders. Shoulders that looked thinner, sharper. She walked across the deck, picked up a fly-swat and stood gazing out over the garden darkness.

"You look like a traffic warden."

"That's not kind, Dad," said Robbie, appearing to say goodnight.

"We can't always be kind, son. Sometimes it's better to be…"

"Cruel?"

"Truthful."

The boy withdrew.

Canada came from the ether; there was no mumbled harbinger that Lachlan could look back on and say that he should have realised at the time. He heard her telling the boys one hot Sunday evening. The word 'secondment' caught his ear. How would the boys comprehend that? Walking fiercely onto the verandah he stood, holding the fly-door open, incensed by her betrayal. Kathy looked at him hard. He turned away.

"What does it mean?" said Robbie, into an evening suddenly brittle, and she told them the offer had come up for her to do a 'six-month secondment'. Lachlan's antipathy for the word burst into bloom. In Canada, on Vancouver Island, working on government law and privatisation.

"Six months?" wailed Merrick.

"I know, darling. Six months is a long time, but it will go quickly."

"Not when you're eight," said Lachlan.

She held the younger boy to her. Robbie's brow furrowed.

"I've not agreed to go yet. It's only an idea."

Robbie's eyes were hooded.

"It's just like Daddy doing a teacher exchange," she ventured.

"Only that would be for a year and that would mean we would all go," countered Lachlan.

He gazed over the garden; his flowers were cowering.

Later that evening Lachlan and Kathy sat across the kitchen table.

"If I don't go now…. It's such a great opportunity. If I turn this down it will not look good."

He said little as she expanded on how she would advise the government on selling off assets. There was a case at present involving diamonds in Yakkatan, a province near Alaska. Lachlan pointed out that Kathy had never been remotely interested in jewellery, reminding her of the episode when she was twelve, which she had told him soon after they met. She had been surprised that her father thought she'd like the necklace. Didn't he know her better than that? Didn't he see her expression on receiving it? He tricked her with the box, of course; she'd no idea what was in it. And felt cheated when the trinket emerged. That was the moment she felt saddest at being the only child. She had no kid sister to adorn with the twinkling stones. The colour was frightening, a sinister marmalade that didn't wink when she turned it in the light, just stayed like a poisoned sweet in her uneven hand.

It wasn't her birthday or a significant occasion other than a Sunday: they had been to church, as usual, in the morning, and it rained suddenly on the way home, streaks of grey rope striped flat on the windscreen. She noticed because for once she was in the front, not straddled eternally between two seats, crouching up into featureless conversation, unsure whether to contribute.

As soon as she'd opened her father's gift, he went out, without changing, to the Melbourne Club. She supposed that was unusual on a Sunday. Her mother was interstate, visiting a cousin. So she was the only one in the house. She'd told Lachlan of the incident one day when they were shopping in Bourke Street, passing a jeweller's. What she didn't tell him was that later that day she took some scissors, and cut the string of the marmalade necklace.

Thunder rumbled round the marriage for three months, during which Kathy remained adamant that she must go to Canada. It was 'time-out', and she would be back after six months. Jo was lined up as a support team, Kathy's parents having co-incidentally chosen that time to retire to the hills outside Adelaide. She realised, of course, it was unusual to leave her children, but it was precisely those blood ties that would bring her back.

The three months were laden with barbs.

"Did you see the footy?"

"No, I missed it."

"Shame; it was a great game. You came second, though. Pity."

Lachlan knew the result from his car radio. He'd love to have been at the game.

"You have to make time, Bard."

That made him angry. "Well, you managed to. Don't tell me there was a sacrifice? Another tele-conference wih Vancouver? Or were they all watching shinty?"

"It's ice-hockey, as well you know."

"No, it's not, it's shinty on ice. All muscle and muster, no chance for finesse. Just like the Yanks."

"They are not Yanks!" exploded Kathy. Suddenly she was in spasm of temper, beads of perspiration surfacing at the side of her eyes, mouth closed. "That's just the comment they loathe. It's so uninformed, so predictable."

Lachlan stuck to his guns. "The Canadians do well out of America. Don't tell me they bite the mighty hand that feeds them?"

"Actually, they feed themselves."

"Actually, they don't. I was reading an article the other day. Three-quarters of Canada's resources come from Uncle Sam. If anything, it's more so."

The fly-screen slammed shut. Robbie was on the deck. He eyed them both, then turned and left them to it. The fly-screen banged again.

That was one of the last times they argued. A date was set for Vancouver Island. It rolled at them all like a silent juggernaut. Two cases were packed, sitting ready in the hall. Kathy ordered a taxi around lunchtime on a warm November day, two weeks after Merrick's birthday. She saw them off to school with Jo, rang her parents and sat down on the verandah, cupping hands round a coffee long-since cold.

Then she had gone.

E-mails dashed home frequently – at first. Canada was a beguiling country. She was working harder than before and the days were rushing by. The messages in hard black type were addressed to them all. Lachlan longed for a hand-written letter to see again the way she shaped her words. He remembered a colleague at school who had lost his wife and then regretted having thrown away her letters. Because he was so determined she would survive, he had nothing left in her own hand. In time, Kathy's e-mails became fewer.

Often Lachlan regretted his coldness, his dampening her enthusiasm, his being on the defensive. He had avoided communication with Kathy from the moment she spoke of secondment. Should he have encouraged her career as she did his? Would that have made the difference?

His guilt raged most when the boys avoided questioning him, not when they plucked up courage to ask after their mother. *She was still their mother.* His answers were lame, his solitary thoughts more so. Something was prising itself open inside him...

And then she must have met Adrian. Jo, recipient of Kathy's Canadian adventures, had to act as cipher for Lachlan and his sons. At first hurt, stunned and confused, Lachlan later felt relief, although the anguish for Robbie and Merrick was impossible to assuage. A Rhodes scholar at Oxford, Adrian had the temerity to proclaim himself an 'atavistic Anglophile', (more hard words for the boys), who was carving a colourful career in politics. Vancouver Island was the seat of Canadian Government; their meeting was hardly a surprise. Adrian was aesthete and athlete. Ultra-fit from jogging, swimming and squash, he swam with dolphins regularly, rescued stricken swimmers, was purer than driven snow. Divorced some time ago, with no children, he fitted Kathy's cravings neatly. He encouraged her ambitions, minimised her guilt at leaving the boys, and provided a suave shoulder on which she could recline.

It was a mistake to send Jo the photograph of Adrian. Merrick recognised his mother's hand on a rare letter when at the Newcombes' and reached to open it while Jo was out shopping. The photograph fell out: a handsome, dark-haired man, arms crossed, on a beach. Behind him, a little girl in a swim-suit was staring disconsolately at an airbed that must have punctured. It was the expression on her face rather than the hunk of manhood in the foreground that Merrick remembered. He told his father about the photograph and Lachlan insisted on seeing it, which he later regretted. Robbie refused to look. The man belonged in a catalogue or a sports shop window. Both boys were silent for days afterwards until Merrick ventured, "He looks squeaky clean." Lachlan did not know where Merrick had heard the expression.

"So, what's the story with Mum then?" ventured Merrick over another soulless supper. The question had been waiting to surface for days. Lachlan looked at him, aware of the courage the boy had summoned up.

"I'm not sure, son. Maybe she's not very well at the moment. She seems to have lost her sense of perspective."

"Perspective?" queried Robbie, ashen-faced.

Merrick started to sob. None of them slept that night.

Her next e-mail was hurtfully bright and chatty. She had spent a weekend in the Rockies and seen a bear at close quarters. She (not 'they') had canoed on Lake Louise, a place where she would return with the boys. A brief sentence at the end alluded to the chance she had been given to extend her time in Canada, but, of course, she was coming home.

Then she had sent a postcard from Alaska, where she was on a cruise.

'Having a wonderful time here. There are whales around the boat all the time, and the views are stunning. Yesterday there was a small fire in one of the engines, but luckily it didn't last long. Staying in Juno, an unusual place. One day you must come here.

Lots of love from Mum.'

Lachlan noted the absence of personal pronoun. He mentioned the card to Jo, who told him Adrian had friends in Juno.

That was nine months ago. New challenges in mining and shipping law had claimed her attention. Prompted, no doubt by Jo, she came clean about Adrian in the only e-mail addressed to Lachlan alone. She was pulled in three directions, she claimed. Her children, (not family), her career, and her guilt. The only way to rectify the problem was for the boys to move out to Canada. After all, they were 'her' children. That communication came the week before they left for England. Lachlan did not reply. Her deception and their abandonment were complete.

CHAPTER EIGHT

'Our Country's Good' is a challenging play. It tells of a party of convicts transported to Botany Bay with the First Fleet in 1788. Once there, the governor realises the convicts have nothing on which to focus other than soul-breaking work; he decides to channel their rough energies into a performance of Farquhar's 'The Recruiting Officer', directed by one of his lieutenants, and, against the odds, they succeed. The work had a resonance with Lachlan, whose family had enjoyed a far less hazardous transportation among the last of those Brits who came out to Australia with a £10-assisted package. Those sentenced to the ends of the earth nearly two hundred years before, often for no more than stealing a loaf of bread, and many of them no doubt innocent, had won his admiration, as they fossicked for survival along the raw coastline of what is now one of the most scenic harbours of the world. For those sent to Tasmania it had somehow seemed worse: the descriptions Lachlan read of Port Arthur's gaunt prison had been passionate; modern post-cards of the place in brindled light had not succeeded in removing his awareness of what had been suffered there. Recently a maniac had gone berserk one summer afternoon, gunning down thirty-five people, most of them innocent tourists. Lachlan wanted to set his production in Hobart Town not Sydney Town; it was more remote, starker, but the play held too many specific references to Sydney in Brodie's view, so he concurred.

As a student he'd once been on the production team for a three-month run of the play in one of Melbourne's larger theatres. It was a necessary apprenticeship. From initial sketches for the set, the designer had then constructed a model box that made clear his plans. He was an ambitious man, whose previous production of the play had centred around a twenty-foot tree. Having taken a silicon mould from a real tree, he covered it with fibreglass castings to give the texture of bark, and made a feature of foam pebbles, individually painted. It had been a huge team effort involving pneumatics, hydraulics and traps that Lachlan knew were not at his disposal now. In his small acting space any sophisticated set changes, trap doors or trompe d'oeil effects were limited; they were aiming for simplicity. In the middle of the theatre, now adapted to be 'in the round', was a pile of sand from which rose one un-forgiving central pillar: ship's mast, flogging post, gallows. Lighting did the rest.

Casting this play was more fun than he'd thought. It was a trove for male and female actors, as Brodie was quick to point out. Having chosen the play, casting was the next hardest task: after that, rehearsing was easy. Discussion, argument, stubborn refusal, blind faith and tenacity mingled in a crucible of intrigue, and Lachlan had to admit that sharing the direction rather than working solo had resulted in several of his better productions. Brodie's skill in organising at first made her seem fitted to being the producer, but to her that was the secondary position; she had the vaulting ambition that she was determined to air as director. So they had carved out an understanding.

They talked over a picnic lunch, fixing the female parts first. Mary Brenham had the most lines; both of them felt Third Witch had earned her stripes. Lady Macbeth would be an arresting Liz, upon whose 'lying' the play later turns. Duckling was harder to cast: apparently sensual, intuitive and kind, her rôle left something else to be plundered: Lady Macduff deserved a chance here.

"Let's see your list of men," said Lachlan gently. He

perused the neat writing on vellum and they agreed on several, his main objection being her choice of actor to play Wisehammer. This character, a man from Gloucester arrested for the theft of a cake, had to be young in Lachlan's view. Had to love words. By no means the largest rôle, Wisehammer's vocabulary was pivotal: he taught himself new words from the almanac, helped by Mary Brenham. The scene with just the two of them comprised tender moments, in contrast with so much army brutality.

"Who do you reckon? Angus?"

Lachlan paused; that trump card was for a later game. "Ross, actually."

Brodie was silent.

"I had him for Ketch," she said after a moment.

"Macbeth should be Ketch. He'd hang convicts well. And he's had the practice recently. Provided he doesn't go walkabout on stage again."

She nodded. "And Ralph?"

Ralph Clark was the hero, the lieutenant whose task it was to show that the play could work with convicts. The man was fundamentally good, moral, measured, meticulous, not the challenge every actor would seize. It was not only schoolboys who identified with Iago, Heathcliff or Judas. As a schoolteacher, Lachlan had found it difficult to convince his charges of the depth of strength 'good' men held; the word was glossed over, almost mocked. Recently a preacher at church had taken as his theme the Samaritan, whose goodness is well-known. But not always plumbed. The sermon had stirred Lachlan's thinking.

"You don't mean Lennox?"

Lachlan thought hard. Lennox might be ideal.

The last weekend before the new school year Lachlan was keen to spend with the boys. He booked a squash court for Saturday morning and watched Merrick flail helplessly after his brother's confident shots.

"I'll play Dad next," the younger boy was quick to say when the game was over. Robbie nodded and moved to the next-door court to practise alone. When he played his elder son half an hour later, Lachlan came out on top, but only just.

"Next time, Dad," said Robbie, glinting. "Unless you want to carry on now?"

Lachlan resisted the challenge with, "Time for the cinema," and the boy savoured a moral victory.

The film was unusual, a spy story that started, inevitably, in New York, then changed ground to Tokyo, ending up in Vancouver, with shots of Whistler that were stunning. The dénouement was icy, unpredictable and clever.

Over an afternoon drink at home Lachlan noticed Merrick was subdued. "Is he okay?" he asked Robbie.

Eyes gazed back at him hard.

Lachlan twigged. Vancouver. He found Merrick in his room, staring blankly at his encyclopaedia of sharks; his face was smeared.

"You still miss her, don't you?"

No response.

"I do understand."

"You don't miss her."

"Doesn't mean I don't understand."

"You never told us why."

Lachlan leaned forward, sensing Robbie at the door. "Oh yes, I did. Several times actually. It's not easy to explain. Not even to myself, let alone to two young boys."

"I'm nearly fifteen," rang out behind him.

"One young man."

"It's not as if she cheated on you," said Merrick, eyes clouding. "Or ... did she?"

Lachlan shook his head.

"She got more and more busy at work."

Silence.

"She felt her work needed her."

"More than us?"

"I think so."

"Why didn't she ask us?" said Robbie. "She never hinted until it was too late, until she'd decided. We couldn't stop her then."

"Dad didn't want to stop her."

Lachlan began to be aware of his breathing.

"That's not exactly true. I wanted her to stay for you, for her family... she said she had to take time out and she'd come back."

He waited for the inevitable question. But neither boy voiced it.

"And you're out so much ... it feels like being adopted when we're at the Newcombes. Emily gets on my nerves."

"She's a girl, Merrick. She's bound to!"

"And we always have bought food. Why can't we have home baking like other kids. I know you work hard, Dad, but..."

Lachlan broke the silence. "I do understand that you miss her. And how you miss her. But it was her choice."

"We had no choice." This from Robbie. "Did we, Dad? She chose to go and she said she was coming back for us."

"Nearly two years ago now. Two years, one month and..."

"...however many days," finished Lachlan.

"And I don't like Kerryn. Have to be honest. Nor does Robbie. He said she's..."

"Enough." Lachlan had never asked Kerryn to the house, but the boys had met her often when she was in Melbourne. The wicked step-mother syndrome was no fairytale.

"We need something to look forward to," said Robbie. "It needn't be huge."

"We're going to England in June. You'll see Rebecca, meet new friends..."

"...and spend days waiting outside a prison."

"That was..."

The doorbell rang. "Thank you, Lord," said Lachlan

under his breath. Robbie went to answer it. He came back with Hetty, who was clutching her shopping bag.

"I wasn't sure you'd be in," beamed the visitor. "Always worth a try, though. How was the squash?"

"Good," said Robbie. "I almost beat Dad."

Hetty continued to beam. "I made some fresh bread this morning, and there's a chocolate cake." Lachlan avoided the boys' gaze. She lifted the cake like a famed jewel from its tin and cut three generous slices.

"Thanks, Hetty," said Robbie, munching.

"Merrick?"

"I'm not hungry."

Late on the Sunday evening, Lachlan pored over the play once more. He had read recently that it had been performed in an old jail in Perth, where the playwright had assisted in the venture. Re-reading her comments on prisoners' endeavours with the play, Lachlan thought of his twin in custody twelve thousand miles away. Communication with Iain was a matter of urgency now, but the trip to England was too far away in his mind. Seeing the play put on in an English jail would have been fascinating. 'Our Country's Good', with its clever pun in the title, was exciting and sinewy, as it developed the power of conviction over tyranny. A prison setting would dilute its idealism, making 'good' appear in sharper focus.

With Dave and Jo, he had wrestled over his thoughts on goodness, and how it fitted the concepts of a loving God. They were no strangers to hardship, even tragedy: Dave's mother had died of cancer, cruelly young, while Jo's brother, to whom she was close, had been badly injured in a cycling accident, that left his face disfigured. To this day Jo could not understand how another cyclist could inflict so much harm: motorbikes, yes, but a light-framed racing bike was too slender. The man he hit, a postman, on his more cumbersome vehicle, had died. All three of them realised that Fate did not dispense pain in neat portions; having once been blighted, you were no more immune than anyone else.

Hetty and Thomas Hardy agreed. The adopted god-mother relished talking with Lachlan about the whims of fate, quoting from the Wessex novels with wisdom and ease. As a seventeen year old, reading 'The Mayor of Casterbridge' for the first time, Lachlan remembered he and his friends claiming volubly that the author exaggerated: coincidences could not be as prevalent as in Hardy, nor could the events of a life be so cruelly shaped.

"Ask me that again twenty years down the track," the teacher had instructed, and they had taken that as a way of being repelled. Lachlan stored the instruction. Now he was well down the track he believed only Dickens could be accused of being over-liberal with the synchronicity bird. And the happy ending.

The boys were ready for the return to school. Robbie, on the cusp of Year 9, was not as keen as his sibling four years beneath him; to Merrick every day at school harboured the chance of piracy, plunder and challenge.

Lost in thought well after midnight, Lachlan was dwelling on the single parent's tag. Parents' interviews, end-of-year concerts he could manage because he always knew other people, but it seemed out of kilter to be dashing, alone, into shops for last-minute necessaries. He felt conspicuous, vulnerable, sensing those in the shop were aware of his lack of confidence, worn like a new badge.

At the end of that first February day, he made a point of being home when they trooped back from school. Merrick arrived, hot, and relieved, his nostrils showing the remnants of a nosebleed; he'd been having a lot lately. The lad said little, went to his room, came out changed and picked up his Gameboy. Robbie, arriving home later, was full of news.

'New English teacher, Dad. A Kiwi. Can you imagine? Hobbsie for Science, 'Miss Cherrynose' for Maths and

'Blazing Percy' for History."

'Who's your tutor?"

"Hobbsie. That's good."

Lachlan shared his son's feelings; Jim Hobbs was a fine man, who had led climbing expeditions all over the world. He would be a strong influence on Robbie.

Hetty rang later to see how they'd fared and the three enjoyed a quiet evening in. "No T.V. on the first night of school," Lachlan had said a couple of terms back, and that was now a tradition. He cooked a roast, and the lads made in-roads into a new tub of ice cream. Calm had, for the moment, returned.

The read-through of 'Our Country's Good' revealed a new talent: Gritty Meg. She was only in one scene of the play, towards the beginning, but she lifted it at once with sharp understanding of the humour. Brodie and Lachlan caught each other's eye; they were not alone. Angus' eyes were on their way back to the page as Lachlan scoured the circle. Meg's humour had so far lain unearthed. He mentally added Meg to the crowd scenes, and was wondering how he could invent more action for her; this was tricky as the characters ignored her in the play, spurning her brutally, even by their own coarse standards. The woman playing Meg was not well-known to Brodie, or to him; she had arrived a few weeks previously and been grateful for the walk-on Gentlewoman in 'Macbeth'. There was something reassuring about her, and something that invited risks. She would make a good mother in 'Wolf.' A director had to engage talent in time.

'Our Country's Good' had nineteen parts, but doubling was possible; Lachlan sorted that out early. Taking a part for the read-through was no guarantee of landing it; sometimes the whole projected cast was altered, but this was usually the stage when things fell into place. 'Wolf' had a fair number of parts, as had 'The Government Inspector'. He and Brodie

91

had planned to give some of the company a break at the end of May, aware it was not ideal timing. Winter in Melbourne can be hard: fine for those able to jet out of the place, but few of the actors were that fortunate. The new season opened in mid-August, with rehearsals for 'Death of a Salesman' from the second week of July. Winter evenings were just when The Tinderbox should be hauling in audiences like whitebait; it was essential to select plays that would appeal.

Lennox was as focused as Meg; he liked the rôle of Ralph and read with zeal. Angus was quiet, apparently content with the unexciting Campbell, a drunken Scotsman. Over the tea-break Meg chatted with Brodie. Norman appeared with chocolate biscuits, and the Company seemed relaxed. As they resumed, Lennox sidled over to Lachlan to say he had an appointment at six; could he leave then? Lachlan was not a man for suspicion: "an appointment," seemed to him furtive. But the way Lennox clung to his rolled-up script was clear indication he wasn't giving up his part; Lachlan nodded and the actor resumed his place for a time. When he'd gone, Lachlan was about to read in, when he leant forward.

"Meg, could you read Ralph?"

Brodie approved of the move, the rest of them maintained their energy levels and Lachlan savoured the final scene for its mixture of pathos and wit. Farquhar and Wertenbaker knew their craft. For once, the company parted crest-high on the wave.

He could procrastinate no longer. A letter to Iain was long overdue. For a man to whom letters were life-blood, he felt uncomfortable. He had not heard from his twin for seven months. Rebecca had written, more than once; she received no reply. She had gone, with Saul, to visit him one November afternoon, an afternoon utterly without colour she called it in her next letter to Lachlan, but Iain preferred not to see her.

It was harder for her being in the same country. Distance lent a sort of perspective, but one with which Lachlan was not at ease: Australia was only twenty-two hours from the U.K., a thought away, essentially, but it was not that simple. In this case, distance made him feel more responsible, though he had done little to show it.

He bought an airmail letter; it had a finite amount of blank space. But it was flimsy. He needed the right place to write it, as well as the right words. Usually words flowed rapidly, but now his words were laborious, rusting, even as he penned them in his head. Thinking of how to say things weighed him down. Iain was a quiet man, turned increasingly inward lately, not easy with himself. But he was still a brother. And a twin. Lachlan was unsure of censorship rituals at the prison, but the letter had to be composed.

He chose a Monday morning early in February; the sun was insistent, but this was the time earmarked for the deed. More thought than he dared to admit had gone into the selection of venue; he decided on the Botanical Gardens, into whose maze of paths he could retreat. Arriving at one of the South Yarra gates he felt conspicuous, the precious letter clamped in a paperback. He chained his bike to the railing, and sauntered self-consciously inside. The café by the oval pond would be a good spot.

The shrubbery was seething colour, varied and unusual, but he passed it in a trance, head down, arms seeming larger than usual as they flapped by his sides. Did he always give the impression of a demented scarecrow? Hitching up his backpack also seemed abnormal, and he was conscious of his breathing as he padded down to the café. Not many people were here: Canada geese strutted to and fro; a couple of seagulls squabbled over a crust, both birds with two legs, he noticed; a golden labrador lazed in the heat, nostrils alert. He rounded the corner, when who should he bump into but Angus beetling out of the café after an early breakfast.

Under the actor's arm Lachlan saw the rolled-up script. The two exchanged greetings, and parted, Angus looking over his shoulder and half-waving the script before he disappeared behind a gum tree. Lachlan nodded, smiling. Synchronicity again.

He ordered a pot of tea and sat down, extracting the air-mail letter like a court exhibit. Angry at his pedantry, he made a small smudge under the pre-paid stamp. A young waiter came out sporting an apron in racing green, and placed Lachlan's tea on the table.

"Is it bags?" asked the director.

"I'm sorry?"

"Tea-bags? Only if so, could I have another one?"

The young waiter nodded and went inside. Weak tea was one of Lachlan's pet hates, along with people getting up during the credits in the cinema, napkin-rings and loose change. Kathy's pet hate had been predictable: burly men whose shorts were wedged below the Plimsoll line. A second tea-bag was delivered gingerly into the pot, looking for a moment like one of the fly-ties he'd seen Dave working on at home. There was no further excuse; he picked up his pen.

Progress was not quick. The boys and his work at The Tinderbox he had covered before the first fold in the skimpy paper. Across from his table a cheery woman in smart straw hat looked sympathetic at his anxiety. Concentrating hard, he wondered if he could ask his brother questions. England was no police state, though wariness was best. What he most wanted to ask was to do with Harry Cudmore; that enquiry would have to wait. But he told Iain he was coming over in June. The second fold was kilometres away. A couple interrupted his gaze, acting out some domestic scenario sotto voce in front of him, and he paused. The tea was cold, but it slaked his thirst. A cake would help, and he settled on a piece of shortbread.

He remained still; mixed in with his anxious struggle to

carry on with the letter was a sudden feeling that he had slowed time down; he was usually its pawn. So much of life was a paradox, conflicting emotions present simultaneously, not just joy and pain but surprise and readiness, dread and excitement, future and past. He had to get on to the back page of the letter. A young girl swung by and he looked up.

"How are you?"

Because he was writing to England he took this as a question, not a greeting, just as he had when first arriving in Melbourne years ago. "Good," was the expected reply, delivered in a rough, clipped manner by Aussies.

"Fine," he found himself lying. "You?"

"Fine, also," came the reply. "See you later."

This phrase was not the reminder of a previous arrangement, but an indication that conversation was going no further. For some people it was a command to leave, not inviting contact but severing any chance of it.

"Words," mused Lachlan. He thought of 'Hamlet', and the Prince of Denmark's fine crafting of them.

Forty minutes later he had made the back page, just. He folded the gummed edges with care. Raising the offering to his lips like a communion wafer, he was stung by the blade in the edge of the paper. As he licked the flap, a trace of blood could be seen in his saliva. He felt no surprise, just posted the letter in the first box he came to. Once written, a letter had to be got rid of at once. It was another of his quirks.

CHAPTER NINE

The firstborn. Kathy used that phrase: her 'firstborn', even when she was leaving for Vancouver. From the boy's birth she'd been a caring mother, bringing the child with her when others hired a sitter. Robbie adapted well, never threatening to wield a despot's sceptre, even when it looked as if he'd have no siblings. Kathy had stopped work happily, looking after her quiet, thoughtful charge. He had not grown out of an unusual expression which made him appear anxious, his brow wrinkled in permanent concentration. Fair-haired, solitary, he took things seriously; there was a scar under his eye where he had toppled over 'as a yearling,' Lachlan used to say. Like his father he was left-handed: unlike Lachlan, he had an ear for music, playing the piano with gusto from the age of five or six. He was not a natural sportsboy, but he clung on, attaining a sort of mastery. At kindergarten he took control of daily diary entries; drama appealed to him from the start.

The photo taken of him after his first day at primary school was treasured, a small ice-cream stain giving him away down his smart white shirt, narrowly missing his red and white tie. In the picture he had the furrows on his fore-head, as if he wanted to see into the middle distance.

Merrick had arrived ten weeks earlier, on the eve of the Melbourne Cup. Lachlan, a regular attender at the race that stops a nation, had been concerned he wouldn't make it to Flemington, but he did. It Happens won that year, at generous odds; it was one of four horses he selected. A year later, on Merrick's first birthday, Iain had been over to

96

Melbourne for the Spring Carnival. The favourite for the Cup romped home cheekily, but neither twin had invested. That was Iain's last trip.

At first Kathy said she wanted a rest from church every Sunday. She still went to communion on Feast Days that fell in the week, and kept up with friends in the congregation as before. In church with the boys, but without her, Lachlan wondered how she was spending the time. She was not one to lie in with the papers; in fact they had no Sunday paper, a 'waste of trees.' When the men came back from church, she was initially at home reading, later at her console in the small room they both used as a study. It got hot in there, so one week she had suggested it would be easier for her to go into work. Lachlan jarred, hearing that. But she had gone into her office every Sunday from then on, eventually remaining there all day.

Apart from her Sunday disappearing trick, life had, for a while, continued on its well-worn rails. She was rarely late home in the evenings, unlike her husband, who ran games teams after school, as well as matches on Saturday mornings. In addition, Friday was his night on duty in the boarding house; from his point of view it was a good night for duty, the boys were relaxed at the end of the week and there was no immediate work pressing. His counselling skills had developed and the house parents for whom he worked were generous with their whisky at the end of a long day. That rankled with his wife.

So Friday evening and Saturday became Kathy's domain. People called in, Jo, or friends from work, passing en route home, but the boys were her priority. She made the boys a fiendish Saturday breakfast. Lachlan joked about 'Supermum' and she laughed. But gradually it became an obligation; she couldn't throw her heart into the meal, and before long she begrudged it. By then Robbie was involved in matches, leaving early with Lachlan. She had hurled the washing in, used the drier no matter the weather, then gone to watch Merrick in his Little League game.

She herself was a Melbourne supporter. The Demons. They played at the M.C.G. and as a girl she cherished the ethos of that sacred sporting venue. She was at home in the Members' Stand, where the young aristocrats went, joked about the tight-fitting shorts worn by her idols and took to wearing business suits rather than casual gear. But between the third or fourth quarter, her lap-top would appear, then be slipped deftly away.

Lachlan barracked for Carlton. The word 'barracked' seemed more apt for her, he felt now. 'Barrack-room lawyer.' The deadlock had shown in their support for their team; disguised as friendly rivalry in their early married years, it had shown cracks when Lachlan's rehearsals at school had denied him the chance to attend a Carlton v. Melbourne clash. Rehearsals were not easy to arrange: evenings were possible with boarders but not day students. So Sunday evenings from seven p.m. had become prime time, another branch lopped off the ailing weekend tree. Kathy gritted her teeth.

A cleaner alleviated her Saturday morning pressures, and Sunday lunch they ate out, she joining them from the office, usually late; her attendance at the boys' matches dwindled, and she was unwilling to seek a compromise. One day Merrick's team had been selected to play a match during half-time at the M.C.G; they had gone to watch him, Kathy cheering loudest when Merrick was among the first to leap through the huge paper hoop at the start of the real match. Lachlan caught Robbie's eye: his furrow was deeper than ever. He had not cheered. Astonishingly, his mother had brought her lap-top to this game. Robbie watched her as much as he watched Merrick; she missed the little fellow's big moment but lied, convincingly, when he greeted her with his gap-toothed "Did you see me, Mum?" Robbie kept his counsel.

The months flickered by, Kathy edging inexorably further

away from her family. She was not a great cook, but knew where to buy food. Money became easier to spend; the cleaner now came twice a week, and, if Kathy could pay to have anything done, she would. The only skills that earned her respect were in her job. So the pattern developed.

Robbie was an unusual child, stranded sometimes on an island like the squares into which he'd jumped in one of the games they'd played at Scouts, 'Man The Lifeboats'. Inheriting his father's antipathy for technology, especially the ''puter,' as Merrick had dubbed the curse of automata when young, he was happy to bury himself in books whenever possible. But he was not anti-social; he chose his mates with care, chief among whom was Harry Newcombe. Harry and he understood each other, while Emily was good company when they needed it. He tried not to ignore Merrick, but that was not easy.

And he had his stamps. Iain had started that on his visit to Melbourne, furthering Robbie's interest when he sent him the album he'd kept as a boy in Aberdeen. Lachlan felt mixed emotions when he watched the boy unpack the carefully wrapped gift, its green customs sticker clinging on to the fold of the brown envelope, that blazed with new stamps. Since then the boy had spent hours with his hobby, keeping the treasures in an old biscuit-box, once orange and black. Many a time Lachlan came home to a sink floating in stamps ripped hastily off envelopes, sometimes before he'd seen the letter. At first Robbie had collected every stamp there was; now, he concentrated on The Commonwealth. He'd soon be amending that, Kathy had said, not without a ripple of smugness. The boy hadn't registered. Rebecca was the boy's greatest supplier. She went out of her way to dispatch new issues of stamps across the globe, making artistic tableaux of colour and shape on her letters. When she was abroad it was a bonus, more ripped ears of paper skimming the sink.

The boys devoured videos, though Lachlan was adamant

they avoided American detritus. One evening, ten days after his letter to Iain, when the boys were ensconced in an animal documentary, the phone rang. Kerryn. As usual, she was full of verve, sorry not to have spoken for a while. Mutual, thought Lachlan, as she chattered on. He told her of the company, the boys, his plans for England, whereupon she reiterated what she'd said in Sydney: Lachlan should catch up with her friends Sam and Pauline Stanbury in the Lake District. He demurred a moment: was it possible to 'catch up' with strangers? Kerryn was insistent; the couple lived in a lovely old house they had inherited, Sam's family having owned Hawkthwaite since 1700 at least. Kerryn had been there the previous year: 'an idyll' she pronounced it. She would e-mail England at once, and alert the pair.

Lachlan's resistance weakened: the Lake District was not far north of Chester. It would not preclude his attempt to see Iain. There was a pause on the line.

"Well, why not?" he concluded, and the call ended with laughter.

The video over, boys in bed after lively chat, Lachlan sat down at the table to write to the Stanburys. It was a far easier letter than the last one written to England. Kerryn was a girl of her word; her message had flexed across the wires of the world in no time. Lachlan pictured her friends' ancient homestead in what Aussies always termed 'The Lakes District.' Stone walls were a feature, he knew, but perhaps that was The Peak District. There would be a pub nearby, probably an inn called The Shepherd's Fold, The Queen's Arms, or The Black Hawk. Australian bars were not unlike Scottish ones, but the English were different. Quaint and cosy, he knew from experience. Rebecca and Saul spoke of their 'local', whose ale he had sampled, real ale. It was just a pity they served it warm.

He kept the letter brief. Rough dates were enough, and he stressed he and the lads could sleep on the floor or in a tent. He used Kerryn's 'catch-up' expression; it would hardly cause anguish. And he concluded that they would not overstay; typically apologetic, Kathy would have said. The letter sealed, he was in the mood for more. St. Paul was unflagging in his epistles; Lachlan could manage another, this one the most relaxed, to Rebecca.

Nipping into the kitchen for a beer, he caught sight of a recent addition on the calendar; Merrick's exuberant scrawl denoted a party on the coming weekend; he went to far more than Robbie. Lachlan paused. The prospect of teenage parties for his elder son did not fill him with relish. He realised Robbie's birthday would fall in England and felt relief. For his thirteenth the boy had been happy to go to a footy game; the fourteenth could prove interesting.

Lachlan's thoughts were firmly rooted in England, and his pen scampered over the lines to his sister. He shared her ability to write as she spoke; another joy to him was the chance to avoid punctuation, a chance he only took up with Rebecca. Their father had been a good letter-writer, but Iain was the best of all as a boy. Somewhere the zest had gone quiet.

The letter raced on, details and the odd witticism peppering paper that disappeared too quickly. He found himself talking of his own birthday, his fortieth, that loomed on the last day of March; he had no plans to make merry, but Dave had already dropped the lightest of warnings.

'It's a Monday," said Lachlan.

"Is it indeed?" Dave knew full well. Lachlan was ill-at-ease about his own birthday; like Christmas Day it held a compulsion to be more colourful than other days. Boxing Day, and other people's birthdays were better.

Back in the kitchen he counted the weeks till they left for England: eighteen. They would ferret by, and he'd need to book up. Money obstacles he was good at surmounting, but the ten thousand dollars air fare would hurt. He signed off the letter, dashes rampant, and sought a stamp in his wallet; it looked dull by comparison to those on her missives.

It was just after eleven, noon in the U.K. He was seized by the desire to ring her, to have an instant word. Then he realised she and Saul would be at work, but he was in the mood to leave a message, on spec. Kathy had said he was not spontaneous enough, and he felt rebuffed. 'Makeshift rather than spontaneous,' was the phrase. He dialled the number in Chester, picturing the phone on their yellow kitchen wall, and at once heard Saul's virile tones on the answer-machine. Lachlan spoke till the beep, avoiding news he'd put in the letter, and went to bed content.

For once he had a good dream. He was in a log cabin on a long sandy beach. Cormorants sat on a once-grey rock, now white with their crusted deposit. Jazz music toned in the distance and he was staring at a poem he'd written, a serious poem, about the ribbon and lace of words. Across a redundant wood stove sat his companion. Lachlan started to read the poem aloud, slightly self-conscious; his companion gazed at the stove. Nearing the end of verse three, Lachlan found himself wanting to cough, the feeling sat in his rib-cage: by verse four he was chortling until he could hold it no more: both of them burst into laughter, rocking, sustained laughter, pouring out of them, leaving them helpless and drained. Tears dropped on to the worn rush-matting; once again the companion's identity was unclear.

Waking up, there was a moist tear down the bridge of his nose. He felt good as he went to wake the boys. Robbie was reading in bed, Merrick still deeply asleep.

At breakfast Robbie had noticed his father's letter to England.

"Can I write to Rebecca, Dad?"

The boys felt a kinship with their aunt. Lachlan slit open the envelope and handed it to the boy.

"And, yes, you can read it."

Robbie smiled, brown eyes gleaming. He'd have read it anyway, and made a comment, not immediately, but some-time, over the coming days.

Rebecca was largely responsible for the elder boy's continued interest in letters, despite teasing from class-mates for whom e-mail was the only communication. He'd told Rebecca this and in her reply she compared letter-writing to a game of tennis: you needed the groundstrokes and knowledge of the sport, but there were many different ways to play a point. Best of all he'd thought her analogy on time-outs between games; they gave you thinking time in which to plan a strategy. And you looked forward to penning your reply, in due course. E-mail was instant, convenient, easy, but, like Lachlan, there was no comparison, for Robbie, to the receipt of a letter from the other side of the world written by a warm hand, entrusted to unknowns to deliver, emblazoned with stamps.

'The Scottish Play's run was coming to an end; houses had been fair, on some evenings good, matinées a waste of time. But the last night was always an occasion. Lachlan enjoyed dressing up in black tie. Robbie had asked to see the final performance and Hetty was happy to bring him. Merrrick was with a classmate, for a sleep-over and the beach the next day.

Lady Macbeth excelled, screwing unusual courage to the sticking place, no hint of failure entertained. Lachlan's eye met Brodie's as the actress left the spotlight and he nodded his admiration for both women. Female psychology held the day. Lennox was firing, Duncan stopped limping, the Gentle-woman was understated, as always. But Angus needed a challenge; Lachlan's anticipation grew into impatience.

The party went well. Brodie's partner was increasingly at ease, unlike his predecessor, who had spoken only to Norman, Lachlan remembered. The old retainer himself enjoyed last nights more than anything, walking around with the red wine, 'a good wee drop this, Lachie.' Brodie and the Porter had a lengthy discussion, punctuated with mirth, until Duncan lost his footing for a moment, grabbing the arm of Third Witch, who was eyeing up Ross at the time.

She would be a strong Mary Brenham in the next play, Lachlan decided. Lady Macduff was first to leave, but by then it was after midnight. Lachlan mentioned to Angus they might have a beer next week, and the actor agreed.

The Tinderbox had one week before 'Our Country's Good' opened; the Monday was spent round a table, discussing logistics. There were so many stages of preparation, once the social history of a play had been outlined. Lachlan and Brodie saw flexibility as essential. Music was an integral part of this production, and a retired teacher was giving his time. Brodie and the wardrobe mistress had spent hours on the women's costumes for the final scene, so different from the rest of the piece, when they wore only convict weeds; at the end they dressed for their performance of 'The Recruiting Officer'. Discussions could last all day; it was important the company had the chance to speak up. 'Dare to try' had been the motto of Lachlan's first school, a philosophy he embraced.

It was interesting to see several of the troupe take on the persona of their character: Lachlan waited to hear Meg spice the conversation, but she stayed quiet, disappointing him a little, saving herself, no doubt, for her rôle. Ralph Clark was still struggling with his inherent goodness; Mary Brenham had found hers, and Angus was itching to flex his riding crop, as the army captain.

This meeting ended soon after lunch, and, after conferring, the directors decided on an hour's rehearsal in which the actors would swap rôles: Ralph was the only one not keen, but Lachlan told him it would benefit him to play one of the more brutal officers, put his goodness to the test. They broke for a sandwich.

Just before reconvening, Angus came up to Lachlan.

"About that beer."

Lachlan looked at him; there was no point in delaying.

"Tuesday?" he suggested.

"Sounds good. Should I bring that script?"

"Why not?"

That evening Robbie had a tennis fixture; Lachlan arrived as he began his final match. The opponent was tall, sandy-haired, with a decent serve. Robbie held his own for the first six games, but had his service broken in the seventh, after which the lanky boy raced away with the set. Robbie shook his dangling hand and came over to his father, eyes shielded against the evening sun.

"Not great, Dad."

"Not bad, though, at least at the start. He's got a much greater reach."

Robbie smiled; he would not be a six-footer, and accepted the fact.

They stayed chatting on the grass after the other boys had gone home. Lachlan could tell Robbie was pondering something. He avoided the direct question, talking of his lessons, including maths where he was struggling, then moved on to his mates. There must have been a bit of ribbing, perhaps about his books, but he was anxious about his Easter tennis match. Would Lachlan take him to Torquay down the Ocean Road? It was still several Saturdays away, but he liked to have things clear in his mind.

"We could make a weekend of it, Robs. Camping. About time we did that again."

The boy nodded.

"But can you get a Saturday off work? I know it's always a big night at the theatre for you."

"No night's that big. We'll have a boys' weekend on the Great Ocean Road. You and Merrick can cook."

The boy looked up at him. The furrow in his brow was not there. Lachlan watched him walk across to get changed, towel over his shoulder, eyes down, thinking. For all that his theatre engaged Lachlan, the boys' dramas mattered most.

CHAPTER TEN

As Lachlan stepped up onto the Newcombes' verandah that Sunday evening, he heard their grandfather clock strike seven. Sure enough, its hands showed ten past. The boys had been here since after lunch, while he spent the afternoon doing chores. Hateful task. In Aberdeen the Sabbath was old-fashioned and sacrosanct; now Sunday should be for plundering.

Jo greeted him warmly, Hetty in her wake.

"Lachie, James." A dark-haired man offered his hand.

"You're the locum?"

James nodded. Lachlan knew one of Dave's partners was on long-service leave. "Dave's at the surgery. Shouldn't be long. Beth Dixon's coming," informed Jo, handing Lachlan a corkscrew for the cold Chardonnay in his hand. Tom Dixon, an ex-school mate of Dave's, wrote poetry in his spare time and was in Launceston for a conference; his wife was a sharp wit, enjoying her new challenge as a head-mistress.

The bell rang and Beth swept in. They moved to the patio at the back, passing the boys engrossed in a video with Harry. Emily was in her room, doing prep. She was very bright, without precociousness and even at eleven put schoolwork first. On Lachlan's last visit she had treated him to the gruesome tale of Aggripina, the poisoner in Ancient Rome.

Beth was in full flow. Hetty winked at Lachlan, who noticed James already comfortable in the ambience. Twenty minutes later Dave was back, bringing out a feisty bottle of

106

red, which was uncorked as the barbecue was fired up. Jo and Dave were inveterate games players; one famous evening had been enlivened by a game Dave had to confess came from America. Its concept was hardly a game, more a series of questions, one of which asked players which profession they'd have chosen if they had not followed their current career. There were only the four of them that night and Kathy had enjoyed the game more than anyone. Dave started them off.

"Whale-watcher," he declared; hoots of derision rocked the deck. But he was serious and had then gone into great detail on his fondness for whales since first seeing them off the coast of New Zealand. Kathy had thought watching was a prelude to the kill, but Dave was quick to insist he meant having his own boat, warm weather, short hours and a life of no cares. Jo was astonished, her answer was more predictable: vicar's wife. Dave nodded eagerly, but Kathy was wary. "Too much answering the phone for a husband who's never there." Her words were crisp, not acidic. Not then.

"And you, Lachie," asked Jo, fingers skimming the top of her glass.

"Doctor," he replied, to assorted grunts. "But I'd have been hopeless, my science is dire."

"And you'd have been too involved," observed Dave. Lachlan expected this caveat from Kathy; from Dave its veracity was easier to take. He dwelt for a moment on the answers they'd given. Dave would have been a great watcher of whales.

They were aware Kathy had not answered; so was she, tasting the moment with dry lips.

"Well?" offered Dave.

Kathy sat back, eyes firm.

"I think I'd have been a prison governor."

There was silence. Then Dave laughed his full-blooded roar, but Kathy was serious.

"You'd have been good," said Jo.

"I know," clipped Kathy, eyes still firm.

Lachlan remembered the moment, not a blitz of warning, nor even a shudder of resentment; his hands had merely registered pins and needles. And he had seen Dave's expression.

This evening looked like escaping game-free. Hetty was in her element with the young; the Dixon wife was entertaining, Lachlan chatted with James, whose home was in Port Macquarie. Dave left the table for a few minutes, and returned with a box in his hand.

"I thought we'd got away with it," Lachlan ribbed him.

"Is this new?" enquired Hetty.

"It's not actually," rejoined Jo. "But we haven't played it very much."

In addition to coloured couches, plastic triangles and two or three packs of 'Treatment' cards, the inevitable board unfolded to reveal six separate areas through which players must speed. There were general knowledge teasers, plus questions on medicine, literature, science, film and history, two green dice and a set of instructions, hardly thumbed.

Hetty, as matriarch, rolled first, and they were soon embroiled. Best moments came when a player was sent for 'Treatment', and thus enabled to draw one of the alluring cards. The first couple of questions seemed harmless, the third, taken by Beth, had a yellow asterisk on it back: that meant they must all answer.

"Which player do you consider had the most rebellious childhood?" asked the card. James guffawed; Beth sat back in her chair.

"This game works best with folk you know really well," smiled Dave, looking round. "But strangers can just let go with their answers; you'll never see these people again, James, so don't hang back."

Beth looked round the circle. "It has to be you, James," she decided.

"Thank you," came his reply. "But I would say, you, Jo."

"I'd have to agree with that," twinkled Hetty. "Close thing, though, between you and Lachlan."

"You're wrong. It's Lachie." Dave's voice rang with daring.

Jo was enjoying herself. Lachlan wondered for a minute about the fate of her charge at school; there'd been no chance yet to enquire. "It's a hard call," piped Jo, in no hurry to declare her hand, "but you're the least rebellious now. I reckon you were the most rebellious then." She turned to her husband, squeezing his arm.

One answer to go. Lachlan took in their expressions. "That last comment is a shrewd one, Jo, as we'd expect. It's good psychology, as we'd also expect. But nothing can mask the fact that one of us round this table had a more than rebellious childhood. I know, and they know, it was wilful." James was not so keen to guffaw now; his youth stood out all of a sudden, he was not so suave. Dave's eyes didn't flinch. Beth was excited; it was a different sort of evening for her.

"So it has to be Hetty," proclaimed Lachlan, ashen-serious for a second, till he could hold it no longer. Laughter cascaded round the deck.

"Are you all sane?" Harry's head appeared out of the window, Merrick underneath, trying to see out.

"Not for a moment," answered his father. "Beth has to go for some treatment, that's all."

"Fruit cakes, all of them," could be heard as the head then withdrew.

"Coffee?" asked Jo, standing up. Voices murmured assent.

"Good game, Dave," said Beth. "Who's winning?"

A quick glance at the board revealed Hetty streaking away.

"Am I?" said the matriarch. "I'd no idea."

Lachlan was amused; she was not used to lying, but her

eternal modesty had got the better of her.

"No idea in the world, had you Hetty?" said Lachlan.

"You seem to be last, Lachie," said Jo, returning with a tray. Newly broken pieces of chocolate could be seen peering over its precipice. Dave lit a few candles. James' eyes fired up.

It was some time before another player needed treatment; the next victim, Jo.

"Which player would confess quickest under torture?"

This was more serious. After a silence Dave spoke first.

"Tricky one. I'd go for Beth or James. Maybe James. Just."

Hetty looked almost troubled. "No, it's me," she confessed. "I'd be hopeless under torture."

"I think you'd be quite strong," encouraged Jo.

"I reckon Lachlan," said James. None of the others commented. There was an edge to things now. Dave was right. The previous question held kudos; this one, hastily-wrapped shame. Dave was filling glasses, but only Jo held out a glass.

"D'you want to stop?" Dave asked into the air round the table, taking care not to point the question at Hetty. They did not, though a tacit agreement was reached that the next treatment question would seal it. The couches sat on their squares, Hetty's still ahead, but only just.

The dice landed; one couch moved on. James broke the deadlock, and reached eagerly for a card. Checking the card before reading it out, he breathed with relief.

"Which player will go to bed tonight with the biggest smile on their face?" Lachlan thought of Kathy and how answers would differ if she were with them on the deck.

Jo answered first. "I think Beth," she said. "She's got a whole day's game-plan for the next Staff Training Day. You'll see."

"She may well be right," responded the headmistress. Such an innovation would not be unwelcome in her view, dyslexia workshops had long run their course.

James played safe. "Dave, because he's got away with his game." Youth had shown its hand again. Lachlan avoided Hetty's gaze.

The others were thinking, eyes moving round the deck; candles burned. A mosquito darted into the hallowed circle, then thought better of it.

Hetty's eyes were quite screwed up now. "Difficult," she said, "but I'll settle for Jo; she's had a restful weekend after all."

Lachlan knew Jo slightly better; he was aware that, while what Hetty said was true, Jo would also be thinking of the morning and the week ahead. His witnessing of her anxiety over the boy caught with ritalin had shown him her devotion. For once Hetty might be incorrect. But she was Beth's answer to the riddle, and despite her demurring smile, there was also a wave of pride.

Lachlan and Dave were still to go, biding their time. Lachlan yielded first; there was a danger in waiting too long, adding weight to an answer; it was only a game.

Robbie appeared on the deck.

"Two minutes, son. Tell Merrick."

"I think it has to be you, James", came Lachlan's answer. James stirred, unsure if he was a victim of Lachlan's Christian principles or of a nudging joke.

"Why?"

"Because......" began Lachlan, "Because smiles are his job. And I think he's enjoyed himself tonight. Right?"

The locum hesitated for a second.

"And the Maestro…?" Hetty's gaze had gone back to Dave, who clearly had not reached his decision.

"You, Hetty. For no reason at all."

They all stood up, James quieter than hitherto. Hetty and Beth were gone in a flurry of kisses. Lachlan picked up his younger son and put his arm around Robbie.

"Till soon," he shouted back up the steps. And he heard

111

the clock strike one.

During the week progress on the next play was staccato. They were all aware they had little time, and, in some members of the company, this came out as panic.

Not Angus. He was quiet for the first two days, but on the Tuesday evening, arriving early at the Southbank bar to meet Lachlan, he was unusually perky.

"I know what it is, and the answer's yes," he said almost before the beers were down on a small, round table, that rocked disconcertingly until Lachlan put a wad of napkin underneath.

Over the weeks Angus had spent time on the script, and sensed the opportunity of an unusual play; his instincts locked. Lachlan was not surprised; he had put out tenders in the way he spoke of the play, Angus was astute, and gut feelings worked in the theatre. They conversed in detail; Angus' understanding of the play was keen. Lachlan let his actors have full input into their rôles, but it was unusual to have an actor with such a sharp focus at this early stage. Angus liked the play's dénouement, and asked questions about it. Lachlan told him of the production he'd seen, stressing how theirs would be equally stirring.

"Better get a tan, then, for when I'm on that table," reasoned Angus, suddenly pausing as he mulled over its complexities. Something in the actor's words made Lachlan more excited than for some time. They pondered Brodie's hostile reaction to the piece, Angus risking the view that its feline element would not go unappreciated by Lachlan's co-director. They grinned. The more Lachlan thought of the play, the more he wanted to be under way with it. Angus was a confederate, not a risk.

He stood up, clasped the glasses and went inside to the bar. When he came back, the conversation swayed away from 'Wolf.' A girl came out and smiled at the two men. Lachlan observed Angus' reaction to the girl.

"We must do this again," said Angus shaking his hand. Watching Lachlan disappear up the steps, he downed a last drop and reached for his script. Could he be satanic in savagery? Angus was not sure.

A letter with unknown handwriting and a nondescript stamp was waiting in the mailbox: Pauline Stanbury had replied by return. Lachlan read it before he entered the house. Written in a generous hand, large loops hanging down the page, she said they would be delighted for Lachlan, Robbie and Merrick to visit them in The Lakes. He handed the letter to Robbie. The boy eyed the stamp with disappointment, then read the letter with interest.

"Sounds good, Dad."

"What does?" Merrick burst into the room.

"Have they got animals?" he asked on learning the source of the letter. "What sort? Probably just sheep and things. We've got them here."

Robbie told him there was no mention of animals in the letter, but they'd probably have dogs, chickens and possibly a horse.

"Chickens mean foxes," he said eagerly. 'I like foxes."

"Not more than sharks?"

"No". The reply was wary; his fad was running its course.

"Does Mum know we're going to England?" asked Robbie, suddenly. Lachlan shook his head. She would know soon, he surmised.

"She may not like the idea!"

"Why not?"

"Because she's not been consulted about it."

"Should she be? I don't see why?"

"But you have to tell her, Dad."

Merrick went out, returning with his homework book. Having a father who had taught was useful sometimes, constricting at others. Robbie sensed this was the former and vacated the room. He needed a hand later on.

The run-up to the opening of 'Our Country's Good' proved languid. Next day the convict scenes were addressed, the women proving more competent than the men. Brodie went out of her way to intensify their warm-up, and received small recompense. It was still hot, but the weather was not the sole reason for lethargy. As she observed to Lachlan, the females in the piece had more space in which to flesh out their characters. Robert Sideway, an instigator of ideas, with great powers of persuasion, seemed unable to act as the catalyst today, and the rehearsal slumped. By six o'clock there was no point in continuing; little had been achieved with the male convicts and their female counterparts were bored.

On Tuesday the officers' tautly written scenes went better. Angus was impatient, to Lachlan's eyes, Lennox biddable, the rest wooden. Lachlan was reminded of the performance where real prisoners played the officers and suspected they threw themselves into the brutality with gusto. The vision of Iain in a convict's smock flashed through his head. Lachlan was no stranger to chasing unwanted images from his brain, but only recently had he been successful: the secret was not to waste energy. Chase the dragons slowly, trident and net. The picture of men in prison stitching hessian mailbags had stayed with him since boyhood.

By Friday it was clear the weekend would have to be spoiled with rehearsal. Over a drink by the river Yarra, whose mud-brown silt looked more depressing than usual, Brodie, Norman and Lachlan made a quiet trio. They knew the story: "It'll be all right on the night," was not a philosophy to be embraced. Lachlan had become accustomed to smiling at school when colleagues had reassured him about his latest production. There, they had been right: in the tiny ponds of school drama energy compensated for expertise and he had a willing audience. The outside world was not so kind.

Brodie, who'd planned a weekend with her partner down

at Barwon Heads, was philosophical. Lachlan was angry: the boys needed his time. Norman, unusually for him, was the most perturbed. They had tried games, gimmicks, innovations and more; the only course left to them was a series of runs-through, starting at nine the next morning. Robbie needed transporting to a match. Merrick was at a loose end for both days; there was a limit as to how much Lachlan could put on the Newcombes. And Hetty.

Silence permeated, punctuated by casual talk from other tables, where customers shed the skin of the week and stretched into two and a half days' repose. Lachlan thought of Rebecca and her Friday evenings; despite being eleven hours behind, she was nearer than he to respite. He hitched his shoulders and gave Brodie a clenched smile. It was not returned.

"Another beer," said Norman, trying to be genial.

Both shook their heads; they had plans to make. Once, Lachlan had played the lead in a staff and pupils' production; there were many lines to learn, at which he proved vulnerable, but the joy of being responsible only for his rôle was immense. No schedules, big decisions, forward planning, dilating egos, logistics and money, just turning up when called, being the part, and making his exit.

On the tram his spectre broke cover. He had been expecting it. Most people breathed naturally and without thinking. When the spectre came, Lachlan was denied such ease. It had started in a cinema, when he realised and admitted to himself that Kathy was going: an awareness of his breathing that rendered him tense, then heavy. The film was not tense; he was, and assumed he would shed the heaviness on leaving the cinema. He did not. Nor did it desert him on going to bed or waking next morning; on the contrary, he was heavier still. In trying to describe it, at first to himself, then to friends, finally to his doctor, Lachlan failed dramatically. His mates were puzzled, Jo holding her breath for a while, then concentrating on him as her breathing took over automatically. Dave said little. Had any patient had this, Lachlan asked? Several patients hyper-ventilated in the chair, but that was not the same thing. Many sweated, trembled gently or went red in the face during treatment, but all were restored to a sort of calm within minutes. Lachlan's heaviness lasted for days, and when it subsided, his muscles took over the action without his thinking about it, so he was unable to say when it stopped. Only when it returned. In times of tension, such as now, he was not surprised; he simply waited for its strictures and laboured on, but sometimes it struck when he was far from tense, at a party, reading to the boys, in the shower.

A second visit to the doctor was disturbing. The medic. admitted he'd not come across the 'syndrome' before; 'syndrome' hit hard, plumbing new, different levels of tension. Valium was prescribed, which Lachlan had left perched on the chest of drawers behind a paperweight given him by his Year 11 on leaving his last school. Finally he had succumbed, taking two of tablets late one evening. They made no difference. Since then he had seen a couple of people, one of whom advised him to welcome the feeling, not push it away. He'd never gone down that track; by that token he'd be blinking and swallowing consciously, or smitten with eternal hiccups. He'd learned to live with it, saying that others had far greater afflictions, but at its keenest he was crippled by it, and quite afraid. People breathed and went about their lives; he had to remember to breathe, then go about his.

His only consolation had been Heathcliff, in 'Wuthering Heights', a warped hero but an ally: after Catherine's death he described his inordinate suffering, and the fact that that he had to remind himself to breathe. But for Lachlan to mention he'd found solace with a figure of literature, albeit a profound one, would invite whispers of concern when he left a room, friends breathing out fear.

The tram screeched loudly and came to a juddering halt.

A small girl had stepped out into the road at a busy inter-section as the lights changed to amber. A car turning left had missed her by inches. The girl was standing in the road, white-faced and wobbly. A passer-by walked up and cradled the child against her stout frame.

"Worst place in the whole of Melbourne for accidents, this junction," muttered an old woman in ankle socks. Other passengers stared out of the window: dusk was approaching. Daylight Savings Time was imminent, and with it the end of summer. The start of old age, thought Lachlan, seeing March 31st in red on an otherwise black-figured calendar. Brakes were noisily released, the girl walked away into the dusk, still held by the woman. No one else had lent help. People didn't. Not in cities. Country towns were different, like Scottish villages. There'd been a fishing tragedy in the Orkneys only a few weeks ago, four young men drowned, eternally cold in a raging black sea late at night. Another needless accident, inconsolable loss.

When the tram came to his stop, Lachlan took a deep breath and stood up.

CHAPTER ELEVEN

"Meg's good," said Hetty in the interval. They were crammed into The Tinderbox's tiny bar, two weeks into the run. Hetty had turned up one evening, tapping Lachlan on the shoulder as he stood waiting for the start. He rarely went for a drink in the interval, but, when Hetty was in, they had a tacit agreement to meet up.

"She is," he replied, smiling at her sharpness, not spoiling for her the fact Meg had not another word to utter. He had put the actress in the crowd scenes in Act Two, where she made her mark without the obstacle of words. They chatted about the play, Hetty flicking back a fetching headscarf that had no doubt been sent across the Nullarbor from Perth.

An arm touched him in the mêlée, then a hand struck him on the cheek.

"Kieren!" he beamed. "And Johnno..." Ben was completing the trio that fought their way through the small space. In fact, it was a quartet.

"Lachlan, Rachel," said Johnno, indicating an open-faced girl with red ear-rings. He shook hands. Hetty bade farewell, leaving 'the young' to themselves.

"You're as good as your word," he nodded, genuinely pleased they had taken up his offer to see the play. "The production's got a little way to go, yet."

"Don't apologise," said Ben. "You did that with us and there was no need."

All three, after their involvement in Lachlan's last school play, considered themselves doyens of thespia. Rachel followed the bolting conversation with studied calm. It was not clear to which of the three she was attached, if any.

A tiny bell, almost unheard, was sounded by Norman.

"If you'd like a drink after the show," laughed Lachlan, making his way backstage, "you'll be welcome."

"Sounds good," said Kieren, "after one of your endings." His mischievous smile hovered after the quartet had gone; in the realms of the sharp, Hetty had a rival.

Lachlan hadn't taught all the boys, only Ben, but, in the boarding house on Friday nights, they had been the instigators of mirth, exchanging banter until long after lights-out. Johnno was an interesting character, reading law with a sure tread. He knew his own mind and was disarmingly honest. Ben had joined them in Year 11 from a country school: with his steed, Noble Gambler, he was an equestrian of some standing. Unlike his two friends, university was not automatic for him; at present he was dallying with the army.

After the performance the bar was not quiet, the five of them spilling round a table, whilst Brodie, her partner, more smartly dressed than normal, and Norman were seated on bar-stools. Conversation raced, at first on the play, then their university jinks, Lachlan's boys, England and beyond. Kieren had once asked about Kathy; Lachlan told him, mincing no words.

In that last Year 12 class there was also Lydia, perhaps the brightest student Lachlan ever taught. Her creative essays had been so good he was afraid of not understanding them. She never said anything in class, preferring to store thoughts and present them on paper, crisp as a secret. At the end of the first term she had been absent; this happened again late in the next term, and when she had not re-appeared in term four he was anxious. He rang her at home, where she assured him all was well; she would be back in school next week. She never was. But she stayed in his mind. He casually asked Kieren if she'd been sighted. But no: the secret had turned in on itself, like a conch.

Rachel looked at her watch, and Ben sensed it was time to leave.

"You might like the next play," said Lachlan, shaking hands. "Unusual, just up your street."

"Should we get a season ticket?" Johnno was there first, but Kieren's expression told he had a similar quip.

"Concession for students, past pupils free," he said instead.

"See you later," said Rachel, gently. "And thanks for the drink."

The four of them walked into the night.

"Like a lift, Lachie?" He turned. Brodie's partner was excelling himself,

On Saturday Dave took Robbie and Harry to a footy match. Lachlan was glad; it gave him the day with Merrick. He deliberately made no plans.

Merrick was more robust than his brother, though equally serious at times. With his close-cropped hair and outsize front teeth, he presented a gutsy figure. At present he was keen on black T-shirts. Rebecca would not miss that detail. A shark emblem alleviated the black today, and sharks were on the computer menu as Lachlan walked in.

"Aren't they beautiful, Dad?"

The screen showed requiem sharks near Mexico's Isla Mujeres, a lethargic species, even when divers swam close and touched them. The next picture was of a diver with his hand in the mouth of a blue shark.

"Blue sharks attack victims of shipwrecks and plane crashes," said Merrick. "Look at their fins. So streamlined."

"Streamlined," said Lachlan, but the boy was now intent on the angel shark, sandy-coloured with pebble-like markings. Lachlan had to admit they were compelling creatures. On the news the previous week an epaulette shark had been washed up on one of the Sydney beaches, a fact the authorities had tried to conceal.

Best of all to Merrick's mind was the great white, a shark of rare intelligence, whose favourite food was sea-lions, sometimes mistaking them for humans. As a lover of words, Lachlan would have gone for the tasselled wobbegong with its great camouflage, found off Western Australia.

"Too good to stay in," said Lachlan. "What shall we do?"

The boy swung round in the chair Lachlan had given him for Christmas, chubby elbow resting on his well-scarred knee.

"Swim?"

"Sounds good to me."

The pool, newly-opened, was gunnel-full of shouting children and harsh Melbourne sunlight. Lachlan thought he'd made a mistake, but it was Merrick's choice and there were doors open to a patch of grass outside, where they could escape the crowds.

In the water Lachlan watched as Merrick hurled himself into the pool; he was fearless. He was also a menace, his splashes substantial. Where Robbie was cheerfully sensitive, Merrick was straightforward: as long as his life didn't change, he was fine. That had emerged well before Kathy's departure.

"Shall we do lengths now, Dad?"

For a chunky boy he moved fast, good exercise for Lachlan, and they negotiated six lengths with only minor mishaps.

"I could do with some goggles," said Merrick back at the shallow end.

"Me too," laughed Lachlan. "When's your birthday?"

"Sooner than yours," lied the boy. "Which reminds me......Well, are you?"

"What?"

"Having a party? Everyone thinks you should. Hetty, Harry, Dave, Jo, Emily, Robbie ..."

Lachlan paused. There were thirteen days to go. "We'll

see."

The boy looked at him hard.

For lunch he thought they'd have a change. Eating on the pavement beside a main road is not a good prospect in cities; in Melbourne things are different. Having left the car, they trotted along until they found a Greek restaurant with blue and white checked tablecloths fluttering in the breeze. There were only two tables, both empty. Merrick chose the four-seater to give them more room.

He looked at the menu quizzically; the names ran round his lips.

"What's taramasalata?"

"Fish brains or fish eggs, more exactly."

He smiled. "I'll try that," he pronounced.

"And a glass of ouzo?"

Eyes stared into his. "Course."

Lachlan's Greek salad excited no envy from Merrick; instead, he began to ask his father questions about their trip to England. He was disappointed not to be going to London, especially as they landed there, but was told it was too expensive, and too busy. Devon held promise for its sailing, golf, swimming and moors.

"There's a famous prison there," blurted Lachlan before he could think. The picture of Iain came back; he by-passed it for a scenic view of Widecombe-in-the-Moor, which he'd seen in a magazine. He explained they might go on into Cornwall, a rugged land of smugglers, castles and full moons. Merrick was happier; the notion excited him. They would then move on up to Chester for a week with Rebecca and Saul.

"She's keen to see you," Lachlan told him. "Remember?" There would be much to do when staying with her. It was the last part of the trip that concerned the boy, staying with strangers in the English bush, who had no children his age. What would he do all day?

122

Lachlan considered his point. These days kids hardly had a childhood, rushing on the conveyor belt to experience, 'missing the meaning' as Eliot would say. And here was his son trying to extend his childhood, exactly what Lachlan wanted for both boys.

"I'll give it some thought," he replied. Pauline had mentioned a birds of prey centre nearby and a tiny railway, along with some sort of fête he remembered. "They may well have a computer," he added. "Only heathens don't have that."

Merrick looked up quickly: it was not common for his father to mock himself. They smiled, and Lachlan felt part of him lurch forward to England; another part was already there. A Greek lad brought out the bill and stood waiting.

"Efharisto."

Merrick spun round. "I suddenly remembered it from my visit to Greece twenty years ago," said Lachlan. Merrick affected not to be impressed, unlike the waiter, whose day was made. He proceeded to tell them that of all languages Greek and Arabic were unique because their words came closest to the meanings. Take 'love', for instance; in Greek there were at least four specific words for that. The waiter took the money and retreated into the café.

Merrick looked at Lachlan's plate that was not quite clean. "You don't usually leave anything, Dad."

It was true. But Merrick's chatter burst forth. He'd just been learning from Emily about Aggripina. And he was away, lavishing macabre details of her exploits on to his helpless father. She'd given assistance to Nero, but had then got on the emperor's nerves, for trying to share the throne with him.

"Whatever made you think of her?"

"That bit of food on your plate. Aggripina was a taster as well; that's how she started in poisons." The waiter had returned and stood back, listening. Lachlan thought there must have been some great Greek poisoners, but decided not

123

to ask.

"It was the Tower I wanted to see in London," chattered on Merrick. He wasn't worried about palaces, cathedrals or museums, but the Tower appealed with its ravens that never flew away. "And didn't one of the kings build a maze?"

The two of them walked back to the car; Lachlan put his hand on the boy's shoulder, but it was slipped off. The lad continued to prattle on. Once in the car, they decided there was just time for a film; that would put chatter on hold.

Lachlan's birthday sprang towards him. It had a leering expression like Punch before he hits Judy hard in the confines of their striped canvas stall. He had always thought these shows savage, while everyone else laughed. There had been one on the beach in Aberdeen, hastily assembled by a man with a moustache, whose eyes weren't quite straight. He played to small audiences and, once the show was over, hoisted the stall onto his back and trudged up the beach. Lachlan watched when everyone else had turned away; it was all part of the performance to him. Contrasting emotions were aroused in him: not laughter, but sadness for Judy and anger with Punch. Why did she take it? They didn't have Punch and Judy in Australia, but he'd seen things that had brought up the same feelings, incidents in the street, live things, not theatrical. Some days at rehearsal he wanted to run out of The Tinderbox, never thinking again about fake constructions of 'reality'. He wasn't the only one; millions faked reality in their own way, anything to fend off real life. A man he met once was talking about soap operas on television, other people's real life into which viewers could invest energy that kept their own reality at bay. The man said soap operas should show life as it could be, not as it was. Circular thoughts swept round Lachlan; always at the centre was a certain date.

It being on a Monday that year absolved him of the need to stage a weekend party. When Dave and Jo finally spoke of the landmark, he was still reticent. The boys mentioned it in passing, only aware of forty as a number. Like sixty. Eighty-seven. Lachlan shuddered. Male menopause was bandied about on all fronts these days, drawing attention to a process that had been coped with by most men in history. Lachlan did not know what he was afraid of. Sagging muscles he'd noticed when shaving, a crease in the flesh on the side of his chin, also sported by a barrister in a programme he'd watched, an ageing barrister, fifty at least. Bodily fall-out lay ahead and he was seeing Dave at the surgery more than before. Keeping fit he managed half-heartedly; unpredictable hours at work was not a convincing excuse. Friends had passed the milestone, appearing no more ravaged than before, but the scythe was being sharpened, the tender thread stretching imperceptibly each dawn he survived. Shakespeare was ironic: age could wither Cleopatra. That was her tragedy.

"Let's get it over with, then," he said to Jo the night the question was removed from the dustsheets. It sounded more as if he was talking to Dave in his surgery. "A barbecue, low-key, with the kids. I'll buy the meat." Painless. Soon over. Not allowed to be memorable.

"Anyone else you'd like?"

A pause. "Beth and Tom, now he's back. Perhaps not James," remembering their games evening. "Hetty of course. And maybe Lynch." Lynch Campbell was an ex-pupil, a carpenter, who sometimes helped with sets for The Tinderbox. Lachlan had been in touch with him about 'Wolf', where a good carpenter was essential.

"I'll do the wine," said Dave, waiting to see if the guest list was going to be extended. It wasn't. Kathy had been a great one for parties in their early days, but lapsed after a while. He wondered about Kerryn, but mid-week for a barbie was indulgent. And he still wasn't happy about the boys where she was involved, refusing to admit they might warm to her. Jealousy, as yet stillborn.

The late autumn birthday was cool. At the theatre he worked on 'Wolf', juggling ideas, then had a long discussion with Brodie. She was unaware of his birthday, which made him feel furtive, almost unclean. Too late to say anything now, but the degree of discomfort surprised him. He wanted to leave early to be at the butcher's, but it was almost seven when he walked from The Tinderbox.

As he was about to enter the shop, in a quiet back street of the city, he bumped into a man with one arm. The window was a frieze of colour, and Lachlan had been standing outside, gazing at the display. As the man passed him, Lachlan looked involuntarily at the man's stump, so like the cuts of meat on display. The man saw his gaze. Lachlan made a late weak attempt at a smile, but too late. He felt bad about staring at the deformity, wanting the moment back to redress it, so was not alert when the butcher, a large man full of jokes, asked what he'd like. 'The last few moments back,' shot through his head. To know if the one-armed man sensed my thoughts. Without concentrating, he bought sausages, ribs, chops and steak. But he didn't enjoy the experience and found the butcher's jokes crass.

"Have a good night," rang out behind him as he left the shop. Again, the birthday had touched a nerve.

The boys were in ebullient form when he picked them up and they drove to Hawkthorn companionably. Robbie had homework to do; Merrick had none. Usually the boys ate with Harry and Emily, but tonight Lachlan suggested they ate together.

"What's the homework, Robs?"

"English, not a problem."

Jo had blown up a few balloons on the deck, 'discreet', she termed them; she and Hetty were caressing a large salad in the kitchen.

"Happy Birthday," said Hetty, handing him a small parcel. 'I know you don't want a fuss." He opened the book, and thanked her. Dave came out of the bedroom doing up his belt and gave Lachlan a hug.

"Beer, mate?" The two strolled onto the deck.

An hour later they were eating and laughter spilled around. Dave had shown his hallmark skill in choosing the wine, and he made a quick toast. Surprisingly Lachlan felt moved; standing up, he spoke briefly and raised his glass in thanks.

"No games tonight?" ventured Hetty. Jo shook her head. Lynch looked perplexed. Robbie had stayed at the table while the other kids left: he was enjoying the pace of it all. Lynch told them of some furniture he'd just made for friends out of driftwood combed on the beach; his current project was a dining-room table. Lachlan listened.

"We may need a table for this new play, Lynch; it's got to be strong, mind."

Lynch nodded. It was Hetty who brought a spark to their talking. She was reading a book on Pontius Pilate and wondered what he would have been like to meet. Opinions differed.

"Who would you like to meet?" she twinkled at Dave. "Anyone in history."

"Or literature?" asked Lachlan.

"Or literature."

Dave flashed in. "Alexander the Great."

"Why?"

A recent programme had retraced the steps of Alexander, pinpointing the scale of his challenge and the depth of his mythical energy. Ever since hearing the story of how as a boy he tamed his father's horse, Bucephalus, by facing it away from the sun, Dave had been entranced by the King of Macedon's son. As a teenager, he'd read as much as he could on Alexander the Conqueror, who died at thirty-three, and his enthusiasm had not dimmed. The eulogy sparked a strong reaction, Tom Dixon feeling he was myth not man, Hetty asking what had happened to Alexander's mother, and

Jo, once she could force her way into the conversation, arguing that he was a hideous misogynist. Lachlan looked at Robbie. Alexander's treatment of animals brought the argument into relief; that led on to Hannibal, censured for his Alpine crossing with elephants. But no one wanted to meet him.

"I think I'd like to meet Boadicea," said Beth. "Think of those chariots."

More opposition, the Iceni's warrior queen likened to the makers of 'Ben Hur' with no regard for horses.

"Lady Godiva, more like," said Tom, but he was challenged on all sides by the women, as a militant element crept in. They diverged for a moment onto the glories of the modern Coventry Cathedral, which Lachlan made a note to visit, and this led Beth to speak of the Guggenheim in Bilbao she'd seen last year.

"Deviation," said Lachlan reaching for the red wine. Beth swung on him, demanding to know his answer to the question. Lachlan was not quite ready, but after a second's thought came out with Oscar Schindler, which led to heated exchange on Thomas Kenneally's novel, and the film.

Lynch had been quiet, soaking in the views around him. When at last he saw an opening, he plumped for the cyclist, Hubert Opperman. There was laughter from Dave, a slight frown on the women's faces, but Lynch was able to expand on the feats of the man from Rochester, Victoria, the gold country, who held the world record for twenty-four hours cycling, a staggering 820 miles. Lynch painted the man with fervour. Then sport lurched in, icons and heroes that Robbie heard with a glow. Harry appeared briefly, but when Hetty brought up the character of Judas Iscariot, the boys slipped away.

"I've always had a lot of sympathy for Judas," she declared. Beth questioned her freely, Lynch joining in, too.

"It all comes back to that carpenter," he smiled. Would they like to meet Jesus?

Jo was sure she would, Lachlan agreeing, with hesitation. Tom wondered if he could envisage the Christ in human form, then, sensing he was serious and not quite comfortable with that, quipped that a meal would be enlivened by the presence of J.C.

Hetty noted how Jesus responded to hospitality in the Bible. She would speak with Judas first, then meet with his Master, a prospect that fascinated. In the realms of literature, however, she chose George Eliot's Casaubon, so she could at last say what she thought of him.

"There's a test for those Christian principles," said Lynch, not unkindly. When Mr. d'Arcy, Iago and Betsey Trotwood had run their gamut, the others sank back in silence.

"Thanks," said Lachlan a short time later. "I've rather enjoyed it, in the end."

But All Fools' Day was still welcome.

CHAPTER TWELVE

Two days later Lachlan dropped the boys at school and headed for a swim. At this time it was quiet; he'd get a lane to himself. The lifeguard greeted him with a friendly nod.

"Not seen you here for a while."

Lachlan explained his schedule, ending with a veiled reference to his recent landmark. The lifeguard nodded, bouncing a float on his knee.

"You don't look thirty to me."

In the water Lachlan felt more like fifty, then settled into a rhythm as his limbs began to co-operate. Today was the first full rehearsal of 'Wolf.' The play was a risk, where his ideas were shadows that refused to stand still. They needed to gel in the coming hours. Pool lengths were devoured, as he pumped up the physical strength to stimulate the mental. But, when he climbed out, he felt drained of ideas, his mind like a plate left out in the sun.

"Big day?" asked the lifeguard, still bouncing the float.

"Bit too big," replied Lachlan, absorbed.

His absorption lasted. Driving past nondescript shops, traffic lights turned red. Waiting, his eye fell on a billboard.

S.O.S. COUPLE IN SOUTH VIC.

He wondered who was seeking them and why? It could only be bad news. As a boy in Scotland he'd heard messages on the radio when a voice, hinting at doom, urged the finding of a long-lost family member, thought to be abroad. Lachlan tried to imagine telling this person there was a message for him. But the man would sense he was looked for because of death; death was the only thing that made sense of the looking. He might weep, uncontrollably. He might ask questions, avoid them, or just stand still, unable to assimilate feeling as the sad words circled around outside him, waiting to gain access, then be indelibly registered.

The words of the radio message were powerful ......"last seen in the vicinity of...... medium height, brown hair...... get in touch with this number......... where his mother, Mrs ....is dangerously ill."

Did they ever find their quarry? And what happened if not? His thoughts swarmed around death. It was said to be the worst thing of all if there was no body, no dead shell to burn or put into wet ground. Lachlan remembered the case of an estate agent who disappeared and was never found, but many others went quietly, without newspaper klaxon. The statistics were huge.

A loud blast on the horn from the man behind stirred him and he moved slowly forward. The man, in a red car, sped past with a look of disdain. Lachlan had better get used to the nasty side of human nature, immerse himself in it. 'Wolf' was not a feel-good piece, and now that he was on its threshold, he felt different from how he had felt in the planning.

Plays that explored savagery were not easy. As a teacher there was only one play he had directed twice, 'Equus', the psychological study of an adolescent who committed the barbarous act of blinding six horses with a metal spike and was placed in the care of a psychiatrist. On the first occasion he had co-directed the play with a man he knew well. It was only months before he met Kathy. They had been blessed with a strong cast and despite hard moments – he remembered the boy who played one of the extras breaking down suddenly in a late night rehearsal, but never saying quite why – the play had gone well. But, five nights after the play, the boy playing the actor who perpetrated the

131

deed, had broken out of school and run away. They found him on a train, in a siding, sixty kilometres away, just sitting there, rocking gently to and fro, eyes half-shut. Lachlan felt responsible, though, in the end, the boy made a full recovery. He had thought carefully about doing the piece again; it was only due to the persuasion of a Year 12 student that he had yielded, and this time he brought in a psychiatrist friend to assist him. All had gone well with the help of this psychiatrist. But when Lachlan took his lead actor home, after the last performance, he had been greeted at the front door by an elder sister.

"How could you do that to my brother?" She stood there defiant. Lachlan answered the question honestly and in detail. But the begging of the question disturbed him.

And now he was about to do the same thing again. Angus was no schoolboy, but nor was he savage.

The car park at The Tinderbox was full, hardly a good portent. He had to park round the block, which made him late for his meeting with Brodie.

She was sitting in the cramped office as he walked in, sweating. A black clipboard sat imperious on her knee. But she was in equable humour, which he hadn't expected, and they set to work. Both knew how challenging this play was. For today, the feminist side of Brodie sat quiet; she had been focussing on the best way for Angus to approach his rôle, and not made as much progress as she'd hoped.

"First rehearsal's crucial," she said with authority. "Thirty-five minutes to go."

Lachlan outlined his thinking and the clipboard nodded. Brodie was new to a play of this nature, her most virulent stage passions having been stirred by 'Who's Afraid of Virginia Woolf?', a piece Lachlan resolved never to touch. With 'Wolf' it was important to stimulate positive reactions from the start; certain members of the company were 'against' the play, but he hoped they would respond to strong

132

handling.

By 11.55 most of the actors were in the building; the crunch was imminent. Only two were missing, one of them Angus. Lachlan had just started on his planned introduction when the actor arrived. He looked unkempt and asleep.

Brodie took over for the warm-up. They stretched lips and limbs, massaged noisily, and lay prostrate, imagining themselves on top of a lofty peak, gazing at the view. It had long been Brodie's ambition to have her actors fall asleep during this exercise.

She began by asking for simple demonstrations of emotion, a clearly defined emotion, elementary task for actors. Gradually the range of emotion was extended until the focus dwelt on anger.

"Play an angry scene," she coaxed. "Let's see the rawness."

Two of the company enacted scenes; the others watched silently; now and again there was a peal of laughter, cut off rapidly, or an aborted snort. But evident rage was not loath to well up.

"Now," cajoled Brodie, "This time let's hide the anger." The atmosphere changed: what had been obvious and unsubtle now became hushed and intense. It lasted far longer. When finished, the actors watched each other sharply, till the last pair exhausted their tiny scenario.

"Let's see yours," she said quietly touching her nearest player on the shoulder blade. "Who's involved in the scene?"

"A wife visiting in prison the man who stabbed her husband."

Lachlan winced.

"Go."

The couple seized their chance. Complex emotions were enchained under the surface. Angus, on the other side of the room, moved quietly closer as the mime gathered propulsion: the wife's pupils were tiny, her hands shaking

133

slightly. The murderer was angry too; she'd interrupted him, made him remember. The end of the scenario lingered in all four eyes, before a gavel came down with their exits on opposite sides. The empty space glistened.

"Next," said Brodie. "Minor domestic, and let's add another passion."

The pairings murmured for a minute, then began to shuffle around the premise of an idea. Lachlan watched their faces: different sorts of concentration, levels of endeavour, nuances of self-consciousness. They moved silently across their limited space, each piece an unplanned dressage test, as floating bodies fought to express feelings shrouded in life. About five minutes into the exercise, Lachlan heard a stifled cry, and a female figure moved quickly from the room. He waited a moment, then crossed after her, finding her outside, leaning on the lintel. To his surprise it was Meg. A hand was sweeping back a strand of hair that Lachlan saw held more grey than he'd noticed. She looked forlorn, denuded of the strength that was so much part of her last rôle. Lachlan touched her shoulder; the hand left her hair and was still. Neither spoke.

"Thank you," said Meg after a moment. "Caught me off guard, that's all."

Lachlan did not ask questions. He moved a pace back, allowing her to pass inside. A demon stirred in him, then folded itself away. He breathed a couple of times, then went in. His vision of Meg's distress needed edging out, but it left him unsure if other seeds had been sown. Angus now seemed involved. From this angle it was not easy to decipher his chosen passion. Lachlan changed position. Looking over at Brodie, who ignored him, he could tell things were not going badly, but these were foothills only, not even base camp. And despite the readiness of some to participate, the stance of three of the company betrayed more than idle questioning.

"Let's break for ten minutes," said Brodie, and shoulders

sagged around the room. Meg went for air, joined by Lennox. Third Witch came in at this point and briefly apologised to Lachlan for her lateness.

"Heavy stuff?" she asked, putting down a string shoulder-bag, into which she reached for a shoe-change.

"Look…."

"No worries. I'll pick it up."

Once they were all back, Lachlan suggested a look at one of the early scenes in the play.

"Any humour here?" Meg quipped. Brodie looked up sharply. Meg read Lachlan's face, assuring him she was fine. One of the challenges was how much they should involve the whole cast in the deep emotional parts. Lachlan decided to work that one out with Brodie at the end of the day. In the meantime, he took Angus into the office, opening the small fridge for water to pour into two paper mugs. He hoped the fridge would harbour ice: it did not.

By 4.30 everyone had had enough, most of all Lachlan. After his talk with Angus over the beers, he had been looking forward to the follow-up. But, in the confines of the office, Angus was ill-at-ease, impatience brimming, fingers tapping on his shoes. It was not the right time for in-depth evaluations of cruelty. But it had to be done.

"Will I often be rehearsing solo?" was his opening salvo.

"I don't think that's a good plan."

Lachlan unclenched his fingers and avoided a direct answer. His half-hearted shrug of the shoulders did little to move their conversation along a path already redolent of ambushing tree-roots. On a muggy afternoon in early April, not far from the city centre, he was forcing a discussion on tearing apart façades in order to play a rôle that questioned everything about conformity and 'normal' life. The man sitting across from him, gazing at the door, had to be made capable of acting on instinctive impulses which society repulsed. He had to allow himself to express the in-

135

expressible, letting out forbidden things, opening up channels that consciousness preferred to keep locked. How was a man to get into that rôle?

Angus looked at Lachlan, waiting. The seeds of anger were in them both.

"Ever hated anyone?" asked Lachlan, aware as he spoke that his words came out with little conviction. His mouth was dry.

"No."

Lachlan looked above his actor's head, where two exuberant masks peered down on him: one black and white daubed in red, aboriginal; the other tangerine and blue, a grotesque green tongue protruding from large lips. A forelock of ginger hair hung over the nose, which was bulbous. Lachlan felt an urge to hold the mask over his face at Angus. There was more life in the masks than the person sharing his room.

"Are you sure?"

Angus stared at him coldly.

"This is shrink's talk. And you're not crash-hot at it."

"We have to start somewhere."

"Oh, yes?"

"Angus. There must be someone."

Silence.

"A teacher? An ex?"

Hesitation filled the room.

"Hatred's strong."

"Hatred's what we're about. If not, just give me someone for whom you felt, just at one point, a level of antipathy."

Angus uncrossed his legs. Another pause. "O.K." Lachlan disguised his relief. "There was one student at drama school. We never got on. He put people down all the time, mainly me, was always looking for bad motives. Said he assumed people were worthless unless they proved themselves otherwise."

"Bit of a cynic?"

"Everyone's a cynic."

"Did it bother you?"

"No."

"Why do you think of it now, then?"

"Because…" The word cut off.

Lachlan held out his hands in an attempt to dispel the tensions rippling between them. He needed another approach.

"Shrinks say we dislike, even hate people because something in them is a characteristic we'd like to have."

Angus' eyes showed their first expression of interest. "Do they?"

"Did he have something?"

"Hmm."

"What was it?"

"Intellect."

He assumed Angus was mocking him; an eyebrow went up, and he realised he'd been wrong. Angus leant forward, a less hostile position. "Same old story. He came after a girl I was seeing. Not for the girl. To bait me. He succeeded."

"And the girl?"

"She wasn't stupid. I assumed they were sleeping together, and I knew he had urithritis."

"How did you know?"

"He told me."

"And were they?"

"Perhaps only once. He lost interest. So did she, in me I mean."

Lachlan nodded.

"Is there anything there you can tap into? His using women? You?"

Angus was showing flickers of assistance. The incident had been some years ago; he hadn't thought of it since. But gradually he delved down into feelings. Lachlan no longer felt pressure to probe. Angus liked the idea of hating a person because of the trait that one envied. This was a peg for new thinking. Rekindling the experience, good things came up, too. He'd met the girl again some years later; she was married to an army officer. He felt protective of her, despite that, and asked questions about her little boy, born with a club foot.

Lachlan nudged his actor back to the vindictive side of this fiend. "Could you be cruel, as he was?"

Angus paused.

"Could you put a kangaroo out of its misery, after it was hit by a truck?"

"I think so."

"And a horse?"

"No way."

"What's the difference?"

Angus tried to explain; it wasn't his answers that mattered, it was the exploration of concepts not usually probed. He still rated Lachlan's psychiatric manner below zero, but had no experience of the couch himself.

More silence.

Lachlan wondered if he should leave Angus to dwell on these things. The actor sat back, his fingers no longer tapping. In his view, he thought, the worst cruelty of all was people who abused children. It seemed almost common-place these days. Lachlan thought of his boys. He entrusted them to friends, he had to, but how did he know he could trust the friends? In business, people were wary; in friend-ships, accepting, surely an invitation to treachery, betrayal?

"And what about rape?"

"What about it?"

"How savage is that?"

Angus swallowed. His girl-friend had told him soon after their meeting of a time she'd come close to being assaulted. It was a Friday night in Sydney. Returning from an evening out, she noticed a man in the entrance to the grisly block of flats where she rented a room with three girls. He was black. As she stepped into the lift he came in after her, just as the doors closed. In reaching for the button marked 6, the front-door key fell out of her hand. She picked it up, and turned round slowly. The level-indicator flicked from 3 to 4 and he was undoing his trousers. She screamed. He lurched over her and pressed button 14, which took him a second. The lift flashed 5 and was starting to slow down; when it opened, she could see the light under two doors on her floor. Her flat was in the corner, furthest away. In the lift, screaming had been useless; it was again, now. She tried a different tack, reasoning with him quietly. No one stirred in the flats. She walked backwards towards her front door as the panther advanced on her. She was conscious only of his bright yellow T-shirt as she haltingly told him she would ring the bell and her friends would call the police. He hovered, stared, then withdrew silently. She turned and fell on the door, pressing the bell, twice. Daring to look round, she saw he had disappeared into the stairwell. Her relief was sobering as she turned back ready for the door to open. But it did not. Her friends were still out, and it was at that moment her fear reached its zenith. All energy had been devoured; if the man sensed she was vulnerable still, he could destroy her. She waited. Twelve minutes later she distinguished the chatter of girl talk and two of her flat-mates stepped out of the lift, unfollowed.

Lachlan heard every word, imagining if it had been Rebecca. Words fell short, inadequate. The man, it later emerged, had done his lift-trick on five previous occasions, always wearing a yellow T-shirt, which was what the victims concentrated on, so they were unable to give a telling description of his face. Two girls had been raped, on two other counts the man was guilty of actual bodily harm, and one girl had been terrified but untouched.

Both men were silent; the see-saw had tipped, now Angus was in charge.

"Do you feel uncomfortable?" he asked, a hint of relish in his voice.

"Yes," said Lachlan before he'd finished the question. Angus had only to admit that he, too, was uncomfortable, and the balance would shift back. But he was in no hurry. The silence drew on.

"I think we both need to visit our dark sides," said Lachlan in the end.

"Sounds like a bad lyric. And what about the danger?"

This was tense. Lachlan knew what he meant. Any answer less than convincing would give Angus match point.

"Yes," he answered, carefully. "You can't open yourself up too much."

"So I should work with other actors." The gloat was tiny, visible.

"Or with me?"

"And Brodie? What does she think about all this? Does she agree I should open up the channels? Bury myself in excess? I like the idea. A mandate for depravity. Perhaps she'll make it a threesome, play the victim, play the scourge."

Lachlan switched on the fan; he should have done so when they came in. Stalemate. With his students a moment like this had come, and gone; it was easier then. Was Angus acting? The possibility came to Lachlan; he looked hard at the man. No give-aways. They stared on. And just before Lachlan averted his gaze, a muscle in Angus' left eye twitched, once.

"Can we rehearse somewhere else next time?"

"Where would you suggest?"

"The abattoir."

Lachlan suddenly felt stirred.

"Not a tender place," continued Angus. "We could just have a look in. Then move on to a cockfight perhaps. That adds the illegal element to our cocktail. Live sex would complete our voyeurs' afternoon in the interests of art."

"That's only simulated passion," said Lachlan," not a bubbling mass of the real stuff, like we need."

He stood up. Looking out of the window he saw a billboard being pasted up: two models, all of ten feet tall, beamed plastic smiles across an unwrinkled cherub in its stroller. The bottom of the poster was yet to be revealed.

"What's it going to say?" he asked Angus, now also standing up, his gaze on the pavement below.

"People eat children, beware," came the reply.

Lachlan kept his own answer to himself, let Angus have the last word.

You're a cruel bastard, he thought as Angus wafted his way downstairs. *And maybe a better actor than I dared hope.*

On the way home, he stopped at the indoor market. Its rows of burnished fruit, cold to the touch, did little to assuage his rawness. At the vegetable counter he found himself twisting a root of ginger in his hand. It looked corrupt, symbolic of his afternoon.

"You want that, too?" said the oriental behind the massed bands of colour.

"No, thank you."

Unaware of what he'd bought, he picked up the boys from Jo's and suggested they went for a walk through the park. Robbie was in high spirits, analysing his day; Merrick hummed to himself, rapping a stick along tree trunks as he passed.

Round the corner an elderly lady conversed with a girl in school uniform. The woman moved away, greeting them. "Never thought I'd see that in a Melbourne park."

Robbie stopped in his tracks: two feet away from him an albino ferret on a lead arched its back like a rubber-band.

"What's its name?" said Merrick, moving nearer. The ferret skittered away.

"Kylie," said the girl, unsmiling. The ferret ran round her legs, ensnaring itself in the lead.

"Weird," said Merrick, but Robbie had already moved off.

Lachlan caught up with him, the boy still narrating his day. Back at home, Lachlan let the boys have their showers and took a glass of water into the front garden. The temperature was perfect.

"Am I disturbing you?" came a voice over the gate, a voice melodious and out-of-place. A girl's face peered after the voice, her hair short, framing a smile.

"I wondered if you knew about the new phone deals."

Lachlan listened to her Irish lilt as she described a deal he could ill afford.

"Sorry," he said. "I've not much cash."

"Not a problem," bounced the reply. There was a smile, and the voice was gone.

"Dad!"

"Coming." He threw the last of his water on a dying fuchsia and entered the house. It was cool. But the girl stayed in his head; how could anyone but a madman want to harm someone like her?

"What's for tea, then?" The boys looked up as he entered the kitchen. He made two quick decisions: "Spaghetti," in answer to them. And he would send Angus to the zoo.

CHAPTER THIRTEEN

There was a funnel-web spider on the carpet in the hall.
Lachlan, coming out of his room, saw its knotty spindle, and
was about to take off his shoe when he noticed the shadow
of Robbie's arm moving slowly from his room into the hall.
In his hand was a folded newspaper. The boy kept the paper
at arm's length, concentrating hard, then lifted the spider up
off the carpet.

"Good man, Robs."

Startled, he looked round, and the spider dropped off its
launch-pad, landing on Robbie's foot. As Lachlan moved
forward, the boy flicked it off with the newspaper and it lay
on its side. Lachlan smacked it hard, then gently picked up
the inert body. You could never be sure they were dead.

Robbie watched him move down the corridor with
unnecessary stealth, then heard the fly-screen bang. When
he was seven, a redback had landed on his shoulder in a
holiday house they were renting near Port Arlington. Kathy
saw it happen; Lachlan was with Merrick at the shops. There
was nothing to grab, and she had advanced on the spider.
Putting one hand on Robbie's left shoulder, she flicked the
beast with her finger, not hard enough; the spider bit Robbie,
and he yelled. Lachlan had taken the car with him. Kathy ran
next door and asked the man, a stranger, if he could run them
both to hospital.

Lachlan remembered coming back to an empty house,
where he spent anxious minutes before the man next door,
back from casualty having abandoned the pair, came over in
his own time and told him the story. His blasé air infuriated

Lachlan; driving to the hospital, he narrowly missed hitting a blue heeler. Kathy had been more flustered than he imagined, but the boy was seen, swiftly, and treated. He was allowed home half an hour later.

Around the same time a colleague at school told him how she'd flared up in a French lesson on 'Phèdre' over the prospect of somebody harming her kids. She knew then what was meant by revenge. Hearing her say this in the corner of their stuffy staffroom, he identified with her feeling. If anything ever happened to the boys…

Robbie was in the kitchen having cereal when Lachlan came back in, the newspaper still in his hand.

"Sorry, Robs," he said. "I should have left you to it. You're quite capable."

Robbie looked up from his crowded bowl but said nothing. There was a vestige of fear in his eyes. Lachlan put his arm round the boy, who studied the back of his cereal packet.

"What time's your tennis?"

"You know, Dad. Ten. I told you last night."

Lachlan sighed. He moved to the calendar with its chill picture of Chester Cathedral against a gun-grey sky, early primroses, fragile, in the foreground. In two weeks it would be Easter. The Saturday was Robbie's match in Torquay and though The Tinderbox played the holiday weekend, Lachlan could escape for a couple of nights. Dave and Jo were taking their children to Phillip Island.

"What're you looking at, Dad?"

A bleary-eyed Merrick cannoned into a kitchen stool, chubby fingers rubbing his eyes.

"Nothing."

The boys looked at each other. 'Nothing' was never what it sounded. They waited, knowing Lachlan would speak again.

"I mentioned to Robbie we could escape down The Great Ocean Road over Easter weekend."

Robbie's eyes narrowed. "You mean after the tennis?"

"After the tennis."

"But where?"

They had no shack in Lorne or Apollo Bay, and bed and breakfasts were not cheap. Scanning the next page of the calendar, Eaton Hall with a dusting of snow. Lachlan thought of the Dixons' place. But they were bound to be using it.

"Time we left," he said quickly.

In the Monday rehearsal, Angus was prickly to begin with, truculent later, a nightmare by the end. Brodie was working on improvisations with the full cast, Lachlan having included Angus with the others for the week. But the actor smarted. For the first exercise, in pairs, he made himself the odd one out, looking helplessly at Lachlan until Brodie stepped in to partner him. He leered at her when she drew herself up to her full height, and promptly did the same. For the next interchange, he appeared to join in with his group, only to stand, hands on hips, and reject their suggestions. Brodie bridled.

Lachlan walked out of the rehearsal, hoping that would deprive Angus of an audience. In the office, cramped and sterile as usual, he opened a cluster of bills. The phone rang: Kerryn. She was ringing to ask how the birthday had gone. He told her, without enthusiasm, leaving her like a drum with slackened skin: she'd intended to say she was thinking of a trip to Melbourne to stay with her sister and see Lachlan and the boys, but his edgeless voice dissuaded. He put the phone down, speared with a sudden sadness.

Brodie burst in.

"I don't know what you've done to Angus."

"Nothing." A part of him was pleased that Angus' new antics were not restricted to him.

"I gave them a break. Said you'd do the next spot. One o'clock." She picked up her bag and walked out.

Angus was ready before one, stretching like an athlete, exaggerating. He ignored Lachlan, in whose head 'prima donna' swirled dustily round. Lachlan had cast him; there was no going back.

The other actors could not fail to notice: some showed disdain, the majority puzzlement. Improvisation held no rules; Angus was using it to make choices not usually made, to say and do the unthinkable. After one display, of cruelty, which achieved its desired effect, the actor looked from Lachlan to Brodie, then back.

"That's what you wanted." A pause. "Isn't it?"

"Let him play his game," decided Brodie, a decision that rankled with some of the cast. Meg's face conveyed she wanted to help, but knew not how. Angus, alienating everyone, was in danger of breaching trust with his fellow-actors. And Lachlan, as Angus was aware, was unsure what was happening. They broke early; the co-directors sat on the floor. Lachlan suggested giving the actor some sort of ultimatum.

"Sounds like a newspaper story," said Brodie. "Ultimatums don't exist."

"Yes, they do. People give each other ultimatums all the time," he answered back. "On stage and in life."

She looked at him, a piqued schoolmistress. The problem was no nearer to being resolved.

That night Lynch rang: he could start on the stage furniture next day. Lachlan gave him details: the blood-legged table created interest. Most stage furniture was made in pine, topped with plywood and painted; this piece called for more skill. Brodie's idea had been to make the table in pine, but leave its legs hollow. That meant they could be filled with water. At the four corners of the table a phial, or balloon, filled with stage blood, could be released by the actor as he writhed in torment: red swirls in the water would prove effective; in seconds the whole table-leg would go red.

146

Lynch listened, unsure if it was quite that simple. But he'd be in next day to start work. Lachlan felt a shoot of hope in the production's deadlock, but quashed it at once.

Hetty rang just as he was turning the boys' lights out. She'd not heard from them for a while; would they like roast lamb after church on Easter Sunday? Lachlan told her of his Great Ocean Road plan, which wasn't certain to happen.

"Leave it to me, Lach," she breezed. "I'm seeing Beth at Women's Group."

"You ripper," said Lachlan quietly as he put down the phone.

"Who was it?" called Robbie.

Lachlan was about to say "No one." "Hetty," he shouted back. "She says time you were asleep."

A muffled chuckle from Merrick got a snort from his brother. Lachlan picked up his novel and took out the travelled bookmark. It once held Tom Roberts' painting, 'Shearing the Rams: 1896'; now all you could see were the remnants of not-so golden fleeces and a pair of bulging fore-arms, pink with sun. Starting to read, he got no further than two paragraphs down the page, then gave up. He could remember nothing at all of the tale, so he put the bookmark in at Chapter 1 and went to his room.

Five days later they were driving over the Westgate Bridge. Hetty's magic wand had been potent; the Dixons were spending Easter with Tom's brother in Yarra Glen. Merrick jingled a rust-crusted key. While Robbie was warming up for his tennis match, Lachlan bought two boxes of food-stuffs. Three hours later, they set off in search of the Dixons' place. Rehearsals had been fraught, but there was reassurance from Brodie, and, once Lynch had started on the carpentry, a fact not unobserved by Angus, there was a ray of promise. Meg was coming up well as the mother, and Angus had shown signs of injecting venom into his character rather than at his directors.

Father and sons sped past Anglesea, Merrick craning to see if the ubiquitous kangaroos gambolled across the golf course. He couldn't see them, but there was much to occupy him, including surfers overtaking at speed. They drove under the log marking the entrance to The Great Ocean Road, and Lachlan felt his spirits climb a notch. He'd not been to South Africa, where The Garden Route vied to be beaten, but for him there was no road like the Great Ocean. Hairpin-bends meant slowing for another view, the sea indigo ahead, then beside them, surfers bobbing on its crests, dots of punctuation seemingly still. The beaches held hardly a person, just layers of water lolling up pinenut-coloured stretches of sponge.

Robbie pulled down the visor, checking his upper lip in the mirror. He caught Lachlan's eye and looked out of the window. Merrick's feet drummed into the back of him until Robbie glared round.

"The shack's called Ivory Towers."

"Crass name," said Robbie, still looking out of the window as if to disclaim his new knowledge.

"What's 'crass', Robs?"

"You are," he replied. "What does it mean, Dad, Ivory Towers?"

Lachlan explained, not entirely to the boys' satisfaction. "It's a joke," he added. Two serious faces met his.

A bird dipped in front of them, and did not come up. The sun bore into a sea now black in another light. Lachlan tried hard to relax, a feat the boys were accomplishing without trouble. The coast would soothe him, though it might take a while.

They stopped, overlooking a beach, and got out, shielding eyes against a sun gaining rigour every minute. The boys watched a distant pod of surfers, Merrick hoping for a shark alert. Turning back to the car, Robbie noticed a bird caught in the radiator grill. He lifted it out, gently, holding it in a sweat-stained palm. It was strikingly green. Underneath, its feathers turned muffled brown, over legs that could never have carried it. The boy was silent. He put his finger on the dead creature, on little white marks round its eyes, like archery targets, letting the fur comb back softly against him. Turning it over he, found the bird no longer looked top-heavy, its spindle legs folded up in formation, as if un-damaged. There was no mark on its skin. Robbie cupped it in both hands, then looked up at Lachlan with sadness.

"What shall we do with it, Dad?"

Lachlan was unsure. Looking at it, he felt the bird's colour go deeper.

"Put it on that rock," said Merrick, with a force that surprised the two poring over the body. Lachlan imagined the talons of a sea eagle descending onto the hapless bird, bearing it away to a lofty crag. A fate like that struck him as fitting.

Robbie walked slowly over to the rock, picking up a blown-off gum tree branch as he went. He dextrously laid the bird down, then put the branch gently on top, vestige of a burial. Merrick watched. A dragonfly buzzed in his face, unexpectedly loud. His brother climbed back into the car.

He's just like me, thought Lachlan. Once, soon after leaving university, he and a mate had been driving in the Otways. A young labrador had sprinted after their car; they braked and avoided the animal. But when they started off again, the dog had kept with them. Despite driving slowly, they could not shake it off. Suddenly it ran right into their path. There was a thud, and no more. They waited, certain the beast would reappear; the force of impact had been nothing to speak of. But it didn't, and when they tiptoed to the front of the car, the young dog was dead on the track. The men were stunned, Lachlan stroking its neck in disbelief. It had a collar. Gingerly, he found its address, and they put the dog on the back seat.

It belonged to an old couple in a ramshackle weather-

149

board house. Lachlan left the dog in the car and they approached the door, fearful. A tiny old lady opened it before they got there; her eyes told them she knew. Nothing was said. Lachlan's friend picked the dog up and carried it along the path down which it had so recently bounded. He handed it clumsily to the old man who had appeared, tears on his rivened cheeks, arms trembling. As the dog was transferred, the old man stumbled for a moment; the weight was too much for him. But he would not be helped. The two young men walked away, muttering unwelcome, facile apologies. Back in the car they debated what to do. It was impossible to drive away. Uneasily, they settled on money, joining forces from tattered wallets, unsure how much to offer. Already the gesture seemed insulting; they could think of nothing else.

Slower than the last time, they walked up the path. Lachlan knocked on the door. No answer. Sad eyes watched from a darkened room. His friend motioned him round to the back door. There they stopped short: the dog lay stiffening, on the back steps, flies buzzing greedily over the carcass. The men folded some dollars, easing them under the animal's collar. And they left. In his head Lachlan heard the gentle old couple cursing them, using words hitherto not allowed to be touched, words that struck into the utterers more than the cursed. Getting into the car, he stole one last look at the puny house. Nothing.

Pulling out of the scrub where they'd parked, Lachlan told his sons that story. They listened hard, Merrick asking questions. Robbie's brow was furrowed, Lachlan knew without looking. They drove on over tiny bridges on sharp bends, each naming a creek: Random, Fantail, Armstrong, Pickering, Stump and Lochinver, a name that appealed to Lachlan. On his first view of the Ocean Road, soon after they'd come to Melbourne, when they still had no car, a friend of his father's had driven the family down to Lorne one hot Sunday. Lachlan was sick, twice, holding hard on to a charred metal barrier by the side of a sharp bend. His head swirled, he had pins and needles, his stomach was blowing away.

By mid-afternoon they had found Ivory Towers, a dumpy, lost-looking house, its blinds eternally drawn. But it was cool inside. They unpacked the food and went straight down for a swim.

At Easter Sunday communion the vicar reminded Lachlan of someone; he could not remember who. It was raining as they sat in the small white church on the main street. Two rows in front, a woman in a wheelchair angled herself to see the pulpit, where the silver-haired preacher was speaking with quiet force. He mentioned a book on the Resurrection; its author had been an atheist setting out to disprove events of the first Easter, but ended up a believer, and wrote that book instead. Lachlan sensed the boys imagining a huge boulder being rolled with great effort away from the entrance to a non-descript cave. Then there was the mystery of the disappearing gardener, and the disciples' discovery of a loin-cloth smelling of hyssop and dry blood. This pastor was a polished speaker, not avoiding the full weight of how pain from Black Friday turned into glory serene; it was more riddle than paradox, a man's return from the undiscovered country, whose threshold no being had crossed. Death brushed across Lachlan's temple. Rain was inching its way down the windows. A hymn book fell to the ground, Merrick surreptitiously squeezing his eyes round to pick out the culprit. Lachlan was aware of Robbie looking at him; he smiled at the boy, who looked away quickly. The woman in the wheelchair let out a faint sigh; millions more sat awaiting similar release.

Nearing the end of his homily, the vicar sidetracked for a moment; his granddaughter had that week shown him a dreamcatcher. Merrick looked for his father's reaction. Had he probed, he would have seen a moment of scepticism:

how could a pagan Red Indian contraption have relevance to the Paschal message? Logic crumbled slightly, Lachlan felt, as the vicar suggested Christians could hold on to the good things in their life of service, but let some things go, destructive things, resentment, grudge. He recovered to end well, like a gymnast back on the mat with his last flourish, and announced the offertory hymn. Hands appeared at Lachlan's belt, then returned, clenched, to warm pockets.

The communion rail needed a spot of carpentry, Lachlan noticed, as it took his weight when he knelt, a boy on each side. In his palm the wafer was elusive, a fact noticed by both boys, who stood up after their blessing and strode back to the pew. At the altar-rail Lachlan was calm, his head cleared for more intimate prayer. The wine tasted bitter, his thumb leaving a print on the cold chalice that faded as he looked. But he did not stand up: for several seconds he stayed kneeling, thoughts whirring, calm gone. An angel stole over his grave.

"The Lord draw near to you, and comfort you," said the vicar, placing his hand on Lachlan's head. Not quite the conventional blessing. He looked up, to find he was alone at the rail, the vicar nodding with a kind expression, chalice and platter already folded into a house of cards on the holy table, the organist stuck with his hands held out over the keys, awaiting the nod. No one moved. Lachlan crossed himself, put his hands on the rail and levered himself to his feet. A Coleridge verse spun in his head, and he walked down the aisle, calm restored. The boys combined embarrassment and intrigue as he edged past Robbie and knelt down, crossing himself once more.

"Hymn number 110, 'Jesus Christ is risen today'." The organist burst from his time-frieze, setting free squeaks, whirrings and a collage of sounds, not exactly in harmony.

Outside, it was raining harder. The boys sped to the car, but Lachlan called them back, wanting to take up the church's offer of coffee. That did not go down well. Hands slunk back into pockets, smiles withered. Coffee was already poured on a trestle table, and Lachlan indicated orange juice on the counter. The biscuits were plain.

Their torture lasted twenty minutes, after which Lachlan jogged through the rain to the car, the boys ambling after him. Lachlan had spoken with the vicar, who was just back from Vietnam; his son was constructing a bridge there. A wonderful country, he said, about which people knew little, distant rumbles of an echoing war. The boys had been befriended by a family with three children, who promised to look out for them on the beach.

"Unlikely in this weather," said Robbie.

"But it's good weather for a roast," replied Lachlan. "We'll cook it tonight."

"What about this arvo?" asked Merrick. "What are we going to do then?"

"Port Fairy."

Eyes rose to the sky, bodies slumped back in their seats.

Port Fairy allayed their fears. Largely free of developers, it boasted a colourful harbour, wide roads, and an excellent teashop, into which they retreated under strengthening rain.

"Just our luck," said Robbie, looking out onto a pair of swish yachts.

"Devonshire tea for three?"

The waitress smiled at Merrick, returning with a plateful of warm scones, home-made jam, and King Island cream, oozing at the sides of a white dish overwhelmed by its cargo. The scones were slain, instantly, hands diving for the jam, Merrick first.

"Careful," said Lachlan.

They looked at him.

"You're in danger of enjoying this tea."

It stopped raining during their meal of Paschal lamb; next day was going to be a scorcher. Sleeping late, they swam in a gentle sea, then devoured a picnic in the dunes. In the afternoon was the Great Eastern Steeplechase at Oakbank, which Lachlan was keen to catch. The boys did not share his enthusiasm.

Serendipity smiled. As they were about to leave the beach, the family from church rolled up, and was happy to have the boys stay with them. Lachlan walked to the betting shop to watch the race, remembering again the time he went to Oakbank, in South Australia, for the Von Doosa Steeplechase, held on Easter Saturday. Nestling in the Adelaide hills, it was a picturesque course, but he had no camera, and regretted it. Regrets grew as he was leaving the course, when he caught the sunset framed in a tree fork. A photograph not taken, but with him for good. He'd used that phrase to Hetty, 'photographs not taken'; she'd said they were better, like words unsaid.

This year's renewal was a close race, and, though Lachlan did not have the winner, he was content as he left the smoky atmosphere of the betting shop. Nearing the beach, there was no sign of the boys, till he saw the mother from church looking out to sea. A small speedboat motored along with four people in it, three of them small. Behind it, a tyre skimmed the waves to shouts of glee that could only belong to Robbie.

"They seem to be enjoying it," said the mother, placing her little girl down on the wet sand.

"Dead right," answered Lachlan. The boys had wanted a spin on a 'biscuit', a spin that he, boatless, was not going to gratify. He stood and watched Robbie buoyed along at speed, then saw Merrick, fearless as ever, change places with his brother. The father waved and the boat surged forward again, a small hand held up in greeting. Boats were a boy's dream, though they hadn't been his. Not after leaving Aberdeen.

They locked up the house, which no longer seemed dumpy.

Dusk was advancing on The Great Ocean Road. Despite that, clusters of surfers still hung in the water, awaiting the last wave of the day. As they sped past solitary houses, the remains of a bush fire could be seen in the trees. Lachlan turned away. Lights were starting to come on in a couple of the houses that were not holiday homes. He wondered what it would be like to live in one of those houses, always sea-bound, enclosed.

"What're you thinking about Dad?" said Robbie in the back, his eyes bright in the mirror.

"Nothing," chirped Merrick, quick as a bird.

Lachlan pipped the horn: they were just crossing Roaring Swine Creek.

CHAPTER FOURTEEN

Lachlan was seventeen when he started not sleeping. He'd known it would happen, a spectre just out of range and biding its time. It was May, crepuscular nights banking autumn to winter. He had not dozed off. Towards five o'clock, just past the time of lowest metabolism, hour of birth and death, he went into his parents' room, standing in the doorway, very still. His father was awake, as always.

"Dad, I can't get to sleep."

The bedclothes arched and his father sat up, hands round his knees. They spoke in quiet tones, his mother sleeping on, stirring slightly. The vicar reassured him, told him not to try so hard, then held out his arm, touching Lachlan's. But Lachlan's father fell short; he didn't take his son back to his room as Lachlan now took Robbie, tucked him up and gave him a glass of water. Then, Lachlan padded back alone to a room grown marginally lighter, lying there till the alarm rang at its usual hour. Other people didn't sleep, they told him, didn't sleep a wink. But that only meant they languished until one or two. He did not attain sleep. Sleepless nights dropped hints in the evening, like random shots from a zealous Swiss border guard. In the morning, he got up, his T-shirt drenched in sweat, like his pillow-case, drawing on sleep from previous nights, pretending. The panic attacks came later.

Angus had not been away on the Easter weekend, a fact made clear by his bored expression. Lachlan greeted him with a handshake, odd English custom, on which the actor commented.

"Scottish," said the director through a fettered smile.

Brodie was late, unusually, and the company warmed up without her. Lachlan knew he had to run the savage scenes, stringing them together with an energy undercut by the time of day. A pity he could not sprinkle a vestige of his boys' enthusiasm from the previous afternoon. Meg tried to emulate Brodie, but Lachlan was relieved when his co-director walked in briskly.

"Anyone seen my script?"

Heads shook numbly.

"Have mine," said Meg. They carried on, Brodie suffering Angus' ravages as she summoned up energy to fuel him in what looked a lost cause. But gradually his levels rose. He moved with force more feline, he shook rage off instead of speaking it, he menaced. Brodie's eyebrows showed.

"Don't stop him now," mouthed Lachlan.

It didn't last, but it had been there. Lunch was the inevitable sandwiches, during which Angus sat across from Lachlan, legs loose; there were holes in his green tracksuit.

"How are your kids?" he asked, chasing a tomato round his finger, looking gauche. There was a pause, then Lachlan told him of their weekend, receiving the obligatory, "Lucky you." Angus had stayed at home and watched a documentary.

"Surprised it wasn't on my schedule," he baited. "Big cats and all that."

Lachlan laughed.

"Anyone ever told you you laugh like a kookaburra?"

"Only you," said Lachlan. "And I take it as a compliment. Largest of the kingfisher family, remember?"

"Of course," returned the actor, resuming his guard.

"You'll need a hyena's laugh. Can you do it?"

"You sent me to the zoo. Remember?"

If only he'd smile, thought Lachlan. Brodie had been

watching. She moved over to discuss the afternoon. Lynch's furniture was looking sturdy; Norman was keen to try it out. That meant the final scenes. It was time to find out if Angus would roar... .

Anzac Day fell on a Sunday. From Aberdeen, Lachlan had shadowy memories of English Remembrance Sundays, black sombre figures laying wreaths at a monolith stuck in the ground somewhere in London. It was always raining. The words lingered in him, solemn and resonant. 'The eleventh hour of the eleventh day of the eleventh month.' Number eleven obsessed the English: he remembered his father telling him one hundred and eleven was a notorious cricket score. But the symmetry of elevens puzzled him; why had Britain waited to sign the Armistice in a mirrored hall in France? He knew why now, because Brits had to plan everything meticulously, they could never simply be. But then he did not know; puzzlement turned to anger the day he learned that Wilfred Owen, whose words boiled in Lachlan's head from first hearing, had died on Sunday 4th November 1918, when the War was really over, only waiting for a bureaucratic seal. One more life added to the waste of millions.

An Englishman had taught him Wilfred Owen, starting, not with poetry, but with the telegram that arrived at the home of Owen's parents on the Sunday morning following their son's death, 11th November, bad timing, for the church bells were pealing out the end of the war. The teacher told of a boy on a motorbike arriving in Shrewsbury with his black-edged message. To Lachlan the bike had a side-car, empty, underlining the blank words addressed to Tom and Susan Owen, late of Birkenhead. Lachlan found Owen stark, visual, honest, where Sassoon was prissy, sarcastic, calculated. It might have been his teacher's bias coming through. But where were the Australian poets, he asked? Gallipoli was the most well-known battle, but so many

Aussie volunteers died elsewhere in the Dardanelles. Many had fought in Flanders, but traces were hard to find. Lachlan needed to know why. And had they written poems?

In a second-hand bookshop in Sydney he once found an Australian novel on The Great War; its title came from 'Hamlet', like so many titles. The words on the fawn spine ran away to the top of the shelf, but he could complete the quotation. The book had first been published in an expurgated version because of its language; that, too, had a title from 'Hamlet', from the same speech. The author, Frederick Manning, was born in Perth and went to England in 1911 to study. When war broke out, he joined up, seeing action at Hill 60 and Ancre in 1916. Constant heavy bombardment and mustard gas affected his nerves, but he survived the war, staying in England, near Cambridge, where Rupert Brooke had lived. At the end of the 1920s, in a country ravaged by the war and its aftermath: the influenza outbreak, that killed more than the Germans had slain; the General Strike, and the Depression, giving a whiff of what the 1930s would deliver, there was a great surge in war writing, and the Australian finally wrote his book. He told of men fighting parasites and sickness, scrounging possessions, speaking coarsely, suffering always, carrying responsibility for which they did not ask and which was never acknowledged. It fuelled Lachlan's fascination with 1914-18; he directed 'Oh, What a Lovely War', read 'The Accrington Pals' and 'Behold the Sons of Ulster Advancing on the Somme'; next season he planned to direct 'Journey's End'. Brodie would find it hard to handle, a play without women.

In Australia, Anzac Day, commemorating those who died, fell in April. When his family had moved, thirty years before, leaving Scotland in December, arriving 'Down Under' in February, they witnessed more than once the sight of veterans from action marching with blazing medals to war memorials in Australian country towns.

In their church this Anzac Day, flags were borne to the altar, where they hung dispassionately, fading colours in the stain-glassed sun. Merrick was gushing half-heard questions; Robbie simply watched. Hetty sat across from them in a smart cream suit; she should have a medal too, thought Lachlan, for a different sort of courage. But he checked the thought; courage was finer without signposts.

As one of the veterans marched to the altar to retrieve his flag at the end of the service, he stumbled and went down. Fear lurched at several in the congregation before the man was taken out, red-faced and whistle-thin, his flag handed to a younger man, made clumsy by having to carry two. The boys' gaze was held to the moment when the procession disappeared behind another fading curtain at the back.

"How's 'Wolf'?" said Hetty brightly, stooping up from kissing the boys. Lachlan told her. "Why don't you look in before we open?" he added.

"Can I look in too, Dad?" from Robbie.

Lachlan paused. The answer was no. But there were ways of saying it.

On 'Wolf' Lachlan had gambled. But not on Lynch, the carpenter who worked for The Tinderbox for a favour, not a fee. He was an unsung man. Lachlan almost expected to find nail marks in his palms. His hands were his greatest gifts; they dashed off a regular array of stage props. He was patient and understated, a man who looked into, then beyond you, trying to save you from something, perhaps yourself. With close-cropped hair and generous elbows, he was fit, not muscle-bound, but spare; he loved his rugby, but willingly gave it up for a crisis at the theatre. He'd roamed for a while, then capitulated to the voice that said he travelled too far too often. He was his own man.

Lachlan had not known Lynch as a child. He thought of the scene in 'Ben Hur', when the protagonist was marched in chains through some remote Judean village. A boy of twelve watched the procession. He rushed into his house, where the camera lingered for a moment on the corner of a workbench spread with tools. The boy grabbed a cup of water, and ran out into the baking-hot street, holding up the water to Ben Hur's lips. A Roman centurion knocked it away, whipping the prisoner, who trudged on. Later in the film the rôles were reversed when Ben Hur held a cup of water to Christ on his way to Golgotha to be crucified. Lynch was the young boy, still running out with the cup.

Brodie was demanding more from him. The lobby of The Tinderbox was underused, she said; a display would help no end. Would Lynch help her devise and build a display depicting scenes from a play in each decade of the twentieth century?

"When for?" he asked, suddenly tired.

"July?" she ventured, lips held apart. "We would pay you for that."

Lynch looked at the floor. "August?" he offered, unusually hesitant.

Lachlan felt Brodie nod. Lynch picked up a saw and moved back to his table.

Angus had heard the previous exchange; rather than slope away, he came out of the half-darkness, script in hand.

"You're not enough of a bastard, mate," he said to Lachlan.

Brodie stared at him. So did Lachlan. In the background, a chain-saw started to scream.

Lachlan got home just after eight. The house was quiet. The boys sat in the dining room, elbows akimbo, poring over a smudged piece of paper.

"Robbie's helping me with difficult homework, Dad," said Merrick, clearly waiting for the next piece of dictation from his brother. The task was a challenging one: in an unexplored country, a couple of hundred years ago, he had to plan his expedition team for a period of two years. Ten people only, excluding him, were allowed. Lachlan looked to see who was conscripted already: Doctor, Carpenter, Blacksmith, Artist and Sailing Master. Then they had got stuck.

"You'd need to eat," said Robbie, and Merrick wrote down, 'Chef.'

"Just call him 'Cook'," said Lachlan. "And how are you going to get there?"

"Ship, of course."

"Steered by?"

But the boy was already writing, 'Navigator'.

"I'm the Captain, Dad, of course".

"Three left", said Robbie with purpose. His own Year 5 curriculum had omitted this exercise; he'd have traded capital cities for its challenge.

"What provisions are allowed?" Lachlan asked, pulling up a chair opposite the boys.

"Fresh water, meat and fish are already there, Dad," replied Merrick. "Natural resources."

"You still have to find them," warned Robbie, who was ignored.

"We can take soap, salt, pill-boxes...."

"Pill-boxes?"

"For insects. Pins, string, sealing wax, needles, fabric, a Bible and 200,000 nails. Also iron rods, to act as ballast, and buffalo skins."

"They're essential," said Lachlan biting a smile. Robbie picked up his irony, and sat back.

"What about the evenings?" asked Lachlan. "No T.V., videos, Gameboys."

Merrick curled his mouth in disgust; it was unthinkable. "We'd talk," he said, with purpose. "Discuss the day. Write journals. Sleep."

"You could take a magician," said Robbie, with a touch of the facetious. "He'd keep you entertained."

Merrick looked to his father for comment.

162

"I think magician is a tad luxurious," said Lachlan. "Why not settle for a story-teller or writer? He'd be reliable."

"He'd also have to be good."

"Fair enough. He would be."

"A teacher?" risked Robbie.

"He'd end up walking the plank."

"Be ambitious," advised Lachlan. "Take someone no one else will think of."

"Whaler!" shouted Merrick and this time his pencil was undenied. "You can live off blubber for years. And think of its uses, hundreds of them."

"Name twenty," said Robbie, who was again ignored.

"One left," sighed Merrick after a rapid count. "Come on, Dad".

"I think you should find it," said Lachlan, rising to turn on the kettle. "You've done well so far." Flicking the switch, he paused to survey the boys. Both sat silent, concentrating, wanting the idea first.

"Dentist?" enquired Merrick, not fully convinced.

There was a pause; he hadn't hit the jackpot. Robbie thought the doctor could handle teeth as well.

"Masseur?"

Same response. Pouring hot water on a particularly limp tea-bag, Lachlan was thinking hard. It was a good exercise.

"I still think a magician would be unusual," said Robbie ruggedly. "If you can't think of anything else."

"I can."

"And that is…?"

Lachlan knew he'd soon be called on for a casting vote; he wasn't sure he had it.

Merrick's eyes flashed and he started to write, swerving the paper away from his brother, who swerved it back the moment Merrick finished.

No reaction caught the silence. Lachlan leant over the table, reading upside down.

'Botanist', it said.

The last scene of 'Wolf' Lachlan set in a castle. To Australians the castle was a concept from film. Lachlan could not imagine life without the exploration of many castles in his Aberdeen childhood. His first remembered castle was half-buried in snow one winter Sunday when they arrived to plunder it. Not a footprint had been made, and the sun, rare visitor to east coast Scotland, had crisped up the scene. It was a castle still occupied, a large red Jaguar parked by a cellar door, unlinked to anyone by footprints. The grounds were spacious to the pair of twins, with prospects for 'hide and seek', and Lachlan felt freed there, a feeling that came back when looking at a photograph taken that day. Iain was in the foreground, Lachlan just behind, mis-shapen snowball in hand. In the far distance Rebecca had just toppled into the snow, a maroon heap for posterity. Lachlan knew exactly when the photo was taken, by his mother, unusually. Returning to the car, alone, he had noticed fresh footprints that led to the back of the Jaguar, then round it to the cellar door. Someone was watching them. On subsequent visits the castle was robust, more real, without a Jaguar parked.

His mother's favourite castle was, he was told, the most ancient of all, though without crenellations. There was a sweet shop across a small road, selling postcards, fudge and something he didn't like the taste of, mint-cake. His mother bought Rebecca fudge, thinking it too childish for growing boys. Iain was happy with his mint-cake, savouring the long drop to a bleak hillside below. One table sat embarrassed by the small space left for cars; Lachlan used to hope it would be occupied when they drew up. It rarely was.

For a long time his own favourite castle was up a long, straight lane cut off by the sea. No one ever went there, except his family, because cars had to be left a mile away and hampers borne among the necessary raincoats, hats, umbrellas, picnic-rugs and sandwiches folded in their bread bags, ceremonious. There wasn't much colour in those

Scotland days except at his castle, where juice was truly orange, plums cardinal purple, eggs blinding white.

His father liked to visit a ruined abbey, spectacular from a distance, and gaunt close-up. In one crumbling chamber a bland voice, not even Scottish, related tales perpetrated in and near the abbey, which his father appeared to find comforting, especially when music played to signify the tale was over. The place lacked drama for Lachlan, history watered down, a sin. He asked himself why his father loved the place, not wanting to find the answer; it might have lessened things.

And then they went to Dunnotar. This was a full-blown castle, still breathing despite sterile notices announcing to visitors what its craggy joys once housed in secret. It sat on the sea, commanding as it once repelled. Other than from the ocean, it was accessible only down a wide sward on which Lachlan once slipped in his haste to gain the entrance. Turn right, across the moat, still rain-decked after the years, and there was the draw-bridge, in the mind's eye. Stand there, and you saw through the doorway to the walls of the keep, moss-drenched but sturdy, moist with the caress of a wind thrashing east from Glencoe. There was a small booth housing an ancient crone, tidy tickets on two spools, 'adult' and 'child'.

Leaping through, under the archway, freedom, not captivity, called. It was not clear which way to go, around the keep, up boot-worn stairs, or down, where scullery maids once looked at armoured knights from flagstones cold to their feet, while fires roared in the Great Hall, bowls simmered, flaming torches crept up walls blackened with their signatures.

Lachlan never went the same way twice; nor, it seemed, did Iain. Often they were a long time before meeting on a three-foot parapet, beside the cellar door, or in the abbot's vestry, hidden like a valued toy way-up stone passages of stairs. Perfect for 'hide and seek'. There were no cleaners here. The sea gazed at them, through arrow-slits, or fallen mason-work, across the low wall of the kitchen garden, whose booty would have been tinged with ice, most months of the year. Lachlan dreamed of jousting there on horses drawn from the imagination of the Greeks, transformed into centaurs as they pawed the ground, then reared Lippizaner-like, before the charge.

This was a boy's domain. Iain revelled in it as much as Lachlan, his glee more verbal, more acute. Once there was a sunset that neither lad forgot. Their fights were mighty bouts, as they rolled interminably across spaces of open green, the odd stone baulking them, catching an arm, drawing the longed-for blood. 'Hide and seek' was seek and kill; there were no truces now. At night Lachlan willed himself to dream of the castle, of galloping up to it, bruised scroll in hand, or charging away, pursued by arrows on fire. He rarely did. But always came the prospect of a return, next Sunday, next Bank Holiday, next time, the entire battleground theirs for the waging. Never had Lachlan been so proud to have a twin; fighting him was taking on yourself in irreversible combat, to the death and back. Epics had their kernel in Dunnotar, Shakespeare had surely been there.

When he heard the family was moving to Australia, something he'd gathered was drawing near but held no reality, Lachlan's first thought was for Dunnotar. He was ten now, and could go on his own. Or with a friend.

"Take Iain on Saturday and be careful," said the vicar reaching for his scarf, climbing into another rain-starred night. But Lachlan had other plans. He was going to introduce Jonathan to Dunnotar; his final gesture before they parted.

They went on the bus one driech Saturday, just the two of them, Lachlan blazing with pride to show off his sacred ground. He brought a duffel-bag, slung over his shoulder, its fraying rope rendering the bag a liability. Once inside the keep, he opened up the bag's treasures to his friend, having planned for days the route they would take. Another family was at the castle, which he had not counted on, and they took time to meander away, but once they did so, Lachlan was Highland Chief. Jonathan followed him, asking questions, which Lachlan loved; he tried to slow down the tour, to make it last, realising he and his friend would soon be thousands of miles apart. How could they go through life without seeing each other again?

Finally, they reached the parapet and stood, bright eyes fixed on the sea beyond; for once it had turned blue. A cormorant flew overhead, silently; Lachlan prayed it would turn into an eagle, conferring majesty on the day. Only a seagull returned, eyes empty and unlived-in, as they always were. He cursed, then ran down to the grass. A blue sign blared: TOILETS but not for long. Without the eyes of parents, Lachlan tore the sign out of the ground and lobbed it over the high wall. There was no splash. He started to dig with his hands at the wet mud, covering himself with dirt and worms and clay, purging he knew not what. Jonathan stood transfixed.

When Lachlan was ready he pointed to the duffel-bag left upright like a feeding wallaby on the grass. He motioned to his friend to pass it over. When it landed, he yanked the rope, which finally broke, and delved inside, holding a silver tin aloft.

"What's in that?" whispered Jonathan, suddenly present at a ritual.

"Time-capsule," said Lachlan, putting it into the earth. Jonathan was silent, perplexed and feeling chilled.

"One day we'll come back and dig it up," said Lachlan with fervour.

"How will we remember?"

"We will. Here, help me put the earth back over it."

They did not speak as the deed was being done. Then trooped out of the grounds, catching their bus in the nick of time; returning home, silent.

Three weeks later Jonathan had left Aberdeen, Dunnotar and the capsule. The Stacey family set off for Australia soon afterwards. Lachlan thought of the capsule religiously for a while, then occasionally, then hardly at all. Now he remembered only planting the silver tin. What had been in it, he was not quite sure.

CHAPTER FIFTEEN

The last performance of 'Our Country's Good' repaid investment. Brodie was pleased with its unsentimental dénouement. Lachlan was not surprised: the play symbolised her triumph. For him the best scene remained the gentle exchange between Wisehammer and Mary, a scene with little action, carried by words. He envied writers' reverence for words, whereas for Brodie strong characterisation was paramount. Well-crafted characters, she claimed, were more rewarding than real ones; there was a mystery to be solved. Lachlan disagreed: real people held more mystery.

"But theirs isn't worth solving," she argued. "They cover up the mystery with skill, showing only certain sides to a gawking world." He countered that because we are limited in our cover-up skills there is more chance for the mystery to remain.

"I don't want it remaining, I want it solved," she retorted.

"Then you'll be disappointed."

"I'll take the risk."

"And where's your sense of romance?"

For a second she missed his irony, then walked briskly out of the room. Left alone, he thought of Dave's belief that nice people were boring, a belief he did not share. The two men had become heated about it at a recent barbecue.

Brodie came back with knowing look and incipient smile. They were to meet the company and explain developments. 'The Government Inspector' would be a winner; there remained the problem of how to handle the three weeks during Lachlan's time in England. Holidays for the company had been abandoned as impractical, so Brodie had ideas for readings, impromptu performances of short plays, and pieces like 'The Hollow Crown' that could be staged with little pain. In a city where experiment held sway, gambles could pay off: much would depend on other theatres' programmes, as yet unreleased.

The troupe was, in the main, positive when Lachlan broached the issue. Two of them had written one-act plays, which they could offer. Meg had wanted to play a feast of Queens of England in one night, but others of the company poured scorn on her suggestion.

"So we slip back, mainstream reduced to the fringe?"

"Yes." Brodie was defiant.

Silence coloured the air. Lachlan mooted another meeting in three days' time, and the company broke up, leaving him anxious. He had called a rehearsal of the final scene of 'Wolf' for ten o'clock that night. Late rehearsals didn't often disappoint; this one threatened to be the exception.

That left an oasis. Slipping out into the Melbourne afternoon he was surprised by rain. As he stopped and looked at it an umbrella hit him in the small of the back. Mindless weapons, umbrellas. In Aberdeen umbrellas had only ever been black, now every colour proliferated. Australian rain was purging, but rarely soaking; it made him feel comfortable, sheltered. Walks in the rain were a joy. He thought of a time when he'd taken the boys for two days to a resort in the Whitsundays. They arrived in searing heat, but the next day graced them with tropical rain, sheer, slender organ-pipes stretched by the gods and sledging down like arrows, bouncing off the pebbles, invitingly warm. The boys exchanged glances at Lachlan's staying outside, writing at a table, only inches from the rain, enjoying it. But they'd slouched to the swimming-pool, aware that the rain wouldn't last. And it hadn't; patches of blue were there in the light grey mist; the sun was having an hour off. In

Aberdeen it was dark, drenching dirty rain, stored up in never-emptying cisterns of no mercy, lashing life from all in its wake. Dampness in clothes, in hair, in books, towels, blankets, invading everywhere. People imbued with cold accept it, like tragic victims, never spared. Melbourne rain was not the spiritual life-giver of The Reef, but it was better than Aberdeen.

Another person bumped into Lachlan, angrily, no doubt wondering why he stood there in a crowded city street, gazing at the firmament. He was unperturbed, enjoying the memory of a night when he stood staring at the stars from a Melbourne jetty. It wasn't a good night for star-gazing, but something troubled him; he found an echo in the skies. To his annoyance a figure had sauntered near to him and he prepared for inevitable questions on his sanity. But they never came. Unable to bear a different sort of tension, Lachlan had finally looked at the figure, who, still looking up, said simply, "Humbling, isn't it?" He had mumbled a reply, then moved slowly away. The figure continued to inspect the skies, alone, on some primeval guard.

Hetty was minding the boys at home but, as he walked in, warmly wet, it was clear all was not well. Merrick was in his room, the computer a blank screen.

"Robs?"

"In the kitchen. With Hetty. There's still a lot of blood, Dad."

Lachlan nodded, mouth at an angle, his body heavy. Walking into the kitchen, he imagined a hundred happenings; what he saw was oddly still. Hetty was standing up, hand on the door of the fridge; Robbie sat, wan, at the table, a hanky stuffed in his mouth.

He took the hanky away from his mouth, revealing his bruised front teeth. Blood still sat on the other teeth, and his lower lip had been stitched in black. Lachlan looked at Hetty then put his arms round the boy. This was one thing he had dreaded as a boy: the loss of a front tooth.

"How did it happen, son?" he asked, clearing his throat as the words came out weak.

Robbie looked up; his eyes were strained. "I didn't see him, Dad," said the boy. "I had the ball, he must have come up from behind to tackle and I landed on his boot. It doesn't hurt... now."

Merrick was in the doorway, one hand on each side as if to push the framework further apart. Questions blazed from Lachlan, leap-frogging each other to be asked, but he said nothing. Hetty, who had arranged to be at home when the boys returned, had received a phone call from Jo and gone to collect Robbie from Dave's surgery. Merrrick had been at Harry's, as usual. "The school secretary rang David," continued Hetty. "She had to act fast."

"Can't eat steak, Lachie," the last word spoken with zest. "Pasta, maybe. But no roast."

Lachlan sensed Merrick about to say he'd be able to eat twice as much, and stemmed the boast.

"I might just go and ring Dave," he said. Hetty put a bowl of spaghetti in front of Robbie and sat down once Merrick had been served, the Book of Job in her head.

Dave told Lachlan the full story. Robbie had known at once that his front tooth had been propelled out of his mouth, then gone cold, unable to prevent a curious tongue from confirming the fact. The hole was enormous. His coach had been helpful, squatting down to try and find the tooth as soon as he had reassured the boy all would be well. He crouched on to all fours and began scanning the ground, running the left side of his thumb through blades of grass still sharp after summer. One such movement unearthed the chunk of enamel; he quickly placed it in his handkerchief, then into his tracksuit pocket. Robbie was tense, heart thumping, his mouth warm and cold at once.

"Who's your dentist, Rob?" asked the coach.

"Dave Newcombe. He's my godfather, too."

When the phone rang Dave had been doing his paper-work, typing up his day's notes onto the computer for the patients' record cards, jotting down on paper things that came into his mind for the next day. Hearing the news, Dave cleared his preparation table and moved unfinished notes to one side. He didn't know Robbie's rugby coach, who walked in holding an orange beaker of milk.

"The tooth's in there," he said. "One of the parents said that was a good idea." He looked at the dentist for approval.

"That's right," replied Dave, putting an arm out to Robbie and managing a clumsy hug as the lad climbed into his black beetle of a chair. His lip was swollen, encrusted with dried blood; he tried to smile, but found it too hard. Dave squatted down, and looked carefully at the lip, the tooth's socket torn, still seeping blood. He was aware it was starting to hurt.

"I'll rub some paste on to the gum, Robs. That'll help make it go numb." He reached for a strawberry-flavoured spray, then prepared the local anaesthetic.

"It's going to hurt, mate. I can't do it properly without a spot of pain."

He reached into the mug, extracted the tooth and washed it in saline solution.

"The quicker we put it back, the better." Dave had to decide whether to root-treat the tooth, and take the nerve out, which meant more pain, or to push it back as soon as possible. He chose the latter course.

Grasping Robbie's head, he tilted it to an angle, then injected the gum above where the tooth should be. Robbie's eyes filled with tears as he fought to keep still. Dave washed the tooth with a three-in-one syringe, sizing it up in the socket, from which it stuck out a couple of millimetres.

"Hold still, Rob." Dave pushed the tooth home hard, blood oozing onto his fingers. He reached for a piece of blue articulating paper to check the bite. So far so good.

"I've got to make a splint now, mate, fix this front one to your teeth to stop it moving, and embed it in the gum." He took a thin piece of ribbon-gauze from the open drawer and roughened the surface of the two teeth either side of the replaced front one, then washed it off with the syringe, sucking out the water.

"Keep your mouth open wide, and try not to put your tongue on those teeth; they need to say dry. I'll put a bonding agent on the back of your teeth." Bonding agent sounded like something from a spy film to the boy. Dave shone a bright light on the back of the teeth, which set the varnish at once. His curing-light beeped after fifteen seconds.

"Now, Robbie, check you can close your teeth together."

Gingerly, the boy did so.

"Job's done," said Dave, pushing his mask down over his chin. "I'll just give you some amoxicillin, they're antibiotics to make sure there's no infection. Cleaning your teeth will be tricky for a few days. I suggest a teaspoonful of salt in warm water to swish round the mouth, gently. There'll be a bit of pain."

Robbie nodded. "I've got a match on Saturday. Will it be okay to play?"

"You'll need a new gum shield; your old one won't fit. I'll make you a new one…"

Robbie's face fell.

"…on Friday, ready for the match."

There was little food at home; Lachlan sped on his bike to the supermarket. He was due to meet Lynch at 8.30, then prepare for the rehearsal. Returning, he saw a letter from Rebecca on the hall-table; it would go unopened for now, stamps untouched. The ansaphone struck in: Brodie was caught up; she'd have to miss the rehearsal. A message from Tom Dixon asked if he could borrow Lachlan's complete Shakespeare and could he drop round to pick it up

174

that evening? The phone rang again, Hetty sweeping it up in front of him: Harry Newcombe, to ask if Robs wanted to come round.

"I'll stay the night," said Hetty, firmly.

"Hetty, you are a star," said Lachlan. And he was back en route to The Tinderbox. When he walked into the theatre, Lynch was not there. He arrived minutes later, his face apology enough.

"You need a beer," said Lachlan. "Not here."

Along the pavement was a bar; they sat outside, glad of fresh air. It was the same bar where Lynch had told Lachlan his story years before. Lynch was a New South Welshman, so he supported The Blues. Born in a small town on the coast, like many Aussies, he grew up at the beach, surfing from the age of five. He remembered his father giving him a leg-rope one February birthday. At seventeen he went to Sydney for a while, then back to Casino, working in an abattoir, good money, not good people. In the boning-room, cool after slaughter, for three long years he sliced the meat, and put it into crovac bags. Then headed off to The Reef. He was there some months, waiting at table, which he hated, but he gained insight into people. There was little carpentry done then. Western Australia was his next gambit, bar work in Fitzroy Crossing, four hundred kilometres inland from Broome, and desert-hot. He served aboriginals and ringers on lost cattle stations, and it was rough. The ringers were all big boys, soaking up triple rums greedily, holding out a fragile glass for more.

Then came the carpentry, when he moved to Melbourne, renting a room with students, sharing a workshop in a garden shed. He worked long hours, to the strains of Matchbox 20, Midnight Oil, Hoodoo Gurus and Hunters and Collectors, emerging after dusk with calloused hands. It never struck him to ask the students what further education was like, he'd learned enough on travels. He joked of winning the lottery, but dreaded the reality. He was simply

175

content. One day he'd drink coronas on Tijuana Beach. Lachlan wanted to introduce him to Dave, but when he mentioned it, Dave seemed to shy away, telling Lachlan that he and Jo were getting a puppy. Lachlan felt insulted for Lynch.

When proposals for 'Wolf' were drawn up, the carpenter saw everything matt black, his favourite colour. Even as Lachlan told him of the play's harsh motifs, Lynch's hands were sketching shapes, corners, shadows, all blood-dark. The challenge grew in him.

The central stage feature of 'Wolf' was a portcullis, whose serrated shadow hung throughout. At key junctures in the play it moved down; by the end it was on the ground. Dotted around its threatening bulk were large metal studs, as if on leather, gleaming. Thin shafts of light shot through the holes at times, indicative, in the beginning, of a conscience, soon snuffed out, and, later, of openings to redemption, stifled by the anguished Wolf. Lachlan wanted to keep the symbolism, though Brodie argued it was overt.

Lynch saw the symbolic possibilities he could create: his central table, scene of the final agony, as well as the ritual place of rape, was an altar, a small white crocheted cloth thrown over it. Sharp lighting picked out a crucifix on the portcullis, whose jagged points were spears. Skulls for the lead actor were a problem. No one wanted a simple mask put on by Wolf to signify his savage alter ego. Lynch suggested three masks of varying size, on strings that dropped from the flies into which the main character walked to drench himself in evil, get his fix. One mask was blank, one held the innocence of a lion cub, the other simply lines criss-crossing on the template of a skull. The idea worked, in theory.

For the feline character's movements they moved as far away as possible from the pantomime animal, though Brodie was adamant that some humour was essential to this play. Images of blood-dripping lips above a creature

176

squatting on its haunches like a friendly Akela at pack drill ensured comedy was not far away. But the more Lachlan went into the play, the more convinced he was the cruelty should stand alone. Aboriginal corroborees held the key for him: there a man danced his traditional measure in celebration, utterly supple, in touch with the earth throughout. Angus had been working hard on this; it was in his mind when he went to the zoo on Lachlan's insistence, but he found it hard to rehearse cold. He had to convey how a man came to lose all humanity, sacrificing it for unimaginable depths of the bestial.

His feline shape was crucial. Lachlan approached it by degrees, first getting his actor to move with the grace of a centaur, then inculcate a level of myth, like a unicorn. But the unicorn did not work, it was too friendly an icon, too revered.

"How about a walrus?" said Angus in sardonic tone. "Just keeping the humour in," he added, which earned him Brodie's scowl.

Lachlan's antipathy for cats was not shared by Angus, who had been weaned on them and had three at home. He scoffed at Lachlan's view of them as sly and arch, defending their inscrutability as vital for the hunter's life. Lachlan took the bait; cats leapt at those who did not like them, then stalked away content, tails up, strutting their pencil-sharpeners as they did to randy toms outside. Domestic cats, preened and self-satisfied, he'd come to loathe. Feral cats were worse. These were on the increase in cities now, like mangy foxes; Lachlan heard of a labrador, its throat torn out by feral cats, who personified destruction. That was what this play had to communicate. Angus was in danger of communicating kitten-play, stray balls of wool in nurseries, bobbing down stairs, chased by pets be-ribboned, and well-stroked.

"Your fondness for them ought to help," Brodie said. "Use it to get inside them, then turn that inside out."

Lynch, watching, lifted his head up at that. It impressed Angus too, leaving Lachlan, for a moment, lost.

The lighting was crucial. Blue-grey day began the piece, backed by metallic music, taking time to fade. Fresh pink seemed clichéd for the carnal scenes, but mixing yielded a raw, honed colour, with hints of orange in its grain. The subsequent deep-red could not be improved on, giving way to black before the final scene. At, and after the end, dry ice under dull green fire writhed up through gaps in the portcullis as an inert figure faded on his slaughter slab of guilt.

Lynch set the lights. His plot was not ready, but robust enough for rehearsal. Meg, calm and excited at once, arrived with the girl Wolf wronged before he raped. Her part in the scene was not huge. Lachlan knew Angus would arrive last, which he did, two bananas in his hand. He was quiet. Lachlan liked late rehearsals and kept instructions to a minimum: of the last three scenes, he'd run two, then pause, and go for the last one. Only Angus was in the final scene.

The actors limbered up, shaking limbs, twisting their heads, then still. There was a focused silence; time blurred. Shouts from the street below rang loud for a moment, a car door banged, the vehicle moved away. Lachlan turned off the fan. A throat cleared in the near-distance as Lynch moved to the console.

Scenes of sexual savagery Lachlan did not find easy to direct; they were often gratuitous and badly written; sex scenes in novels were the same, though usually amusing. But 'Wolf' was different: it was urgent writing on the deepest themes: desire, betrayal, insanity, and what – if anything – was left. In one play he admired, a young man was taken into the home of a penniless couple whose daughter was handicapped. In the dénouement the lodger raped the helpless girl. It was too explicit. Lachlan preferred to give his audience uncomfortable knowledge of what had to come; it wasn't what Wolf did, but how he set his mind to it.

178

The rape scene was harder for the girl. She said little, knowing the purpose of the beast was intractable. But, she was cold, no foil to Angus tonight. Brodie had sensed a bad rehearsal and kept clear. Angus paved his way behind the third mask, the skull: his body calmed between lust and destruction as he drank in evil from his unknown source. He came out, metamorphosed, ice on his mind. Having ravished the girl, he slew her briskly. The lights dimmed, the girl stole forward to watch with Lachlan, and Meg stepped into the darkness. The penultimate scene was a quiet one, essential contrast, as the beast sat alone with his mother in a low-lit room. She knew what he must do, her face clenched into sorrow, wizened, stained with recognition. And with shame. The girl, by Lachlan's side, watched in terror, light reflecting off her chiselled features. If only she could look like that on stage, thought Lachlan, catching her expression.

Meg was acting well, no hand-wringing or stifled screams, simplicity incarnate. Angus drew strength from her, gentleness pestelled to mortar. His feline moves were convincing as he pounced across a stage made smaller in his wild intent. Meg turned from him to the mirror, in that trice her face was magnified on the portcullis; her son just turned away. Slowly, Angus drew himself onto his hind paws, eyes stiller than moons; he was shaking. Lachlan could see Lynch scanning the script to mix the final scene, as Meg, sitting at the table, sank her head.

Dilemma. Lachlan had to choose: either he let the final scene run on, or he stopped it, destroying the intensity.

"Hold it a second, Angus."

The actor turned on him, blazing; he was in the rôle, the hardest rôle, what was the director doing? Lachlan felt the lack of Brodie like a punch, his hand still raised to end the scene. Angus walked peremptorily past him, anatomical impossibilities hanging muttered in the air. The girl looked away. Meg lifted her head. Lynch remained buried in the script. Lachlan was burning now. Justifying his decision was irrelevant.

Lynch got up and walked out after Angus. There was no noise except the buzz of a spot-light, fiercely yellow. No one spoke. Then two figures walked back into the theatre. Eleven o'clock bleeped on the girl's watch. Angus was subdued now, having reached for a banana, devouring it in three eager bites. He looked through Lachlan into space.

Lynch broke the stale-mate. "We had a word outside," he said.

Lachlan had to say something. "It's that journey back into yourself, coming out of yourself at the same time, not easy. Do you remember those advent calendars as a kid? Each with a number on the window, leading to the nativity picture on Christmas Day? Imagine you have a wicked equivalent of that. In this last scene you're opening windows one at a time, only they get progressively worse. You're opening the last window for yourself, and for us, at the same time." He paused. "Come here a minute."

Angus thought about it, then moved to Lachlan. One stage-light was on, into whose splashed beam the director guided the actor. "Just one more risk. Keep your eyes closed, then look up for a second at the light."

Angus did so. Wary, not at ease.

"Now look away. You've got shapes behind your eyes you want to get rid of. Try and let them stay there. Pursue them if they slide away."

Both men were still for a minute or two. Then Lachlan sat down.

"When you're ready," he said.

Angus blinked as the light went down. He walked to the back of the stage and undressed, putting on a hair-suit skin hanging on a lone peg. Lynch dimmed the lights. Neither the girl nor Meg had gone. Breathing was heard.

A dim blue light grows and Wolf stands still. In front of him a hefty tree-trunk blocks his path. An owl hoots some-where close. Wolf bends down on all-fours surveying the

180

obstacle. Then he prepares to lift it from his way. It is immensely heavy, going to defeat him. But one last effort holds, he splays his haunches, and with sharp breathing gasps, he lifts the trunk, holding it in front of him. A scorpion must be inside, for suddenly a finger sticks out from his hand; he's been bitten. The tree-trunk falls, but Wolf's path is clear. He holds up the finger and starts to suck the poison from its niche.

But then he stops, change reflected in his face. The hand, a paw, comes clutching at his face and scratches hard down the side of his cheek. Blood creases the skin, he puts the paw into his mouth and sucks. Light flickers, then a spot beams on his face: whiskers protrude. The light pans back, showing his body fragile against a portcullis' might. Its spokes descend a notch.

And all the time his table waits. The end of his journey is here to meet him; feline nemesis is his. At last he is the beast: he springs onto the table in a single bound; another leap and his back is to the audience. A tail swings. He's making an odd noise now with his tongue, not purring, but something earthier. Another light, this time red, sends coals on to his shrinking form. From across the stage an arrow of green hits him broadside; he turns again. The portcullis slips down one more ratchet, rasping in a sudden gust of wind. Wolf's head is raised; a siren starts to sound, but he hears nothing. His paw is raked with pus; it suppurates. Veins bulge where no veins were. And slowly, imperceptibly, he starts to scratch. The light snaps out, a gust of wind roars through the room, the table starts to rock.

When the light comes up it is piercing. Wolf is on his haunches, reaching up. The portcullis has nowhere to go and grinds, agonised. He is scratching harder now, tearing at his face, his chest, his every limb. His noise begins again. Strobe-light lingers; there is no reprieve. His animal skin is cast off, leaving him naked as he starts on his own flesh. His noise is frightening, borne up by the wind. Fingers are

181

claws, ripping at his helpless naked self; his face is fire, screams come from somewhere else.

The final sound is not feline roaring but a human hollow cry, then he crashes back on the table, grief eating him away, his soul flayed open, body just a cork.

The table legs are choked with blood. Then the light snaps out, the beast is gone, the actor heaped, exhausted.

No one applauds. After some time the girl walks quickly out, followed by Meg. Lynch's eyes roll towards Lachlan, who is staring at the table. A tread, and Lynch is gone.

Lachlan feels heavier than he has ever been. To step forward is, for a moment, beyond him. In the darkness he hears Angus crying a few feet away. The table moves. Lachlan's teeth are tight against his mouth. He finally moves towards the other man, hand outstretched. It touches Angus on the shoulder. Lachlan moves his hand gently along to the collar-bone, trying to squeeze the space where no flesh is. Pins and needles make him impotent. He tries once more to squeeze some comfort into the prostrate form, but fails. What was the Wolf stutters in tiny spasms, red-raw, still bleeding, and the crying does not stop...

CHAPTER SIXTEEN

When Kathy stopped going to church, suddenly, one autumn Sunday, she surprised them. It was a schism he'd seen growing, but it still shocked him with the cleanness of its break. She had no reason, cooked up no pretext, just came out of the bedroom as they were about to leave. Merrick had one sandal dangling from a newly-broken strap, Rob was pressing a book into his side, spine outwards.

"I'm not coming today." And that was all; she turned and went back into the room, leaving the door to ebb back in the draught like Caesar's messenger withdrawing from Cleopatra.

The three looked at each other, stunned. No one spoke till they were in the car.

"Robs, did you know Mum wasn't coming to church today?"

"No." Pause. "Did you?"

"No. It's a bit of a surprise... isn't it?"

Merrick was silent, sitting up between the two front seats, hands on his knees.

At church the first three worshippers they saw asked where Kathy was. Lachlan just said, "At home," with a dryness in the roof of his mouth that came back when the question was asked again, several times. From that day he felt the victim of a family tragedy. He was apprehensive of their return home, but she was at her best when they walked in, served up a strapping meal, asked in detail about church, then loaded the aged dishwasher, humming, which Lachlan never appreciated.

And the schism grew, though some weeks she went to church, as usual, her smile satisfying the more curious, as it used to satisfy him. Then, one week when she stayed at home, they returned to an empty house. Merrick was unconcerned, Lachlan cold to the stomach, Robbie instantly afraid. Some minutes later the phone rang: Robbie was there first.

"Where are you, Mum? When are you coming home?" He put the phone down, relieved. "Half an hour she says, Dad. Can you fix the salad?"

Can you fix the salad? Innocuous hint, preparing a husband and two sons. She walked in smiling, twenty-five minutes later, but at once her mobile phone bleeped and she moved away to speak. Hints were bludgeoning them now.

"Where were you, Mum?" said Merrick, the moment she pressed the off-switch on her phone.

"Where do you think?" she asked.

"I can't. That's why I asked."

Robbie was looking at her with his furrowed frown, but she ignored them both, concentrating a gaze onto the garden.

"At work, of course. Where else?"

Where else? Lachlan, with his loathing of rhetorical questions, bit his lip. "Is there any lunch?"

She kept her eyes on the garden, with a lot of effort.

"There will be when you get it."

Not if, when.

And that was it. Kathy's work on Sundays was established as paramount from that day; she was rarely at home on the Sabbath afterwards. In the office to which she had transferred a sort of faith, she was ever-present. Her firm had set up a weekly teleconference with Vancouver Island, home of Canadian government. In an office Lachlan never saw, three Australians sat tuned in to a large television. On the screen was the image of ten Canadians around a table. There was the odd flicker, an occasional sound delay, or rapid staccato movement reflected in a static voice, but, that apart, communication was in sway. On top of both televisions sat a camera, relaying pictures across the world. Sunday morning in Melbourne was Saturday afternoon on Vancouver Island, perfect timing.

It was perfect timing, too, that meant Kathy was soon offered a job with the Canadian team, a job where she would not only 'sit on a bonus', but earn shares almost immediately. Government Law was her thing; she would be foolish to resist.

Telling Lachlan was not hard. Telling the boys was different. Her crime, to a husband's thinking, was telling them she would return within the year when her stint was up. There had been a time when she didn't lie. Light years ago.

When Lachlan reached home, it was gone midnight. He had caught the last tram, thoughts in the stars. Two lights were on. In the living-room he found Hetty still fully dressed, asleep on the sofa. A luke-warm cup of tea sat untouched on the nearby table. Robbie's bedside lamp revealed the boy asleep on his back, mouth closed, handkerchief fallen on to the duvet. His left hand guarded the swollen lip, its black stitches visible. Lachlan pushed the hair from the boy's forehead, feeling it damp to his touch. The echo of a bruise slept gently over Robbie's eye. Lachlan was very still.

Looking round he saw the room tidier than usual. A fistful of stamps floated in a bowl of water, most of them face-down, soggy brown envelope remains waiting to be peeled away. Three paperbacks were also face-down, two with a bookmark close to the end. Like his father, Robbie hated finishing books; he often felt cheated.

"Why are endings never good, Dad?" was a constant question that Lachlan could not answer. He found himself looking at the boy's carving of three fishing boats against a sunken sea, framed in wood. The boats were painted white and green. Only the other day Robbie had been kneeling up on his bed, carefully tying one of the strings with which the boats were fitted out. Lachlan hadn't noticed the intricacy before: tiny nets for landed fish, red jibs holding slender coils thrown over them in readiness for hoisting. Two of the boats were bottle green, almost black, the middle one a lighter shade. "Racing green, Dad," said Robs, "Like those flash English sports cars." Lachlan said they should go on a fishing boat in England. Robbie was not convinced.

"What will we do all the time?"

Lachlan did not reply, just looked at him and shrugged his shoulders with a smile. The string Robbie had tied up that day was loose again now, hanging over the boat, spoiling the symmetry. Lachlan left it there and walked quietly from the room.

The ansaphone flashed twice: he'd get the messages next morning. Angus flashed into his mind as he squirted tooth-paste from a dying tube on to his brush, and flashed out again in a trice.

"'Night, Lach," came a voice from the sofa, peaceful, tired.

"'Night, Hetty. Thank you."

He left his door open for Robbie, in case.

Reading the previews of 'Wolf', for once, excited him. But Brodie remained absent. She was never crook, and he wanted her to see the play at this point. Hers was one of the messages that night, the other being Dave to see how Robbie's tooth had taken. When Lachlan rang Brodie back, her partner answered, sounding protective; her virus gave him cause. She sent her best, not love, and he returned it, wondering how the guard would let his message through.

For their production after 'Death of a Salesman' the actors needed the relief of a comedy, but Lachlan was still bothered over his choice of play.

"Try two casts," breezed Hetty. "Try three."

He had not taken the idea seriously at first, but mooted it warily at a Brodie-less meeting of the company, and was surprised to find that it had mileage. Two actors said it was precisely the experimentation they should be doing.

Meg was a stalwart. The meeting over, she walked up to him, shoulder-bag in her arms and praised the concept. "Have two casts, then mix them," she offered. "I was in a whodunnit once, in Ballarat. There were ten of us in the cast, and the play had three endings. We only decided in the course of each performance which ending to go for. Quite cunning, really; it all hung on the positioning of the cigarette lighter. At a key point in the action, any one of us could place the lighter in a certain spot and we'd run that dénouement. People could come three nights running and see the same ending three times"

"Didn't that make it a power struggle," asked Lachlan, "everyone fighting for the lighter, night after night?"

"Exactly," she replied, eyes flashing. "That was what made it so exciting. We used to plan strategies way before the lighter's moment. It made for sharp playing, I can tell you."

"Not to mention a thrill for the theatre-going public of Ballarat," chimed in Lachlan, and Meg walked away, laughing.

"Any news on Brodie?" she asked, turning at the door, and bumping into Norman with two mugs of tea.

Lachlan shook his head.

"I'll give her a call," said Meg. "At least I'll get a sentence from the hunk, if not from her."

"Very chatty this morning," said Norman, holding one of the mugs out to Lachlan.

"She always is," replied the director. "She's a doll."

Norman nodded sagely, his top lip testing the surface of the tea for a warmth it never had. To his surprise the blood-filled table legs had worked well, but they needed to order more 'blood'. Lachlan sanctioned the request, still thinking of Meg's idea. It was growing on him.

May moved on wheels. Robbie's tooth seemed fine, and Merrick asked a feast of questions about the English trip. One Sunday, after church, Lachlan suggested a cycle ride, with picnic. It had been a glorious autumnal morning, but by the time they set off clouds were banking up. The choice of picnic site was a fiery one, Lachlan's Botanical Gardens suggestion deemed dull. They settled on Caulfield race-course with its sward and scenic lake. Merrick was ready in a flash, his new red helmet sported like a trophy.

The breeze was stiffening as they left; it rose as they pedalled out of town, hitting them head-on when they crossed the muddy Yarra. Lachlan, cycling hindmost, watched Robbie with the realisation that his bike was too small. His coming birthday was good timing. There'd be a second-hand bike somewhere.

Merrick's hand-signals were a joy to watch, exaggerated and prolific. Robbie overtook his brother, up on his pedals, wind blowing through his sleeves, deforming him.

"Watch the tram tracks," shouted Lachlan into a heedless breeze. The tracks were thin, easy prey to cycle tyres if a pilot was unwary.

The racecourse was almost deserted, its flowers nodding, a set of starting stalls redundant by the 1200 metre mark. An elderly couple stood, regaining breath, against the plastic rail, the wife smiling at Lachlan as he passed. The husband looked concerned. But already Robbie had reached the lake and was climbing out of his rucksack, both wheels spinning on the discarded bike. Merrick was inspecting his elbow, blessed by a mosquito.

"You'll live," said Lachlan.

Over lunch that drew rare compliments from both boys, they spoke of England, now less than two weeks away. Still disappointed not to be seeing London, Merrick screwed his face up on hearing again his father's reasoning. "One day," was not sufficient recompense. Devon and Cornwall sounded colourful places, but Rebecca he could not remember very well, and The Lakes contained no mystery for him. Robbie was quiet, thinking of the Stanbury boys, late-teenagers, who might be home at Hawkthwaite; possibilities lurked there. Lachlan told them more about Rebecca, adding to the picture gleaned from her bright letters, finding himself suddenly moved at the thought of their reunion.

"Saul's an odd name?" said Merrick, into nowhere. Lachlan agreed; Saul of Tarsus was changed to Paul, and Dave had said the name put him in mind of a black pimp.

"What are you smiling at, Dad?" Robbie's expression was keen, his tongue touching the tip of the mended tooth.

"Just something Dave once said," replied Lachlan. The boys exchanged glances, then raced on with questions about water-ski-ing in the The Lakes. Lachlan had only dim recollections of the names, Ambleside, Coniston, where water-speed records were tackled, Windermere, Bowness; those lakes were different from the one for which they were bound. Mountains rose out of Wastwater he said, England's highest mountains, and the views were stunning.

"Can we rock-climb?" asked Robbie, again thinking of his chance to follow in the Stanburys' slipstream.

Lachlan had received no reply from Iain. He'd not expected one, but hoped. Rebecca's latest letter, opened by Robbie in his urgency to purloin the stamps, had glossed over their brother, concentrating on the plans she had for Chester in late June. She'd clear her books of patients for four of the days, though Saul had only the weekend free. Lachlan wanted to meet their friends and knew the days in Chester would be colourful ones, a fact not easily transmitted to his sons.

Pauline's enthusiasm for their visit to The Lakes was stirring. Kerryn told Lachlan on the phone one day that Pauline hailed from Northern Ireland. Kinship between

Ireland and Australia ran deep, increasing Lachlan's desire to meet the woman. Sam sounded a man of strength. Lachlan pictured a latter-day Gabriel Oak, huge forearms, with a farmer's weathered ruddy skin. The village fête would be on while they were staying, and their labrador sounded a good companion for Lakeland walks.

The wind had dropped, and sun emerged again as they picked up their bikes. In the near-distance, a racehorse trotted back to the course stables, lone equine figure on this day of rest. They cycled out of the racecourse complex and crossed the wide main road. A horse-box jolted along in front of them, fragile, as it crossed a mine of tracks. A grey tail hung over the back, unkempt. The bolts looked as if they could shear off at any moment. Lachlan had once passed a horse-box fallen on its side, the horse still trapped, whinny-ing with fear. Worse was told to him by a mate with whom he'd gone racing: the floor fell out of a horse-box, causing carnage to the two horses inside. Their legs were ripped to pieces on unforgiving tarmac; both had to be put down. Merrick's face suggested he feared something similar about to happen now. One by one their bikes overtook the faltering vehicle, and eased back to the left side of the road.

Half a mile further on, Lachlan shouted at the boys to go left, an instruction not heard by Merrick, who sailed on. Lachlan caught up with him and they rejoined a patient Robbie.

"Are we going to Dave and Jo's?" he guessed.

"Why not?" returned his father. "We'll grab a chocolate slice and call in for arvo tea."

Leaving the bikes against the verandah, the three walked up to the fly-screen. There was a loud snort and something ballooned up the darkened hallway, crashing into the screen.

"Molar!" came Harry's voice, and the boy emerged with towel and huge grin. Against the door, a young golden retriever gasped for air.

"You didn't tell us," said Merrick, still taken aback.

It had happened fast. Driving past the stray animals' home two days before, Dave had called in, idly, and returned home with the yearling dog. Merrick's face craved the same for his family, but Lachlan already shook his head.

"Not when we're off to England," he said firmly, and the posse moved out of the darkness. The kettle was on, Jo clearing up legions of the weekend newspaper, Dave's hedge-trimmer buzzing busily in the garden. The boys disappeared with Harry and Molar, and Lachlan grabbed his familiar chair at the table.

Jo looked tired as she narrated recent events. School was hectic beyond belief, and she'd been troubled by two students ringing her at home. Dave had lost his temper one evening, rare occurrence, and she wondered if they needed a break.

"A holiday would be good," said Lachlan.

Jo winced. "We've got a week down at Lorne. I'd rather go further, somewhere new, but Dave's quite happy where we always go these days. The ritual gets to me there; he's gone there all his life, and it's enough for him. Not for me, though."

Dave came in, licking a healthy scratch. He'd heard Jo's words. But Lachlan sympathised with Jo; he was not a fan of ritual.

"How's the tooth?" asked Dave, when Lachlan wanted to challenge him on Lorne.

"You did a great job, buddy. Thanks."

"Time's the important thing," replied the dentist. " Hetty was on the ball, as always."

Lachlan nodded. His thoughts were miles away, transported on a whim of which he was not aware. "Could we talk about Iain?" he heard himself say, hand fingering crumbs around the uncut chocolate slice. Without waiting for an answer, he was pouring out feelings, speaking unmoulded thoughts, voicing the fear, shame, guilt and lack of comprehension so long stored in the attic of his mind.

191

Dave sat down to his left, eyebrows raised so as not to stem the flow. Jo was professional now.

"It's not the past, that's hard enough," said Lachlan, aware of his breathing once more, "it's the present. These last few days I've woken up thinking of him now, at this moment, nine hours behind us on some international clock, but still existing, raw as us. I wonder what his days are like; how can I not know? Is he alone all day with just a bucket except when stepping into a crowded yard? I know prison's a punishment, but who says how deep the punishment can go? He's hardly likely to see the prison governor for a cosy chat or tutorial. Films don't help, sanitising, disinfecting, building up, not taking down mystique. But all I have are celluloid tapestries and those childhood pictures of mailbags sewn by prisoners in navy blue overalls. I don't even know if they wear uniform now.

And what about his minders, warders, whatever they call them now? They're unlikely to bend in obedience to a prisoner's rights. No, they're violent, using brute force as a means of control. Think of the crimes these men commit, extending the circle in the guise of moral order. Bad things happen in prison. Those warders can be bullies, sadists, thirsty for assault, the only influences on a prisoner's life. It's the isolation I keep thinking of. Iain in the cell, the shower, strip-searched at random, powerless to resist... an individual without the barest privacy, with no protection, no one to whom he can appeal. Child molesters, I'm told, are kept apart in prisons from other inmates because of a distorted, quasi-sense of morality that makes their crimes intolerable to criminals. Same with murderers. I shudder to think of the risks attendant on a prisoner from fellow captives. Risks everywhere, lying in wait like painted gremlins in some endless computer game, greedy to contribute to the highest score.

And if the prisoners do complain, what then? Instant re-trial in front of a sympathetic judge, erudite barrister on tap, jury biddable as in some fairy-tale TV play? No. Just unheard complaints, then taunts, abuse, ganging-up by the prison officers, adding insults to a bank of injuries, biding their time. In charge of sleep, meals, work and exercise, the officers are in control, so violence and hurt can be prepared, then unleashed... all in the name of 'discipline'. I can't say 'justice'. Moral agents with no conception of morality... Can I get a drink?"

Jo stood up, her face inert, but Lachlan was at the tap, gulping down the not-yet cold water in frantic bursts. Dave looked more uncomfortable than she'd seen him for a while: he averted his gaze into a garden suddenly bereft of birds. Lachlan hiccupped, then held his breath, eyes clenched shut. Jo moved to the fridge and fished out three cold beers, taking off their jagged tops with a tea-towel. Dave picked one up, and carried it to the sink.

"Cheers, mate," he said, attempting a wink.

Lachlan hiccupped again. "Cheers," he said a few moments later. "Want to come to England?"

Ten days later Dave drove Lachlan and two eager boys to Tullamarine airport. Brodie had returned to work, and her return had sparked harmony. His casting of 'The Government Inspector' sparked unexpected enthusiasm. 'Wolf' was attracting audiences and Lachlan's efforts to implement his ideas for the weeks after that were meeting with some success. 'The Hollow Crown' had worked in its early stages, and a part of him was keen to to start work on 'Death of a Salesman' on his return from England.

Kerryn rang with a final word on Sam and Pauline. Hetty had fled to Perth, too soon in Lachlan's eyes: she was an astute packer and he missed her help. The boys were eaving school a week early, Merrick missing one party, which did not go down well. Robbie stacked his case with books. Lachlan had spent an hour the previous evening sorting through the selection, trimming it, then adding clothes; it was an English summer to which they travelled. He threw in Rebecca's last letter to remind him, on the plane, of her enthusiasms, found scripts he was considering for the spring, and rang Dave; they were as ready as they'd ever be.

All four were silent in the car. For the past few days Lachlan had again felt not that he was flying 12,000 miles to a northern clime, but that a part of him had left; it was already there, beyond the journey, safely home. Emotions outran the hour-glass.

Outside the airport Dave shook his hand. "Any time, Lach, you know that. Same with the boys. We'll have them any time."

CHAPTER SEVENTEEN

Arriving with the sunrise into Heathrow airport, Lachlan was surprised to find blue skies and a hint of warmth. The second leg of the journey had been lengthy; fourteen hours since their shower in Singapore airport.

Initial warmth was tempered by dull formalities: they met starched white or Indian complexions, none of which smiled, and blank expressions on airport workers, for whom he felt sympathy, as they chased litter through eternal dawns. The boys were tetchy, half-awake, rubbing their eyes as they leaned against immigration desks, unsure how much effort they needed to make.

The hire car disappointed them; nondescript brown, it felt cramped, with no room for stretching limbs. Before they were on the motorway, both lads were asleep, missing the flag-decked bulk of Windsor Castle proud against the sky.

Lachlan's resolve to stop at Stonehenge looked futile, but he stuck to his guns, guessing the boys' sleep would be fitful. Robbie was awake as they turned off the motorway, but questions did not flow. Lachlan parked some distance from the stones, and they walked towards them, the boys with hands in pockets. It was clear this should be a brief pit-stop, Lachlan pushing down the fear that this reaction might be repeated for the next three weeks. There was a dearth of interest in both his sons. He drove on towards Devon.

The farmhouse sat on top of a valley, views stretching ahead of them down to a sinewy river, and across to the flinty outcrops of Dartmoor. Robbie had spotted a 'Bed and

Breakfast' sign by the lych-gate to a village church. It was mid-afternoon, quite warm, and they needed to stop travelling. A comely farmer's wife, with pinned-back black hair, greeted them, her rustic intonation causing wariness in the boys, a wariness that increased as she ended consecutive sentences with the words, "my lover."

It was an old-fashioned house to young eyes that had not encountered anything antique. The landlady led the way up a tight staircase, chatting merrily. On the landing Lachlan stopped, looking down into a shed of cows, like an unwieldy crossword in their shifting black and white. A dog yelped in the lane; a baby smeared with milk tottered into a puddle. The boys were bounding on twin beds, Robbie's hand fingering a fabric he had never seen, rough to the touch, constricting. The farmer's wife launched into the history of her sister, newly emigrated to New Zealand, which, she presumed, was very like Australia. "She's never seen animals like it," confirmed the biddy, "sleek, healthy, burnished in the sun. I expect you've been to New Zealand."

Without waiting for a reply, she led Lachlan across the landing to a room boasting three windows, with a view over the orchard to a small town some distance away.

"There's a good pub in the village," she nodded, "and I do a full English."

"Full English?" asked Robbie.

"Breakfast. Bacon, egg, sausage, tomato, mushrooms, black pudding... the works."

Merrick pulled a face; he picked up the magazine that lay on an unusual piece of furniture and riffled through glossy photographs of seals and otters on the Scottish coast. Not a shark in sight.

The woman had gone, leaving them in a vacuum. "Quick walk?" said Lachlan. "We'll have an early tea, then bed."

Emerging from the wide front door at the end of a hall festooned with family photographs, they heard dogs barking by the milking shed and saw the baby, again about to fall headlong. An old rusty car had breathed its last and now squatted among nettles by the ill-kept wall. There was a pond that hadn't housed fish for some time and a mattress coiled itself around a rusty fence.

"So old," said Merrick.

Lachlan laughed.

When they arrived outside it, The Cock Pheasant was locked and barred. It was 5.53p.m. They peered through a window, seeing only darkness. The inn sign, newly painted, swung in the breeze.

'Not exactly welcoming. Is the whole country like this?" Robbie's expression was resigned.

On the dot of six the bolt of a door was released and two faint orange lights were seen inside. A burly man stood by the door, making no attempt to move as Lachlan ducked his head and went in.

"What's 'liquor'?"piped Merrick, reading aloud the white letters on a black background above the door. "Licensed to sell 'liquor'."

"Beer, of course," said Robbie, coming back to look. It struck him there'd been other names above the words but they were painted out.

The boys struggled with a steak and kidney pie; Lachlan finished it, amused by the English idea of 'steak', and all three were in bed before dusk.

"What's a 'knave', Dad?" said Merrick. Lachlan looked down and saw a grubby thumb planted by the number 5. The trio was enjoying a day at Newton Abbot races.

'ARRANT KNAVE 8 years old, carrying 10st 12. Red and green quartered colours, red sleeves, black cap. Ridden by T. Scollop. Second last time out.'

"A rogue or rebel... can be a thief," his father replied. He had the swift mental picture of jam tarts whisked off a plate by someone dressed as a playing card.

"Am I a knave?"

"You certainly are."

"Is Robbie?"

Lachlan looked over towards the paddock where his elder son was burrowing his way through shirt-sleeved race-goers to get a better view of the runners.

"You're both knaves," he said, taking his chubby hand, which Merrick resisted.

There were nine runners in the first race, headed by a recent course-and-distance winner, Lurking Shadow. He had twelve stone and a top jockey, who would know how to get the best out of him.

Arrant Knave was a chestnut with four white socks ... unlucky in racing, but that hadn't stopped good horses like The Minstrel. He was sweating a little in the heat of the June afternoon, but not as much as a dark bay sporting yellow blinkers, number 6.

The boys watched the sleek, powerful machines walk regally by. The top weight certainly looked fit, but Arrant Knave would be worth a small wager. Good name, too. Lachlan was surprised Merrick hadn't gone to ask him what 'Arrant' meant. The memory of a Shakespearian villain shot into his head, only to be chased out by a fair-haired figure in striped trousers like a clown. Hamlet, of course.

A bell rang, and sparks of colour that he hadn't seen enter the paddock sprang up onto the backs of their steeds. One was a girl, he noticed ... not Arrant Knave. A grey snorted, dropping dung that looked golden as it walked away from them toward the paddock exit. Merrick looked up instantly, roguery behind his excited grin. Robbie raised his eyes to the heavens and led the way past the ambulance room to the course.

An assortment of men was standing on what looked like fish-boxes rippling money in their hands like tired playing-cards. They were shouting now and then, but what they said was hard to decipher.

"Arrant Knave, Dad," said Merrick with defiance.

Lachlan looked at Robbie, knowing he would play safe and go for the favourite.

"Mine's Lurking Shadow." The words came out with emphasis directed at his brother.

Lachlan scanned the race-card quickly. It had to be Arrant Knave. His grandmother told him years ago that third letter 'r' in a horse was always good. Merryman II won the Grand National in the year he was born. It didn't always work, of course, Arkle, Mill House, Crisp, that great Australian chaser, and it only worked with famous Red Rum if you spelt it backwards ... MURDER. He'd thought of that sometimes; what was the name for a word spelt backwards? Palindromes had always been favourites with him, acronyms less so. He placed the boys' bets, adding his own modest wager on the Knave, and returned to his sons, Merrick's impatience now obvious.

"Where d'you want to watch from?"

"The finish." "The last fence," came out together, and Lachlan realised the clash of wills would last all afternoon.

They ended up halfway down the final straight, Merrick leaping up and down on the plastic rails, T-shirt sleeves flapping in the breeze.

It was a good race. The grey led, after skewering slightly at the initial hurdle, and as they flashed past on the first circuit Lachlan sensed the red and green colours in mid-field. Lurking Shadow, with purple and black diabolo, was just last, biding his time, conceding the weight.

There was a faller at the downhill hurdle, and, as they turned the bottom bend, Lurking Shadow began to take closer order. A train crossed above the course in the opposite direction to the horses, and Lachlan envied its passengers their view.

Over the third last there were three horses in it, the dark bay, Arrant Knave and Lurking Shadow. Both boys now used the white rail as a vaulting horse, screaming encouragement to their selection.

At the last the bay had fallen away, destined for third, and Lachlan found himself shouting loudly for the Knave whilst Robbie screamed for Lurking Shadow. Both horses strained for the line; spectators heard the creaking leather and harsh slaps landing among veins surging with effort.

"Photograph, photograph..." said the loudspeaker and Lachlan was mildly irritated that it was a woman's voice...

The boys looked up at him, both sure their number would be called.

There was a pause.

"First, number one; second, number five; third, number six." Another pause.

"First, Number One, Lurking Shadow; second, Number Five, Arrant Knave; third, Number Six, Machismo. The distances: a short head and ten lengths. A short head and ten lengths."

Robbie knocked Merrick into the rubbery rails.

"How much, Dad?"

"Not a lot. He was favourite, remember."

"So how much?"

"Just a couple of pounds, plus your stake back. Better than nothing."

'Not enough."

"Did I do Arrant Knave both ways?" said Merrick.

"Both ways?"

"You know, to come second or third?"

"Each way."

"'Both ways' is better. Did I?"

"Sorry, no."

"Did you?" asked Robbie, side-jumping to Lachlan's right, and almost colliding with a St John's Ambulance lady, who looked cross.

"No."

"You should have, Dad. I would." Robbie looked twice his age as he said it. Lachlan wondered what he'd be like at eighteen; serious, cautious even, and he hoped not too correct.

"How much?" yawned the bookie from beside his weather-worn sign: 'Andrew Jarman, Plymouth.' Lachlan passed him Robbie's ticket and old hands shot back with three tired coins. In Robbie's grasp the coins would rejuvenate.

The third race was a steeplechase, different from anything in Australia, where jump racing was in decline. Birchwood fences stood up stiff, black, and unforgiving to a height of 4'6"; unlike hurdles, horses could not slick through these. 'The black ones,' a trainer had dubbed steeplechase fences. Lachlan and the boys walked across the course, on grass that sprung, to inspect one of the obstacles. It was the last fence and looked severe, on a slight upward incline; the thought of jumping it at thirty miles an hour was hair-raising. In front of the stands, past the finishing post, was the water jump, a much lower fence, on the landing side of which was four feet of muddy water. Merrick could not imagine a horse clearing the fence, and insisted on staying to see it done. He had decided not to bet on this race.

"Stay with him, Robs," said Lachlan jogging off to a straggle of bookies with the elder boy's determined choice. As he came back, the horses were coming out onto the course. Sharp-coloured silks rippled in the breeze, the horses straining at their reins, one in particular pulling the arms of his jockey from their sockets, prancing with energy. Robbie stared at the man's face as he fought to prevent the beast from bolting. He was standing up in the stirrups, tension in every muscle. The wind pulled his jacket from his white breeches; its flapping sound was deafening, alarming the beast, whose eyes rolled white in his head. The man kept hold, just, passing other, more docile runners sticking to the rails

The noise of rattling hooves was arresting; both boys felt fear as the horses galloped towards them out of the sun.

Robbie ducked in before they jumped the fence, Merrick risking another second before he, too, recoiled. In a blur of cracking leather, shouted curses, and equine breath, the horses cleared the fence, one dropping his back legs in the water, losing ground. His jockey swore, gathered up the reins that slipped through his gloved fingers and urged the steed on round the bend. The water jump was only negotiated once.

Merrick won on the next hurdle race, enough to satisfy his thirst for a winner. Lachlan's horse came down. Robbie's fell increasingly further behind and gradually stopped, trotting back through the middle of the course to the alarm of a young couple intent on each other, oblivious.

They returned to the paddock, busy people dashing past them, loudspeaker giving the official result, still a woman's voice.

"How about going to the start for this race, lads?" said Lachlan, consulting his race-card to discover this was the longest steeplechase of the day. "We can see them set off, then walk to the next fence, ready for their second lap."

"It's not motor-racing," said Merrick. "And why are they called steeplechases?" Lachlan was expecting this, just as, on their first morning at the farm, going down to breakfast, he'd been expected to deliver a complete explanation of black pudding. "Pig's bladder," as he'd anticipated, caused a reaction, exacerbated when Lachlan attacked the boys' abandoned pudding, having demolished his own.

"When horse racing started, one man would challenge another across country. The only landmarks to guide them were the steeples on churches. Hence the name." For once, a brief explanation was enough. Lachlan placed their bets, and they set off to the start in the far corner of the course, close underneath the railway line.

They arrived only just before the horses, the animals rippling muscle, snorting down blaring nostrils, coming on them unprepared. There were diamonds on the backs of some, Robbie noticed, put on with a branding iron that would hurt.

It was quiet at the start; only a handful of people watched, and the grandstand was miles away. Two men climbed out of a four wheel-drive and touched their funny hats to a man in overalls struggling with an enormous rubber-band. Merrick flinched as the man stretched it in front of him, fastening the end into the top of a post. One of the men in hats climbed a tiny three-runged staircase and pressed a button, at which the elastic-band whip-lashed across the track. No one seemed concerned, not even Merrick; he was leaning on a squeaky bending rail trying to take a photograph of the runners as they circled twenty yards behind the start.

Robbie savoured the atmosphere. One horse almost touched him as it walked round, head held high, flecks of sweat edging out from under the saddle. He looked up; the jockey was pulling his goggles down, but managed a nod at the boy. In front of Lachlan, one of the hatted men was straining at something under the horse's saddle, the jockey almost upright, taking his weight off the horse. It was the conversation that held Robbie's attention. Short grunts from one man resulted in laughter from two or three others, then another curt remark rang out, a couple of swearwords, another grunt. One of the jockeys was young, left out of all this; he walked round in silence, tapping his whip against his thigh. Then he pulled his goggles down over his eyes. A roll-call was held: the hatted men looked at their watches. It was eerily quiet.

"All right, jockeys. Come in steady." One of the men had again climbed the little staircase; he pressed the button, and the horses were away, bunched rumps springing forwards in unison. The man in overalls retrieved the rubber-band, as the men in hats climbed back into their vehicle. Robbie was taken aback by their lack of interest in the race.

"Come on," said Lachlan, and they were under the

running rails, striding fast towards a fence in front of which was a wide ditch stopped by an angled piece of wood. This made the fence wider, though not higher, and more formidable than the water jump. Already the field was passing the stands, tiny model horses with inert dwarves astride them, racing through a tunnel of noise that would increase on the next two circuits.

Robbie stared at the jump. What if the horse missed his footing, ending up in the ditch? He prayed that wouldn't happen, as the horses thundered nearer.

But it did. The horses were moving quicker than ever as they approached the fence; the leader stood back and cleared it with four lengths to spare, his jockey's hand raised, as the reins slipped from him. He snatched them back, galloping on. There was a simultaneous mêlée of thuds, swishing limbs and crashing twigs, punctuated by a moment of silence, in which one horse, not rising at the obstacle because his foreleg was still in the ditch, hurled itself through the frozen mass of birch, crashing onto the turf, legs flailing, one horseshoe glinting in the sun. The jockey was thrown a long way ahead, plummeting into the ground like a sputnik, instantly still. His black jacket with a white cross on it looked for a moment like a beached penguin, crumpled and inert; Robbie realised it was the young jockey. Two ambulance men, after checking there were no more horses jumping the ditch, ran towards the prostrate figure.

The horse lay prostrate too. No one ran to its assistance; it was rocking awkwardly on its back, eyes glaring wide. A car sped along the track that lined the course, and two people jumped out. One ran to the horse, clawing to take off the cumbersome saddle. A member of the public ran up, holding down the horse's head, the animal now frantic in its agony. For a moment none of the other spectators moved. Lachlan sensed the fence had to be jumped once more, on the final circuit.

"Perhaps he's only winded," said Lachlan, lamely,

knowing that was more likely to happen at the final fence, when a beast was exhausted, having given its all. Things were happening all at once now: a figure ran out of a small hut with flags in his arms; he dropped one, but ran on, to the other side of a fence, shouting at the few stunned spectators on the landing-side to lend him aid, sticking crossed poles into the ground, the warning that jockeys should by-pass a fence. Would they see the signs with the sun in their faces, wondered Robbie? Already the field was turning out into the country one last time, unaware of the drama unfolding. A man ran across the course with what looked like a stretcher rolled up tight, dark green. The ambulance men were levering another stretcher underneath the injured jockey, his head now slowly moving.

Lachlan felt sick. The horse's saddle and number-cloth were extricated, its blue 9 upside down, turned into a 6; they were desperately trying to take off its bridle, whilst at the same time pulling in a desperate attempt to get the animal onto its feet. A black and white chequered flag was brandished from side to side, as the remaining runners by-passed the fence and thundered past, one jockey cocking a look down to his left, then racing on. The men by the horse looked forlorn. Another official jumped from the newly-drawn-up four-wheel drive and ran to the beast that was gasping, its sides straining for air, then blistering as the lungs were filled. A head shook; a tense lad ran up holding a sponge, mouth clenched; the stretcher was rolled out into screens that were hurriedly put up around the stricken horse. Robbie and Merrick looked at Lachlan, then turned away. A train chose that moment to pass, hooting with a lack of tact.

No one moved. The screens covered almost everything, but a chink remained. People avoided it, looking and not looking. There was no sound, then the slam of a tractor's door and the horse ambulance struggled backwards towards the scene, its driver leaning out, head into his elbow, gauging the distance. After two attempts, when he was satisfied with his reversing, he jumped out. A winch appeared, cold as a noose, dangling down till a hand reached up for it. Then came a rattled, drawing sound that lasted. As it ceased, the screens were quickly taken down and folded, to be carried back to their secret lair. The tractor pulled its heavy cargo away, bumping along with no noise, and the crowd, released, began to move from its trance.

Robbie ducked under the rail onto the course. The jockey had been placed in the ambulance, which was slowly moving away. The boy saw no blood, no marks, just flattened grass through misted eyes. He felt tight in his chest; saliva had deserted him.

Death hi-jacks a day, then wrecks it.

CHAPTER EIGHTEEN

The seaside town rippled in the sun as they drove along its promenade. 'Built like Rome, on Seven Hills', boasted a poster. Lachlan suspected Rome was the warmer. There was a bustle about the place: on crisp, mown greens white figures moved in unerring lines, then suddenly squatted, earnest, beside a collection of heavy, dark brown balls. Gardens opened themselves to a deft breeze wafting over a pink, stuccoed sea-wall; cafés sprawled on to pavements, also pink; tiny flags licked, now and then, against large white hotels.

School holidays had not started, but there were children on skate-boards, young teenagers hovering by traffic lights in the thrall of walkmen, toddlers idling behind purposeful parents, who kept turning round, dazed. After a car park had been found, Robbie and Merrick sprinted to the front of a large amusement arcade. Noise thumped out of it, random litter swirled, its life-span extended by a tired cleaner, his face drawn. Lachlan shook his head; four shoulders shrugged. Merrick raced on, past the town theatre proclaiming the day's matinée of some bright-faced farce. Four taxis stood at ease, their drivers clustered by the bonnet of the first. Two smoked, one leafed through a tabloid, the fourth looked hopeful of a day-long fare.

"A day on the moors?" he said, to the trio, half-jumping into their path. "See the ponies, Dartmeet, the famous Dartmoor prison." In that trice he altered the complexion of the day. Lachlan had been conscious since they landed that he must contact Iain, but had deferred the task. Now there was urgency in him, which he did not welcome. And guilt.

"No thanks," he replied to a face no longer looking at him. Robbie was by his side, aware of some change in his father; Merrick ran on ahead, oblivious. Experience had taught Robs that his father could be shirty if plagued with questions; later, he might probe with more success. Lachlan was torn, again, between sharing a quandary and inflicting it.

By the harbour, seagulls' screeching reached a crescendo; a small fishing smack was cutting through oily water, burly men in giant-size overalls throwing fish entrails in the wake of the boat. The trio stood and watched it moor, noticing the rust that was everywhere, on chains, nets, winches, the handles of plastic buckets, lifebuoys. Huge piles of glinting fish were tipped on to a newly- swilled deck. The fishermen ignored predatory gulls, reaching for rectangular boxes in once-sharp colours, tumbling in more fish. Their expressions were lacklustre. It was a day like any other, bereft of rain, at least. Hands like hemp were intent on gutting larger fish. Lachlan wondered how their night had been, what they spoke about, if anyone out at sea had broken the harsh English reserve with a two a.m. confession or revelation nudging the universe.

They wandered on. A man with a camera was pointing it at Merrick, who looked back, quizzical. He managed a sort of smile, for which the man handed him a ticket.

"In the kiosk by four o'clock," he promised, pointing along the road to a pier.

"Just like St Kilda at home, Dad," said Merrick, man-of-the-world. They walked towards the pier, cafés, more pin-ball machines, eternal seagulls on the railings, another tiny theatre at the end. A whodunnit was playing. Merrick studied the photographs of its holiday cast; Robbie awaited the inevitable, unsure whether or not to be critical. 'In Memory of Murder' held a flicker of promise. Silent, he watched Lachlan buy the tickets for that night.

After lunch they walked to the other side of the harbour, the sun hotter now. A fortune teller's booth sat unvisited, its notices bleached yellow; the lop-sided face of 'Madame Francesca' still vaguely compelling on a faded photograph. Where was she now, wondered Robbie? Another sea-side town; a city, anonymous and cold; a circus? He'd have gone in had she been there, and now checked his palms.

A shout from Merrick ended the inspection, and he saw his brother dart into a small throng of people up ahead. As they neared the group, a gibbet could be seen from which something heavy was hanging. To Merrick's horror it was a shark. He could not speak, thrusting his way through the onlookers. About to touch the denticled skin, he paused, then let one finger move gently up and down its rubbery surface. Strung up to public gaze, the creature's beauty had quite gone; it was a hideous sight.

By the lifeless tail someone had chalked on a slate that the blue shark had been caught in Torbay early that morning. Over four feet long, and weighing a healthy number of kilos, it was the biggest shark caught in these waters for years. Merrick thought of the Japanese catching sharks, ripping off the fin for their soup, then throwing the shark back into the sea, their worst crime of all. Sharks without fins were unthinkable.

Lachlan came up behind Merrick, resting both hands on the boy, who tried to shrug them off, then changed his mind. He reached out once more to touch the shark, higher up this time, still reverential. Its face was fixed and vacant, small chains drilled into the jaw, demeaning it. Merrick looked down at the slate, and with his foot edged it away from the shark. It landed face down; he turned away, in need of a mother's words. Robbie waited till he saw Lachlan move, then followed him, watching. He was usually the one whose feelings ran deep.

A Punch and Judy show on the beach had attracted few

spectators. Lachlan was surprised these still happened, and they skirted round the booth in search of sustenance from the beach café.

The murder play lifted spirits. Two of the actors were convincing in Lachlan's view, and the boys were entranced, sitting back to take in clues, trying to eliminate red herrings, comparing notes in the interval. The plot was a tight one; suspicions walked around the minds of both boys, neither of them keen to declare his accusatory hand, until just before the second act. Lachlan went for the victim's daughter, a wily girl, in his eyes; Robbie settled on the curate, with his ingratiating manner, and Merrick, debating till the lights went down, finally decided it had to be the retired lawyer, a patchwork man of guile and consequence. In the end Merrick was right, his chubby fist punching the air. But Lachlan suspected the shark was not forgotten.

Next morning he went into the boys' room. They had got up with a misty dawn and gone outside. Cows surprised them by the gate, nudging their bulk against the post. The boys stood watching them plod away up the path, then moved on, silent, towards the river. Despite the lack of sunlight, Robbie was hoping to see a kingfisher. When they reached the water all was still, including a heron standing on one leg, watching them from beside a small willow. He was not the only fisherman around. Through the glaze they were surprised by the approach of a silhouette advancing silent, one hand in front of him like a blind man. As he drew nearer, they made out a panama hat, galoshes, a suede waist-coat and a green net. His rod he held out to his side, like a rapier. At first he looked comic, a cowboy dressed for dinner, an up-market Pink Panther en route to – or from – a Fancy Dress Ball.

Merrick heard the galoshes, which added to the figure's mystique. There was something ominous about him, though the heron, eyeing him, was still. The boys stayed silent despite the fact they had been spotted. As he passed them, the figure looked over for a moment, and resumed his tread. It was then the heron took off, its wings folding noiselessly on the slightest breeze. Robbie looked at his brother. The day was advancing. He signalled time.

The cows were coming back from milking, heads raised. Their leader was chestnut under fresh mud, a blue tag stapled in one ear. Most of them were dun or bay, just a couple black with cream splashes. They advanced, tightening into a herd, nostrils damp, huge, cloven hooves and stunted horns. They were clean, sleek as stock in New Zealand, healthy. Merrick was relieved he wore no red.

Through an open gate, up a track littered with stones, was a small building, to which cows and boys walked. It was sunny now and the boys looked across at their companions. Flies crossed arterial strips of bovine nose, then settled in cushions of ears. Between the cows' stubby front legs slack skin shifted from side to side. One animal was flecked like the Ordnance Survey map of Dartmoor they had bought in Torquay, others were brindled, their knee- caps furry, stained with grass. Two were advancing on Merrick, who walked backwards, hands waiting for the cold corrugated iron of the shed. Robbie looked over, concerned. He wondered if any-one was watching them. They'd not met the farmer despite hearing him the previous day; a short curse from behind the hedge, a shout to hasten the dogs. Farm folk always sensed where you were, knew what was happening, tracing alien movements without letting on, appearing by your side, unheard.

The two cows were still close to Merrick, pressing him against the shed, into which a sparrow darted, suddenly. The boy watched them, poised, their heads tilted to one side, both blank and serene.

Robbie walked over, gazing at the beasts; there were sixteen, he counted, all with stumps on their back legs where

211

horses had fetlocks, the back of their knees like shin-pads, wrinkled and firm. Tails moved, as did flies; the day would be warm. Already, pinpricks of heat pierced Robbie's T-shirt; a wasp appeared, then dived into heather clumped up by the wall. Still hemmed in by the cows, Merrick was in no-man's-land, somewhere between fear and excitement, being brave. Robbie wondered if he'd have been the same nearly five years ago. They didn't often get out of Melbourne into the country; once they had, staying on a property beyond the airport, but there'd been a dearth of animals, to the boys' dismay; a lot of possums, not much else.

For no reason the two cows suddenly took off, breaking into a canter that was oddly becoming; another one followed, aimless. Merrick moved away from the shed, mud on his elbow which he scraped at, energetically. The remaining cows began filing into the shelter, pursued by flies, and the heron screeched overhead, planing into the sun. Robbie shielded his eyes and followed it, as long as he could. He still yearned for a kingfisher.

A rumble in his stomach urged breakfast; he waited at the gate for Merrick, who was balancing the last few feet on flints in the trampled grass. They walked up to the house. Inside, a shadow moved across the downstairs window.

Lachlan was in the dining-room, looking at a guidebook while eating his heaped bowl of cereal. "Had fun?"

They nodded, and reached for the juice.

"A reservoir, Dad?" queried Robbie. "That's really exciting."

In the back Merrick grunted agreement, little fingers probing the small silver panel that came out when you pushed one end of it, but had no obvious purpose. Maybe for jewels, he thought, but they'd need to be pretty small. Australian cars didn't have these moveable pockets. England was behind the times.

No one else was walking round the reservoir as the boys

ran ahead, their faces flicking past tall seedheads of fox-gloves. A fisherman cast his line impatiently as they passed and Robbie was reminded of the Pink Panther seen in the dawn.

What a dull hobby, thought Merrick, who couldn't imagine standing still for long. Even if you caught some-thing, it'd be dull. His mind flashed up a picture of the fisherman's hook landing in his left eye: the pain would be unbearable and he would be lifted off the ground, pitched forward into razor-blade reeds waiting to score his cheek.

"Where've you been?" triumphed Robbie, standing on a tiny bridge, suddenly cool as it gloated over a mellow brook. "Look at that post-box, Dad!" Robbie had been amused by red post-boxes in England and there was a glinting, red, in the ferns ahead of them. Merrick sought it, standing still for a second as he fought to establish what it was; it held no friendly mouth for letters.

"B-U-O-Y?" he questioned, one hand now lifted to shield his gaze from the sun.

"It's a lifebelt," reassured Lachlan, coming up behind him.

"What's it doing here then?" It seemed a fair question, since the water's edge was a good thirty yards away. Perhaps that hadn't always been the case, Lachlan explained, but Merrick was not convinced.

"Let's go," rang out a bored voice. Robbie disappeared over the bridge. Merrick stood still, hands entrenched in his pockets.

"Had enough?"

The boy evaded answer. It was going to be one of his days.

"Look, there's a damselfly."

"Weird name," came the retort. "It doesn't even look like a fly." Lachlan suppressed a smile. The damselfly was untroubled in a sea of purple heather and blazing gold gorse. Merrick broke from his recalcitrant stance and ran after his

213

brother, cannoning into him as Robbie pored over the ground on a patch beyond the bridge, shaded by trees.

"I thought it was a toad," he said, pointing to a root in the middle of the path.

"'Course it's not a toad," gloated Merrick. "You're seeing things." A hand smacked his elbow as he felt something land on him. Two wagtails skimmed into the sky.

"I'm hungry," said Robbie.

"So soon?"

"Where are we going for lunch, then?"

"We'll find somewhere."

"A bistro?"

"A pub."

"Why not a bistro?"

"Pub's just as good. Less pretentious."

"What's pretentious?"

"Watch out!"

Merrick was waving two sticks in the air as a family rounded the bend in uneasy silence. No one spoke to the watching trio, and Lachlan asked himself why the English rarely spoke. Was it shame? Lack of interest? Fear of involvement, and laying themselves open?

Robbie looked at Lachlan.

"Poms, Dad?"

"Right."

Now ahead of them, Merrick had climbed astride an upturned log. "What's this log look like?"

"An otter," said Lachlan.

"Giant scorpion," from Robbie.

"Both wrong, of course. It's a dead bear with its paws in the air. You two are hopeless."

"Looks good against the rose-bay willow herb," said Lachlan with a mock seriousness. The boys gave him their old-fashioned look, eyes skywards, then sped away through an iron gate and onto the bridge of a dam, where a red and white open-top Deux Chevaux rumbled towards them.

Lachlan caught up with them both on the bridge; the boys were squatting down, trying to read the dam's construction date. Since landing in England they'd been amused by dates before 1788; B.A. (Before Australia). Here the date was impossible to read except by tracing it with fingers. Robbie's were big enough and for once Merrick bowed to the superiority of age.

"180...6," he declared, leaping up and rubbing his hands together, interest lost as soon as the grit was rubbed off his fingers.

"Bo-ring," returned Merrick, and they dashed on towards the car park, another impromptu race. As Lachlan unlocked the car, he was spattered by gravel from a dirty Volvo, from whose back door, thrown open, a teenage voice boomed.

"I want the radio ON..."

Hunger grew, and the trio bounced along high-hedged lanes towards lunch. Rounding a bend, they were faced by a tractor and Lachlan plunged on the brakes, knocking Robbie, who was in the back, between the front seats. The tractor driver waited for Lachlan to reverse. That collision averted, they then came up behind a pony and trap they had overtaken earlier.

"His wife's in the back now. She was sitting next to him before," informed Merrick the sleuth. Robbie wasn't listening: he was counting fence-posts, hoping for an even number.

The pub car park was full, but an old retainer in faded wine-coloured uniform pointed them right up by the fence. The boys bounded out and led the way past picnickers into The Coach and Horses. Inside, it was cold and dark, but there was a maze of passages into which Robbie disappeared. Merrick and Lachlan pursued him, the boy reaching for his father's hand, but abandoning it the moment they emerged out of the gloom.

"This is truly old, Dad."

Turning suddenly into daylight, they heard the sounds of a piano.

Robbie was at the bar. "They do chicken teddies for you, Merrick." He'd have liked chicken teddies himself, but they were hardly appropriate. "Can I have scampi, Lachlan?" He looked for approval.

Awaiting the bar-snacks, the boys scoured a pamphlet on The Coach and Horses. Way back, the pub was renowned for its potato fair, to which thirsty wrestlers flocked in the late 18th century, around the time of the First Fleet. In 1847 the place was seriously damaged by fire, then rebuilt; many years later it became an important motoring stop, selling petrol in cans outside the stables. During World War Two it was a boys' school, the only one in England with a licensed bar open to the public for the sale of beer and spirits. Robbie chortled.

After a ploughman's lunch, the origins of which Lachlan explained, they drove to a tranquil spot where two branches of the river Dart met up. There were few people there, despite the weather, and Merrick investigated the stepping-stones. Ponies grazed at close quarters, uninterested in tourists, some of whom advanced warily with picnic left-overs, in the face of a notice asking that the animals remain unfed.

It was cool by the waterfall, carpets of moss silting damp to the touch. Lachlan thought of the Otways back home, under whose shade he was always content. These falls were smaller, but water's power was strong in him. The Devon ocean had left him wanting, too genteel, in keeping with the people; he longed for a storm.

Next day they went to Slapton, a long stretch of shingle beach, where the sand fell away sharply, in shelves. Behind the ribbon of road that ran along the beach for at least a mile, there was a bird sanctuary which they explored. It was mid-afternoon when they came across a black American tank, a

216

Sherman, isolated at the end of a car park, set on a cobbled plinth. An amiable old Devonian, sitting on a seat next to the black oddity, told them the story.

In the Second World War the beach had been used by the American allies as a training ground for the landings of thousands of soldiers onto the north-west coast of France. Slapton was chosen because of its similarity to the Normandy beaches, code-named 'Utah,' 'Sword,' 'Juno,' 'Omaha' and 'Gold.' The training was 'Exercise Tiger' – top-secret stuff. Nearby villages had been evacuated, at no small cost to their inmates, some of whom had never before left home. The exercise was on a massive scale.

Huge Landing Ship Tanks were engaged to make a shore assault, using service ammunition, secure a beachhead, then rapidly advance inland. The date set for this 'rehearsal' was April 27th 1944. But things went savagely wrong. German torpedo boats that had come over The Channel from Cherbourg slipped past English navy patrols without being recognised, and spotted the Landing Ship Tanks edging along the south coast. Moving at 40 knots, the 'U' boats fired the first torpedo around 1.30 a.m. on April 28th. Two of the targets burst into flames and sank. Fires broke out on other LSTs, where men were assailed with noise, heat, smoke, blinding flashes of explosion and deluges of water. The LSTs were loaded with amphibious trucks and Sherman tanks, many of which were decanted into the sea, along with men, weapons and ammunition. With confused orders to 'Abandon Ship,' soldiers had to jump on top of men already in the sea, shouting, praying, drowning. There were nowhere near enough life-belts; some men were left in the water for five hours, until daylight, when bodies could be seen everywhere, on and beneath the ocean surface. In all, 946 American servicemen died in the exercise, as opposed to 200 at Utah beach in the real thing.

The English forces were clearly at fault; they had bungled on a massive scale, but no explanation or apology was ever given; the 'authorities' melted away overnight. Casualties were taken to hospital, but never acknowledged; survivors were threatened with court-martial if they discussed the operation with anyone, even the doctors treating them.

"What happened to the bodies?" said Robbie, eagerly.

The old tar paused; a light in his eye flickered , and survived. "Never found," came the reply. "Local people saw men digging in fields...claimed to see piles of bodies in the back of lorries." Another pause. "They say some were buried in the Exercise area as a temporary measure." He was running out of steam now, pressing a stick into the tarmac with his feet. "I think some were returned to America...and there's a cemetery outside Cambridge...Madderley, or Madingley Hill."

"Thank you," said Lachlan. Merrick had been circling the tank for some time now; Robbie looked out to sea. Lachlan turned back to the tank.

A reed warbler landed on the end of the nozzle, flaunting its speckled breast. Behind, the scene was tranquil, water sparkling in the sun. Two small flags, the Stars and Stripes and the Union Jack fluttered in the breeze, on top of the tank.

"Amazing." Lachlan heard Robbie say. "They dug this tank up in 1984, and when it touched the shale on the beach its running gear turned freely. It doesn't look as if it could move now."

An American memorial paid tribute to its countrymen who died in the early hours of April 28th 1944, ending with the words, 'Lest they be forgotten.' Seven or eight wreaths lay on the floor at the foot of the plaque.

Merrick was touching the tank, tracing its giant caterpillar treads. 'DANGER SHARP EDGES' blazed out at intervals around the weapon, together with the less strident, 'Please do not climb on the tank.' A small box for donations sat, almost hidden away, under its belly. The boy tried to imagine the gun nozzle, and then the whole tank appearing out of the waves; casual observers would have had a surprise.

They stayed that night in the Normandy Arms in Blackawton, one of the villages evacuated; the pub was a shrine to 'Exercise Tiger.' Helmets decked the walls next to faded photographs, a trenchcoat hung solitary and sombre. Notices in heavy print told of meetings on November 12th and 13th 1943 in the local village church: land was to cleared by December 20th. 30,000 acres comprising 3,000 people and 180 farms had to be evacuated. In the short winter days farmers had to sell livestock and machinery, but to whom?

Opposite the black notices were caricatures of Montgomery, Eisenhower and de Gaulle. There was a message from Monty to the troops in 1944, next to one from Eisenhower, terming the battles a 'great crusade.'

The publican knew much, which bored Merrick, irritated by his brother's thirst for information on an event so long ago. Robbie was fascinated to hear the villagers had nailed their boxed possessions up in the loft, perhaps in this pub, but when they came back the possessions had gone. He wondered what Devonian folk thought of as valuable, enjoying the notion he might stumble on a locked tin box, or a suitcase with frayed leather straps. The photographs compelled him; farmers, all in black, looking quizzically at the camera as they loaded chattels, tools and instruments onto sinking carts. Nearly all of them had a moustache; their faces were similar; they looked embarrassed, as if caught doing wrong. There was a furtive air to them, and not a woman in sight; men involved in a mystery, yet knowing none of its clues, sworn to an uneasy and eternal silence.

"They walked to neighbouring villages, many to family, some to local towns, ignorant of how long they would stay away, or why they had to go at all." The barman had come up behind Robbie, who continued to stare at the photographs. "Huddles of houses behind the sanctuary lake were alone privy to official secrets, yet still puzzled when truck-loads of Americans began to arrive."

"Did the villagers all come back when it was over?" asked Robbie, without turning around.

"Not all, I don't think."

The boy's mind raced on: seeing families returned home, still baffled by their absence, settling with difficulty into a new silence thronging the air.

In bed later that evening, his own room for once, he sat on the window-sill looking out into the street. A woman was walking her dog; she looked up at him, but didn't smile. He wondered for a second if he should duck behind the flowered curtain, but resolved he was doing no wrong. He would be dreaming tonight, that was certain...soldiers about to jump off shelves of steel studded with rivets, aware of the weight in their arms, looking into each other's dim expressions, subduing questions that bubbled through them. A tank crashing into the water, taking men with it, vast necklaces of bullets made only to grow green with plankton, bobbing helmets borne down the coast. How soon would everything go rusty?

Lachlan lifted the latch of his door.

"'Night, son. God Bless."

"'Night, Dad."

He wriggled under the covers, old-fashioned and heavy. Didn't everyone have duvets now?

He wanted to find out more about 'Exercise Tiger', buy a book on the subject, a real book, not the slim pamphlet he'd seen available free at the village store. And if there wasn't one, he would write it, talk to people in the village, if there were any left, go to the library in Plymouth, do interviews, be an author. A phrase he'd seen on one of the letters downstairs in the pub echoed in him: the deck firing had sent up arching incendiary columns which one survivor had described as 'cruelly beautiful.' In Robbie's head, an acorn grew…

They drove back onto the moor. Lachlan had looked at the map, seeking a place for the promised cream tea. Merrick's stomach was rumbling audibly. Lachlan drove, focused. Ponies were on the road ahead, oblivious to traffic; crows dived on a fresh rabbit carcass; an old Ford rattled past in the opposite direction.

The road ran flat for miles across the moor, whose cropped grass stretched away on all sides. A wayside pub, The Warren House Inn, had wooden bars outside for horses to be tethered, like in a western. Lachlan remembered reading something in the guidebook about the pub's fire, which hadn't gone out since 1845 – remarkable. Away from the steep hedge-guarded lanes, he pressed the accelerator, enjoying the speed. Robbie's hair blew in the wind as he leaned out; Merrick, Lachlan saw in the mirror, was asleep.

Without realising it, they had reached Princetown, its prison sign craving attention from the side of the road, a new notice, white letters on a caramel background, and the outline of a large barred house.

Half a mile to the right, they saw the grim Napoleonic fortress. It was odd that tourists should be wooed to drive up and gaze, ghoulish, at the outside of a building, the inside of which was shunned.

"Are you thinking about Iain?" said Robbie, his first words for some time. Lachlan's look answered his question. Last night's phone call to Rebecca had confirmed there was no news for the visitors. Lachlan had to act. The phone call to the prison was the hardest task on earth. He would ring up tonight. And he would discuss plans with the boys; cloak and dagger stuff never paid off.

They stopped in a village not far away, with a small church, and a green that sloped down to a shop. Cream teas were on hand in the garden of a thatched house with roses spilling from the walls. An old black sheepdog lay on the path not inclined to move. Inside, the darkness swallowed them, as the pub had done, eyes taking a second to adjust. Back in the garden, they attacked a mound of defenceless, warm scones that sank under a tripartite assault of cream, jam and teeth.

The gate clicked, and a wheelchair was pushed into view by a short-haired girl of around twenty. Her arms were white, fragile. In the chair was a youth in his late teens, discarded sunglasses perched on a tartan rug that extended over his lap, even in the heat. His legs were at an uncomfortable angle. Robbie looked quickly at his face; it gave nothing away. As they passed the table one of the handles knocked against Lachlan's chair. The girl looked mortified, the boy merely bored. But it was he who apologised, his face turning from wariness to a half-smile when Lachlan muttered, "No worries."

"Australian?" said the boy, who must have preferred to pause and chat for a moment. But the girl pressed on, leaving Lachlan's "Fair dinkum" to be spoken to the back of the boy's closely shorn head. They disappeared into the house, the wheel squeaking as it caught on a doorpost, to the girl's annoyance. Robbie looked at his father.

Ten minutes later they walked down the path, bees buzzing round them. By the gate was a garden gnome fallen on its side. Lachlan moved it against the wall with his foot; it angered him, it was grotesque. Robbie noticed his gesture, the second time that day that something had been moved along the ground. He was about to comment, when he saw his father's face. Lachlan was, for a second, oblivious. He had heard his echo again.

CHAPTER NINETEEN

Chester was all black and white. As they drove round its approaches, timber façades could be seen through gaps in more modern buildings, before they passed under the city walls and turned left into Prince's Street. Rebecca and Saul's house was on the right, in a tall narrow terrace squatting close to the road. Cobbles intrigued Robbie as he climbed out, stretching; looking up, he saw them bend round out of sight, rising gently towards the centre of Chester.

Saul was not as expected. A sturdy frame filled the doorway, but he was softly spoken with a ready smile. Rebecca was in gardening kit, hair tied back, sweat-shirt strewn round her waist. The house was littered with paint pots, many of them crouching under dust-sheets, the odd one standing defiant, a strip of kindling denoting its colour. They went straight into the garden behind the sitting-room at the end of the house. Geraniums in terra cotta boxes blazed on window-ledges under the evening sun.

"You'll have a drink," said Saul, disappearing along the patio beside a crooked wall.

"It's all so old," said Merrick, gazing at the backs of houses, whose irregular windows had perhaps been on the same level once, but now seemed like a series of paintings hung at different heights.

Talk flowed, and the boys sat listening, glad of fresh air at last. Rebecca did not look like their father, but certain mannerisms were echoed as they watched. Now and then the boys looked at each other. It was odd seeing a woman so relaxed with Lachlan, teasing him, then serious when their uncle's name came up. Saul said little, and was in no hurry to start up the barbecue. When he did so, the sun had just started to turn pink.

"No whingeing from you Aussies," he laughed. "It's not easy for an amateur watched by three 'pros'."

But he was no amateur; the barbie passed its test. Robbie commented on the fact that it was still light at ten o'clock.

"Longest day today," answered Rebecca.

"And the shortest night," rejoined Merrick, suddenly sage. "It doesn't stay light this late at home."

No one stirred, the boys happy not to be ordered to their beds.

Church bells woke them, pealing close at hand. Only Robbie got up straight away, peering down from his attic window over the wall, even more crooked at this angle. The lack of alignment pleased him; so much of England had struck him as symmetrical: houses, fields, even the people. Chester was different; he liked the place.

After breakfast they headed for the city walls, which could be walked in their entirety.

"Left or right?" said Saul as they climbed steep steps to stand on top of one of the city's ancient gates. Cars trickled by underneath; a muddy canal had long ago lost its struggle with life, now lying inert, and forlorn. Lachlan thought of T.S.Eliot's canal: rats, gasworks, fishermen, something about a Phoenician merchant with mud in his pockets.

"Right," he said, for no other reason than that he'd spotted a second-hand bookshop tucked in against the parapet, lashings of wire holding in paperbacks bleached by the sun.

'Closed on Sundays', apologised an equally faded notice.

"Now there's a relief," said Merrick, looking up at his father.

"It's open tomorrow," said Rebecca, her first false move in Merrick's view.

The wall afforded views that changed rapidly. A snatch of the cathedral gave way to the garden of a pub, then they were up against the back of a town house, its pebble-dash bruising any shoulder not on its guard. The canal followed them listlessly; a mallard surfaced in a sudden splash of action, thought better of it, and dipped back down.

The music of a hymn caught their ears, and, turning a right angle on the wall, they could see the cathedral's glory. Steps went down into the graveyard and Merrick led them down. Shadows and sunlight made for sharp edges. Rebecca took off her sunglasses, blinking, watched by the keenness of four eyes.

Robbie tried a large door-handle, to no avail. The buttresses protruded a long way out from the building, festooned in moss, chilling to touch. A female tramp sat on a bench at one corner, her swollen hands striving to undo the knot in a bread bag. Lachlan wondered if she had tied the knot, or picked up the remnants from a rubbish bin. Absorbed, she did not look up; a walking stick, gashed and weather-torn, rolled a few inches along the bench by her heavy woollen skirt; a sparrow landed for a moment in the space between her and the nearest gravestone. There was no music now. The cathedral looked black, lead gutters every few feet, dark slabs of paving, more shadows. Robbie wondered how the place would be in an English November, and shuddered.

Rounding the final corner, they were confronted with a party of tourists, jabbering like rooks around a helpless guide. Different languages hurled themselves at the man, who was unsure in which to reply.

"Speaking in tongues?" risked Saul. Lachlan smiled. They ducked round the mêlée and went inside. For a moment, silence engulfed them, with space and coldness. They were decorating here, too, it seemed, full-blown tombs draped with cream dust- sheets.

"Spooky," whispered Merrick.

Communion had begun some time ago; a suited man came towards them, indicating they could slip in for the rest of the service. He seated them at right angles to the chancel on the front row, which gave an unusual perspective. Lights blazed as in a theatre on white and red-clad figures, moving gently in preparation for the sacrament. Robbie liked the brilliant turquoise of the kneelers; it was the best colour he'd ever seen.

The distribution of bread and wine was approaching. Lachlan was struck by how much the cathedral had in common with racing: spectacle, drama, colour, sound. He bent his head, praying past visions of exercise yards, cells, and wire mesh stretching tight across each floor of the huge vault that made a prison.

A tide of communicants came up to receive the sacrament, most kneeling solemnly, some standing, unable to kneel down. There were serious faces, sad expressions, not a lot of energy, some faces reminding Lachlan of particular people back home. Sensing the flow about to cease, the visitors stood up quietly, advancing the small distance to the altar, waiting. Rebecca's teeth locked for a second on the coldness of the chalice; released, she looked up, then bent her head in thought.

The final hymn stirred Lachlan's shifting memory; he recognised its tune down the boulevard of years, which left him confused, stifling a skim of hurt that rose to the surface and lingered. When the procession went out, Merrick watched it to the end as he did players disappearing down the tunnel at the end of a 'footy' match. The priest and servers were organised; he wished he'd seen them process in like players emerging out of the tunnel in neat lines, with spruce kit, the captains holding a mascot's tiny hand. He'd like to have been a mascot, too late now.

The organ played on at the end of the service, as the congregation slowly left. Their small team moved to the front row of the nave to view the cathedral. Lachlan loved the names: transept, baptistery, quire, Lady chapel, cloisters, refectory. Merrick was looking up at the ceiling, where gold bobbles stuck to the vaulted roof like Ferrero Rocher chocolates flung into the air and stuck.

They walked down the sides of the edifice, confronting ancient plaques and sepulchres of fading names. Every so often a television set reared up above them, obscene and incongruous. The names on the plaques also drew admiration: Hugh Lupus, Ommanney Wrench: 'learned, ingenious, upright'. Robbie wondered what he was really like. Tombs were everywhere on the walls and floor ("Is it blasphemous to tread on them?" asked Merrick); coats of arms punctuated the tombs, enhanced by shards of coloured sunlight beaming through windows of stained-glass, fragments of spirits shattered over time.

The cathedral's charms began to pall for the boys soon after they went into the small chapel of St Werburgh, where two candles flickered, lonely, by her ancient shrine. The walls and ceiling had been restored, revealing the brilliance of medieval churches. Lachlan looked up at the roof bosses, suddenly cold. Castles, monasteries, cathedrals intrigued him in a way museums never could.

Sunlight surprised them as they walked past the font, invading the stone in harsh metallic lines. Outside, the foreigners had disappeared. So had the tramp, the boys noticed, as they rounded the corner, back towards the city wall. Merrick ran ahead, zigzagging over outsize paving stones, stopping just once to decipher the mouldy carvings on a slanted gravestone, inviting as a buried seesaw.

Here the wall was not so narrow; through the buildings Lachlan caught a glimpse of a green expanse that could only be the racecourse. Someone trod on his grave. To the left, an artist had set up his display of paintings, too twee, too ordered for Lachlan; all the frames were the same, all views similar. Saul gave them only a flicker. Rebecca went up to Robbie to answer his intense questions, her stomach suddenly rumbling; a bold look from the boy made them both smile, and Rebecca saw for the first time her mother's eyes in him. She recognised traits in friends, especially when they skipped a generation; it was harder to spot resemblances in the family.

Robbie was looking at an ancient print of the city's West Gate, imagining Roman soldiers, bearded, bare-legged, the helmets slightly skew-whiff, a pelt of fur round their neck, sandal straps winding up their calves, and in their hand the spear topped by a golden eagle astride the letters S.P.Q.R. What had they done all day? Sport, undoubtedly; pottery, and a great deal of digging. He fancied the shields they carried, rust tinged with gold, all of them gladiator fans for the matches of their day. History interested him; he liked Chester more and more.

It had clouded over by the time they went for lunch into a large pub nestling under the walls. No one else had ventured into the garden, where they sat down, awaiting a drink. Merrick was frowning, Rebecca noticed; he looked seriously concerned, but, feeling her gaze, he looked away and the frown fled. Another family trait. She wished sometimes she was not so observant, so quick to isolate an emotion, freeze it and, later, distil. People at work noticed it, more envious than they admitted, but they were wrong to covet the foible: she needed to tell them that.

Veteran cars slipped up the road ahead of them and under the gate, en route to a rally on the other side of the city. Two hearses were caught up with them, both empty, the drivers in casual clothes, not mourning dress. The voice of a young French girl shrieked out somewhere from a room in the hotel up above them; Merrick sought to locate her.

The adults were silent for a moment, glad of a drink. Days like this took care of themselves, even with two boisterous boys. Lachlan shifted in his seat to dispel thoughts of leaving his sister at the end of the week; they'd not yet been there twenty-four hours. Saul chatted to the boys, lunch came in its own time, a newspaper was glanced at, more veteran cars drove by, and they moved off, aimless, calm.

Chester boasts its Rows: a second layer of shops above those at street level, 'like a double decker bus,' said Merrick. Not all the shops were old, but every so often the black and white timber reappeared in a façade or marked a balcony from which to peer down. Nearing a bookshop at ground level, they were aware of a voice clamouring for attention: passers-by had stopped, and a crowd was gathering up ahead. In and out of the crowd darted a stocky form, also in black and white, urging people to stand and view his act. Lachlan looked around him: some shoppers scuttled away, but many were content to watch. The man's patter was good, there was energy in his squat frame, something compelling. The boys were caught up in the crowd, till Robbie moved away, seeking access to the first floor, where he'd have a better view. Merrick stood his ground. The actor asked for volunteers, seized on two men and pulled them from the crowd to muted applause. The men stood, embarrassed. Passers-by were caught unawares in shop doorways, and encouraged to view the actor's show. His audience was growing all the time. Rebecca edged in front of Saul for a better view; when it wasn't forthcoming she saw Lachlan's eyes indicate Robbie, leaning forward from his royal box, so moved away to join him.

The two volunteers now had their moment: the actor used them as landmarks for a series of gymnastic moves, executed skilfully and fast, bringing warmer applause. The crowd was starting to relax, as the performer was well aware. Two chains lay on the ground, picked up by the volunteers on cue and wound round the actor as instructed. Badinage filled the air until the chains crossed his abdomen, which made shouting impossible. Some of the crowd ventured forward, a move encouraged by the object of their gaze, now thoroughly enchained and locked into his metal prison. He kept talking, quieter now, asking people how long his Houdini act would take to accomplish. He accepted suggestions and kept on shortening the time. A clock was placed on his up-turned box, but the actor was in no hurry. The crowd edged nearer to him, Merrick wishing he'd joined Robbie, but too proud. Saul lifted him on to his shoulders; someone groaned behind.

The actor was only whispering now, his chains seeming to bite into him: the audience was quiet. The clock was set at ninety seconds. He began to jive, cavort, wriggle, all the time maintaining his banter with a crowd won over by charm. A shoulder shook itself free to a small cheer; the actor danced on. It was terrific theatre, and he knew it. The other shoulder burst from its shackles, but time was evaporating; there was no applause. Robbie concentrated hard: an elbow emerged and the shaking grew frantic. 'Ten...nine...' it would be touch and go. On 'six' the chains fell from his waist; 'four' saw them at his knees. He was smiling now. On 'two' his ankles were released, and he stepped out, miraculously, as the clock struck, to hearty and sustained applause. He ran across the crowd, did two full somersaults in the air and landed close to the box, whipping out a cap from under the clock. Bowing wildly, he stretched the cap in his fingers and jumped onto the box.

Applause was still fulsome, his smile taking in the semi-circle that surrounded him. He bowed again, then ran forward.

"Now comes the moment," he cried. "The test of tests. So don't break my heart; it makes you look cheap."

A woman laughed raucously.

"Take out your donation," he urged. "Fold it up neatly." More reaction. "You've been a great audience. Don't spoil it now."

The crowd murmured, amused by his repartee.

"Children," he appealed, quieter now. "Ask you parents for a little money. Every little counts." Mutters ran through the crowd, as a couple of people sidled away, embarrassed.

"That's mean," said Merrick to Saul, quietly.

"If your parents aren't putting money in your hand, it means they don't love you!" A pause. "No," he added, revelling in his smoothness. "No, it means they're not your parents." Lachlan smiled, handing Merrick a 50-pence piece. It found the flat cap fast.

"Thank you," beamed the actor, completing his circuit. The cap soon had to be held in both hands; he lifted it above his head and waved it. Some coins escaped, but he took no notice, for the moment. The crowd began to fade.

"I want to talk to him," said Robbie, who'd joined them from his eyrie, and he walked across the precinct, putting two stately pigeons to flight.

The acrobat was wiping sweat from the tops of his arms. Veins bulged blue in his paleness; stubbled cheeks suddenly looked gaunt. A woman came up to him, cigarette in hand, but said nothing, To the man's other side was a skinhead with a wisp of 'beard' not quite central to his chin. They looked expectantly at Robbie, who was suddenly unsure of himself.

"It was good," said the boy after a moment, taking in the unusual trio, uncertain what he was going to say next. The man rubbed his forearms, then passed the towel across his brow.

"Where d'you train to do that?"

The man handed the towel to his skinhead mate.

"I trained as a gymnast," he said, in a Cockney accent that Robbie liked. "Competed for G.B. a couple of times. Then joined a circus when I was eighteen."

Robbie nodded. That seemed to end the conversation. He needed an exit line.

To his surprise the punk spoke. "These people," he said, his arm making a feeble effort to indicate the now empty space. "They look so sad. They've earned all this money to go shopping, now they go shopping and they look so sad. Like trout lifted into another world."

231

Robbie stared at this philosopher. The woman, perhaps the acrobat's mother, flicked ash over a pigeon.

"Smiles are odd things. The more you give away, the more you get." The pigeon clattered past them and Robbie thought about opposites. Men of the street could be wise, clearly.

"You Australian?" asked the woman.

The boy nodded. "Cheers, then," he said, "Thank you." He walked back to where Lachlan stood, waiting, aware that the street players would not give him a second thought. He didn't turn round. Seeing them counting the cash in the cap would profane the experience, and he knew they would comb the pavement for the dropped coins.

There was no sign of Saul, Merrick and Rebecca. Lachlan and Robbie sought them. The lad caught sight of a lane leading off the main road: Poor Street. He liked that. He'd already seen Feather Street and Crook Street, which made him smile.

"G'day," said Merrick bursting out onto another black and white balcony. Robbie made as if he'd not heard, then sprinted up the nearest staircase for a counter-attack. A sunburst took Lachlan by surprise, and he bumped into a young girl as he looked up. The girl said, 'Sorry', without conviction, and he watched her trim figure slide away from him. There were attractive women in Chester.

That evening they ate in, amongst the débris. Saul was renovating the front room, originally a lounge, to make Rebecca's treatment-room; she had been sharing a physiotherapy practice near the river, but her partner was due to move, so it was time to set up her own business. The lounge was now to be situated at the back of the long narrow house, through the dining-room. French windows would lead into the garden; Lachlan imagined the tranquillity.

Standing on the lawn he looked up at the random attic windows where the boys had a room each. In the coming days the wall between the two rooms would be knocked down, creating a studio for Saul. Tools lay everywhere, encouraging Lachlan to imagine the house that had been run as a B&B by the previous owners. His mind swam back to their house in Hawthorn: the thought of still being there in ten years time, when the boys had grown and gone, was not one that appealed to him, unless a new partner was found; life as a single parent became lonelier in time. He'd always envisaged re-marrying, but for the first time, in the muted colours of this small English garden, feared he might not.

Turning towards the back door, he hoped to see the boys bursting through its dark space, but all was still. A sudden sense of loss hit him and he spun back, angry at his layers of wild sensitivity. He wondered whether to go up and fetch his paperback, but was too restless to read. Shadows danced on the confines of half-framed thoughts and he closed his eyes to dismiss them. But he failed; something held sway, a magician's top hat bounced in his eyes, as if the man holding it had completed his trick but now refused to do it again. Still no one came through the door into the garden. His mind on white rabbits, Lachlan forced both hands into his pockets and walked slowly towards the house.

"Funny men in ancient costumes. Dancing up and down, with ribbons everywhere, banging round, hollow musical things like two pizzas joined together."

Merrick was holding court.

"Tambourines," laughed Rebecca.

"Weird people," joined in Robbie. "Made me feel uncomfortable."

Saul looked up. He felt the same about Morris dancers, and was unsure of the origins of this prejudice.

"None of them looked kind," said Robbie, giving the conversation his full attention. "Shifty, more like! You'd make a good one, Merrick. When you grow up."

His brother stared at him, then his face broke into a smile.

"Better that than a street puppet."

Poised at deuce, they were urged to table. Rebecca was good on puddings, and midway through his lemon tart Robbie looked up; next day was his birthday.

"Can you remember your fourteenth, Dad? It's light years ago?"

Lachlan thought hard. "I remember it was a Saturday," he said after a pause. "But not much else. My tenth birthday was more significant, the last one in Aberdeen. I got into a fight by a stream. A woman came out of her teapot house and said she'd report us to our schools. I never thought it was an empty threat. Quite ruined the Easter holiday." His eyes stared at the table. "But Iain," he dwelt. "He knew she'd never do it. Told me I was too much of a worrier. Not a warrior, like him."

Rebecca watched him. She'd never heard of the incident. She'd heard of little at her distance of years. Her childhood was Australia, orange and blue at once, sharp grass, a lot of dust. Space makes a childhood and she'd had realms of it, the way kids didn't now, except in the outback. She'd not visited the Never Never Land of the Northern Territory, but she might. Some day. Her eyes held Lachlan's; she'd wondered why he chose to stay 'Down Under' when she and Iain came home, had assumed he'd not questioned that choice, but looking at him now was like the first attempt at cracking a brazil nut: she saw doubts, anxiety, telegraph wires of questions stretching along an open road, soil red as a wound, in that blinding Australian light.

"Any more wine?" ventured Lachlan. "Never thought it would happen, but I'm getting a taste for French!"

CHAPTER TWENTY

The phone call had to be made. Slipping away from Robbie's birthday breakfast, Lachlan dialled cold digits for the prison; he was tense, realising he'd need a pen, but one was nowhere to be seen.

A country accent answered and Lachlan cleared his throat. He was three sentences into a convoluted explanation of his situation when the voice interrupted.

"If it's visits, you need the control room. I'll put you through." Lachlan was relieved not to be palmed off with the universally smug, 'Bear with me,' the phrase that had become synonymous with those things English that irked him. He loathed the expression, it sounded condemnatory and flip, giving the speaker immeasurable power.

"Control room." A low voice, as he'd expected. Lachlan explained his position and was put through again, this time to booked visits. Unable to face a third curriculum vitae, he waited for the demands: they came in desultory fashion.

"You need a visiting order."

A pause.

"How do I get that?"

"The prisoner sends one for you. It'll take three or four days."

Another pause.

"I'm not sure he knows where I'll be then."

"I thought you said you were his brother."

"I am." Lachlan cleared his throat again. He felt phlegm gathering, and swallowed, hard. "I'll give you the address where I'll be."

"It might help."

Lachlan was not focussed. He knew Hawkthwaite, but his mind was not co-operating to give the village. The phlegm built up.

"Can you hang on?"

"Best to ring back."

The thought of more torture was enough; Lachlan remembered the village, the county, the post code, even the phone number.

"Permission has to be written, sir. Regulations."

"So, I just wait for the visiting order?"

"That's what I said."

"In three or four days!"

"In three or four days."

Lachlan sensed the voice's impatience, muttered, "Thank you," and hung up.

"Who was that, Dad?" said Robbie. He'd been at the door, leaning into the room, leaving a finger-mark on the paint. Lachlan spat on to his hanky and erased it. "About Iain? Are we going to the prison?"

His father's face was serious, glazed.

"Perhaps. Now let's finish breakfast, shall we?"

With a birthday meal planned for the evening, Lachlan had decided to take the boys out for the day.

"A boat museum? Fascinating," said Robbie, but once in the car he was chatting breezily. Visions of steam, diesel and gas engines had been banished once he knew it was the largest collection of traditional canal craft they were heading for. The place was teeming with activity, barges boasting their heritage in sparkling orange, white and blue. The boys were amused by cabins that recreated 19th century cottages, complete with wax models.

"It's all so tiny," breathed Merrick, "so English." He was fascinated by the workings of locks through which boats moved slower than at snail's pace, by the ocean-going ships passing through the Manchester Ship Canal, and by the blacksmith, a man knocking deep red sparks off his odd-shaped anvil, too absorbed to speak to his audience.

"Not as good as Sovereign Hill in Ballarat," said Merrick on their way out of the museum. "But not bad for a country who sent all their best talent away in convict ships!"

"Hulks," corrected Robbie, remembering the opening chapters of 'Great Expectations'. "Good word, 'hulks'."

By the evening they were famished. Saul was delayed at work, so met them at the restaurant, a bistro in town, intimate and stark at once, with a white piano bursting to be played. Pillars of bare brick punctuated the room. Despite it being still light outside, each table had a candle, lit; the ambience was warm.

"Did you ring the prison?" said Saul, just as a waitress appeared, menus in hand.

"I did," answered Lachlan. He wondered if Saul thought that an evasive answer. The action had been put off long enough; what exactly had Lachlan been afraid of? In all probability his brother would still refuse to see him. But it couldn't end there. The next move was harder. Arriving at the prison might still present the same impasse, but there'd be people he could talk with. Deep down, though, he knew that calm explanations from a friendly warder with all the time in the world as to why his brother did not want to see him were whims of fiction. That rejection, outside the prison slab, seen only by a lone visitor or solicitor emerging from one more session with a culpable client, would be final. Nowhere to go from there. He did not want the boys to witness this last rejection, looking up with silent faces to find incomprehension. Better not to let them come at all. Decision taken, he reached for the menu. He risked a look across at Rebecca, and chose boeuf bourgignon.

The waitress took a shine to the boys, laughing as they exaggerated their accents to her. Devilment ran high in them, boys' spirits, ready to soar.

"How was the museum?" asked Saul, just as steaming mussels were placed in front of him.

"Different."

"How different?"

Robbie looked up, distracted for a moment by the size of the sea bass on Rebecca's platter. A man at the next table stood up, his chair scraping on the floor and hitting Merrick in the back.

"It's the history that's different," replied the boy. "We're not used to it going so far back."

"Not just history, dare I say culture?" chimed Lachlan. "I miss that, in Melbourne. I miss being so near to Europe, and the range of things you can do here."

"You'll have to come back," said Saul, which rankled Lachlan. Too much about this trip had finality woven into it. His thumb moved down the glass in front of him.

"Cheer up, Lach," ventured Rebecca.

"And eat up, Dad," said Robbie.

A few minutes later the piano started up, stoked by a girl with frizzy ginger hair. She had no music, and kept her eyes closed, swaying now and then, lost in the sound. Her notes swam round the brick pillars in search of the furthest crannies.

"Schubert," said Rebecca, which caught Lachlan unawares. His sister wasn't known for musical recognition. How much else of the change in her could he discover in the five fleeting days he had left? In many ways she was as he remembered, but the new offshoots fired his interest; she and Lachlan had been too long apart. In the nick of time he shut out a picture of Grouse Mountain outside Vancouver, winding pathways to the summit glanced down on by a dangling chair-lift. He'd not been to Canada, but a postcard sent in innocence by one of the actors he'd met in Melbourne featured views of British Columbia, views that lingered, challenged, chiselled away when his guard was dropped. Kathy still had him in thrall.

Applause greeted the end of the Schubert, and the girl launched straight into another piece. Lachlan raised his eyebrow at Rebecca.

"Give me a minute; it could be Brahms."

"Or Berlioz?" said Saul, with a grin.

"Schumann, surely," insisted Lachlan, as the girl went suddenly pianissimo, eyes tight shut, not swaying now.

Out of the silence grew a waitress bearing a cake with flickering candles. For a grim moment, Robbie feared the bistro was about to burst into 'Happy Birthday', but that feeling was allayed as swelling piano chords rose around him. At least he'd been spared fourteen candles.

"Dad?"

"Not me. Rebecca." Robbie looked over to his aunt, her black hair in the candlelight giving her a look of Lorna Doone.

"Cheers, 'Becca." He demolished the candles and plunged in the knife, alarmed by his gusto in the action.

They sauntered home through darkening streets. Robbie smiled at the waitress' good humour, clutching the remains of his cake. Merrick was silent. Saul whistled as he led the way. The English birthday had been good.

Saul worked all week, but Rebecca had kept odd hours free in the day, including the following morning, when she proposed a boat trip on the Dee. Sunshine flickered across the river as they walked down from the city walls. Lachlan was pondering the vagaries of language: way back in Aberdeen he'd been curious about the Good Friday hymn. 'There is a green hill far away, without a city wall'. To think of Golgotha lacking a wall had meant little; only years later had he understood.

His kids were all energy. Merrick pointed out canoeists near the weir as Robbie scoured more paintings, intent on finding an original. The boat was not crowded and they sat on board gazing at impressive mansions on the opposite bank. As they moved away, a tannoy struck up and Lachlan groaned – another recorded voice to pry into his thoughts. But this voice kept silence for minutes at a time, and all too soon he felt the boat start to turn round. On the way back they glided past two homesteads with a boathouse, and several pubs, by one of which their boat slowed for the voice.

The pub had been notorious. Witches frequented the place. They were apprehended, outside the confines of law, and made to swim across the river: if they drowned, they were innocent; if not, guilty, and burned at the stake. The river had claimed another infamous life, when a boy of twenty had been on his way to the gallows.

"Gallows?" said Merrick.

"Where they hang you," came back Robbie, like a gunshot.

As the executioner slipped on his black mask, the boy had made a run for it; still shackled, his blood was up. Despite his fetters, he had almost made it across the river, only to flounder as he neared the bank and finally go under. His young corpse was dragged out, but the law demanded he be hanged, drawn and quartered, even when dead. And he duly was. The voice went silent. Neither boy moved.

"What a great story," said Robbie.

"Was it true, Dad?" from Merrick.

"Oh, yes. Barbarous people these English."

"Pity he wasn't sent to Australia. He'd have made good with spirit like that."

Rebecca found herself nodding in agreement, then wondering about the boy. No one could know if he'd been guilty. Arbitrary justice, then, as now.

"What was the boy's name?" said Merrick.

"John somebody…Heath, I think."

"I'd like to have met him," regretted Robbie.

"Me too," said Rebecca, as the boat gathered momentum and a crackle heralded the return of the voice.

The notion of justice held sway during that evening's dinner, but then gave way to fate. Merrick had gone to bed, but Robbie listened intently. Saul was a fatalist; Lachlan saw things were not that simple. Even as the conversation began, he was treading through dark avenues.

"As a Christian, you must accept fate, surely, Lach?" said Saul. "'Thy will be done'; isn't that your line of thinking?"

Lachlan shook his head. "The age-old question. A merciful God over a world in such pain."

"But if there's a better world...after this one?"

"There is. No 'if'."

Saul had avoided tragedy in life. Lachlan wondered how he'd react to a harsh hand of cards dealt him. Strong people crumpled, some apparently not strong rose above their grief remarkably, passing succour to others in undreamed-of fashion.

"You mean your parents?" Saul said it. In Lachlan's head trees caved in on him, became torches of fire, then rose up on end and set fire to the sky. There was a deafening sound of timber swallowed by white-hot wind, grenades of bark exploded all around him, black leaves pumped themselves into the cauldron. He heard a siren wailing in the distance, his hands burst into blisters as his shirt was blown from his body into a bonfire moving faster than sound. Thunder cracked the sky, raining down javelins of flame as he fell to the sand beneath him, ripping holes in his side; he was writhing, his temples caving in.

Hands still held across his chest, Lachlan came to.

"Do you still feel blame?" Saul said coldly. "All these years down the track?"

Rebecca put a hand on his arm. "We all do, Iain too."

Saul got up from the table, coming back with three bottles of beer.

"They are cold," he tried, unsure how much humour to let out. Robbie was disappointed. He'd never heard the full story of the bush fire, and thought this was to be his chance.

The days flicked by. Chester was rich in attractions, and after a day at Arthur's Labyrinth in Wales, they were joined at lunchtime by Rebecca for a tour of the city in an open-top bus. She was between patients. It was grey again, the distant rumble of an aeroplane fading slowly over Birkenhead as they climbed to the upper deck, where Merrick made straight for the front. Turning, the back of his hand rubbing one eye, he squinted at them impatiently. Kathy's look again. Lachlan mentioned it to Rebecca.

"Will they go to Canada...? To...see her?"

Lachlan nodded. "Next year, I gather. She doesn't communicate with me. They need to go. That's fine. I can't imagine how she survives without them. I couldn't."

"But if you had to?"

Lachlan's eyes flashed, wary.

"If..."

"I think about it. Often. That I'm on a tightrope; there's no safety net, no crowd. I'm holding a long pole at right angles to the rope, one boy on each end. Kathy's the ringmaster, looking up. She has a whistle that keeps being taken towards her lips, then released. In my temples the veins stand out. The boys are happy, though; it's excitement, not risk for them. Robbie's end is heavier, so I have to keep adjusting my hand hold. There's not much resin. The whistle will be blown and the boys will fall into her saw-dust arena..."

"And you?"

Pause.

"I'll get to the other side," He was aware that Robbie had heard the last part of their conversation. The boy looked puzzled. Until recently he'd have questioned; now he looked away.

The bus stopped abruptly, and Merrick, standing up for a

242

better view, felt his teeth smack against the plastic guard at the front of the bus. He looked hard at the Roman amphitheatre remains, picturing gladiators in mortal combat in front of a primitive grandstand, where men in togas straightened their thumbs in readiness for the kill. The racecourse beckoned beyond them, sun glancing across windscreens as the last of the veteran cars prepared to depart.

Rebecca alighted near her practice, leaving the others to complete their journey. Later, they sampled the Roman experience of Deva, highlight of which was an extensive archaeological 'dig'. Merrick pulled up an ancient nail, but threw it back, disgruntled.

Setting out for the zoo two days later, they met a blind man being guided down Prince's Street by a girl who smiled at them. Lachlan's 'G'day' was answered by a nod from the blind man. Merrick shut his eyes and walked up the street, hands just held out from his body. Robbie watched him. Overheard, rain clouds were gathering; there was a chill in the air.

"Autumn already," muttered Lachlan, and a passing executive, briefcase in hand, gave him a wider berth.

Lachlan was thinking of Angus, why he'd sent him to the zoo in Melbourne, not gone with him. There'd been no word from his company while he'd been away, which was not a surprise, but didn't stop him wondering about his actors. Angus' performance in 'Wolf' was making him a commodity in Melbourne; he could be snapped up at any moment.

The zoo was a full day's adventure, whose highlight for Merrick was six black rhinos, one of whom was to be sent back to Africa as part of a conservation plan for the threatened species. Two elephants were pregnant, though it was not easy to tell, and Robbie enjoyed the komodo dragons, together with the birds of paradise. As they were leaving, he spotted a sign offering members of the public the chance to be a keeper for a day.

"Terrific, Dad."

"Terrific, son, and an exorbitant price. £150...that's $375."

"Worth every cent."

"And whose side –"

"Yours, Dad," cut in Merrick. "Imagine feeding all those animals. I'd love it – just for the day."

They were passing the maned wolves, bred for the first time in 1999, whose distinctive smell was hard to avoid.

"Feisty," said Robbie.

Saturday evening ambushed them. They'd spent the morning at the Military Museum with its exhibition of four regiments in Cheshire. Suddenly the end of their time with Saul and Rebecca was at hand.

They sat in the garden with drinks, Saul having lit the barbecue, waiting for coals to glow. The boys were quiet, Robbie helping Rebecca make kebabs; Merrick, un-characteristically, with a book on his knees.

Iain hung on the confines of his brother's mind. There were misconceptions about twins. So much between them had been shared. Iain was still the closest person to him: he knew how his twin would deal with things, which was why he fought not to picture his brother in prison. In youth they had the same tastes in people, women, sports, with subtle differences picked up on by close friends. They liked space, not always the case with twins, having been to the same schools, in the same classes when young. University saw them severed for the first time, bringing with it relief. Constantly being compared annoyed both, relentless head-to-head competition for which they hadn't asked: competition for their parents' congratulations, unwitting competition to be recognised when they were seen alone. Inevitably they enjoyed playing tricks on people unsure with which twin they were dealing, Lachlan getting more mileage out of the deception than Iain; as young boys he'd been the one more irritated at always being dressed the same, two trophies to be paraded. Since teens they had dressed as differently as they could.

Iain being the elder, albeit by those eleven minutes, ploughed the path that Lachlan then turned into a road, with the benefit of a few doors opened in the interim. The grass was trampled down for him; he could go further down the path, as Iain was aware.

At fifteen, Iain had his appendix out in a large hospital in the city. For the first time Lachlan was without him, for almost a week. The operation was not straightforward; tests were done, 'cysts' and 'tumours' mentioned in anxious expressions, from which Lachlan was excluded. He felt cheated. Iain's problems had begun on a Friday evening, just as they were about to board the ferry to Queenscliff. He was silent one minute, screaming in unbearable pain the next. They watched they ferry set out across Port Phillip Bay, awaiting the ambulance from which Lachlan again was excluded. No one asked about *his* pain, a jabbing guilt in several parts of his body at once, sweat in the small of his back, muffled screaming out of the range of human hearing.

When Lachlan went to the hospital halfway through the week, he knew how his brother would look, saw confirmed in his eyes a level of pain he could gauge, sensed what his twin would not say, pushing into the silence a hot block of bravery, though Iain wouldn't call it that. Lachlan was reluctant to leave the single room, fearful, because Iain wasn't in the ward where patients looked better, less white. Lachlan had later been in a ward like that for one night of his life, after breaking his arm, a night affording luxury and freedom, for he knew next morning he'd be home. With Iain there was no guarantee, not even after another operation when a cyst, not a tumour, had been removed, after which he'd come home pale rather than white, and tumour-talk had ceased.

Lachlan was the first to have a serious girlfriend of whom he was proud, the daughter of an Australian swimmer, herself a bright mermaid with long, blond hair. He was enamoured for months until one summer camp when she changed her allegiance. During the months Iain felt a shift in their fraternal bond; he was the one cheated now, the one to whom things were not explained. The girl was friendly to Iain; he, too, found her physically attractive, but she treated him more as a younger brother than as an elder twin. Through it all Iain realised he'd have been as his brother was, had he won the girl.

At university the road forked. Both were looking forward to the parting, yet, when it came, they hated it; they had no idea what it would be like to venture solo. But they were still linked as if by a fisherman's wire, strong, invisible, of infinite length.

Long before Iain went to prison Lachlan wondered how one twin would react should the other fall from grace. It was harder to accept misdemeanour in his brother than in himself. He could not explain why, nor could Lachlan ask if the feeling was mutual. For all their differences, he valued Iain's judgement more than that of anyone else. When he knew he was in serious trouble, Iain warned Lachlan early, feeling guilt, aware of the consequences; his brother had to know. Lachlan's reaction was hard to chronicle: anger, disappointment, hurt, uncertainty and grief leap-frogging endlessly, set off by the desperation to understand. There was no judging; Lachlan had to get inside his brother and understand why, seek a comprehension whose seeds were in his brain as much as in Iain's, blast the crazy paving and have it land in another sequence, where its rocky shapes made sense.

They were on opposite sides of the globe, but distance was not tyrannical in this; they needed communion, not words. If Iain cut the rope, there was no one else, one hurt meant both were hurt, which could explain something in

Iain's silence and reluctance now. Not that he couldn't share the hurt, but that he had to take it on himself. Iain's faith had lapsed; he was on his own now. Women he treated roughly, few names lasted more than a couple of months, and of recent friends he spoke not at all. Horse-racing friends were all tinged with corruption, wads of tired notes drawn from back pockets by a dirty thumb. A criminal record could not be shed like a slough.

Iain was stubborn. Where the young Lachlan had a temper, Iain's patience slipped through tenacity into obdurance, hardening by hairs' breadths until beyond approach. He was unreachable, and Lachlan had to admit it.

"You look like a man in need of some red," joked Saul, emerging from the house, with Robbie in pursuit, kebabs held out on a tray. There was no sign of Merrick.

"He went to pack," said Rebecca, seeing her brother's searching eyes. "Said you looked so intense." There was a pause. "You did."

"I'll fetch him down." He heard Robbie's intake of breath as Saul bent to flatten the white-hot coals for a plate redolent of red meat, and was back in a moment, having met Merrick at the foot of the stairs.

No one mentioned it was their last night, but there was more silence than usual, more space to hear the spitting barbie, dealing with its victims in the late night garden where rain was kept at bay.

Next day was cloudy and cold. They went to communion in the local church, which was muted, with only a small congregation. Lunch was eaten inside, looking out on the crooked wall, whose plants had lost their lustre.

The hired car was loaded up in preparation for Lakeland.

"Hate goodbyes," said Rebecca as she led them to the open front door. Saul hung back, reticent, his frame filling the doorway one last time.

"There'll be a crossroads," Lachlan assured them, catching his cheek with a frayed sleeve.

Then they were gone up the Prince's Street cobbles, under the city wall and into the mesh of fast roads that would disgorge them in Cumbria. Saul and Rebecca stood awhile by the door, then went back inside, where Merrick's book confronted them on the carpet. Rebecca stooped to pick it up, stifled a tear, and held the book to her side. A hint of prescience touched her shadow on the wall.

CHAPTER TWENTY ONE

Hawkthwaite sat back from the road, an inviting house of grey stone, snug and rustic. The road from the village dipped away sharply, then ran between low hedges to a bridge, under which the small river flowed through unfenced fields; they could see its course, over the flat land. The name of the house was just recognisable in flaked crimson on a once-white five-barred gate, perhaps the original drive. Carriage horses, turning down it, snorted in Lachlan's head. These days the road ran on, then took a sharp bend to the right at the foot of the drive. Pebbles spun as Lachlan turned into it, Pauline's careful map no longer clutched in his hand, and there was the scrunch of tyres on gravel.

Just before the house a large beech tree stood, blocking the building from view for a moment, the track swinging to the left before landing them on cobbled stones in front of flower beds adorning the house. Lachlan turned off the ignition, stretching slightly. No one came to greet them, and they climbed out of the car, suddenly nervous. The air was sweet with honeysuckle, a chicken ran under the gate ahead; to the right, under the guardian tree, was a home-made barbecue, unused for a while.

"There's a message for us," bubbled Merrick, seeing a note twirl on the front door. He ran across the cobbles and returned with it held tight in his fist.

'Back soonest. Make yourselves at home. P.' he read. "Let's go in then." He turned the brass handle and they went inside, Lachlan stooping a little to avoid low beams. The house smelt of countryside; on the right was a small lounge with embroidered guard up against the fireplace. Tiny water-colours hung on the walls above a small brass foot and two bells. On the left was a kitchen, its black cooking-range smelling of new bread, with small windows, a pipe on the table, binoculars by its side. The strap was worn with use. Two postcards in autumnal colours were perched on a shelf in the recess. A clock ticked on the sideboard.

Looking through the window Lachlan saw a black labrador panting along the drive, followed by a woman in an orange anorak, the lead swinging in her hand. He went into the hall and opened the door to the stranger he felt he knew. An Irish accent was unexpectedly warm. The dog sniffed round the two boys and Pauline introduced Merlin. Within minutes they were sitting in the small parlour. Pauline was a fine cook, her homemade sponge soon devoured by the boys. Sam was in the village, but he would find them, she said, struggling back into the anorak for the promised tour. Outside, bees feasted on hollyhocks lining the house and Lachlan saw the year 1739 etched in stone on the house's façade. Looking closer, he saw more dates: 1750, 1896 and – finally 1575. He smiled.

"Always been in the family," said Pauline, following his look. "Always will be, I reckon."

They walked through a gate, past a kitchen garden, where an upturned watering-can boasted POISON. Merrick caught Robbie's eye. The path led down to a hen-house, chicks and hens scrabbling for pieces of grain, four cockerels watching, aloof.

"There's a fox about," said Pauline, "cunning as an Irishman." Lachlan liked her smile and easy gait. Merrick was hoping to shut the hens away at night and catch a glimpse of the fox. They strolled on, fields opening up; ahead of them was a copse framed by barbed wire.

"Over there's the old garden," pointed Pauline, "and there's a tree-house when you want an adventure." Her words spun two heads. "I'll take you there later."

Robbie made a mental note to go there on his own; a guided tour would spoil the mystery. They walked towards a hedge with one narrow gate, set deep. The boys climbed it, impatient; Pauline and Lachlan swung over too. On a narrow path, almost overhung by brambles, shadows floated and ebbed in the breeze. It was hot now. Lachlan rolled up his sleeves, glad of the warmth; the boys were out of view. Down to the left was a barn, recently renovated, with chestnut wooden doors, outside which stood a piece of rusting machinery.

"The iron horse," said Pauline. "Still works. Yes, you can have a go," anticipated Merrick's question, as a jay dived down to the stream, its flash of blue lasting a second longer in Robbie's instantly closed eyes. Rooks circled overhead; Merlin appeared out of tall grass, and they moved on. Through the wood Robbie thought of badgers; he'd be up here again at dusk. As they ducked under the wire to come out of the wood, Merrick was snagged for a moment: Pauline dug out his wounded T-shirt.

Cows glanced at them with little interest, overhead she pointed out a buzzard, and up ahead they saw an unusual rock formation jutting five or six feet out of the rough ground.

"Volcanic lava," said Pauline, sensing from his reaction that Lachlan was not a man for geology. He smiled, lifting Merrick halfway up the rock on which Robbie stood proud. It was a captivating view: distant scree-tops like sand dunes, the palest brown, behind which soared two peaks. "Tallest mountain in England," affirmed their guide. "And in front of it is Wastwater, the deepest lake of them all. We'll go there one day; there's a good pub at the head of the valley. And a tiny church. There are climbers buried in the graveyard from way back. Before Australia," she countered, not missing a streak of indignation in Merrick's face.

Sam was a true countryman. He heard them returning and came out in black wellingtons, cloth cap and with the firmest handshake. He was an open-hearted man, who knew little of the New World. Lachlan had brought four bottles of Australian Cabernet Sauvignon. "You'll be a true red man in a few days," he said, handing over the booty.

"And I'll get you to do the barbie," Sam replied, pulling a wedge of mud from his giant thumbnail and flicking it into the empty fireplace.

After supper, closing the curtain in his room, Lachlan was aware of his breathing again, a sudden drain on his relaxation that hit him without warning. The confrontation with Iain was imminent. Not to have it would be worse. So far he'd met with rebuff, failure, alienation, but his twin brother had to be seen, and the days were falling away.

"You know the tree-house?" Merrick's words at breakfast next morning caught Robbie off guard.

Pauline nodded. "You want to see it? I'll take you."

"It's all right," said Robbie quickly. "If you tell us where it is, we'll find it."

"More fun," chirped Merrick.

Pauline told them and the boys set off at once. Climbing up round the side of the house, they found a mower had forged a single track through the long grass. Sam had said the long grass needed scything, to give the fox less cover, Robbie remembered.

The track disappeared under heavy foliage. Up ahead was a blown-down trunk, with a stile leading to the wood, but their way wound left, under more branches, into a clearing. A wooden house nestled on stilts, logs stacked underneath it, the sunlight dappling through. Casual planks lay against the tree-trunks; there were ferns on the ground. On the roof of the tree-house Robbie saw 'Cricket Club' in faded paint.

Access was via a ladder festooned with cobwebs. Merrick rushed up first and his head pushed into the shelter.

"There's felt in there, all covered in leaves," he said with disappointment. The rest of his body climbed up and was gone. Robbie, on the other side of the tree-house, stood still, listening to sounds in the undergrowth, making the most of this short-lived freedom before his brother emerged. A twig crackled to his right, then another. He longed for a glimpse of deer.

Wednesday was market day in the local town; they set off early. Leaving Sam and Pauline to their animals, Lachlan took the boys to the square, a pedestrian zone. Despite the heat, stalls were doing a healthy trade, and Robbie wasted no time in locating a stall boasting soccer mementos. Merrick was quiet, hands buried in the pockets of his commando shorts, thumbs strumming against the waist band as he hummed to himself, in another world.

Lachlan knew shopping was not possible when the boys were in tow. Already Robbie had darted behind a stall laden with Lycra shorts and lurid T-shirts. Merrick saw him disappear and the younger boy's expression showed him planning to outwit his brother; he sped through the gap in the canvas, leaving shiny pink halter-necks trembling from his spring. Then he appeared a few stalls away, scanning the foreground for a sibling he knew would be in hiding, and well concealed. Lachlan picked up a paperback, skimmed its reviews on the back page and held out a pound coin that changed hands slickly. When young, he'd written a story on a day in the life of a penny, and could still remember the end of his essay, when the well-travelled copper had fallen into a hungry gutter, leaving him bereft.

He was hungry now, and collected the boys, intent on a display of watchstraps.

"No, you don't need one," and the trio walked on.

At the corner a group had clustered; it was watching a smartly dressed man in a bowler hat who stood stock-still. Did every town have street theatre, Lachlan wondered? White braces tight as cello strings, a white bow tie and white gloves added to the man's splendour. Only his eyes moved, occasionally. Something about his expression was disturbing, more like a ventriloquist's dummy than a person, and the dark eyes bore into anyone affording him more than a cursory glance.

His hair was greasy and slicked back, making him look taller, and his expression, beneath the hard, fixed stare, alluring. When he moved, after at least ten minutes in one frozen pose, the change was marked, almost violent, despite its lasting only the fraction of a second before his unreal glare once more took hold.

The black and white costume was smart, and cloaked in menace; his gloves added a chilling touch. Just then a butterfly with orange wingtips landed on his sleeve; he made no attempt to hasten it away.

"He looks like a burglar," said Merrick, "except you can't see him breathe."

"I can," Robbie affirmed.

"You would," came the rejoinder. Robbie said nothing.

"Let's get lunch, can we now, Dad?"

"Sure."

Lachlan led the boys away from the statue, glad to avoid the moment when it stepped back into reality, picked up the receptacle thrown down for idle cash, and walked away, a mundane human. The receptacle was a violin-case of frayed and faded velvet. He turned one last time, and saw the braces rigid between bobbing heads.

"Robbie! Nip back and put this in the statue's case."

"Now?" said Robbie, surprised.

"Why not?"

Lachlan's eyes followed his son as he sprinted back through the crowd; the boy was back in a trice.

"Does he move when you give him money?" asked Merrick.

"Course not."

"I would."

Lachlan looked at the boy. "I know you would." He

stepped into a flintstone of shade.

"This place'll do," said Lachlan, and the boys sped up the staircase to a terrace in the sun.

Having given the prison the Stanburys' address, Lachlan anticipated a letter enclosing his visiting order on their return from town. But there was no letter awaiting him at Hawkthwaite. He felt the disappointment rise in him. He'd known the chances were against him, but he'd hoped. When the boys were out, walking the dog, he picked up the phone and dialled the prison. The same lack of welcome, and he was put through to booked visits. Trying to avoid sounding rejected, he explained he'd received no visiting order.

"If the inmate won't see the visitor, there's nothing the staff can do," rang out the voice, with more than a hint of satisfaction. Lachlan tried again, his explanation sounding increasingly desperate in his own ears.

"You could talk to the Wing Senior Officer," said the voice, finally. "He's the man responsible for the welfare of individuals on his wing."

"Can you put me through?"

"I'll try."

The phone rang out, but no one picked up, and the switchboard didn't come back to him. Pensive, he walked on to the top lawn behind the house. A kestrel interrupted ablutions on the telegraph wire to eye him. Lachlan felt his eyes tighten for a sharper view, aping the bird, a young one. Two white butterflies crossed over in mid-air, diverting his gaze. The kestrel watched.

Some time later, he rang the prison again, this time reaching the Wing Senior Officer; the man's dialect caught Lachlan off guard, but he was sympathetic.

"I'll have a word," he offered, once the explanation was over. "No promises, mind. But I'll have a word."

The man rang back later that evening.

"Mr Stacey? No go, I'm afraid. Mr Stacey isn't keen on

the visit. I did try."

Biting his lower lip, Lachlan breathed hard, asking the man to have one more try with Iain. "Plead with him if necessary," he found himself saying, just as Pauline crossed the narrow hall, her fingers round a gin. She entered the parlour noiselessly.

"Anything you can do," said Lachlan. "I can't say if I'll be in England again." Blackmail, he was aware, as he replaced the phone. Iain would be contemptuous of that.

It was the dental records that did for the killer. A man in Cornwall had strangled his wife, then trussed her up and bundled the body aboard his light aircraft, or so the story went. Knowing that Wastwater was the deepest lake, he executed his plan: to fly over the lake at night and let the weighted carcass fall into the depths below. He chose a risky night, fog clinging to the tops of the screes, visibility poor. But he had reconnoitred with care: the deed was accomplished and he flew home confident of his coup. Unbeknown to him, though, there were ledges far beneath the surface at the sides of the lake; by ill-fortune the body came to rest on one of these. Eventually a fisherman's line snagged the parcelled torso, nudging it from its perch and, over days, it rose from the depths. Spotted by a passing farmer, the parcel was lugged ashore and unwrapped, the list of missing persons scoured and dental records checked. By a lovely irony, the pilot himself was a dentist.

The boys were agog as Sam narrated the saga. Lachlan thought of Dave.

"No such thing as a perfect crime you see," said Pauline, passing round a capacious crumble, its contents garnered in the grounds.

"There must be," said Sam, and a lively discussion ensued, during which the Stanburys' son, Edmund, arrived home and sat down with a pint of Guinness. Robbie was calculating the chances of the dentist's bad luck: he must have thought he'd got away with it until the phone call or knock on his front door some months later. The adults moved on to discuss conscience, at which point Robbie and Merrick slipped outside. The air was still, a distant farm dog barked at an unheeding sky, bats flew from the eaves.

"Chickens!" came the cry from inside, and Edmund loped into the darkness, followed by the labrador.

"Want to come? There may be carnage!" They were soon by the gate that led to the hen-house. A rooster crowed, making Merrick jump; there was a scuffling, a hen darted over Robbie's foot. The door was open and some of the poultry inside.

"Looks like we've been lucky this time," said Edmund.

They walked back to the house, Merlin sniffing ahead of them, the sound of laughter emanating from the open parlour window. Looking in, Robbie thought he had never seen his father so relaxed as he talked with these new-found soul mates, a whisky in hand.

He and Merrick were sleeping at the back of the house. Edmund told them how he used to shoot rabbits from their window which overlooked a lawn; away to the left there were hundreds of rhododendrons, their blooms just visible over a part of the grounds the boys hadn't had chance to investigate. In the olden days it must have been the main access to the house, up the long grass drive at the foot of the bridge. Robbie imagined horses and carriages powering up at the end of a journey from London, their passengers, dressed like characters from Dickens, climbing down, exhausted and hungry.

Merrick was still at the window, waiting to catch sight of the fox. On arriving in the room, Lachlan suggested they went to bed, adding that there was a large bookcase in his room from which Robbie could choose a book. The boy was away some time; he came back with three, and started them all.

It was pouring with rain from the early hours. Tight in one car, they drove through fierce weather, rattling over cattle grids, aquaplaning as vehicles came at them going towards the village. Merrick was again amused by out of the way post-boxes; blazes of scarlet hidden in ivy-clad walls, as if no one had unlocked them for centuries. They were climbing a steep gradient when a cow faced them on the road, not one of Sam's, but he recognised the beast and phoned his neighbour on the mobile, impatient at the man's delay in answering.

The youth hostel looked bedraggled as they swept past, then suddenly the great lake was there in front of them, a bruise swelling over the rain-spattered vista. Two hikers gazed up as Sam slowed to avoid drenching them further; the girl looked friendlier than her mate. As he drove down-hill the windscreen-wipers moaned at the speed with which they were expected to work. Where the road flattened out, water was seeping across it; the shoreline had vanished, visibility was nil. Clouds came in and out of focus overhead as Robbie, in the back, saw them distorted for a moment through the reflection of Pauline's glasses. The water was getting deeper on the road, the place becoming eerie as light sank away around them.

"Never known it this bad," said Sam, large hands resting on the wheel, which looked inadequate, like a dodgem car's that spun and took you nowhere but backwards. Lachlan was glad he was not driving.

The car park held one car as they drove into it. Rain had abated slightly, but puddles remained, blown in the gale. Stepping out of the car, Pauline put her foot in one. Robbie was impressed by her self-control. Around them greyness engulfed all; the puddles blew water. Robbie wondered where the occupants of the other car had hidden themselves. It was hard to discern the church, but Sam led the way up the path, the gate banging noisily in the wind.

Merrick came across the grave of an animal and stared at

the inscription. Lachlan put his hand on the circular iron door-handle; in this weather it was clammy and cold to the touch. The noise, when he turned the handle, surprised him, a throated sound that hung in the dank air before dying away. Mould could be smelled everywhere, and wax, and dried flowers. Pauline straightened two of the flowers that were spilling on to a thin carpet by the small altar; there was a Bible open at 'Revelation' on the carved wooden pulpit; a list of names, handwritten; a key. Other than the main door there was nothing to lock; perhaps it was the key for a collection box out of sight. Rain renewed its assault, landing on the ancient roof and spilling from gutters down windows of pale stained-glass. Even in midsummer there would be no piercing sun for this church. Lachlan said a quick prayer, finding, at the end of it, that he was holding the scrap of paper with the names in his hand. He looked at the last name; Michael Childs. Age-old shepherd, teenage climber, publican from the Wasdale Head, fell-runner, visitor? Lachlan would never know. He prayed for Michael Childs, and replaced the paper, which blew down to the floor at once. Robbie swooped down the steps of the pulpit and placed it under the key on a table beside the altar, unadorned save for a wooden crucifix, its INRI carved with an inventive hand.

On the way back, the water had risen on the road running beside the lake. There was silence, Sam concentrating as he drove, Lachlan beside him, scrutinising the weather.

"Always rains for Eskdale Show," said Pauline.

The village fête was an event built up with some importance by the Stanburys. Even taciturn Edmund had mentioned it, fleetingly, as a source of possible amusement. Terrier racing had grabbed Merrick's imagination, but there were three days still to go.

The buzzards intrigued the boy. He was watching from an upstairs window that looked over to the mountains, and

259

thought he saw one circling over the wood. The previous day's rain had left an echo in clouds of gunmetal grey, so he was not quite sure if he'd seen the bird or not. Buzzards preferred a warm summer's day, he knew, when they could tease the thermals, spiralling to a great height. They came to the fells many years ago, Sam told him, feeding on carrion, earthworms, beetles and the odd jackdaw. Often they had a brood of one chick, hatched from a beautiful egg, growing up to twenty, or twenty-two inches in height, with a wing span of over four feet. Since myxamotosis and the subsequent lack of rabbits, buzzard numbers had declined, so Sam and Pauline welcomed the birds to Hawkthwaite, where they appeared to use the same nest year after year. Sometimes in September the Stanburys were treated to striking aerial displays.

"For all their acrobatic potential, they are lazy, preferring to scavenge rather than kill." Merrick listened to Sam, relishing his tale of a young buzzard Edmund had found one day with a broken wing and fostered for a time. A part of Merrick wanted to see a crow attack on the buzzard.

The present pair was nesting in a silver birch, which was unusual; their home was typically the oak. Sam showed the boys a picture of the birds, the pale circles under their wings looking like markings on a plane. Robbie had taken the binoculars up to the wood at once, hoping to lie low and see one. The days were flicking by…

The Roman fort seemed worth a view, although prehistory was beyond the ken of the boys. But, arriving there up a hairy, zigzag track masquerading as a road, dismay hit them both hard. There were not ruins, just stumps, piles of dull rubble that gave no hint of a life having been lived in them. Sam made jokes about the New World's lack of history; Merrick found them in poor taste. He had been ready with convict quips, and prepared a couple of sharp answers, but things never materialised as planned, people made their comments using different words, altering emphasis, catching him off guard when he'd thought he was primed. Adults took a sad pleasure in that. He kicked up large tufts of grass high in the so-called ruins. Below him a solitary car fought its way up the endless chicanes to the crest of the hill; he fancied watching a motor-bike race down, more exciting by far. The adults were absorbed in talk, this time including Robbie, who'd become too grown-up for Merrick's liking on the trip. Edmund wasn't as interesting as the lad had hoped, except when speaking of his predatory escapades with wildlife.

Way down the valley he could see the lake, looking leaden. There was not enough to do here, and he missed Rebecca. She noticed the occasions when he felt his age, and endeavoured to do something about it. His Mum was like that, he remembered, but it was a long time ago. Pauline was doing her best, which made him grateful, but it wasn't the same. A sheep showed alarming energy in clearing a nearby tussock, which startled him. Before the drizzle started, he had known when it would come. Exactly when it would come.

At last the skies cleared, and they woke up to sunshine. Merrick leapt from his bed and wrenched open the curtain in his quest to see game. A starling had landed on the lawn. Merlin was barking; a stray chicken pelted over the broken-down wall, then thought better of it. Merrick hurled himself on top of Robbie, getting an elbow in the mouth, which repelled, for the moment.

Downstairs, Pauline was looking serious. The fox had struck again, four hens slaughtered and dragged down the path. Merrick was embarrassed by the deaths and stood silent in the hall, unable to pass Pauline, who was shouting at Sam. He wasn't sure if he wanted to see the débris or not. Something had disturbed the fox, or he would have continued his needless butchery. Pauline was trying to work out what the disturbance had been. Without her glasses she looked different, not as friendly somehow, although younger, less able to command the situation.

Robbie bundled downstairs, almost cannoning his brother into Pauline. Sensing the tension, he turned on his heel, and came down the back stairs, once the priority of servants. He was on the lawn not long after, saw a hen half-hidden in the foliage, and raced towards the dog, both of them ready for a morning's activity. When Sam shouted for the dog, the boy changed direction and made for the henhouse. The sight of the three other brown birds, who'd been healthy the day before, took him aback: their necks were broken, heads torn awry, feathers trampled on. Was this why people hunted?

Sam came along the path, ashen-faced. "See what happens?" he said, gravely. "We got too engrossed in conversation last night," he added, as if to explain his negligence. Robbie felt a jab of guilt; he'd been in the wood, watching for badgers the previous night and forgotten about the hens as he returned. He suspected Sam might spot his guilt, and avoided the farmer's look. Again, Sam's big hands swept into action, dragging the dead birds off the floor. They were too defaced to eat.

"They should have got the old cockerel," he said suddenly looking out into the countryside. "Time he had the chop. Sunday lunch maybe." Robbie did not understand how he could envisage adding to the slaughter; it seemed to underline the fox's victory. A kestrel hovered above them. The hens that remained were appearing, emboldened by human presence; the old cockerel leapt on to an oil drum, defying Sam's death sentence on his quivering comb. The sun had disappeared now. There was a chill in the breeze, and the chance of more rain. Looking out at the screes, Robbie was concerned to find they were not in sunlight, hardly a good omen for the show.

262

CHAPTER TWENTY TWO

The Jockey Club was formed in 1750. Influential men interested in racing and breeding horses needed an organisation to stand for integrity, honesty and fair play. They rapidly assumed authority for devising and implementing the Rules of Racing. More recently, the British Horseracing Board took over responsibility for the business side, leaving the Jockey Club responsible for discipline, security and anti-doping measures. To become a member of the Jockey Club requires a deep interest in racing and a commitment to promoting its well-being. There is a wide spectrum of talent: owners, breeders, ex-trainers, ex-jockeys, journalists, bankers, lawyers and businessmen.

The Jockey Club's Secretariat deals with everything from jockeys' safety and medical treatment to intricate legal matters, and preventing skulduggery. These men are based at Portman Square in London. Their foremost concern is security, so the Jockey Club has a small army of investigating officers, ring inspectors, betting intelligence officers and stable guards, some of them ex-policemen, others recruited from within racing. Doping is the ever-present threat, for which the Horseracing Forensic Laboratory at Newmarket is central. Newmarket, the 'headquarters' of English racing, also houses the Jockey Club's rooms with wonderful paintings, where members can stay, as in any private club.

Of the 120 members of the Jockey Club, half are honorary, including sheikhs, and half are younger, working members. The 'Old Boy' network is starting to fade, though perks, such as dining in Newmarket, remain. Increasingly, there is an international element to the Jockey Club as more and more horses are campaigned overseas.

When Iain Stacey came back from Australia, his interest in racing led him to meet a South African Steward's Secretary, who introduced him to handicappers, auctioneers, clerks of the scales and several vets, among them Harry Cudmore.

The gambling appealed to Iain. He soon established a bevy of racing friends with whom he travelled to all parts of England, his boast being that he had seen every course except Pontefract. Northern courses held a definite attraction, among them Kelso and Hexham. He met Harry Cudmore at Newcastle races; Cudmore was a vet in West Yorkshire with a syndicate share in several racehorses. One of this syndicate was an up-and-coming trainer, Seth Vincent, who wasn't averse to a flutter, despite the rules. Vincent's stables consisted mainly of flat-racing horses, but he had three or four jumpers, for fun. It was one of his horses, Stone Cherub, in whom Iain was persuaded to buy a share. Stone Cherub was a chestnut with three white socks, a characteristic on which some of the syndicate held reservations, knowing white socks to be unlucky. Stone Cherub ran without distinction in claiming hurdles, often ridden by an apprentice to reduce the weight on his back; his best placing was a distant third at Sedgefield one May Bank Holiday, when only four completed the course.

In his next race, at Hexham, Stone Cherub was a rank outsider in a field of nine for a selling hurdle. Minutes before the race he was backed heavily in several Northumbrian betting shops, his price falling from 50 – 1 to 20 –1 at the 'off'. In the race, run on dry ground the horse was not reckoned to relish, Stone Cherub was tucked away at the back of the field, his usual position, until the third last, when he began to gain ground. At the second last, he jumped cleanly, and, coming round the final turn, drew close to the leaders, both of whom were tiring. In a battle of heads to the line Stone Cherub was just in front at the post, a fact it needed the photograph to confirm. After the race, the horse was sold to a vet friend of Harry Cudmore. The stewards inquired into the running of Stone Cherub, but bets stood: Iain, Harry and others made a healthy profit.

All racehorses have passports, carefully checked after ringers were detected in the past. Recently all racehorses have been fitted with a microchip to prevent substitution. But technology had not been quite so snappy in 1995. Cortado, a young chestnut recently arrived from Ireland, with three white socks, had not run before in England, but Seth Vincent realised the horse had potential; the lure of a coup was too much for Harry Cudmore, who ran Cortado in place of Stone Cherub. There was no doping, just substitution. The Jockey Club Secretariat investigated Cudmore, who claimed full responsibility, and was 'warned off', which meant he was not allowed in any stables or on any racecourse in the country. But he could still be a pernicious influence. And Iain had caught the bug. He was in debt, gambling without restraint.

In recent years racing has become an international business. Where British horses were once campaigned almost entirely at home, with perhaps the odd sortie to Deauville, or fashionable Longchamp, which stages the Arc de Triomphe, Europe's mile-and-a-half championship in October, frontiers have been pushed back. The Breeders' Cup in America, the Emirates' World Series in Dubai, huge prizes in Hong Kong, and Australia's Caulfield and Melbourne Cups attract horses from all over the world. And pundits travel widely to view these races.

Iain revelled in international circles; he was personable, informed and easy-going, with a keen knowledge of southern hemisphere racing. He was seen as an authority on

265

the training methods employed 'Down Under', which are different from those used in Europe. He also began to develop an interest in breeding. He visited studs outside Newmarket, intrigued by the covering sheds, how stud grooms spoke of their equine charges in reverential tones, fiercely guarding the privacy of money-drenched couplings.

Ireland is home to the world's finest racing stock; Iain's visits to the Emerald Isle became increasingly frequent. The hospitality appealed to him, he had a sweet tooth for barn-braic, or fadge, and his Celtic temperament was at home. On one of his trips he bumped into Seth Vincent at Tattersalls' Sales in Dublin. That night, over Guinness in The Manor House, on the outskirts of Naas, the pair hatched a plot.

In the U.K. equine covering starts on or around February 14th, (Iain was amused by the Valentine's Day trigger) and extends to late March or early April. In Australia the season runs through September and October, so fashionable, healthy stallions do both stints. Iain and Seth's plot sounded facile: buy a decent stallion in Ireland, fly it out to Australia, have the horse die in transit, claim the insurance, then substitute a lesser stallion for duties in the southern hemisphere, for which hefty covering charges could be demanded. Using their contacts, Vincent and Iain had found a decent horse, formed a new syndicate to buy it, raced it on the flat three times without 'putting it into the race', and convinced the owners it needed to go to stud. But then a vet, Cudmore, discovered the horse would be no good at stud; it was 'firing blanks'. With what seemed a long face, Seth bought back the horse off his syndicate for £10,000. He promptly insured it for half a million pounds, and flew it out to Australia.

The hardest part of the scam was to convince the stringent Australian authorities the stallion had died en route, for which a veterinary certificate was essential. A dodgy certificate needed a dodgy vet. Harry Cudmore had been warned off racecourses and stables, but he hadn't been warned off aeroplanes landing in Sydney, with a dead stallion on board. Iain must have attacked his meal in the pub that night with more appetite than for a long time.

After that, events moved quickly. Iain still had contacts in New South Wales: he spoke to a stud in Scone, a celebrated breeding centre, five hours north west of Sydney, arranging to bring a 'top' stallion for duty at the start of September. Meanwhile, racing friends in Victoria found him a stallion similar in colouring, markings and confirmation to the one that Vincent had earmarked for their coup.

The ex-syndicate stallion was flown to Sydney with six other horses. But on the flight it panicked; in order not to upset the other horses, already fractious, the travelling vet, Cudmore, had no option but to shoot it. Two young customs officers on their three a.m. stint at Kingsfield Smith airport were smothered in paperwork, and the carcass was quickly disposed of. Two days later a substitute stallion arrived to take up stud duties in Scone under a false passport, provided by Cudmore.

They had almost got away with it. But the stud groom into whose care the horse had been placed at Scone had smelt a rat. Iain and Vincent's middle-man, put in charge of the operation in Australia, fell out with this groom, who came from the Czech Republic, but had worked with horses in Lambourn. He was genuinely fond of the beasts, and had a highly developed sense of honour. Radik Egorov was suspicious about the stallion's passport, and the middle-man was not able to answer the groom's probing questions. They argued, so Radik had gone to the Australian Jockey Club, who in turn had referred the matter to Portman Square. Iain, Seth Vincent and Harry Cudmore stood trial for serious fraud, deceiving the insurance company and claiming money off Australian breeders keen to send mares to a prestigious stallion. The verdicts on all three fraudsters had been unanimous: guilty. Each of them was sent down for four years. To separate prisons.

For Lachlan the fact the trial was taking place in London had been hardest to swallow. Strong feelings had surged in him from the moment Rebecca had phoned; he knew he had to see and confront his twin. During the trial he had often been on the point of jumping onto a plane, but the boys could not be left, despite Dave and Jo's offers to mind them. Only after the conviction had Lachlan been able to approach the situation with rationale. There was nothing for it but to visit Iain in prison in England, taking the boys with him.

When Edmund had taken the boys in search of deer, Lachlan sat down in the parlour with Sam. It had been a fine day; the farmer stretched out his legs in the small room as Pauline brought in the coffee.

"Tell us more about Iain," she urged, handing their visitor a large mug with 'Lakeland' emblazoned on its rough finish.

"Not sure where to begin," said Lachlan. "I don't feel I know him at all these days. Not since…"

The room was silent.

"Since the death of my parents – our parents," he went on. "We never had a chance to talk that through. He went back to England just a few days after the funeral, came back, briefly, for Merrick's first birthday, and that was it really. Next thing I knew he was involved in swapping a racehorse…and then in worse trouble."

He took a swig of coffee, and told them the saga of Cortado and Stone Cherub. Halfway through, Merlin padded in and rolled over in front of the fireplace. Sam reached out and rubbed the white blaze on the dog's chest.

"I think the hardest thing," Lachlan continued, "was that he didn't learn his lesson. You'd think having burned the fingers once…"

Pauline was clutching her coffee, deep in thought.

"Easy for us to say," she murmured.

Sam was silent, his dog stretched at his feet.

"And what would you have said to him?" ventured Pauline.

"Good question. I felt so many conflicting things at once. Anger, of course; disappointment, that ever-emotive word. Frustration, that I was unable to help in a concrete way. And an odd sense of …pride, funnily enough."

"Pride?"

"Misplaced pride, crazy really. But I felt that he could have used his daring and his brain to achieve something admirable rather than despicable. My father would have been incensed."

"Good job he didn't live to see it," Sam contributed.

"Oh, he sees it all right," said Lachlan. "Imagine what his soul might feel. Responsible in many ways."

"Responsible?"

"Yes."

Pauline's teeth clenched. "But as a Christian…"

"Yes?"

"…he'd understand… and, presumably, forgive?"

Australians know a bushfire day. After weeks of hot, tinder-dry conditions, fire is inevitable. There is an eerie feeling of apprehension, and of mourning. Pine and eucalyptus trees give off a highly flammable vapour. Sparks blister into life, driven by a furnace of wind at terrific speed, feeding the frenzied appetite of fire. Blazing, blasting, jumping, this fire radiates heat and hot ash, creating a wind of its own. Flames rush through the air before the trees catch fire with terrifying force. Eucalypts bend in the wind like catapults. Birds leave first, screeching warnings into the smoke; animals are on tenter-hooks gazing up at the sky. Telegraph-poles have a singing, ringing sound. The sound of heat is in the land, the sound the Aboriginals feared for their dream-land. And people withdraw, distracted, waiting for fears to be confirmed, aware of the power of fire. Radio stations are given over to reports on the fires. But before these reports come over the airwaves, people smell fire. The smell carries quickly, blown across thousands of hectares. Children are gathered in, everyone is on red alert. Despite understanding the language of bushfires, and the signs given by nature, people wait – helpless. No one leaves the house. All are watching or packing, prior to evacuation. The quiet, eerie sound grows. Then the siren blares... People walk quickly to a meeting place, perhaps the town oval; they know what to do. Firedrills are rehearsed twice a year on Sunday mornings. Snakes go down to the river, as far from the fire as they can, thereby creating another danger, for, as the fire advances, some people throw themselves in the nearest water. Others make a dug-out and lie in it, covering themselves with wet blankets, and they wait...

The Ash Wednesday fires of 1983 were devastating. The ferocious wind, intent on destruction, blew roofs off houses, preparing them for slaughter. At one point the whole of southern Australia was on fire, with blazes in South Australia, Victoria and New South Wales. One woman was cut in half by a blown sheet of corrugated iron as she ran down the street. There were other grim tales. A policeman directing traffic saw a car go through with a dead child in it. The child was his. Thousands of animals were killed, including a koala, which, burning and desperate, had blundered into a house. Millions of trees were razed to the ground, reduced to black stumps or charred trunks, like Lowry people. These were the fires from hell; it was days before many of them were brought under control. The town of Cockatoo was virtually wiped out.

The extent of destruction was immense but, as it passed, people emerged; churches opened their doors, food was delivered, a sense of community grew strong, as in wartime. Solitary figures stood on silent hillsides looking over the desecration. Their sorrowful God had passed over them, as in the Old Testament. Gradually they drove through skeletal forests with grey ash on the ground, the odd log still glowing in the moonscape, and already trees started to

270

regenerate. The black trunks threw out green shoots. Tree ferns grew back quickly, conditioned to the bushfire scenario. A newspaper printed the aerial photograph of six or seven burnt-out houses with one in the middle quite untouched.

But six years later the fires struck again. Lachlan's parents had gone up to Dandenong. It was January 6th. Epiphany. After the rigours of Christmas, they decided on a three-day break in the house of some parishioners who were overseas. Summer was raging, drought measures had been brought into force. Lachlan kept thinking of his mother's asthma; the smoke would have made her suffering worse. She had been found by the small swimming pool, face-down, a charred and wizened drumstick, easy prey to thirsty flames. His father had been clearing the gutter that was filled with leaves; Lachlan imagined him astride a stepladder, but there was no trace of one. The vicar was not recognisable, a savage cremation with no time for prayer.

It had been a high fire-risk day. They would have awakened and known at once. Gazing from the window, inertia was palpable, the helpless, vulnerable feeling. They were already grieving for their own loss, for other people, for the land itself, as they waited for the evil presence to arrive. The evil wallowed in their fear. Lachlan's father had once told him the worst time of day for fires was late morning with a windy afternoon in prospect. He had, Lachlan knew, hosed down the house, drenching walls, roof, gutters, then keeping them sodden, looking up to the sky where he glimpsed only a red glow through smoke of a colour he had never seen. Had the fire burst up the drive? Or surprised them from another direction? The way fires jump had been the single greatest horror for Lachlan. He tried to picture his parents' panic in order to understand: they had not experienced a bushfire before, though they warned their children often, more so since Robbie's birth. The boy was two and a half.

Lachlan was at the beach, when Kathy thundered up in the car to tell him. He noticed Robbie was not strapped in. She'd been listening to the radio; there was a fire up in the Dandenongs, an hour away. Lachlan drove Kathy and Robbie home, then he sped north. On the outskirts of the small town he met a roadblock, and, despite his urgings, he was not allowed through. Flames were roaring up the hill-side, cinders and huge smuts blew in the air. Lachlan drove round the town; again his route was blocked.

"For your own safety, mate," said a yellow-vested fire-man. Lachlan paced the tarmac, already melting in the heat; he was impotent. Some time later he saw the firefighter walk past, wiping his brow, holding his helmet in blackened hands. There was no specific news, and no way Lachlan could discover any details. He was restless, tense and certain at once. The firebreak was moved towards him; irritated, he reversed the car two hundred yards.

By six o'clock he was racked. Exhausted firemen walked away, to be replaced by others, many of them volunteers. They looked young. Lachlan rang Kathy; there was no news.

He waited till after 10 o'clock, when the road was opened again. He could not picture the house, had only the address given him by his father in case he was needed by his flock. Not in case his molten body needed finding for identification. The streets were filled with people, many clutching possessions and suitcases, wearing empty masks for faces. Policemen blew whistles; civilians bumped into each other. Lachlan felt searingly alone. A fireman asked what street he sought.

"Quallong," he muttered.

"Up here, I think mate. I'm not sure exactly which road it is." The man sensed Lachlan's fear. "Want some company?"

"Please," came the faint reply. Lachlan cleared his throat. "Yes, please."

They turned into a wide road. No one was in sight. The

omen bit into Lachlan's chest.

"What number?

Lachlan knew it was number eleven, but could find no voice. Certainty and futility welled inside him. He shook his head. Six houses had been destroyed, among them number eleven. A woman stood in the darkness, silent. Her dog came snorting down the path at the side of what had once been the wall of a house. Lachlan stood still. The firefighter put his hand on Lachlan's shoulder and started to walk up to the embers. The dog barked, twice. The man switched on a lantern that Lachlan had not seen in his hand. Seconds later its ray darted over a tarpaulin on the blackened grass. Lachlan turned away. The house next door was unscathed.

Identification was hardly possible. Kathy accompanied her husband; no words were said. Two days later Iain and Rebecca landed from England. Lachlan gave the eulogy to a packed church. He was twenty-nine, exactly half the age of his father. Iain went back after a week, Rebecca stayed for three. Lachlan remembered none of the arrangements, the practicalities, the detail, only endless cups of bitter coffee as they stared into the void. Alongside grief he came to feel two things. One was raw anger, when it was proved the fire had been started deliberately. Perhaps the arsonist had gone home, satisfied, to watch the fire on television. The other feeling was harder to define, something to do with bitterness at the irony of the Epiphany fire: frankincense for worship, and myrrh the sweet herb of death. But his Christian faith had been shaken to the foundations.

Over the ensuing years Lachlan was unable to make sense of the tragedy. He dwelt on it. Once the fire had been started, it would have gathered speed within minutes. Soon it was leaping over tracks, across farmland, jumping roads, fanned by an evil wind. Witnesses said the noise was worst, a human banshee at the top of its scream.

He knew his father had no experience of bushfires, but

would have remembered how leaves that had gathered in the gutters, tinder-dry, aided the course of the ball of flame. Standing on top of a step-ladder to gather leaves, he'd have been ripped to the ground by the heat. The house was destroyed in seconds. Of their mother's last moments they had no knowledge: worst of all would have been to see her husband licked by flame before the fire turned sharply in on her, defenceless as she stood. There was no pool at 11, Quallong Street, but, even if there had been, hurling herself into it would have done no good. Fires were voracious and unpredictable. Some people had escaped certain death when a blaze suddenly blew onto a different course at the whim of the whipped-up wind. Northerly. The one word, heralding doom.

Iain and Rebecca being in England, it fell to Lachlan to face the embers. He bore the knowledge alone for five hours. It was not the time difference that made him hesitate before ringing his siblings, not the disbelief, or shock, but a compulsion to keep it to himself, as if by doing so he could negate the news, or at least control the effect it would have. Rebecca was twenty-five. She had just gone back to England to seek physiotherapy work, and on January 6th, had been at a friend's wedding. 'Hamlet' reigned in Lachlan's mind, with funeral and wedding reversed in a trapped echo, beating his ear drums, stopping saliva, making him breathe.

As time went by he came to realise the best way of honouring his parent's memory was to live with greater fervour than before. But there was no escaping the pain…

"Well," said Sam, breaking the silence in the small parlour. "Who's for tea?"

Lachlan was aware of heavy rain outside the window. He had been absorbed in his story. It was the only time he had spoken the entire saga out loud. Pauline shifted her position on the sofa. And then he saw Robbie.

"How long have you been in here?" he asked, clearing his throat as he spoke. The boy shook his head slowly.

"I don't really know, Dad. About half an hour, I ..."

"He slipped in a few minutes ago," said Pauline. "You were engrossed."

Lachlan saw the furrows on his son's brow; the boy was gazing at the brass fender. Outside the rain grew heavier.

"Where's Merrick?"

"He went to bed, I think," said Pauline.

Lachlan nodded.

"You'd better go, too, son," he said to Robbie. The boy did not move. Sam's foot kicked the door, and he came in with tea and flapjack.

"Torrential," said Sam, nodding towards the window. "It's not rained this hard for a long time."

Pauline pulled the tray towards her and began pouring the tea. Rain smote the windows with fury. Lachlan swallowed, exhausted from so much talking. Robbie continued to stare at the fender.

He had finally heard the story of the fire.

CHAPTER TWENTY THREE

Behind his eyes, tiny shadows stood like imps, waiting to dance out and bait him. This feeling cut slices out of his confidence, and energy was needed to cover up his dread. How did dread exist on a morning such as this?

All around him, sounds could be garnished like summer fruits: grasshoppers, like gently demented spin-dryers that cut off suddenly; crickets, waiting for their chance to resound; blackbirds in the wood; the chirpings of a thrush, warm and mellifluous; a distant waterfall; even more distant car engine, and, rarest of all, silence. Robbie had never liked clocks, ticking in sombre and rigid control; they cut out the spontaneous.

Up in front of him the screes of Wastwater stood in a bluish haze; yesterday they had been clearer. The haze was accentuated by shades of green. His brain tickled. Once, asked about his favourite colour, he'd flashed, "Red." The reply shot back. "So what are you angry about?" Truth was a reflex action. Most people took their time, and came out with a guarded response, keeping truth at bay like an unskilled matador, desperation covered with years of practice escaping from drugged bulls. Drugged bulls don't think.

A vole shot across the path in front of him, a tiny white butterfly danced on the spot and he was reminded how the day before a red admiral had landed – and stayed – on his shorts.

"It thinks you're a flower,"said Merrick. The admiral had remained still, vaunting its colour in the sun.

The path traversed nimbly by the vole was a single curving track mown out like a rustic athletics arena in an otherwise wild part of the garden. He waited, wanting the fox to pad into view and face him, all of a sudden. They'd said it was a grey fox, a vixen, with cubs to feed. The decimated chicken population was on his mind. The previous day, to others' amusement, when the consensus of remaining broodies had been eight, he'd counted nine. Much as he hated carnage, and had locked up the chickens with rigid care in the evening, he badly wanted to confront the fox. In one of the novels he was reading, a boy's imagination mingled with reality till the borders lost control; he wanted to live that conflict, feel the two forces and let them bear him along in their union, unsure where one started or the other ceased. The red admiral spun back into view, then was gone.

In contrast to the twinkling colours on this side of the garden, he knew that on the other side, hanging in a tree, was the head of a deer not long dead. The fox had feasted on its carcass; so had the family labrador. Now just the head remained, its antlers imposing, its smell rank. The first thing he thought of was 'Lord of the Flies', but a split second after that came the thought of a grey vixen rolling in the deer's now-rotten flesh, adding its vulpine musk to the already rancid aroma of a corpse not properly hung. No one knew how the deer had died, but for the boy its rotting head rendered it heroic status. His mind buzzed with symbolism: savagery, abruptness, flies, quivering knees, innocence, carnivores and sunshine. He felt a thrill of ownership, as if the animal were his.

A large cloud scudded overhead, blanketing the sun. Robbie was staring down into blackness, and, as the cloud passed over, slowing down somewhat, he saw the skeleton emerge back into the light, antlers last. Elephants tusks came at him, a rhino horn trumpeted up an African savannah, swordfish swam. In the distance he heard a female voice call his name, which reassured, and he gently reached up to touch the deer's head. A tinge of yellow crossed his vision; the goldfinch had watched his every move. He rubbed a scone of mud from his fallen sock with one deft flick. Would a smell on his hands give him away? He walked out of the old garden, closing the gate with care.

The vixen could come back that night.

By the time they reached the car park for the fête it was raining steadily, cloying English rain that permeated clothes, especially water-proofs. Lachlan missed his dry-as-a-bone, feeling vulnerable in an old Barbour of Sam's. But he was amused, donning the English uniform of countryside green. Merrick's hand appeared in front of him, open and pink, eyes just avoiding his father in anticipation. Robbie watched across a car bonnet; he was walking with Pauline, whose glasses were misting up despite prodigious efforts to clear them every four or five yards; under them all the ground squelched satisfyingly. Robbie avoided comment.

Stall-holders seemed oblivious to the drenching. Water fell down off-white canvas held up by dirty ropes, over which now and again people stumbled for a moment. One man cursed beside Merrick, who was unable to translate his oath, resolving to ensure none of the guy-ropes proved his undoing. Pauline went to a trestle table beaming with home-made comestibles. Robbie wondered which items she would purchase, surprised to see her plump for the oddly-shaped gingerbread figures, several of whom were missing an eye. But she spurned the tall chocolate cake. He took his eyes from it quickly so she wouldn't see his disappointment, yet had the feeling she had seen anyway.

"What's terrier-racing?" said Merrick. Fastening the Barbour, which lacked more than one button, Lachlan kept one hand to his throat, while with the other he led Merrick through the quiet crowd. In a pen surrounded by corrugated iron, four brown and white fox terriers chased each other round the end of a makeshift track down which they had run pell-mell, unaware of 'lanes' marked out by bitten string. Numbers were painted on their rotund backs.

"I like number 4," shouted Merrick into the wind. Owners forcing a smile struggled to recapture their shrieking dogs, one of which cleared the side of the pen and darted under a thorn hedge. Its handler, a plump woman with rosy cheeks and no hat, was unamused as she stood straddling the corrugated iron, hefty footprints embedding themselves. A knitting-needle marking the finish-line had been knocked flat and broken in her exertions. Merrick looked up to catch Pauline smiling, gingerbread men now sodden in her ungloved hands that looked chafed. A man with his weight on a crook announced the next race would be starting in five minutes.

"Going to be chaos, Dad," said Robbie, surveying the canine stadium. "Look, the ink on the numbers is running in the rain."

He was right: number 1 was the only distinguishable terrier as the rain splattered down on them. Robbie saw a fresh dog being placed at the other end, by the start. Unfair, he thought, but nonetheless gave 50p to a small man handing out numbered slips of coloured paper, indicating the chosen dog. Merrick had kept his eyes on what was once number 4: his money went on that warrior. A serious-faced woman at the start looked over to the hedge into which the truant had fled, but seeing only the bootmarks of the sturdy rosy-cheeked handler, abandoned her attempts at a full field and dropped a large red handkerchief into the mud, where- upon the dogs leapt free of crouching handlers and dashed for freedom, tumbling over the weakened string, burrowing into each other. Robbie's dog was not one of the crowd; finding itself alone towards the end of the course it stopped, looked around, and stood shivering, not keen to move at all.

"Come on, you good thing," shouted Robbie, irate at the dog's defiance. Two contestants emerged from the mêlée and shadow-boxed each other down the course before one of them got bored and bounced past the prostrate knitting-needle.

"That's mine!" roared Merrick, though its number was merely a blob. He ran with his ticket to the small man, whose betting slips were now redundant, and returned, hand clasped.

"How much?" said Robbie, turning away from his triumphant sibling.

"Enough," came the reply and the winnings were stashed into his wet pocket.

"You dropped one," said Pauline, kneeling down to pick up a 50-pence piece. "Every little counts."

The fortune-teller's tent was abandoned; she had seen the weather coming. Most of the onlookers were on their way home; it would not clear up now. A row of windcheaters huddled together on a rack, above gloves in plastic bags and flat caps, one of which Lachlan tried on as they passed. Both boys saw him; neither spoke: not even their father would be that stupid. But Merrick turned round again a few seconds later, to make sure. Tractors and farm equipment stood help-less in the rain; plastic bags rippled noisily; still the ground squelched. In Pauline's hands a gingerbread man shed his head, which gave Merrick peculiar satisfaction: he waited for the others to be dismembered.

"Looks like we'll have to postpone the barbecue ... sorry, barbie," said Pauline, with a rueful look.

"No worries," answered Robbie, "there's still tomorrow." Mentioning it, he realised that tomorrow was their last full day in Lakeland. Feelings filtered through his head, strong feelings that needed to be kept apart, not allowed to conflict: he was keen to be home, but Cumbria was making an impression on him. Next time he wanted Rebecca to be with them, not to displace Pauline, but complement her. He felt a need to fix the date of this next time, have it in his head, a surety when he went home, something to aim for. Hadn't his father said this was their big trip, no chance of another for years to come? Robbie could come back on his own, at uni., before uni., whenever he could raise the airfare. He climbed into the car thinking of this, another time capsule, in which he'd be secure. Lachlan and Pauline chatted with gusto: did his father miss a woman's presence as much as he did? He needed to find out.

Back at Hawkthwaite, a brightly painted car announced that the Stanburys' other son, Neil, was back for the weekend. He was working up in Keswick with his girlfriend, and only came home intermittently. Sam introduced their Aussie visitors, and they set off for the village pub.

Neil was an extrovert, enjoying his year off before university; he was a great man with kids, forging bonds without effort, sensing the whims of the young. Within minutes of their arrival at The Poacher's Bag, he was introducing the two Aussie boys to the complexities of shove ha'penny. He lit a fuse in Edmund, too, who paired up with Robbie. Outside the rain had relented, clouds of charcoal grey were less opaque, but the wind wailed on.

Lachlan was finalising plans with Sam and Pauline. No word from Iain would not defeat him; he'd decided to send the boys home to Melbourne on the day planned, while he stayed in England for one final attempt at gaining access to his twin. Sam was more dubious than Pauline, who was sure the Newcombes would honour their offer to look after the boys.

"I only need three days," said Lachlan, unsure why he was being so persuasive. "And then I'll be back, more settled, a happier man." Sam was still to be convinced, which angered Lachlan: after so much internal agonising, all he now called for was a rubber-stamp.

The arrival of Cumberland sausage ceased plans.

"He loves being devil's advocate," said Pauline, fingering a chip whose life expectancy was halted as she spoke.

Sam looked up, brown eyes focused on Lachlan. "Christians don't go for that, do they?"

"Oh, I don't know. A good Christian will relish the combat."

"And you are?"

'Not quite such a good Christian."

"That's duff," laughed Pauline, extracting another chip, this time from under Sam's well-stocked steak and kidney pie.

"And you call that steak?" probed Lachlan.

"Best rump."

"Sirloin's the best, not rump."

A bulging plate of vegetables landed under their busy mouths.

"South African?" teased Lachlan.

"Cyprus," answered Pauline, quickly, whipping the wind from Sam's sails.

"You know we've got a lemon tree in the orchard?" he challenged Lachlan.

"Next to the orange grove?"

"Avocados in the old garden."

Robbie pricked up his ears.

"And cumquat on the top lawn."

"Game Sampras," triumphed Lachlan, and the air rang with laughter.

Unperturbed, the foursome continued apace.

When the boys went to bed, someone, probably Neil, was intoning 'The Magnificent Seven'. A tumbler of Balvenie malt sealed the evening; another one, the night.

"The last day," said Merrick as they walked across the fields to early communion in the 17th century village church. There was a pause. Lachlan knew well the dangers of trying too hard to make a day tingle; for this one he would be a paragon of calm. Sam had been due to accompany them, but a difficult calving before dawn made that impossible.

282

There was no sermon at early service, which pleased the lads: there was no choir, which displeased Lachlan. A cluster of worthy village dames glanced round as the trio entered, Lachlan's "Good morning" sounding unfamiliar to his sons. The vicar was a serious cove, intent on briskness; it was not much more than half an hour before they rewove their steps to Hawkthwaite.

The smell of bacon assailed them long before they stooped through the small front door; Pauline waved from behind a generous frying pan and Merlin came bounding to greet them. It was a Jane Austen return from church without the landaus. Sun streamed in through the kitchen window, but clouds already hovered over Seascale.

"God bless us all," rang out behind them as Sam tramped on to the cobbles and shoe-horned his feet from loyal wellingtons, the gesture slaying Merrick's curiosity as to the use of that particular piece of wood stacked under the porch.

They devoured a hearty breakfast, home-grown mushrooms adding to the feast. Pauline suggested a roast meal up in the dining-room that evening, a rare honour, which left the day free. The motor museum, yachting on Ullswater, and the Ravenglass railway were summarily rejected, Lachlan remembering his resolve. Pauline had a bowls match and the older boys would be hors de combat until noon, but Sam pronounced himself eager to join them.

"Something we'll remember," ventured Robbie, who wanted to stay as near to the house and grounds as he could. Sam looked at Merrick, who stayed silent.

"Muncaster Castle?" he suggested. "There's an owl centre there."

Nods stole round the table.

The castle dated back to the beginning of 13th century, not an easy fact for the lads to assimilate. The turn-off into Muncaster grounds was a nasty one; only the week before there had been a serious accident, Sam explained, as he waited to enter the drive, lips pursed, thumb tapping impatiently on the steering wheel. Once out of the car they were confronted by signposts: Creeping Kate's Kitchen, Carriage House Gift Shop, Wild Flower Meadow, The Owl Shop, Wildfowl Pond, Baby Changing Room, Owl Tours. Only the last-named held fascination, and they walked quickly under a turret.

To Merrick's despair, the birds were all caged; he hadn't expected that. The enclosures were copious by comparison with some zoos, but to him a cage was a cage. Robbie was equally unimpressed, standing rock-still as paths diverged. Ahead of them, a keeper made his way gently into one of the large pens. Merrick moved away from the others to the little owls. He liked the name: *Athene urctua*, and read the information solemnly, disturbed that the birds were still declining in Britain. Robbie preferred to see the birds, then read the information; he was taken by the severe eyebrows low over glistening yellow eyes, giving the birds an expression both quizzical and fierce. Merrick moved on to the barn owl.

The keeper came out of his cage and looked at Lachlan: there was a hint of threat, as if he was angry that he'd been spotted. In his hand was a shovel. Sam picked up a hint of tension in the moment, looking from one man to the other, mystified. Then the keeper moved away; his was a supple form, that covered the ground in large, loping strides, using the shovel like a walking stick. Bats hung in Lachlan's memory and were not dislodged.

"Thought I'd seen that guy before," he said in answer to Sam's gaze, and shrugged. The barn owl, *Tyto alba*, with its heart-shaped face, was endearing.

"We get it in Australia, Dad," chirped Merrick, "all over the world in fact. And it's knock-kneed; look!" Further scrutiny of the bird told them of its varied vocabulary: purrs, hisses, yells and screeches, and that its nervous system was the most complex and advanced of any owl. The bird's habitat was threatened not only by so many barn conversions and repairs, but also because, under intensive farming, field edges have been ploughed to the limits, and strips of old grass-land gone for good.

Robbie's attention wandered. The keeper was behind them now, about to enter the buzzard's cage. There was a reluctance in the boy to see in captivity a bird he'd watched wheeling free. The man entered without fear; he no longer held his shovel, and in his hand was a plate of raw meat. Two buzzards watched him from high up. He was nimble, climbing effortlessly on to a tree trunk to remove a piece of debris that must have come through the roof. With that movement the bat flew down in Lachlan's brain.

"Recognise the keeper?" he said, glad to have laid the ghost.

Merrick looked up, but Robbie was quicker. "Of course – it's the puppet. 1 saw him as soon as we came in."

Merrick couldn't understand their logic. The chicken population was decreasing, and here was Sam instructing Edmund in slaughter.

"The old cockerel. We'll eat it before it's too tough. Go and strangle the old bird." Merrick was intrigued, Robbie disgusted. But both went out in Edmund's wake, following him in silence down to the hen-house. The old cockerel wasn't there. Robbie's face blazed with triumph: self-preservation had won. But he reckoned without Edmund's perseverance, handed down in Sam's family for aeons; the teenager now set about combing the vicinity. Two of the younger male birds panicked, colliding as they both sought the gatepost's brief refuge. Edmund ignored them, intent on his quarry. The other hens fluttered clumsily into and out of his way, sensing his blood lust, not sure of his methods. Merlin had come down the path, snorting: Robbie had the idea they were all being watched by a fox.

A cry from the other side of the hedgerow informed them Edmund had sighted the cockerel. Robbie dearly wanted not to see what happened, and dived onto all fours under the hedge. Merrick stood his ground, fixing his stare on the wood to their left. But Edmund's sense of theatre was strong: he carried the squealing cockerel, already spraying black feathers, into the arena outside its shed.

"Thing is to be quick," he said to Robbie, who'd spun round under the hedge. The cockerel squirmed and swerved in Edmund's big hands, but a reprieve was too much to ask. As the older boy's hands sought the bird's neck, Merrick jumped off the gate and walked quickly to the house. He was too late to avoid the sound, though: a loud crack rang out in his wake. One final effort lifted the bird out of its captor's arms and onto the ground, where it ran round in crazed circles, its head hanging down to one side. Robbie buried his face in his numbing arms, hating Edmund, and admiring him. The bird collapsed, attempted to get up, then fell in a squirm of feathers onto its side in the black dust. There was no dignity as it lay twitching. Why didn't Edmund put it out of its pain? He merely watched, satisfied, as Robbie watched, horrified. Finally he stepped into the arena, the scuffed ends of his toe-caps landing a cruel touch to the scene. Robbie wanted to assail Edmund with steel caps like that. Kick him again and again. The bird ceased its throes of death and lay still, cinders on its wing. Edmund walked forward, but at the same time Robbie scrambled up from out of the hedge, not wanting to witness the boy's moment of triumph. By the time he was outside the hen-house, smacking his hands to get rid of the straw, mud and droppings, the evening meal was hanging from Edmund's calloused hands as he walked away, even his back view exultant.

Five minutes earlier Merrick's return home had not been anticipated by Lachlan; as the boy bent to use the quaint boot-remover, he heard his father in the parlour.

"So I'll stay. The boys'll be fine. Dave and Jo know them like their own."

"Certainly seem to," Pauline's voice was steady; in Lachlan's, the boy detected tremors.

"And it's only three days," he added after a pause. "No time at all, really."

"And if Iain still won't see you?"

"I've tried my best. But he'll see me."

Merrick walked in, hands in pockets. They heard the front door close of its own accord.

Lachlan looked at him, his face asking whether the lad had heard. Merrick nodded, and made for his father's knee.

"We'll be fine," he said, looking across at Sam. "We always are."

Pauline put her mug on the grate and got to her feet. Supper in the dining-room needed to be prepared. They heard Edmund and Robbie walk along past the kitchen window to the back door, and Merrick left Lachlan to finish off his chat with Sam.

The dining-room was like a museum to small colonial eyes. Its temperamental door-handle sometimes denied access, or delayed it, but, once inside, it was unlike any other room. Across from the door a huge french window led out onto the top lawn, beyond which the screes could be seen. Green and gold curtains, a welcome combination for Aussies, hung waiting to be drawn; to Merrick they were as wide as a theatre's curtains he'd seen in books. The furniture was aged, dark and mysterious, but the portraits were most striking, seven of them, also dark but closed-up, denying the mystery, making you prise it out arduously, over time, with which they were in cahoots.

Merrick made for the darkest portrait of all, that presided over an intricate sideboard, hand-carved centuries ago. The background to the painting was darker than ebony; a sword tapered away into it, hilt holding a muted gleam. The man looked uncomfortable, stretching up, like a ballet dancer on points, to attain loftiness and repel the more than cursory gaze. His face was hostile, tweaked at the cheeks for the sake of haughtiness, bushy eyebrows joined over a nose of consequence. It was a woman's mouth, which complicated things, adding a softness quite out of place. An off-white ruff burned the sallow neck, the hair was limpid, lifeless, the waist thin, like the legs. No one had ever sat for the picture; it was made up of composite features, like an identikit picture of its day. This man had never been, Merrick was certain. And he never would be. Except in the eyes of the painter. Merrick looked at a faded gold label in the centre of the frame: Arundel Stanbury 1740-79. Not very old. What had he died of? There was nothing save the dates to link him with the world he had eschewed. Arundel? Merrick rolled the name around; his father would roll the 'r', as he had in christening his sons.

Merrick moved over to the woman. She sat side-saddle on a pit pony, snow unfurling behind her, picked out with tiny dots. Her expression was consciously inscrutable, but the artist had tried too hard, with the result that her expression lost human softness, offering instead a face-pack elusive and austere. It was hard to picture her eating a hard-boiled egg, or moving on the burdened horse. Looking at her was disturbing; Merrick's gaze drifted away, to a dirty red wine glass abandoned on the mantelpiece. Next to it was a photo-graph, a babe in Victorian dress, with no clues as to its lineage. All the expressions were outmoded; they bored him. He was gazing again out of the window, towards the screes, when there was a hand on the door- handle. Merrick did not turn round as the door opened, waiting for the newcomer to be identified, sure it was Pauline about to lay the carved oak table.

But it wasn't Pauline; it was Robbie. He advanced towards his brother without speaking, until he stood at his side. A blackbird swooped down from the tree to their right.

"Did you see how Edmund choked that chicken?" said Robbie, quietly.

Merrick nodded, mouth pursed. "He was impressive," said the boy.

Pauline appeared at the open doorway, unspotted by the pair.

"Want to set the table?" she asked to the back of their fair heads.

"Is the carving knife truly sharp?" asked Merrick. "I think it might need to be."

Later that evening they sat round the table, seven of them, one for each portrait. Candlelight gave the room a different lustre; Lachlan had not eaten in a room like this before, surrounded by ancestors crouching in aspic. Despite their looming departure and his meeting with Iain, he savoured the evening, trying to store it up for later benefit. Pauline, noticed his serious mien.

When the meal was over, Lachlan lingered, now in charge of the flames. He reached for the heavy curtain, yanking it two feet open; at once the flames trebled, skipping outside now, their glow fainter, assuaged. He kept his eyes on the outside flames and blew; two hardy candles fought off the sudden draught and came back to life. A portrait sneered at his attempt. He was in no hurry. Then he gutted the remaining flames with his fingers, and made his blind way to the door. He turned on making contact with the mischievous handle, gazing back into the darkness.

"Store it up, like pollen," he whispered, as a draught tickled his neck, and he made for the boys' landing.

They left after breakfast under a gentle sky. Robbie had got up early, aiming to walk up to Table Rock; hoping to catch sight of a deer, he had hovered in the wood, but without success. Although Pauline cooked bacon and eggs, with oat-cake, black pudding and tomatoes, the meal could not alleviate a heaviness in the atmosphere, and it was with an odd sense of relief that Lachlan rose to collect their bags. Sam was out with the cows, the teenagers still in bed, but by the time Lachlan had loaded the luggage there was the full complement to farewell the trio. Robbie felt sad, Merrick was thinking of the plane trip home and a part of Lachlan, as so often, had already left, but as they nosed slowly down the drive all three felt emotions not dreamed of six days before.

Where the gravel ended, a branch lay across their path; Merrick jumped out to remove it, his reaction taking Lachlan by surprise. A milk-float squeaked past, away from the village, and the car turned out onto the road. Running alongside the edge of the field, Lachlan saw over the hedge the Stanburys still huddled together at the porch as if for a Victorian portrait, hands aloft. A spasm of homesickness reared up inside him. He swallowed. Robbie was studying him hard. Sun hit the windscreen as two pheasants dipped over the hedge ...

CHAPTER TWENTY FOUR

The sun played British Bulldogs as they drove south. Layers of cloud wound round sudden patches of pale blue. Through the village of Gosforth and on to the main carriageway, Lachlan turned right and started to climb the fell road. Views of the sea teased sporadically; Sellafield Power Station loomed, gaunt, in the rear mirror, and always there were sheep at the edge of the road, moving at the last minute. A car hurled itself at them round a sudden bend, its driver bent over the wheel, rattling it with impatient thumbs; tyres slipped where asphalt met heather, and the car was gone over the crest behind them.

"Dangerous," said Merrick, in the passenger seat. "English drivers."

"That was a French car," corrected Robbie.

A nod confirmed Lachlan's agreement, cut short by another wandering ewe. Towards the top of the fell they met mist emanating from high to their left, where it blended with cloud, greyer now. They dipped over the fell summit, and gathered speed downhill, isolated farms standing solitary, as they had for aeons.

"There aren't any people," said Merrick, expecting a caravan of gypsies or at least a gang of rustlers in the growing murk. "Must be market day again already." The week had flashed by; two days and the boys would be in Melbourne.

"Dave'll meet you at Tulla," said Lachlan, picking up Merrick's drift. "And I'll be back three days after you."

"Deo volonte," said Robbie, his head on one side. He'd

taken the phrase on permanent loan from Rebecca, to be sparingly used. "When's lunch?" he asked, fingering the paper into which Pauline had packed ham and cheese sandwiches.

"Much later on," answered Lachlan. He stopped for a caravan to cross an ancient bridge, and drove on towards the motorway.

He'd asked Sam where would be a good place to break the journey; Sam had gazed into the distance, where nothing was visible, and scratched his elbow.

"Kenilworth Castle," he said at last. "I grew up near there: it's a tad out of the ordinary. But, like the Coliseum, you need to walk round it before you go inside." He proceeded to give Lachlan precise directions to the midland town, close to Birmingham's maze of roads.

In the event they came upon the town with ease, coloured flags decking pubs that sat close to a tree-lined street. Traffic rolled slowly past as if quelled by a dose of laudanum; the boys clambered out. Locking the car, Lachlan saw them sprint off towards the castle, its deep red stone burnished by the sun. The mist on their fellside road had long since vanished.

A path led down to the side of the ancient fortress, tall grass stems waving when a gust of wind blessed them. Butterflies whirled through summer air, changing course wildly into unguessed directions. Lachlan liked their random patterns, knights of hazard on fragile wings. He followed the boys along the path, nettles scraping against his knees, and, further down, his feet, where Englishmen wear socks. He saw Merrick take off his T-shirt, keeping up with Robbie as he raced along. The path wound round the ancient keep, pressing against it in a sudden outburst of vulnerability, then dived off left again, this time abandoning the castle for good.

A stile led through tall corn into which the smaller boy disappeared. The path ran true, and Lachlan smiled to think there must be real bush in England, perhaps over the Pennines, or on Exmoor. Just as he thought of taking a photograph with the disappearing castle behind, a cyclist came towards him, his knees touched for a second by bobbing sheaves on either side. Lachlan asked the man if he'd mind taking a photo of them. Throwing his bicycle into the corn, he waited for Robbie and Merrick, who retraced their steps. The back wheel of the bike was still spinning; its whirring was heard in the silence as the man pressed the button.

"I moved," said Merrick.

The cyclist held up the camera to take another shot. As he handed back the camera, Lachlan noticed blazes of eczema on his hand.

"Cheers, mate," said Lachlan. "The castle came out well?"

"Fine," returned the cyclist and picked up his bike, the wheel now almost still. Lachlan took one last look at the castle, and walked on. Another stile led into stubble, where two kestrels had just made a kill; one darted down with a squeal, while the other hovered over a hedge. Robbie wondered how kestrels would fare in competition with a buzzard; he thought of the caged birds of prey back at Muncaster, going through endless days of captivity, days only distinguished by different faces prying into their rusting domain.

"Where are we heading, Dad?" asked Robbie astride a wall, on the other side of which two horses stood guarding their space.

"Good question," said Lachlan. The spinning cycle wheel jumped into his head as he stepped down past the taller horse, a bay.

"Watch the back legs, men", he cautioned, as the two boys brushed past the steeds. Ten minutes later, sitting up against the wall of a barn housing goats, they ate Pauline's picnic.

"We'll just have time to take in Coventry Cathedral," said Lachlan, putting the rubbish bag into his rucksack. "Most of it was destroyed by bombers early in the Second World War; they've built the new one right next to it. People say it's remarkable."

The boys looked at each other; one last English relic they could handle. But only one.

At the entrance the statue showed St. Michael over-coming the devil; it was thirty-five feet high, unmissable from the cathedral steps. Merrick, turning from the ice-cream van, was taken aback. The horned devil was in chains, under a muscled angel with a spear, whose foot was poised just above the devil's belly. Merrick stood by Robbie, whose frown was summoned by the sheer size of the sculpture, as he tried to assess the expression on both faces. The angel's was easier to see but harder to decipher. There was no gloating, rather a wary sense of the struggle still going on. Robbie twisted to see how the devil looked, expecting him to convey a similar feeling. But the horns curled in on his forehead, darkening the eyes. His posture looked oddly comfortable, despite the chains, as if he was contemplating his next move.

Robbie looked up; a canopy straddled the gap between the new cathedral, darkly inviting, and the ruins of the old, clouds dipping where one stained-glass window allowed only shapes to be glimpsed. Merrick and his father were entering the new building; Robbie chose the old cathedral first. Red roses swung behind a small railing, and he ran up the steps into the shell. On the wall ahead of him FATHER FORGIVE was carved in sturdy relief. Robbie imagined the building ablaze almost as soon as the bomb had dropped, and wondered if the pilot knew he had bombed a cathedral. He must have had an inkling, and what then? A surge of pride as he raised his thumb to the co-pilot, a 'rush' as he looked forward to telling his mates on some airfield, near Dresden, that had also suffered much bomb damage, or had he been caught by the last defence of a Birmingham airgun and forced to limp over the Channel for a quiet landing outside Antwerp, his heroism unknown?

Next to the lettered wall, Robbie saw scaffolding, stacked furniture and a mass of orange hemp. Underneath the hemp were clothes, simple, old-fashioned, Biblical, as if somebody was putting on a play. Behind him he saw four lights in a line: had they just been switched on, or were they shining all the time and he'd not noticed? So that was it: there was a performance of sorts taking place in the ruins. He saw more scaffolding, a large cross on its side, and a warning, 'Pyrotechnics in use.' Walking to a poster, he read that a Polish troupe was performing Mystery Plays throughout June. But these were no ordinary whodunnits; it must be another sort of mystery, religious. His father would know. The boy felt at home among the ruins; he saw a tall spire that had survived the air raid. Opposite it was a statue that made him laugh out loud: it was grotesque, a squat monk with Latin sprawling across his front: 'Ecce Homo'. The notice next to the statue claimed the marble came from Italy. Grey banners leaned against more scaffolding, and Robbie moved on to another sculpture, a man and woman on their knees in an embrace. The work was entitled 'Reconciliation', had been cut in Japan, and a notice informed there was an identical sculpture in Hiroshima. In the middle of the open space a truncated flight of stone steps climbed to nowhere. Robbie stood on the top step, gazing through blasted windows to the city's lunchtime buzz. There was an even higher steeple behind the solitary spire, but that was locked in scaffolding, barred from impinging on the splendour of destruction.

The boy turned his head to the new building. On the huge glass screen were figures etched in silver, like brass rubbings risen from the dead. Saints and angels everywhere. There was no sign of Lachlan and Merrick as he walked past two sour-faced ladies, unsure if he was meant to pay. The cathedral was dark; behind the altar he saw a huge tapestry in green with a 'hip' Jesus coming out at you, not smiling. The stained-glass window to his right was spectacular; there wasn't a colour missed out, he realised, as he stared at the blocks of bright light. Crosses he made out, and flowers, daggers, haloes, arrows, but in the middle of it all the light was unpolluted, white, almost too hard to look upon. He wanted to twist the colours into a different sequence, like a giant kaleidoscope, to see what other clues emerged, to bring the turquoise sky out of its supremacy, re-fixing the central blaze.

In front of the baptistery window was the font, a rough, three-ton boulder from a hillside near Bethlehem. Robbie liked its primitive roughness: he liked, too, a Head of the Crucified Christ, hewn from the metal of a crashed car by a female artist in Florida. He looked through the visitors book, where a recent entry showed a man had come back to Coventry for the first time since singing in the cathedral choir in 1939. Visitors books were a signpost to adventure, giving away so little, and so much. The man had come back sixty years later, memories polished to mingle with the newness of things, a final visit before the greatest journey.

The boy walked into growing darkness, past huge tablets emblazoned with Biblical sayings. Only when he was near the high altar did he turn round and see the huge windows of the nave screaming with colour, their secrets not hinted at until the moment of turning. Now the tapestry loomed. He could see the hint of a smile on Christ's face, his body clad in the apron of a carpenter, surrounded by four figures, the Eagle, the Lion, the Calf, and Man, the four figures from 'Revelation' said the notice, along with the fact the tapestry was the size of a tennis court, woven in France. Robbie liked it better now. He moved past a mosaic showing an angel with the cup of suffering, sweat-like clots of blood falling to the ground. A crucifix from Czechoslovakia was dedicated in 1968 to world peace; weeks later, said a small notice,

Russian troops had invaded the now Czech Republic.

The last thing he saw was striking. The old cathedral bells, silent for more than a century, were re-hung in 1987 to mark the new cathedral's 25th anniversary. They first rang out to celebrate Coventry City's F.A. Cup Final win in that year. He saw his father and Merrick sitting on the steps outside; his brother got up and walked towards him. In Merrick's hand was a video which, he boasted, was of a tightrope walker. In 1884 Charles Blondin, the famous tightrope king had been refused permission by the authorities to walk from the parish church spire Rob had seen trapped by scaffolding to the remaining cathedral steeple, 295 feet tall. Last New Year's Eve an eastern European had managed the feat, now recorded on celluloid. Merrick guarded the tape all the way to Heathrow.

At the airport Lachlan had allowed enough time to change his ticket for a flight three days later; he was lucky. He was relieved the Newcombes would only have to look after the boys for a short time. He'd ring them once the boys had gone into customs. Melbourne would be just waking up.

The trio had five hours to kill in the terminal; a lurid, frazzled meal took only twenty minutes. Lachlan had nowhere to stay for the night, resolving to seek out a B & B not too close to the airport. Robbie seized the chance to finish another book, while Merrick fidgeted for hours. He could not understand why Lachlan took this uncalculated risk of seeing his brother when it was clear the desire for a meeting was not mutual. But he said nothing: the boys wished Lachlan luck and would see him Tuesday morning. Watching them walk down the wide ramp to departures, Lachlan thought five days could be a long time, elastic stretched till it burst, abandoned catapult on its side in the wind. With one look behind them, the two faces were gone.

He dialled the Newcombes in Melbourne, to be greeted by a

voice wrenched from sleep. Normally able to calculate the time difference by instinct, this time he had blundered. Lachlan explained the change of plan, apologising for landing his sons on the Newcombes yet again. Dave did not complain. They'd look after the boys. "No worries." For once that expression did not ring true in the jangled noise of Heathrow airport.

Lachlan drove for an hour before he started looking for a B & B. The longest day just past, light was starting to fade as he crossed into Warwickshire. Gone was the urge to find rustic charm; any shelter would suffice. None sprang out at him and darkness lapped up more light. Rounding a bend on the still busy road, he saw a large house offering rooms, and pulled into an empty car park. It was expensive, with modern fittings, no substitute for character; he sat in the bath wrapped in thoughts. Until now tenacity held sway over logic, but, his acolytes no longer beside him, he was suddenly vulnerable.

"Has to be done," he murmured, getting out of the bath.

His night wasn't restful, rain wakening him more than once. He had become tense by breakfast, a clinical affair in a room made over-cheerful by farmhouse plates racked up on an enormous welsh dresser; he felt an urge to hurl his token glass of orange juice at them. The landlady stuttered in too early with a plate of bacon and eggs, covering her faux pas with busy questions. She retreated with the plate, re-emerging cautious minutes later, but by then his appetite had deserted him, a train dwindling into the distance from a station long-overgrown. The toast was devoid of warmth, covered in a paper serviette. A man and woman punctuated his confinement with forced chatter; Lachlan stood up, suddenly, knocking an egg-stained fork to the floral carpet. As he bent to retrieve it, his hand flipped the laden side-plate and toast joined him on the floor. He uttered a full-bodied Australian curse, then smiled at the couple, cut short in their performance, and wished them a pleasant day.

In the hall his hands ran with pins and needles, his right cheek went numb, and phone numbers clashed in his head. Taking out a scruffy piece of paper, he dialled the prison, though he knew the digits by heart, and awaited the voice. But a different person answered this time, brighter in aspect, and put him through. The Wing Officer took time to recall their conversation, then affected concern in relaying that Iain was still not wanting a visit.

"Did you tell him we'd spoken?"

"I did. Yes."

"And he wasn't responsive?"

"That's right. Yes."

"You mean, no," said Lachlan, which was greeted with silence.

"Well, I'm not far from the prison at this moment." He forced the numbness spreading from his cheek down his side. "I could just turn up."

"We don't make promises," said the warder. "He could change his mind, but it's unlikely. In my experience, unlikely."

Lachlan let the phone fall from his ear and stood gazing in incomprehension. When he picked it up once more, the line was dead. He went to his room, packed, paid the woman from a wallet now empty, and threw his rucksack into the boot.

He knew exactly where the prison was, having looked it up on a map months ago, in Melbourne. Looking at the sky, he marvelled at new shades of grey, a tired magician's hand-kerchief that never changed colour, only shade. A motorbike came round the corner, too fast, and the rider corrected his machine, leaning out to the left, his elbow scraping the ground for a second. In the mirror, Lachlan saw him straighten, then accelerate into the next corner, unheeding. Had Iain's risk been reckless or considered? He'd loved horse racing since a country meet in his early teens, but, unlike Lachlan, it was the gambling side that spiked his thirst. And didn't slake it.

He started at the bigger Melbourne tracks: Caulfield, Moonee Valley, Flemington just before uni., abusing the freedom of days, taking his mates, initiating them into the thrills of the turf, cloaking his bets under bonhomie and good entertainment, skills he paraded without effort. On the occasions when Lachlan joined them he noticed his brother's changing coterie, some of whom were older than the Melbourne undergrads, more serious, drinking less, and calculating. After uni., Iain went to England, where he went through a swarm of girlfriends, all lavishly treated, and a series of jobs in public relations. Before he knew it, he found himself on a criminal charge of conspiracy to fraud. The sentence was four years; it had started six months previously and though his brother would not be in jail for the full term, there was only this chance for Lachlan to see him.

He looked at his watch; only minutes had passed since the motorcycle. He was fifteen miles from the prison, in danger of arriving too soon. The boys would be approaching Singapore, already at the end of this day that for him crawled under a snail's brittle shell. Robbie would be deep into a book, Merrick leaning forward in his seat pressing controls with vigour as he gazed at the tiny screen in the back of the seat in front of him.

A pub promised 'Morning Coffee' and Lachlan pulled into its empty car park. But the door was locked. He cursed, just as a human frame came to the other side of the glass and fumbled with recalcitrant keys. Lachlan stepped forward, but his move proved premature: the door was opened only a foot and a sturdy woman told him coffee was served from eleven o'clock. She closed the door smartly and again fumbled with her keys. Lachlan saw her frame vanish from the dark glass; the absurd notion came to him that she was a warder at the prison, and he flinched. He felt hemmed in by his thoughts, her behaviour and the strictures of a mission not begun. Turning his head, his body rigid on the pub doorstep, he saw only his hire car, and the empty car park. There was a sudden longing for company, for an Australian voice, a gum tree. He scratched the back of his neck, and cast a glance at his watch; it showed 10.07. Trudging to the car over loose gravel, his thoughts roamed to Brodie, then Angus, then back to the boys. Their plane would have commenced its descent. He decided to ring the prison once more. There was no dialling tone. Lachlan felt relief; all he was going to do was repeat the same desperation to the same unheeding voice.

He stiffened, purpose swelling in a far cavern of his head, and regained the car; its metallic chunk as he unlocked the doors was offensive. Within minutes he was turning down a lane to H.M. Prison. A chaffinch missed his windscreen just as the bleak building came into view. It was as he'd expected, though light blue notices surprised him. Parking in 'Visitors', he spent no time with thought, walking briskly up the steps to a recess in the glass. Two men kept their heads down on the other side, though he was sure both had seen him. The older of the two got up and sauntered over with a blank expression.

"Yes'

For all its preparation, Lachlan's mind went blank.

"I'm...Lachlan Stacey."

The revelation met indifference.

"My brother's here," stuttered Lachlan.

Indifference turned to boredom.

"So?"

"I've been trying to see him."

The man stared through him. His colleague said something Lachlan didn't catch and the gatekeeper chortled.

"Could I see the Wing Officer?"

The man put ringed fingers on the hatch through which they were speaking.

"You could do."

The phone rang, and was ignored.

"What was your name again?"

"Stacey. Lachlan Stacey. I spoke to him yesterday about visiting my brother. . ."

".. .who you say is here."

Lachlan nodded.

"I'll see if he's free."

The rings lifted slowly from the hatch and the man ambled away. Lachlan was sweating and moved to get some fresh air. A glance over his shoulder showed the guard had stopped to flick through a tabloid. He looked up at Lachlan and leered.

Minutes ebbed away.

"Mr Stacey!"

The Wing Officer slid out from between two grinding gates and nodded at Lachlan.

"Determined, huh?"

Lachlan nodded, seeking the man's eyes that roamed past him into the outside world. Traffic clanked past.

"There is a chance," he said, when he'd seen his fill. "Now you're here. But there's still the formalities. You couldn't see him till tomorrow, even if he agrees."

Lachlan felt nothing. "I'll have one last attempt."

The man looked at Lachlan with a scrutiny that had no room for warmth, and disappeared behind the grinding gate, having nodded at reception for re-admission.

Lachlan's mouth was dry. They won't serve coffee here, he thought, looking past the glass to where both men on the gate had resumed their seats. The one who had not dealt with him looked up briefly; Lachlan smiled, but his action was not reciprocated, leaving him stuck in mid-smile. It took minutes for his lips to uncurl. Outside, a lady in red struggled under her shopping; two youths jostled on the pavement; a post van pulled up with a squeal.

The gate ground again, a portly dark-suited man emerged and, with a look at the skies, scurried off. Lachlan waited. The post van departed with another squeal and the Wing Officer was beside him.

"Right, sir," he said, without emotion. "Let's get this paperwork under way."

Half an hour later Lachlan drove away. It was not yet noon, but he felt suddenly patient, concentrating on his last minute progress, not on having to wait until next morning when he would drive the road again. Now the hours did not weigh quite so heavily, he savoured an unplanned afternoon in middle England. There was a town nearby, to which he drove in search of lunch and liquid. It was not a picturesque place, rows of new houses lining the outskirts with predictable sameness. Pubs were the same, too, but he bought a paper and ordered a bowl of soup in the hostelry that looked least crowded. No one paid attention to him. An hour later he left the pub, booked into a nondescript hotel, for one night, went into a second-hand bookshop and emerged with two novels. He walked out of the town in the opposite direction from which he'd come, saw a stile and ventured down a track to the valley. A deserted farm cast him no glances, and some time later he sat down in a hedge-lined field to begin one of the novels. Set in France, it began with a journey. He read, and dozed, his soul more at ease. It was Friday afternoon.

At the hotel he took a long bath, ate a cardboard pie, and rang the Newcombes. It was 8 a.m. in Melbourne. Jo picked up the phone. The boys had landed safely. Lachlan spoke to them briefly, then had a quick word with their godfather.

"Take it easy," said Dave. "And good luck with Iain."

CHAPTER TWENTY FIVE

Having set off in good time, he was late arriving at the prison. Two tractors had been ahead of him on the switch-back, country lane, and, despite his flashed headlights, they made no concession to his haste. He scrambled into the reception area, expecting to see the two porters from yesterday, but there was not a soul in sight. He drummed on the concrete shelf. At length a man in black uniform approached the grill.

"I've come for a visit," said Lachlan.

"Got your I.D.?"

Lachlan cursed. It was in the glove compartment. He ran back, then presented it to the guard, who did not share his urgency. The visiting order was stamped and handed over, before the man strolled to a button and Lachlan heard the grill grind back. He stepped into a small space in front of a second grill, expecting it to open, but the first gate ground slowly closed, leaving him momentarily a prisoner. His brow was moist. On the other side of the guillotine a warder held a clipboard into his stomach as if he was about to surf on it. He reached for Lachlan's visiting order, then ticked his name off a list. There was no greeting.

Lachlan looked around the space in which he found himself. Off-white walls gave the backdrop for notices, of which there was no shortage. Most eye-catching was the sombre pronouncement, DRUGS ARE A GRAVE BUSINESS, beneath which a red skeleton hung astride a gaping sepulchre. The notice was repeated two or three times round the room. Lachlan counted eleven warnings about drugs and their consequences. One notice had the number '20' chalked up on a square before it continued, 'arrests this year for bringing drugs into this prison.' It was not halfway through the year. Next to this stark fact was, 'Please do not stroke the dog.'

He waited. It was quarter of an hour past the time he'd been given; as far as he could see, there was only one other visitor, a woman. The grille ground back again and three more people, all female, stepped, sullen, into the waiting area. One of the women was old, carrying shame as an extra burden, into the unwelcoming place. The youngest woman held a babe in her lifeless anorak, her arms jingling with jewellery. The third woman was elegant, attractive and smartly dressed, her long sleeves incongruous for a June day.

A burly warder came under a door-frame that resembled the metal detector in an airport; he held a cocker spaniel on a lead.

"Could you empty your pockets, sir," he said to Lachlan. "All but the loose change. And turn off your mobile phone."

Lachlan obeyed, as the man opened a small locker to shut the visitor's wealth away, briskly, pausing to check and then copy Lachlan's name onto the front of the locker with a black marker. There was just the one key, handed back to Lachlan. Three pushchairs lined the wall, with H.M. PRISON on the back in faded lettering. The women were waiting, used to the procedure. But something was holding things up. The women spoke little; he wondered how often they met in this pageant of caring. All the warders were gathered in the reception area, looking up at a screen. Lachlan moved over.

"There's been an incident," said a shaven-headed warder. "Half an hour ago. We're playing back the tape." Lachlan had failed to notice the cameras, which now were obvious. He looked round the room; three steady gazes ignored him.

"There," said one warder, without interest. The man nearest Lachlan pressed a button to wind back the film.

305

When the other two nodded, he pressed again, and they relaxed their stares. There was a whirring noise, a couple of clicks and the sound of pressure released. No one spoke. One of the women, the one with the baby, cursed, and was ignored. The men were now studying a photograph, a 'still' of the video film they'd been scrutinising. More nods, a grunt, and they emerged.

Lachlan was ushered against the lockers, and a warder gave him a pat-down search.

"Could you open your mouth?"

Lachlan obeyed, unsure what they were seeking. The women seemed to be spared a search, waiting by the metal detector. The windows round the room had white bars across them; on the other side of the portal was a green strip of matting with red lines marked on it. The cocker spaniel lay quiet under bare shelves.

"O.K. Come through."

The women waited for Lachlan, who passed through without incident, followed by the old woman. The elegant one was in her slipstream and the dog went straight to her.

"I'm not good with dogs," said the woman quickly. "Shall I come through again?" Lachlan saw the warders exchange a glance as she walked through, more slowly. The dog again made a bee-line for her. There was no barking, no drama.

"Would you like to step in here a minute?" said the shaven-head.

She did as she was told. "Will it be a closed visit?" Lachlan heard her say. A grunt came in reply.

"Get a move on," said the old woman, to no one in particular, her wrinkled face expressionless in its impatience. The baby, hitherto asleep, stirred. A warder led the remaining visitors around the corner into a long room with white regulation chairs. Comfort was not their hallmark. But instead of having to sit and wait, Lachlan was instructed to keep walking. He hung back to let the women past him, then swung into the visiting room.

It was surprisingly large. Low tables crouched between low chairs that were green on one side of the table, purple the other. Dotted round the room, apparently at random, were prisoners decked in red bibs. Cameras roamed at will. Lachlan had not been nervous until now. The women walked on with purpose. The red bibs bothered Lachlan: presumably they were to prevent embarrassment to the prison if another family member swapped places, leaving the inmate to walk free. How many had twins like him? The shaven-head pointed to the far corner.

"Stacey. Over there, sir."

Lachlan zigzagged between tables, knocking his shin more than once. The red bib he'd been pointed towards was not looking round, but staring at the table. Shaven-head tracked Lachlan, who needed to be alone for this moment. As his brother approached, Iain shifted in his seat, looking away from, not towards, his twin. Lachlan stood still, poised on the cusp of a moment he had sought for so long, but which now weighed heavy.

"Iain."

The head turned, familiar as his own; he saw the Adam's apple shift as his brother swallowed, a motion Lachlan echoed without thinking, but the expression when it finally rounded on him was blank. The prisoner stood up.

Lachlan was at a loss. He attempted a smile; his brother looked through it. The stillness circled them both, included the warder standing close by, and seemed ready to stay. It was too late for a handshake now.

"No boys, then?" said Iain. There was a pause. "I was expecting to see them."

"No boys," Lachlan replied. The words sounded crass. "They went back the night before last. They'll stay with friends."

"David and Jo."

Lachlan was surprised by the prompt response. "David and Jo," he echoed.

Across the room someone coughed. Iain rubbed his stubble.

"How are they? David and Jo, I mean?"

"Good. Still working as hard as ever. Jo does too much. Dave fixed Robbie's tooth not long ago."

"You didn't tell me he'd lost it."

"In a rugby practice. He was lucky it was only one."

"You put them in milk, I heard."

"You heard right."

"And Kathy?"

"No news."

"...is good news," Iain chimed in. "You know my opinion there."

"Maybe we share it now."

"Maybe."

"I'd rather share other things."

Pause.

"Such as?"

Lachlan shifted his weight on to the other foot. "Thoughts." Another pause. "Pain."

"You can't do that for me."

"You could let me try."

Iain looked away; the first impasse. Lachlan was surprised it hadn't come sooner. The sun slanted onto a drinks-machine, accentuating its tawdriness.

"Thirsty?" said Iain, watching his brother's gaze.

"Not yet. I will be, probably."

"There's time."

Lachlan jolted; there was not time. His visiting-hour would tease itself by, and then what? An awkward farewell, sealing another impasse? Iain was looking at the table. Both men were still standing; the alternative was too comfortable.

"Do you get enough exercise?"

Iain smiled. "We play football in the yard. And we walk every morning. Grandmother's Footsteps. Not a game, of course!"

"Of course." Lachlan eyed his brother with impatience.

He could share platitudes with warders, with fellow inmates. With his twin it should be different. He wondered how long it had been since Iain talked to a different face, one from outside his confinement. Then he asked him.

Iain looked up; his eyes still held a cold aspect, but for the first time Lachlan got a positive response.

"Cheryl came about three weeks ago."

"Cheryl?"

"A girl from way back. Nice kid. Didn't stay long, but she came."

"Were you glad?"

Another response. "After she'd gone I was. Not during the visit. A lot of pauses."

"I'm not surprised."

"Is this what you're expecting?" asked Iain.

Lachlan finally sat down. "Probably. A few word games, you were always good at them. Even the odd quip. And then..."

"Then?"

"Twelve thousand miles. I can't nip across for another weekend on the off-chance of your being communicative."

"Isn't that the risk you're taking now?"

"Risk? Surely. But I needed to take it."

"Who for?"

For whom? rang in Lachlan' s head.

"That's up to me," said Iain into the stillness that had now settled. "Right?"

Lachlan looked at his watch. Twelve minutes had elapsed. Iain was still standing; the warder moved a few steps away. In the corner the drinks-machine gave birth to a can that landed with a clunk. Thirst crossed Lachlan's mind.

Lachlan thought of Jo and how she might handle this sticky communion. He should have asked her before coming away. For her there would be a plan, a process, an evaluation and another meeting, the same hour next week; he had none of these luxuries, least of all another meeting.

"Iain, can't we just ...?"

"What!"

"Just bypass the guilt. Sweep it away, bale it up for an hour and take the weight off." 'King Lear's words shot into his head:

'The weight of this sad time we must obey,
Speak what we feel, not what we ought to say.'

He'd never thought Iain was comfortable when he lapsed into quotation; now was not the time to see if he'd changed.

The stillness moved down a gear. Atrophy hung in the silence. Lachlan tried another approach.

"I took the boys to the races. In Devon. Newton Abbot."

Iain was foxed. In his brother's mind Lachlan imagined demons playing havoc, pronged forks plunging into the skin of thoughts, darting off, inflicting pain somewhere else in his brain, now reduced to a brittle oasis. Iain's eyes seemed to be absorbing the forks' hard pinpricks, then sending them back, deadened. This had happened when they were children, on occasions less stressful, but Lachlan felt stirrings in the tight air around him. He shifted in the chair.

Iain's leg pushed his chair back and he sat on the arm of it. What was the opposite of deadlock? Two of Lachlan's fingers flickered on his right knee.

"Nervous?" said Iain, his voice a fraction warmer.

"Yes." *You could admit it, too.* It struck Lachlan, finally, that only his brother could devise the game plan.

Iain slid off the arm of the chair and faced Lachlan for the first time. He recounted the whole story of his crime, sparing no details. Lachlan was stilled. Silence dwelt between them.

"It's not the guilt," Iain salvoed, toe in the water. "It's being duped, conned. Into believing people. You like to think your judgement is sound, but judgement doesn't tick on with just the odd flicker, like a speedometer. It needs constant adjustment: assessment of people; when driving cars; making decisions at work; in the family. Judgement should be improving all the time. Not getting worse."

Lachlan looked at him, unsure if an intervention would stem the flow. He nodded, mouth open.

"How's your judgement, then?"

Iain's tangent surprised him.

"Not as good as I'd wish. If I'm honest." The last words caught in his throat. They were incongruous in a prison, came out louder than he'd meant, threatened the stillness. But no one reacted. Lachlan had an urge to say them again.

"Example?"

Lachlan knew the question would come. "Brodie, my co-director," he replied. "I think I got her wrong; she's shrewd, got a head for business, and she's a bloody good director. I was wrong on two of three counts."

"But not too late to do anything about it."

Lachlan nodded.

"There's the difference," said Iain. "I was disappointed in Harry Cudmore, but it was too late. No one's fault but mine. The law may be an ass, it seems so increasingly these days, but if you break it, you take the rap."

"And how is the rap?" asked Lachlan.

"Piece of pie," came the reply, and a cold smile caught in the wings of his mouth. Lachlan waited.

"Mornings are quiet. Afternoons dull. Evenings a rage." Iain was reverting to the Aussie vernacular.

"Any mates?"

Iain shook his head. "Not as we mean. Ninety per cent are on drugs. Not a reliable crowd. A sort of inverted English dinner party scene: predictable types, acting a rôle and going through the moves. Some of them well practised. Most are amateurs. And there's not a great deal of hope."

"And you? How are you on hope?" This was a risk but Lachlan had to push things.

"Can't answer that," came Iain's reply after a few seconds. "Not quite sure what hope is. 'The rack dislimns', didn't Shakespeare say?"

"I'm impressed. 'Antony and Cleopatra'."

"I'd have said 'The Tempest'." Iain was smiling more warmly now.

"There's got to be hope," said Lachlan, in a voice not as strong as he'd planned.

"Has there?"

A bell rang above them. Time had made prisoners of them both.

"Has there?" repeated the prisoner. Other visitors stood up or gathered themselves for the farewell. There was nothing to remember or collect up, just the farewell.

"Have I got to go?" said Lachlan, faltering. The warder came over to him, impassive.

"Just a few more minutes, sir. You've come further than most."

"Robbie would like his humour," said Lachlan when the man moved away.

"Tell me about Robbie."

Lachlan dwelt a minute. "Takes himself too seriously," he said, "but he's a grand kid. Doesn't miss a trick, bit like we used to be." Iain's face was unmoved. "A great reader, sensitive, he carries the world on his shoulders."

"Going to teach then?" No irony.

"I don't know. But he won't stay behind a desk. He's enjoyed this trip, so I expect he'll travel later. But he's vulnerable and not afraid to show it. It took me thirty-eight years to see vulnerability as attractive, not an unsightly birthmark. He's been spared that."

"Because you've taught him."

Lachlan's eyes looked down.

"And Merrick?"

"He's the pioneer, gutsy little fellow, a lot of mouth, no fear, wears his heart on his sleeve."

"Like his uncle, then?"

Lachlan saw a speck of pride. "Pretty much. He'll take a risk; Robbie shuns that. He got on well with Rebecca; she's

312

got a soft spot for rebels."

"I know."

"With causes. Have you got a cause now?"

Iain's look darted over Lachlan's head. "Not really. Not yet. I'll need to be out of here."

"But you can plan."

A pause.

"I can plan."

Lachlan saw they were the only people still conversing. In a far corner he could make out two faces behind a low screen: the men with the cameras. One of them came out from behind the screen and yawned into the empty space.

"So, where to from here?" Iain was staring at him.

Lachlan had no immediate response. He wanted to end the meeting on a strong note, but his mind raced ahead. He'd not planned the coming evening, but suddenly saw himself in Sam and Pauline's kitchen. There was a whole day till his flight.

"You can handle the rest of your term?" His words sounded false, as if he was banishing a child to some distant boarding school. 'Term' had finality, 'for the term of his natural life.' Like 'Hung by the neck until dead.'

"Who knows?" Iain was not going to let emotions stage-manage their parting. "Maybe I'll take up water colours."

Lachlan was unsure if he was serious. "Don't waste it on still life," came out clumsily. There was a silence. Iain scratched the back of his head as the shaven-headed warder began his progress across the room.

"You want the bib?" said Iain, with mischief.

"Too obvious for twins." Lachlan spoke slowly. "Where would you go?"

The answer shot back. "Dartmoor. A house in the country. Long track downhill, through a couple of gates. Old barn along from the house, lone chicken strutting around. A lot of tyres. Moon waiting to come up across the wooded valley. Distant gulls, a woman in dungarees walking out with

313

home-made scones. Toddlers." There was a sort of sob, caught at once.

"You should have been a set designer," said Lachlan.

"So the director could change it all round?"

"Maybe."

The warder stood by Iain. For a moment Lachlan thought he was going to whip off Iain's bib and grant a free pardon; instead, he took hold of the prisoner's elbow.

"Time," he said firmly, the one word cutting pain and relief, like a Wimbledon umpire. In spite of the third party, and the location, Lachlan leaned forward to give Iain a hug. But his feet were in the wrong place, the movement was clumsy, too soon over; there was no chance to cut, and run the move again.

"My love to the boys," said Iain. "Sorry not to have seen them. Next…"

"…time." nodded Lachlan. "Take care." The phrase was lame; Iain and his guard were already heading back to the cell, the bib half-undone.

"Iain," shouted Lachlan. His brother made an attempt to turn.

Lachlan's arm fell in the air. Too caring again, he realised. Always have to squeeze the minute dry. His mind ran blank. Somewhere a key turned in a distant door.

"Catch you later." But the door had groaned shut.

In a novel, thought Lachlan, as he handed back his badge, a friendly face would stop him just as he was leaving the main prison door and say that, having come so far, he was entitled to another visit this evening. But no face emerged. The two grills ground open, then back again. The man in the black uniform ignored him. Once outside, he put both hands in his pockets and turned round to look at the featureless granite building. The air was warmer now. A buxom woman bustled past him and up the steps into the prison. His task was accomplished, but the visit would take time to sink in. Apart from his sudden vision of the Stanburys' kitchen, he hadn't thought beyond the meeting with Iain, had no cognisance of the hour of day, nor of the expanse of time stretching to his plane the next evening. His mind was a barren canvas on which no figure stirred. He found himself with the underside of his elbows resting on the roof of the car. There was a desire to keep consciousness at bay, so he was only dimly aware of an engine starting up quite near to him, then chugging off like a motor boat. Lifting his elbows from the car roof, he noticed indentations in the skin as he rolled up his sleeves. A wasp wove round his head, droning.

In that moment he made up his mind to drive north. To Hawkthwaite. By Australian standards it was no distance, and he was sure of a welcome. Rebecca and Saul would be preparing to leave for their trip to Mallorca; he would call them later on, break up the journey. The boys would be about to sleep in Melbourne.

An hour later he was grid-locked in traffic on the M6, the result of an accident. The air was sticky, with no breeze. Stuck in the outside lane, he opened his door and stepped out. Three or four cars ahead, another motorist did the same. No cars were moving. Searching for his mobile, he punched in Rebecca's number, but was met by the patronising English voice message, informing him her mobile was turned off. Over the hum of the engine, he heard an equally detached voice warning motorists of long delays on the M6, and cursed. The emptiness he had not hurried away had been replaced by a pulse pressing down on him; he was trapped on a strip of asphalt unused to pedestrians, glad only that articulated lorries remained stuck on the inside lane, leaving him a modicum of breathing space. He climbed back into the car and tried Rebecca again. This time she picked up on the second ring; he began relating what had happened in the room with the crouching green and purple chairs.

CHAPTER TWENTY SIX

Having looked at the road atlas, Lachlan saw there was a quicker way to Hawkthwaite. After a pot of tea and flapjack at a cafe in Broughton, where he switched off his mobile phone, he turned onto a minor road. The country opened up as he came down a twisting hill and flashed over a cattle grid. Picnickers stood by a stream, mainly kids, but a woman held up her skirt over her knees, like an old-fashioned postcard with its dubious caption. A post-box just avoided his wing mirror as he swung sharp right, to be baulked by a slow motorist intent on the view. In his rear-mirror he saw the car behind pull out to overtake him, then realise there was no point. The driver looked like Iain. Not far down the road a sign indicated a left turn up a steep incline. The car in front took the turn, too. Lachlan lifted his hands off the wheel in anguish as the car behind roared past, the driver raising his arm in greeting and relief.

Suddenly the road became a challenge, hairpin-bends climbing under dark trees; to his amusement, the car in front accelerated into the switchback. He took the pressure off its beleaguered driver and put space between the two vehicles. A disused track to the right warned it was unfit for motors, while up ahead the mountain range unfolded into view. The sun was hot whenever he turned into it, sheep unperturbed by cars edging by. At the foot of the largest incline he skipped over a second grid, swung past a stately bed and breakfast and recognised the pub ahead. It was a sort of homecoming, and he felt a tinge of glee in not having warned the Stanburys.

Scrunching on the gravel he slowed down to take in the drive and its sentinel beech trees, presiding over arrival and departure. The cows were close to the fence, not under the trees, despite the sun, and he stopped the car beside them. There was the sound of a hammer close by, interspersed with the coo of pigeons. The cockerel struck up in the tree.

"Couldn't keep away then?" Pauline stood on the step, tea-towel in hand, smiling. He walked up and hugged her.

"I'd a feeling we'd not seen the last of you," she said. "Cuppa, or would you like a beer?"

Lachlan asked for the beer, still standing on the doorstep. The sun cut a wedge straight through the flowerbed, slanting down behind the house. Birdsong abounded.

"Sam's mending the water trough," said Pauline. "Would you believe the cows broke off the ballcock?"

"How so?"

"Years of rubbing. Cows love to rub. He'll have seen you arrive, that's for sure."

Lachlan walked across the cobbles to the field. The cows had moved away; he heard more hammer blows and made out Sam's figure by the fence under the trees, the silhouette of an ancient blacksmith at work. House martins whipped in and out of the eaves, the cockerel had gone quiet, and a brisk flutter of wings, followed by a squawk, gave away the hen roosting in the tree by the front door. A chair sat on the lawn, into the sun; beside it, a glossy magazine, its pages rippled now and then by the breeze. The beer was cold, and did him good.

A few minutes later Sam walked up the drive with a broad grin. He held out his farmer's hand, wiping his brow with his other arm, and said nothing. Pauline came out of the house with a beer for him, and the two men sat down on the latticed porch, knees bumping in the confined space. Sam raised his eyebrows.

"Better than I thought," said Lachlan, "but it took time. Bound to."

Pauline had poured a gin and tonic; she dragged the chair over and joined them. Lachlan explained his frustrations with the delay, and how apprehension had given way to calm once he was face to face with his brother. Pauline was amused by the red bibs, which earned her a look of restraint from Sam.

"So, how do you feel now?" asked the fanner.

Lachlan wasn't sure; he'd thought about that ever since walking from the prison, but thoughts still leaped like particles of light. He shrugged.

"Happy to have seen him. But cheated. We needed much more time." There was a pause. He knew his frustration at the brevity of their meeting would grow.

"But it's not a life sentence," said Sam, emphasis on the life. "He could come out to Australia again before you know it."

The prospect hadn't been considered by Lachlan. But something dislodged the prospect before it could settle. He took a breath. Pauline, already down to the lemon, was just thinking of supper when a car was heard on the gravel as Edmund and Neil, back from golf, drove into view. They greeted Lachlan, then disappeared for a shower.

"We'll eat in the dining-room," said Sam, into the silence. "Celebration."

Lachlan moved to the car and took out his rucksack. Entering the kitchen, he saw a large bag strung across a broom handle, suspended between two chairs. On the floor was an earthenware bowl into which liquid slowly dripped. Pauline was making jam the traditional way; the air hung with sweetness.

"Doesn't take long," she said. "Boiled the black-currants up last night, transferred them into the muslin jelly bag, let it drip overnight. All I've to do now is measure the liquid that's come through, boil it up again, add its weight in sugar and then bottle it. You could make great jam 'Down Under' with all your fruit."

Lachlan nodded. "Not sure we'd run to the muslin jelly bag."

"You'd like it here in early September," said Sam. "Crab-apple time. Pauline's wild jelly's unbeatable."

"He just likes shaking the tree," laughed his wife. "You know the one, up by the old barn. We get a good haul, and a lovely colour, too. I cheat sometimes and throw in a few raspberries for colour."

The simplicity appealed to Lachlan. He felt the same out in the bush, back home. Peace of mind, running deep. Stretching his legs to avoid Sam's, he was suddenly restless.

"Go for a walk," said Pauline, "after all that time in the car."

"Or a cycle," suggested Sam. "Bikes are all there. We'll not be eating till eight."

Lachlan plumped for the ride. He walked across the cobbles, avoided one of the chicks that was behind its siblings, as usual, opened the door of the shed and pulled out the bike. It was still warm as he cycled down the drive and turned left over the bridge, where days before two horses stuck their heads out from under dense foliage. There was no sign of them now. The air was thick with chicken manure. A mile up the road he turned off, down the tarmac track to Crag House Bridge, moving over for a tractor heading up towards him.

The last few yards were rutted with stones; there was a car parked in the shade, but otherwise not a sign of life. 'ANGLERS ONLY' said the sign, as he leaned his bike against the bridge, then vaulted the wall and strolled along the riverbank. A kingfisher would make the scene perfect. All was still, save the slowly flowing water, less muddy close-up. Another tractor started up some fields away. Knowing his loathing for shattered silences, Merrick would have spun round to catch his father's gaze. Lachlan looked at his watch; it was just after seven o'clock. Just after four in the morning at home; the boys would be asleep. It was strange not having them with him, not having their questions. Lachlan looked back to the bridge. From where he was, he saw its complete reflection in the river marked by floating leaves. A muted splash diverted him temporarily, but there was no further aquatic activity, and still no king-fisher. A seat to the side of the bridge looked inviting; as he walked towards it, he decided to ring the Newcombes between ten and eleven, once the boys had wakened, to check all was well.

From the seat he imagined a canvas by Constable, with Willy Lott's cottage. This was England at its best. He'd been lucky with the weather and he was going home in time for spring, although Melbourne's August was not often mellow; he'd have to survive that first. Easing his reverie, he was back at the bike. And hungry.

They sat outside the house with sloe gin and tonic, the smell of lamb wafting towards them. Two of the hens strutted about, enjoying peace from the roosters. The chicks had grown even since Robbie and Merrick saw them, their plumage more established. Butterflies danced in the evening light, while, higher up against the house, bats were preparing for take off.

"Mustn't forget the hens," said Pauline in the easy silence.

"I'll go." Lachlan seized the chance, forgetting he was in bare feet.

"Take the wellies." He went across the cobbles to the doorstep and dipped his feet into the vacant black boots. The rubber was cold on his legs, a sensation he'd forgotten. He walked along the curving path, avoiding a freshly-killed vole, past the kennel and down to the hen-house. There was no sign of action, just a muted clucking from inside the aged building. Its green door was ajar, weather-beaten, faded yellow towards the bottom, flaking. Lachlan ducked inside for a second, smelt the fetid air and withdrew. Pushing the door to, he noticed the jamb moved also. At the foot of the door, there was a gap; he nudged a cloven log into the cavity and upended a slate for extra protection. He tried to jam a pointed stake between the door and the stone lintel; it wasn't quite tight, but would last the night. Then he closed the gate, snagging home the top wire. They were going to eat in the dining-room; he'd better change.

He unlocked the door of the room with portraits and slipped inside, wondering how many details of the room were as he remembered. The screen embroidered with birds had been moved, but the dirty red wine-glass was still on the side-board. Beyond the wide oak table he saw through the window to the screes, pink heather sinking in the dusk. There was the same peace in the room, and he glanced round at the portraits, already old friends. It would be good to discern a change in one of them. The green vaulted ceiling he'd not noticed before, nor the number of cushions. Pauline had arranged a spray of dried flowers in red and orange for the hearth, and decanted one of the Aussie reds that stood on a silver wine-stand. Bottles sat on a low table next to an ancient record player; he'd not seen that before.

Pauline nudged the door with her foot, both hands busy with platefuls of food, and Lachlan crossed to assist her. Neil had extended his stay, while Edmund seemed to be at home indefinitely. Sam walked in last, bearing roast potatoes and vegetables, from the garden.

"Did you get food at the prison?" asked Neil with a glint.

"Alas, no," Lachlan replied. "That's why I came back here. Rebecca and Saul have left for Mallorca; I drove here 'on spec', as you say. No distance for an Aussie."

Edmund began questioning him about backpacking in Australia, the idea rapidly promoted in his future programme. Roast lamb absorbed the wine.

"Funny thing yesterday," said Sam. "I took the dog for a walk up to the barn, to check on the Land Rover. Suddenly, the hound went mad, and chased up across the field to the fence."

"Fox," said Neil quickly. Sam gave him a sideways look, then carried on.

"At the fence, the dog realised he couldn't get through after the fox. So he turned back, dejected. Once his back was turned, the fox came out and followed him all the way back to the barn, stopping on the hill, watching him eagerly. The dog was oblivious. He got back to me, and I lifted my arm to pat him. The fox was gone in a flash."

Sam threw back his head, and the others joined in his laughter.

"Hadn't seen you then, the fox?" clarified Lachlan.

"No. I happened to be in green. But the moment I moved..."

Sam laughed on, as Pauline rose to collect up the dishes.

"What's the pud?"

"I just knocked up a crumble. Blackcurrant and apple. That do you?"

"More than," said Lachlan, still smiling, and still hungry.

"You did a good thing. Going to see Iain." Sam's voice had lost its humour.

Lachlan nodded. Thoughts were overlapping inside him; he felt a millstone had been not lifted, but its weight shifted. In one way he'd achieved his objective.

"Listen!" Edmund's voice rang with alarm. Lachlan heard nothing at first, but Sam was on his feet, bounding across the dining-room, leaping the stairs from the hall. They heard him fumbling with a lock, then he was on the threshold holding his shotgun.

"Stay here!" he urged, climbing silently through the french window onto the lawn. They all heard the commotion: hens screaming, cocks crowing in quick succession as panic tore through the air. Neil and Edmund looked at each other, then at Lachlan. Pauline sat motion-

322

less, gazing out. It was almost dark, but they saw Sam approach the edge of the lawn. At that moment, a fox jumped over the wall, making for cover through the rough grass: a half-grown chicken was in its mouth.

Sam rammed the butt into his left shoulder, pivoted, and fired, the noise ringing round, alive. It was hard to see from inside, but Sam was still for a moment, then walked cautiously towards the stone steps that led down to the hen-house. Neil, Edmund and Lachlan moved over the step onto the grass. The fox had been hit in the head.

"Got him this time," said Sam quietly. "He's a wily old dog. See his ragged coat. He was slowing down, that's for sure."

The body had landed in the grass, a pattern of pellets in its head.

Sam said little; unclenching his left hand, he let the gun fall.

"We've lost so many hens over the last few years. Now, perhaps, the threat has gone."

No one spoke.

"Especially that time we lost seven at one go. Tiny chicks, crawling through that crack in the door with the fox eating them whole, one by one."

"There's no guarantee it was the same fox, Dad," said Neil.

Lachlan's thoughts were on the hen-house: his locking up had not been foolproof – he was the cause of these deaths. It did not seem wise to seek a pardon now.

"I saw it up at Table Rock the other day," said Neil quietly. Edmund looked at him. Their father was kneeling next to the corpse.

"What do you feel?" asked Lachlan squatting down.

"Relief.......satisfaction. I hate that word. Once you get close, it's different, it gets personal. He was a fine animal, in the wrong territory."

Silence. After a minute, they heard Sam's knee crack as

323

he stood up.

"We'll dig a hole in the morning," he said. "Leave it now. But keep the dog away from it."

Pauline stood some way back, her shoulders quivering a little. Sam walked past her and into the dining-room. Neil had picked up the dead chicken a few yards away in the grass; he threw it back towards the hen-house, deep in thought. Edmund was nowhere to be seen.

Lachlan stood, hands in pockets. The screes were invisible now; there was a chill. He wondered how his boys would have reacted to this kill.

Neil waited for him where the long grass ended. The night was still, though eyes were on them in the glowing darkness. Together they walked into the dining-room, resuming their places in a different silence. Pauline had cleared the plates; Sam was replacing the gun upstairs. One of the portraits was smirking on the far wall.

There was the noise of a shoe knocking the wood and Edmund came into the light.

"No more damage at the hen-house," he said, avoiding Lachlan's look. "The chicks are all there."

Lachlan said nothing.

"I think we could all do with a malt," pronounced Sam, walking back into the room. There was mud on his cheek, and a trickle of sweat ran down his jowl. He walked over to the sideboard and reached inside. Pauline arrived with coffee and they moved to the sofas, rarely used, Lachlan assumed, not comfortable. The malt was good.

Somewhere in the distance the phone rang. Lachlan was deep in thought, only just aware of his host's getting up to answer the call. He was even less aware of Sam's return, head round the door.

"Lachie?"

The Australian needed stirring.

"Lachie!"

He spun round.

"Can we have a word?"

Lachlan got up with apprehension, aware of the silence around him.

"It's David. From Melbourne." Sam's face was taut as he indicated the phone. Uncertain whether to stay, Sam hovered, his arm on the door-post.

"Dave?"

There was no second's pause as when Lachlan used to ring England years ago, but he could feel tension in the short-lived silence.

"Lachie... It's not great news, mate." Another silence. Lachlan pressed the phone into his ear, as if to counteract its grim information.

"There's been an accident, Lach. This morning, on Glenferrie Road. The boys..."

"Not both of them?"

"No, mercifully not. Though Merrick's in shock."

"Robbie?"

"Yes, Robbie. He... got his front tyre caught in the tram tracks. The driver couldn't stop. Robs went under the tram."

Of all the feelings Lachlan expected, blank loss of emotion was not one. His heart beat into the receiver.

"Is he ...?"

"He's bad, Lach. In intensive care at The Alfred. Best hospital in Australia. They're looking after him well."

"But maybe still not well enough." Silence. "Is that what you're saying?"

"No, it's not. They're fighting for him, mate. It's the head injuries they're worried about." Lachlan saw Robbie's fair hair flash past him.

"He had his helmet on?"

"Of course. They'd had a bit of breakfast after Jo picked them up at the airport. After you'd spoken to them on the phone, they went to lie down for a while, but you know what they're like. They certainly weren't going to sleep for long. The weather's crud, they floated around the house. Then about five Jo suggested a cycle ride before supper. She feels beyond words, as you can ima..."

"He's in I.C.U?"

"Yep. They got him there quickly. Jo rang me and I went straight round to the hospital. Sat with him till four. Then Jo relieved me. Hetty's with our kids. And Merrick's fine. Shocked, because he saw it. But fine."

Lines jangled in Lachlan's mind. He was unable to calculate the time difference.

"What time is it with you?"

"7.15. I didn't ring before because..."

"No matter." Lachlan thought beyond the numbness. "I'm due on the plane tomorrow night. But there's one leaves Heathrow at lunchtime. I'll be on that one."

"...and back here the next night. Evening, rather."

"So many hours."

A pause. "Only twenty-four, Lach if you can get on that plane. I know you've changed your flight once already."

"Irrelevant," said Lachlan. "I'll ring Qantas. They must have spare seats for emergencies." Dave chose not to query his friend's assumption.

The numbness in Lachlan's head was giving way to a tight feeling.

"I'm so helpless," he said. "He needs me."

"Jo's there still. We'll take it in turns."

Lachlan's thoughts refused to be sorted. He heard Sam's knee-joint crack as he shifted feet in the doorway.

"Better get going. Sorry, Dave. I can't be making much sense. Can't focus."

"Lach, just get here," came the reply. Another hiatus. Then they both spoke at once. Lachlan held the phone away, vaguely aware of Dave still speaking, then he let it fall onto the table. Sam walked into the room, his hand rubbing non-existent stubble on his face. Putting his other hand on Lachlan's shoulder, he tried to inject strength into his friend.

"Robbie's on the danger list," said Lachlan with a vacant

gaze. "I've got to go back. Got to reach him."

Sam was mute. He nodded, plotting a strategy. Outside the door there was a footstep, then Edmund appeared. "Is everything...?"

"Just leave us a minute, son," said Sam to a shadow already vanished. Turning to Lachlan he urged, "Let's ring Qantas."

Lachlan stood, entranced.

"I'll do it," said Sam, dialling directory enquiries. The number, when he obtained it, was engaged.

"It was me shut up the chooks," said Lachlan, suddenly, in a voice not his. "I'm sorry, Sam."

The farmer's eyes moved a fraction. "I'll drive you down to Heathrow," he said, firmly. Pauline had entered the room. "Can you rustle up a few sandwiches? And some coffee?"

She was downstairs in a trice.

"Do you want to grab your kit?" Sam's voice was trying to sound calm.

Lachlan looked up at him.

"Your stuff? Then we can get going. In your car. I'll sort something out for the way back."

Lachlan moved away towards the hall. He heard Neil and Edmund's low voices in the dining-room, where the curtains had been closed, and trudged upstairs, past a stuffed owl in a case. He'd never been into an I.C.U. ward, had only T.V. reconstructions to go on. All wires, plugs and empty space. He thought of Merrick trying to take in the shock of seeing his brother crushed by a tram.

Back in the sitting-room, Sam was trying Qantas again. Lachlan sidled past, downstairs and through to the kitchen, where Pauline was busy at the table. Outside it was clear, the stars defined in a northern hemisphere sky alien to him. There was no sound; he'd have been happy to hear the young cockerel, a squeaking chick, the annoying coo of wood pigeon, but there was nothing. The cobbles irritated his feet; he knocked into his bag lying in the middle of the path. Sam strode by to the garage.

"You can be there in six hours," said Pauline, on the doorstep with food and a flask. She put them into Lachlan's hands. "He's a fighter, Lachie. He'll win through. I've met the boy. I know."

Sam started the engine and headlights wove round the trees. "I'll just get my phone," he said, crossing back inside. Lachlan put the provisions on the back seat, then gathered Pauline into a hug. Tears couldn't be held back any more and he gave way.

"We're off, man." He hadn't heard Sam reappear and, before he knew it, they eased down the drive over gravel that now sounded soft. Lachlan did not look round, but he knew through the dark Pauline was waving.

They drove in silence taking the main road, not the fell road. Both men were wide-awake. A cattle truck rattled past outside Millom soon after midnight.

"He's still unconscious," said Lachlan into the gloom. "I think Dave said that. The longer that's so, the less chance of recovery."

"Not necessarily," said Sam, relieved that the silence had been broken. "You hear of people coming out of a coma long after they've had an accident."

'*Coma*.' The word sounded hostile, fatal and unreal. Lachlan thought of Jo sitting by Robbie's bed on a Melbourne day nine hours old already. Merrick at least would be safe with Hetty.

"Let's ring them," he said brusquely.

Sam passed Lachlan his mobile phone, but Lachlan's fingers fumbled. On his third attempt he coaxed a ring from the phone he knew so well. There was no reply.

"Where are they?" he asked Sam. "All at the hospital? Have they been summoned? And I'm not there."

"They'll have gone for a walk. Or some breakfast. Get Merrick out of the house."

They hit the motorway and swung south, eventually

stopping just past Birmingham. It was three a.m..

"We're doing well," said Sam as they entered the service station. Lachlan bit back a response: on a journey of over 12,000 miles they had covered meagre inches. His chest was tight, his breathing a conscious foe.

The place was desolate. Two lorry drivers stared at dry sandwiches, an unkempt couple gazed at each other, giggling now and then. Sam shook his head.

"Not exactly a cheerful time of night, is it?"

Lachlan showed no reaction.

"Shall we go?"

As they came out, dawn was beginning to stir. They bought petrol and drove on. Near Warwick they passed a fox squashed on the hard-shoulder. The men looked at each other. This one had suffered a painful death compared to the quick clean shock administered by Sam to his fox. The thought reminded Dave he'd have to bury the fox on his return. But he kept quiet. He clenched his hands on the wheel and pressed down the accelerator; adrenalin drove now.

It was 6.45a.m. when they reached Heathrow. Sam stretched, having pulled up in a space reserved for taxis, while Lachlan grabbed the sandwiches off the back seat. The coffee was welcome, but Lachlan felt unsure what to do next: the drive had raised no questions, now he had to act.

"I'll just ring Pauline," said Sam. "She'll have taken her phone to bed." Lachlan felt a stab of loneliness, his head hurt somewhere, he needed Sam's strength. A taxi hooted indignantly, making him jump as hot blood rushed to his left side.

"We're not staying," he shouted to the back of a cabbie, who ignored him.

When Sam returned he said only that Pauline sent her love. They parked the car.

Sam took up residence on a bench while Lachlan approached the Qantas desk. He was informed that, far from

329

having spare seats, airlines oversold in the expectation of passengers not turning up: this was the situation today.

"I can put you on stand-by," said the girl, "but we can't promise. If you come back at eleven, we'll know."

He looked at his watch; it was one minute to seven. Four hours of inertia. When he returned to the bench, Sam was asleep. Lachlan thought of Peter in the Garden of Gethsemane. He sat down and dozed; sleep was out of reach. When his friend stirred some time later, Lachlan told him the scenario. Sam made to get up, but was restrained. There was nothing to do but wait.

The clock refused to budge, however hard Lachlan scrutinised it. Eventually the hands teased towards eleven; he went back to the desk.

"Sorry, sir. We can't say anything yet." Lachlan was impatient, explaining why it was essential he took the mid-day flight. The girl was sympathetic, but his plea made no difference.

"Come back in ten minutes."

When he did, things moved fast. There was one seat. A hastened farewell with Sam, the farmer enveloping him, and he was jogging to departures. His twenty-three-hour journey was under way.

CHAPTER TWENTY SEVEN

"Can I get you anything, or are you just stretching?"

The bob-haired stewardess zipped back her curtain, taking Lachlan by surprise.

"Just stretching." But no smile came with his reply. The girl smiled anyway and was gone. He watched her progress down the aisle, leaning over passengers, picking up an empty cup from the floor. He wanted her to come back.

They were not halfway to Singapore, and still an hour behind schedule. Prior to take-off, a towing vehicle had broken down, leaving an aircraft stranded on the runway ahead; they were at a standstill for half an hour. Lachlan had known there'd be some delay. He had no appetite when the meal was served, and knew sleep was beyond him. It was a long haul, and dark now, but he'd been aware of daylight at the start of the flight; in his memory it was dark throughout the journey, or was that the other way, going against the hours to London?

Ahead of him he saw the stewardess talking to two flaxen-haired children, who wanted to visit the cockpit. After recent hi-jacks such visits were not encouraged, but it seemed these two small passengers might be lucky. The boy trotted off behind their brisk guide; the girl hovered, looking back towards her grandfather, who urged her on.

Lachlan's mind cowered on the edges of the hospital. He'd only seen intensive care units on television, lots of doctors, wires, drips, tubes, monitor screens, bleeping insistently into an uncertain silence. How many patients would be in there with Robbie? Would he recognise his son?

A picture of Kathy tripped into his brain. She needed to be told, but not yet, not by him.

Suddenly it seemed Robbie was in front of him, walking back down the aisle with assurance. Lachlan gave a cry. The fair-haired boy looked up at him, his assurance fractured, then sidled into his seat. The grandfather lent his head out and saw the girl holding the stewardess' hand high to avoid sleeping passengers. Lachlan's mouth was dry; somewhere his mind shifted, and he swallowed hard.

"Lovely kids," said the stewardess. "German. Good to use my schoolgirl languages for once." The curtain flicked back again, leaving him in darkness.

The sky in Singapore was the darkest he'd ever seen, like a dead pigeon he'd caught sight of recently, its head down a drain. Lachlan suspected the head was torn off, but did not investigate. He'd known the pigeon would re-enter his psyche.

He wandered around Changi airport, utterly forlorn. A door promising fresh air and a cactus garden led only to the rank welcome of cigarette smoke. He retched, and retraced his steps. No time had elapsed on the concourse clock: green bulbs flashed; he couldn't read the words. Letters riffled noisily, another destination added to the ever-moving list. The bulbs were bleeping; he turned away.

Time yawned, legs carried him back to the gate. Muted conversations were eked out around him. His plane lurched down a runway, its windows suddenly streaked with rain. The sky emptied its womb. Lachlan swallowed ready for take-off, saliva making contact with bile. His brain was reluctant to move.

As they prepared for the final descent into Melbourne, the captain's bright voice informed passengers that they had made up time and would be landing two minutes early, at 6.18 p.m. Lachlan had no reaction. He'd not thought about arriving at the airport, only reaching the hospital. Collecting his cumbersome bags, he pushed a numb trolley through waiting relatives, then felt Dave's arms round his neck, also numb. Neither man spoke.

Outside Lachlan felt cold as Dave took the trolley and pushed it in the direction of his car.

"He's stable," said the dentist into the vacuum.

Lachlan nodded. "Stable." Could mean anything. He clutched the door-handle, waiting for a click.

"It's open, Lach."

He sank into the passenger seat, his hands sheltering pins and needles. Despite flexing his fingers, the tingling remained.

"I want the story."

"The boys didn't seem tired when I picked them up Saturday morning, but Jo suggested they had a quick kip. They'd just woken up when you rang. Robbie was joking about how cold Melbourne was after England's summer. I took Harry to soccer, and when I got back, just before lunch, Merrick was reading on the verandah, legs firing like pistons as usual.

Robbie got up soon after and we had a spot of lunch. Harry had a party that afternoon and Emily was with a friend for the weekend. I had to go to the surgery, but Jo was happy to keep an eye on the lads. We mentioned an early dinner, then the boys could crash out." He winced at his unshrewd choice of vocabulary, but Lachlan paid no heed.

"I went off about 2.30. The boys were restless, so when Robbie asked if they could cycle round the block, Jo agreed, reminding them it was Saturday afternoon, and busy. They'd only be ten minutes...what's the percentage of accidents that happen within a mile of the home?"

Lachlan's eyes stared ahead. The freeway devoured their progress.

"But of course, they were more than ten minutes. A lot

333

more. Jo had been to the gate twice and was anxious. After an hour, she was frantic. She rang me, and I said I'd come straight home, looking out for them on the way. They'd probably lost track of time."

Lachlan's head shifted to stare at David.

"Robbie's good on time. He wouldn't have lost track."

"No, I thought that, too. Then, almost immediately, Jo rang again. Merrick had just called, very shocked, on a policeman's mobile. He was crying, and didn't make full sense. But we gathered he was at the corner of Glenferrie and Barker."

Lachlan knew the junction. Busy, not least on a Saturday.

"I said I'd meet Jo there. She was going to ring Hetty to look after Merrick. It was clear Robbie had been badly hurt."

Lachlan breathed in. A taxi inched past them, going too fast.

"When I got there it was getting dark and I could see little. Two policemen were taking statements outside the church; traffic was moving slowly. There was no evidence of an accident till I saw Robbie's bike against a shop window. Mangled."

Lachlan remembered a day spent cycling in England, where helmets weren't compulsory.

"Another policeman asked who I was, and we pieced together, briefly, what might have happened."

Lachlan didn't move. "What?" came from a voice dry as a Greek hillside in July.

"It was dusk, that funny light." The word 'funny' jarred.

"Bad light," said Lachlan. "Bad light stopped play."

"Robbie was cycling ahead, probably planning to go straight over Barker. Merrick would have been behind."

Lachlan tensed. He'd not known how the accident happened, despite imagining it a million times.

"The police think a car indicated right, suddenly, moving across in front of Robbie. His tyre caught in the tram track, hurling him from his bike. He must have gone over the car into the path of the oncoming tram. The driver would have been starting to accelerate uphill. He braked... it could have been even worse."

The cliché was inept.

"And Merrick saw that happen," came slowly from Lachlan.

"I think so." There was a long pause.

"Think of Merrick's dreams now," said Lachlan.

Dave was silent. They flashed past the bulwark of red concrete that had been recently erected in the name of modern art. It irritated Lachlan. The hospital was five minutes away.

"Tell me about Merrick."

"Again, this is conjecture. He's not wanted to talk. But he saw Robbie sail over the handlebars and under the tram. There'd have been a huge noise as the tram did an emergency stop. When that happens, the tram lets down a 'lifeguard' to stop anything being further damaged by its undercarriage."

Lachlan pictured a scene frozen in time, hushed when the tram's harsh scream cut off.

"I gather a lady came up to Merrick, who stood astride his fallen bike in the middle of the road. The car that wanted to turn right was still there, obscuring Merrick's view. After a few minutes, policemen came up and helped him to the pavement, which was crowded now. There was a wedding at the church. The couple had just come onto the steps when the accident happened."

Lachlan's pins and needles came back. The jarring of joy and grief, with split- second timing.

"The policemen asked Merrick for his home number and, after a moment's thought, he gave ours. Jo was at the scene soon, and Hetty, who was shopping in Bridge Street, followed not far behind. Jo found Merrick first; only then did she see the ambulance arrive. She left Merrick with

Hetty and went with Robbie to hospital."

Lachlan looked across at Dave. "Is he going to survive, mate?" Dave's hands gripped the wheel as, in the mirror, he saw the flashing light of an ambulance careering past. Lachlan saw it a second later, heading for The Alfred hospital, like them.

"He's got guts, Lach. And each hour that goes by increases his chances."

"But he's still in a coma. After two days."

They had reached the traffic lights on Punt Road. Lachlan saw the dull biscuit colour of the hospital.

"I'll drop you, Lachie, and park."

Lachlan did not react. But when the car stopped outside Accident and Emergency he was suddenly terrified.

"He's got guts, Lach."

Lachlan opened the door, and jellied legs struck tarmac. Ahead of him an old man was being pushed along the footpath in a wheelchair by an orderly, and the man's wife. The old man's hair was grey and ginger at once. Several people were walking away; they looked drawn, clutching bags and clothes as if their lives depended on the grip of these possessions. Two ambulances guarded the emergency bay. A man with a cigarette stood gazing into the distance. The Australian flag furled, uninterested. A large woman sighed, "Ah, here we go," and fossicked in her bag. Behind Lachlan, a bus drove away.

Beyond the portico, groups of people sat out in the crepuscular light; one spoke into a mobile phone. A taxi hooted at Lachlan, granting him respite from his thoughts; it hovered, then decanted its cargo. Lachlan looked up; above the doorway was a HAZCHEM sign. A nurse clutching a bucket smiled at him. A car hooted, was it Dave urging him inside? Lachlan stood on the threshold still, moving to his right to make room for a family, mother pushing a pram, father in overalls, with a moustache. Loneliness speared Lachlan, pushing him into the building.

The noise inside surprised him. On his left was a book-stall, next to which a woman stood by a tiny table with ADMISSIONS written on crude cardboard. There was a bank, its bored cashier strumming the fingers of one hand on a bare counter. A man on crutches looked at Lachlan, waiting for him to move out of the way. Phones were in use; a baby screamed; the lights in the pharmacy glared.

Then he saw the reception desk, more like a hotel than a hospital. A poster swam in front of him: Cancer Support Groups. There was a picture of a mixed-race family. When he reached the counter, the woman behind it did not look up.

"Excuse me."

No response.

"Excuse me!"

A tired face screwed up its eyes at him.

"My son. Robert Stacey..." The words blocked them-selves out. "He's in Int..."

"What was the name again?" Past tense.

"The name is Robert Stacey."

"I'll just see where he is... "She started to type his name into a computer.

"I know where he is," whispered Lachlan. The woman looked up sharply.

"He's in-"

"Intensive Care," said Lachlan dryly.

"I'll get a nurse to come and collect you. Take a seat please, Mr Stacey."

Lachlan could not obey. For the last twenty-three hours he'd taken a seat across the world. It was the last thing he could do now.

A male nurse walked to reception. Lachlan looked away, but seconds later the man touched his shoulder.

"Mr Stacey? Come with me, please."

Pins and needles bounced back as Lachlan stood up. The feeling in his left leg had gone. His guide waited at the foot of a flight of stairs.

337

"Don't worry, Mr Stacey."

Winding round stairways, Lachlan was confronted with a dark blue door. Beneath the words 'Intensive Care,' he saw two commands:

WASH YOUR HANDS.
TURN OFF MOBILES, PLEASE

He'd expected pointed calls for 'Silence'. The nurse pushed open the door, and Lachlan was inside.

Later he would relive the moment. He was tingling, in another world. The ward looked like any other, except it had more space. Colours sprang up at him: blue machines, bright yellow refuse bags, grey floor, red lines on it, marking isolation areas. There was much more noise than in a medical ward, which surprised him. He did not know where to go. Two of the bays were deserted, gaping islands of lino with not a bed to be seen.

There was a movement to his left, a curtain pulled back and a figure ducked through the gap: Jo. She took his hand, guiding him to the bed in the far left-hand corner. Lachlan walked into the curtained area, across the red line. At first he saw nothing: the figure lying in front of him was so small he was almost not there. Tubes, drips, monitors made it impossible to connect with the beached human being only inches away. A nurse stood over the boy; she acknowledged Lachlan with a nod, then came forward and slipped a mask over his mouth. Lachlan stared at the figure on the bed. Its eyes were closed.

He willed them to open, to flicker, but there was no response. A doctor came into the isolated area in yellow gloves, goggles and a tunic; underneath his mask Lachlan detected a kind smile.

"If you give me a minute, Mr Stacey. I'll explain how we're going."

Lachlan stood. Above his son's bed hung a steel triangle; there were lots of trolleys, yellow bin bags, a fire

338

extinguisher, several sinks, on one of which a half-drunk mug of coffee sat, abandoned. A nurse was recording information onto a chart. Another doctor came out to confer with the first, being careful to draw the curtains after him.

Jo touched Lachlan's shoulder, indicating she was going outside to meet Dave. He nodded, vaguely. Bleeps grew in intensity near the boy's head; no one reacted. Lachlan was surprised how unhurried it was. Two computer screens gave out demented signals, unheeded. A toy animal perched on top of a screen.

Lachlan turned back to look at Robbie. He was not a good colour; the bruising and swelling made him an object rather than a person. His lips were those of a monster, his face devoid of any trace of life. Swollen mouth gaped up to closed, swollen eyes. There was a bandage on his head with a line coming out, tubes in his mouth, intravenous drips, needles in his hands, pale and small against the crisp fold of white sheets. Hundreds of wires led to monitors, more tubes, ventilators, scanning machines. On the part of Robbie's face he could see, there was no skin, just a raw hole.

He needed Jo to come back. But the door remained closed. Another nurse came in to Robbie, the second doctor holding back the curtain with his forearm, before moving away. The first doctor stepped towards Lachlan, undoing his gloves.

"Shall we go and sit somewhere quieter, Mr Stacey?"

He led the way out of Intensive Care, down a short corridor and into a small waiting-room. A box of tissues lay next to a plastic plant. There were pictures on the wall, more notices. A sink in the corner held tea and coffee next to clean cups. They looked as if they had never been used.

"Would you like some tea?"

Lachlan shook his head. "No, thanks."

The doctor, one hand in his pocket, indicated a specific chair for Lachlan. It was not unlike the chair he'd sat on at the prison.

"What's the story?" Lachlan realised his question was needless.

"I'll try and fill you in." The doctor put his clipboard of notes on the arm of another chair.

"Robert—"

"Robbie."

"Robbie's done himself a fair bit of damage, as you'll have seen."

Lachlan found his eyes unable to keep still, trying to journey round the room on separate orbits.

"When the paramedics got to him there was significant disfigurement, a few broken teeth, a fractured leg and much dessicated skin; he needed oxygen badly. They put him into a neck-brace while trying to establish if the spine was damaged. Then they brought him in here, a 'bells and siren' job, continuing to treat him en route. The most important thing was to relieve pressure on the brain and get the blood flowing.

He got here and we assessed his condition. We put an intravenous drip in, did a whole series of X-rays, then took CAT scans, which photograph a cross-section of the brain. He'd fractured a couple of ribs, one of which lacerated his lung. His spleen was ruptured, so we removed that."

Lachlan's brow furrowed. "Can you cope without a spleen?"

"Easily. Like the appendix, an unnecessary organ. We straightened his leg and put it in plaster. He's got a catheter, too. The head injury is the most serious; we're monitoring that all the time. He may need surgery in the not too-distant future to evacuate any blood clots that could form. When he hit the ground he obviously banged his head, fracturing the skull. We had to establish whether the tram then struck him, causing further injuries. In fact, the tram missed his head, but broke his leg, crushing some internal organs. They should heal in time. His brain injury remains the worry. He landed on the left side of his head, which affects the right side of the body."

Lachlan thought of Robbie's left-handed writing. Minuscule mercies.

"We've been trying to stabilise him and see the extent of the brain damage. There is a lot of bleeding, still. What happens in an accident like this is that the brain, normally suspended in a fluid sack, carries on moving when the skull suddenly stops, and thus gets squashed. There's a lot of haemorrhaging and inflammation, which leads to compression and therefore brain damage. Blood clots form, which have to be evacuated. It helps to keep him under sedation at first."

Outside a trolley was trundled past in the corridor, its noise deadened on the rubber floor.

"And the million dollar question?"

The doctor had been waiting for this. How many other times had desperate parents listened like porous rock as they tried to frame their question.

"Impossible to predict. We need to keep getting through the days. If we can keep him stabilised, he'll have stronger chances. I can't be too optimistic, obviously. But he's a healthy lad. With time, there's always some recovery, who knows how much? There'll be residual problems, but let's deal with them later."

He stood up.

"Thank you," came feebly from Lachlan's mouth.

"We'll do all we can here. Nothing is left to chance. There's no guesswork."

"No, I've seen that already."

The doctor held the door, brown eyes on the floor. Lachlan was unsure if he should shake the man's hand, but the doctor was gone, down the corridor. Lachlan stared again at the WASH YOUR HANDS on the I.C.U. door, then pushed it open. There was more noise now, more activity, phones and alarms ringing, nurses reading flow charts,

341

recording details. A cleaner polished silently in a bay that had been occupied minutes earlier. The toy on top of the monitor reassured Lachlan.

But the form in Robbie's bed lay inert, no more resembling the boy than it had ten minutes before. Lachlan looked down at it. He needed to pray, but chunks of Shakespeare came into his head, from plays not worked on for years. The Psalms were what he reached for, their promises of courage, faith, hope, acceptance of God's will. Their elusive nature was what galled him when Kathy left; it still did, and now he stood, helpless. Acceptance of God's will was a defeat, abnegation. What about *his* will? The will for Robbie to get better, to be made whole?

A young man made his way carefully towards Robbie's bed.

"G'day," he said calmly.

Lachlan looked at him. The man smiled. He was fair-haired, not a doctor.

"I'm the hospital chaplain," he explained.

Lachlan held out his hand.

"I'm his Dad," stuttered out.

The man nodded. "Any change?"

Lachlan shook his head. "If only."

The chaplain looked him in the eye, with a gaze Lachlan needed to read. Had he come to give the last rites? 'Extreme unction', Lachlan knew it was called. His father sometimes used the term, though no one had administered it to him, shrinking to blisters in flame, unable to find water.

"We hang by a thread," said the chaplain, confirming Lachlan's dread. He was unhurried, and Lachlan was struck by his youth, early thirties, perhaps thirty-three, Jesus' age. One of his sandals had a broken strap; the parallel went further.

"You've only just got here?"

"That's right." Lachlan was looking back at Robbie. "I was in England. Seeing my brother in prison." Lachlan had no idea why he said this. It was unnecessary. Another fractured member of their torn family.

"That's hard."

Lachlan looked round at him. Was the man coming out with platitudes, that everything was for the best like Candide's crass tutor, Pangloss?

"You're a Christian family?" Lachlan's eyes focused more keenly. "Your friend mentioned. The dentist."

"He's Robbie's godfather," said Lachlan. Somewhere there was a stab of pride, quashed by anger at Dave; he should have been looking after the boys.

"Would you like me to say a prayer?"

Lachlan's eyes filled; nodding his head was an effort. The chaplain moved round the bed, placing his left hand on Robbie's crowded temple. Lachlan saw a thin wedding ring as the chaplain motioned Lachlan to put his hand onto Robbie, too.

"O God, thank you for Jesus, the good physician. We thank you for restoring health to man's body, and sanity to his mind. You understand pain and suffering, Lord; you know the sting of thorns on your brow, the nails in your hands, the scourge on your back. You know what we are suffering at this moment. Send your blessing down on this man and his son, help them to bear their pain and to remember that they will never be tried beyond what they are able to bear. And that you are with them, even in this valley of the deep, dark shadows. Help us to remember the words of St Paul in Corinthians: 'God is faithful, and he will not let us be tested beyond our strength'. Help us, Lord, help us..."

They kept their hands on the unconscious boy. An alarm went off in the next bay, followed by activity. The nurse came back to Robbie's bed and began to take more readings.

"He's going to need another scan in a minute," she informed, then returned to her notes.

"Do I come?" asked Lachlan.

"There's no real need, Mr Stacey. He'll only be away a

343

few minutes."

The chaplain looked ready to go.

"Have you a moment?" Lachlan asked.

They walked out of Intensive Care into the room where Lachlan had seen the doctor. Its silence was unnerving. Lachlan had a plethora of questions; none came. They sat opposite each other. Minutes later, Lachlan spoke.

"I'm sorry. Can't form any thoughts. No coherence."

The chaplain looked serious. "There are no right words."

Lachlan's eyes lifted.

"I'll keep praying. And I'll be back before too long."

"Thank you," said Lachlan with no energy. "Thank you."

The chaplain walked down the corridor, sandal-strap flicking as he went.

'*God is faithful and will not let us be tested beyond our strength.*' This was the test.

Robbie's bed was empty. Machines bleeped.

"Lachlan," came a voice behind him. Dave. Lachlan smiled for the first time since landing back. In Intensive Care there was nowhere to sit down. They hovered by the nurses' station.

"How did you know where to get hold of me, Dave? I've not thought of it before."

"It was a challenge. We knew you'd been at the prison on Saturday, so assumed you'd stay somewhere en route to Heathrow. But, of course, your mobile phone was off. It didn't seem right to leave a message." The dentist risked eye contact. "Jo and I had no way of finding you. We thought Rebecca and Saul had left for Mallorca. Merrick was still in shock. He'd been put to bed by Jo around midnight, but didn't sleep much. She'd kept looking in on him. Around 5.30 he came into her and blurted out, "Sam Stanton might know where Dad is." We never thought you'd returned, but there was a chance you'd have rung them and they could trace you. The rest–"

"–is far from silence," said Lachlan. He thought of Sam back at Hawkthwaite, mending the wooden gate, driving his iron horse to the wood, shouting at Pauline for leaving the muslin bag in the only place he was guaranteed to catch his boot. Normal family life. That wasn't Lachlan's lot; unlike Sam, he went about life in permanent readiness for tragedy, yet had still been caught unprepared.

"I must ring Sam," he said. A flurry of action in the bay next to Robbie ended with the swift drawing of curtains. Dave and Lachlan moved down the ward.

"Tell me your part. In the accident's aftermath."

Dave was leaning against one of the machines not in use; he looked older. Straightening up, his eyes took on another mien.

"I reached the hospital about twenty minutes after the ambulance. No sign of Robbie or Jo, so I asked a triage nurse, who insisted on knowing who I was. Robbie was in theatre; I'd have to wait. I had so many questions..." Dave faltered, letting Lachlan into a surge of guilt waiting to immobilise them both. The moment passed. "I walked up and down, saw the next admission, grizzly, then the nurse found me and said Robbie was having a scan. I could go and view with the doctor. Their levity as we watched this scan surprised me, three of us gazing from the tiny cabin at Robbie, a piece of flotsam in a cylinder intent on swallowing us all."

There was a squeak of wheels behind them, as Robbie was pushed back into his bay. Two nurses, one at each end of the floating trolley, eased the boy onto his bed. He seemed to be sleeping; perhaps the scan had tired him.

Dave waited a moment, looked at his watch and bade a hasty farewell. Lachlan looked at the boy, then at the machines and back at the boy. His breathing was regular, though Lachlan strained to hear it. The left hand looked bluish around a tube whose function escaped Lachlan. The lower lip fell away slightly; with a gurgle, his boy slept on.

Lachlan could hear muted feet padding behind him, the release of the brake on a trolley. A plastic beaker fell to the ground to his right; Lachlan rose and picked it up, uncertain where it came from. He felt helpless standing with the cup in his hand, both feet on the red line exclusion zone.

Turning to Robbie, he saw his eyes were open. Or one of them was, his right. Its pupil looked out of proportion, while the left eye remained closed. There was a whispered croak coming from Robbie's mouth, now further open than before, and as Lachlan looked at him, the mouth closed abruptly, teeth started clenching and blood came out of his mouth. His whole body was suddenly stiff, jerking out of control, both eyes open, the face pale.

No one came. Lachlan turned round, blood tight in his chest.

"Nurse. Nurse!"

A doctor stepped from the station.

"I think he's having a fit..."

Before Lachlan had finished the sentence the man was beside Robbie, now rocking out of control, teeth rigid, his whole frame thrashed in seizure.

Someone pressed a button, Robbie's bed sped across the lino, people ran quietly out of the room and Lachlan was left marooned in the bay, fists clenched helplessly, mind stuck between gears. On the floor lay the scrunched-up beaker.

A nurse came to him swiftly.

"Mr Stacey, he'll need an operation. It's not unusual. We'll drill into his skull and make a burr-hole to relieve the pressure that's built up on one side of his brain. This can happen."

She began to move away. Curtains swished, sounding like lances plunged deep into stones of hard flesh.

There was still nowhere to sit. Lachlan turned back to the vacant bed space.

"What do I...?" He spoke to an empty room.

Swallowing, he moved to the door. After the action, all

346

was now quiet. The door resisted his weak push, and yielded on the second attempt. Lachlan walked into the waiting-room, predictably empty, its box of tissues mocking, plant preening to an invisible mirror. He walked down the corridor to the operating theatre-suites. Both had a red light on above the doors.

A plastic chair stood to his right. He crumpled on to it, and waited.

CHAPTER TWENTY EIGHT

It was a different doctor who came out of the theatre-suite; he looked pale in the intense strip lights. They could not escape the waiting-room now.

"When Robbie had the scan his blood pressure was low," he began, flexing his hand as he gestured Lachlan into a chair. "Resuscitation caused bleeding to start, and then it clotted. We had to drill into the skull, make a burr-hole, then remove a piece of bone about the size of a fifty cent piece." He held up his fingers to show the size. "We evacuated the haematoma through the hole."

There was a pause. A trolley rattled past in the corridor, its shrunken occupant swathed in tubes.

Lachlan's strength had run out. He stared, unable to form questions in his mind. The doctor stood, touching Lachlan on the shoulder. "It's not necessarily made things worse. We'll just have to watch and see." He waited for the man beside him to look up, then left quickly.

Back in Intensive Care, Robbie was looking peaceful, despite the insertion of more lines. A catheter was plunged into a major vein in his neck, near the collarbone. Fluid ran up the flimsy tube. Lachlan needed to read the monitors; he realised it was vital to keep Robbie's blood pressure up.

The nurse came over. "We'll keep him sedated, of course."

"Of course," echoed Lachlan.

"…except when we assess."

He nodded. "Could you help me read these screens?"

She obliged, explaining, briefly, what they monitored. Lachlan fought to stifle the many questions inside him.

"You'll soon understand them," she said. The medical staff were competent and kind, but no one was preparing him for what was to happen. Reason told him there were no answers yet, but instinct roared at him, be brave and ask the questions.

The nurse moved over to the station. Lachlan gazed at Robbie, who made no noise. His lower lip trembled and his father saw, above the angry purple gum, a hole where the front tooth had been. Lachlan thought of that day again. The tooth had never been quite straight. But better that than a gaping hole.

There was a slight cough behind him; he turned round. He had known it was inevitable, but was still unprepared for the figure that faced him. Neither spoke, and he was aware of a second shape, a man's, with hands askew.

Kathy walked over to the bed. Her ignorance of the red line smarted. The nurse moved round the other side of Robbie's inert frame. Both women looked at each other. The nurse broke eternal silence.

"He's had a relapse. We just have to wait and see."

Lachlan stepped forward, his space violated by the impromptu arrival. Already Kathy was playing to perfection the rôle of anxious mother. She gazed down at her son, reaching for the dull contact of his left hand.

Lachlan turned to the man, still at bay beside the door. He had not imagined Kathy would bring him, too. At least, not to the bedside. The man's eyes did not slide away when Lachlan's confronted him, but stared back, cold, and empty. Something in Lachlan's bowel did a slow somersault and ebbed out of existence.

The nurse was whispering to Kathy, whose face was screwing up in its attempt to take in the information. Lachlan edged a few centimetres forward in case there was anything new. He saw a flicker of Robbie's right eyelid, then nothing. Should they be playing music? Reading him a favourite poem, some unwieldy crank-handle to kick in heart and brain? He felt ousted by Kathy's arrival; the nurse was giving a lot of information. He'd had to endure silence on arrival.

A bleeper went off on the other side of the unit, and two doctors sprang into action, flicking the curtains behind them with the deftness of ballet dancers. There was a distant, whirring sound; something buzzed, and one doctor emerged, eyes on the floor.

Still the nurse whispered. Lachlan sensed Kathy exulting: he could not tiptoe nearer again like a kid in the playground greedy for each morsel of gossip. The nurse went silent, reaching up to one of Robbie's tubes. The man by the door had gone. Kathy sat on the bed, risking a gaze at Lachlan.

"Helpless. We're just…helpless."

He nodded. Anger at her bringing Adrian bit into him, but to question her now was unwise.

The nurse took more readings. At one point Robbie let out a small hiss, which made both parents lift heads and peer harder at the boy. He remained motionless.

"We need to avoid another seizure," said Lachlan. The word 'avoid' was reluctant to be spoken; he wanted to say 'prevent'. But had to be realistic. The vein in Robbie's neck seemed angrier than before, its line bobbing up and down, mocking its task.

"They have to keep his blood pressure down."

Kathy took no notice. The monitor on the wall danced a frenzied message at its captured audience, lay still, and danced again. Faint green lines blew in and out of the picture, a blue dot screamed.

Lachlan edged round the base of the bed; if he made a movement, perhaps Robbie would. He stood behind Kathy, his eye drawn to a ringless left hand. That much she had allowed him.

When Jo crept in some time later the tableau was

unchanged. The women greeted each other, warmly; Lachlan did not look away. Jo's face asked him the needless question; he shook his head.

"How's Merrick?"

"He's calm. I think he's starting to understand now. Keeps talking about the wedding on the steps."

Kathy frowned.

"The one the boys saw just prior to the accident. A couple came out on to the steps, and it must have distracted them. Someone said the bells pealed suddenly."

Lachlan wondered how the newlyweds felt; they must have seen the accident. Doubtless they were now on a tropical island, honeymooning with the sun. With Jo and Kathy at the bedside, Lachlan decided to go for some air. A part of him dreaded confronting Adrian in the corridor, but the bird had flown, and Lachlan stepped unhindered into the night.

He was out of time. Streetlamps gave no clue as to the hour, nor did the occasional car, its lights beaming off the road for a second, then disappearing beyond the hospital confines. A taxi pulled up just as he had done some hours earlier, its passenger hovered, then braved the doorway's maws. Lachlan wondered what it would confront.

Jo emerged, hands in a light jacket pocket; she looked more tired than he had ever seen her.

"I'm leaving Kathy to have some time with Robs."

Lachlan nodded. There was no mention of Adrian.

"It's the helplessness, Jo. There's nothing we can prepare for. No scene-shifting, props to scout for, costumes to alter..." his voice trailed away.

"Each hour he gets through is a new chance," she offered.

There was no reaction. Lachlan looked at her after a few seconds.

"You've been strong," he said, avoiding her gaze. "Can you keep it up?"

"Have to. Question is, can you?" Across the road a car

pipped; someone sat on their brakes. A milk lorry sped past in the opposite direction, harbinger of another day.

"Is Kathy..?"

"...staying with us? No, she's in a hotel off Faulkner Park."

Lachlan knew the one. He shrugged. "She'll want to be with Merrick, too," he conceded. "That's fine. He'll need her." He looked up; Jo was staring at him. "You go home now," he said. "No point everyone driving themselves into the ground." It was an unfortunate choice of words. Images of trams unleashed from their wires, bikes in mid-air, cars lined up to be leaped over by a stuntman on skis, upturned ambulances and a hearse at full speed bucketed around in his head, coming to rest on the steps of a church where a bride and groom stood, aghast, their buttonholes blown away on a wind that smelt of white heat, landing in a line of small white crosses in a military cemetery.

He stifled a sob. Jo's hand reached for his arm and they walked slowly back towards the hospital, its fickle colour starting to emerge against the dawn. Already there were signs of activity. When they reached the entrance, Jo took her hand from his arm, patted it and watched him set off up the stairs once more.

The figure beside Kathy stepped with her into Intensive Care. Lachlan looked up. There was no greeting.

"Where....is he?"

"Having a scan." There was a pause. "It happens...pretty often at the moment. They have to..." Lachlan's voice trailed away. Kathy was halfway out of I.C.U in determined search. The man remained. His hands looked out of place as he sought to do something with them. Eyes avoided contact, on both sides.

Adrian. Lachlan's mind was axed. The man sidled away, but his presence lingered by the door. There was no sign of Kathy. Lachlan was torn between the urge to pursue Adrian

352

and inform him how his presence was superfluous, and the need to rationalise his turning up at all.

He waited.

The door opened, and a whirr heralded Robbie's return. This time he seemed more lively, eyes firmly open, questing round the immediate vicinity of his mobile bed.

"Dad?"

Lachlan touched the bed. The voice was distant, alien, and slow. But it was a voice. Lachlan fought hard not to over-react.

"Did I...see Mum?"

Of the lines Robbie could have uttered on coming round from his coma, this would not have been Lachlan's first choice.

"Yes, she's just arrived. She went to look for you."

The boy's gaze was empty.

"I suppose she was worried stiff – she is your –"

Two eyes fixed on him.

"She still is..."

There was a muffled footstep. Lachlan did not look up. A shadow appeared on the other side of the bed. Lachlan avoided the urge to focus. The doctor eased the bed across the lino to its vacant bay. Lachlan was surprised how large the space was, how it made no effort to swallow its cargo.

"This is Robbie's mother." The voice was not his.

Lachlan walked away sadly. Just what Kathy wanted.

He had no idea what to do. He could not approach another bed and start up conversation with a patient as in a medical ward. If he left the unit he'd no doubt bump into Adrian prowling the corridors like a black bear in search of picnickers in The Rockies.

He stood by the centre station. *Adrian.* No one else would have brought him. Immoral support. Lachlan tried to visualise Kathy's mind-set since hearing from Jo. He'd been hurled into jumbled emotions at Hawkthwaite, fear striding into consciousness, stomach lurching on a demented cycle, pins and needles, dry mouth, awareness of the attempts to hold down his own consciousness. Women were different. Had she kept everything at bay, calmly dialling a travel agent to book an instant flight to Melbourne? He pictured Adrian consoling her, after coming home from a day in Ottawa. Hadn't he thought she might come alone?

Into his head came snatched bars of a pop song last heard twenty years ago: naïve sentiments, brash backing, a carnival's false cheer. The oxymoron struck home. Adrian was a walking oxymoron. False friend. Devil's advocate. Second husband. Kathy was the blood mother. Lachlan's mind was full of these two-word contradictions and the beat of that song grew louder, eluding identification.

Lachlan had a vision of Adrian in Parliament, spruced, slick, smooth, and convincing. He remembered Pierre Trudeau, the erstwhile Canadian Prime Minister. Adrian was in a way similar. Bestriding the Ottawan Parliament like a misshapen colossus.

A little figure walked swiftly into I.C.U. followed by a breathless Hetty, apology sculptured into her forehead. Merrick had no idea what he was to confront. Lachlan was glad he did not see Merrick's expression as Kathy rounded on him, sweeping up his nine vulnerable years into arms that seemed to have grown mannish. There was a cry; Lachlan was unsure from whose throat. He stared at Robbie, savagely willing him to be aware of all that was happening. But Kathy was gone from the room, Merrick thrashing against her frame like a demented tractor. She had her hand over his mouth as they were devoured by the faceless corridor. Lachlan felt Hetty grasp his hand and a distant part of him marvelled. Then she, too, eased out of the room.

Robbie was staring into space, any vestige of his previous conversation gone. Lachlan smiled at him. There was no reaction. Lachlan wondered if he'd ever stared so hard at anyone, willing a response . His hand grazed the boy's cheek, its skin white rather than pink: where had the blood gone? Was it working overtime around his brain, trying to set up a 'pulse in the eternal mind' as Rupert Brooke put it? Literary phrases sped round Lachlan's head. One poet had written 'Death of a Son', about his boy who died in a mental hospital aged one. It was a poem that he'd taught often, one step removed from reality, until now.

He went for a stool and placed it by the bed. He picked up Robbie's hand. The waiting would going to continue. Around him the unit remained quiet. Lachlan felt suddenly alone. He banished the thought; how could he be alone with the stricken form of his son beside him?

When the nurse came back he was aware of her fluid movements; deft and unhurried, she mastered the controls beside Robbie with measured calm.

"Any progress?" he asked.

Her expression tautened and for the first time he felt something leap in him.

"Too early yet, but…"

The 'but' struck him and he let it sink below his consciousness. Logic came sparring at once, fists poised, stance guarded, but the spark out-danced it.

Lachlan looked at Robbie. His pupils seemed smaller.

A new shadow appeared over the bed and Lachlan looked up to see Dave in black T-shirt and khaki shorts. The nurse was pressing buttons, but without the urgency she'd shown before. Robbie's pupils were definitely smaller. Dave looked at the boy, and Lachlan was glad he ignored the subject of Kathy.

"I sense a change, Lachie."

Lachlan nodded. Saying more would tempt fate. Then Robbie moved. His hand shifted a fraction on the sheet, his third finger crimping for a second. Dave stared at the sheet. Lachlan stared at the finger. It crimped again. Lachlan leaned forward and felt Dave's hand on the back of his neck. The boy's eyelids flickered.

"Can you hear us?" urged Lachlan.

The boy's lips stretched; he was on the verge of a smile. Lachlan beamed at him. The boy gave a sigh, then his eyes fixed on Lachlan.

"Dad?"

Lachlan was unsure what to do. He sat for a moment, nodding gently. He tried to find the word 'Son', but could not, so kept nodding, tears in his eyes. He grasped the hand of his boy and felt a tiny squeeze.

Dave coughed. His eyes asked Lachlan if he should go, but Lachlan shook his head. Dave was nodding, too. Dry-eyed, as far as Lachlan could discern. Just as well.

A doctor was standing over them. Lachlan knew the man's lines. "We mustn't get carried away. There is still enormous residual damage. But this has to be a hopeful sign. He has a long, long way to go, of course."

Lachlan refrained from asking details. He walked to the window. The doctor waited. Dave had stepped back; the nurse was still recording facts from her screen. Lachlan wanted Merrick here, with them, not with a mother who'd only emerged when drama was unfolding. It was a test for his Christian principles. A part of him was praying, thoughts all over the place, but intent fixed. Prayer was like that, he'd realised down the years, spontaneous not planned, impetuous not cosy. Not put into words. But going on all the time.

"Amen" said a voice. He turned. Jo stood behind him. He drew her to him.

"It's not over yet."

"I know. But –"

Dave caught Lachlan's eye, indicating he was leaving.

"Where's Mum?"

Lachlan looked down at the eyes that moved slowly across the room. "I'm not exactly sure…"

"She's gone to our house, to freshen up," said Jo, walking round the bed and grasping Robbie's right hand.

The boy nodded. Though Lachlan wanted to discuss

every topic that darted in and out of his head, he knew caution. The three of them were silent. Doors opened and a trolley brought forth a new patient, pursued by an anxious woman in flip-flops over which she tripped. Lachlan knew she was going to. Curtains swished like a bullet and low voices gave way to the buzz of machines.

"Mr Stacey?" Another doctor had entered and gestured Lachlan to the nurses' station, now buzzing with action having lain dormant for some time. Lachlan was worried he wouldn't hear properly.

The doctor was serious. Whatever was the opposite of a relapse had just occurred, but the man still looked grim.

"This is delicate," he said, eyes fixed on Lachlan. "Your wife. We must keep additional trauma to a minimum."

Lachlan felt outrage. The doctor was still regarding him fixedly. "At the moment we need to restrict the number of visitors. If you could do that rather than us…"

He smiled, faintly, and walked away. Jo and Robbie were communicating without a lot of words, so Lachlan decided on fresh air. But despite having been out of the hospital before, it took time to escape. After a couple of wrong turns and superfluous staircases, he found himself walking out of A&E, dodging an admission and the paramedics' gaze. Ahead of him cars passed, unheeding. There were few people. Lachlan realised he still had no idea of the time. An ambulance veered off the road, a girl in a red top stepped from nowhere and almost knocked into him.

Then he saw a figure leaning on the railing, cigarette in hand. Lachlan was unripe for confrontation.

"Any progress?" enquired Adrian. Trudeau flashed into Lachlan's brain. Telling the truth to a charlatan would deny that truth; it could also undo any good that might be happening to Robbie at this moment.

"No, not really." *Father forgive him; he knows not what he does.* "He needs space." There was a pause. "From all of us." *Convey that message to your – to Kathy* was forged on his forehead. But there was no need to prolong the interview.

As Lachlan turned away, he heard the other man come after him. The cigarette flew away. But Adrian said nothing, just walked half a pace behind Lachlan past A&E to the swing door, where he did not hesitate.

"Look –" said Lachlan.

His adversary had donned the politician's beatific smile. It was unwelcome, and inept. Lachlan heard himself swear at the man, who stood, unmoved. He was used to being abused. He thrived on it. The smile had not worn off. Lachlan was going to remember this moment.

"It's not me you should be confronting," said the smile with false gentleness.

Lachlan eyed him. The get-out clause was unexpected. And only a politician could think in terms of confrontation at a time like this. Lachlan shot him an angry glance and turned away. He was suddenly tired. He couldn't remember when he had last slept. Perhaps the hospital had a bed he could lie down on for a few hours. He trudged back towards the unit. Adrian watched him all the way, then lit another cigarette.

It was hot in the bedroom kept for relatives of patients in Intensive Care. Lachlan came to, aware of the sunshine, but not of the hour. His watch told him it was just after eleven a.m.

He put some water on his face, avoiding the mirror. As he reached for the towel, he saw the door-handle move. Jo stood on the threshold.

"Feel better?"

He nodded, wary. His sleep had not been deep; he had the wretched feeling of waking up after only a short rest. He wanted a shave, too much effort.

Jo moved over and sat on the bed. She, too, looked tired.

"Like to use the basin?"

On the edge of words, she declined.

358

"Kathy's….concerned."

Lachlan fought back his anger and waited. "Almost more concerned about Merrick." Lachlan's brow furrowed. "She thinks he's so vulnerable…"

"*He's* so vulnerable?"

Jo looked straight at him. "She says he's no longer responsive to her. She is…his mother."

Lachlan said nothing. There was no anger for Jo, only Kathy. Jo was caught among loyalties, not an emissary from the enemy.

"She's not sure how best to help, Lachie." Lachlan felt his principles grinding together somewhere far back in the brain. Or in someone else's brain. They were talking of a woman once wooed, cherished, woken up with, now a mythological figure with several heads.

"Just get rid of Adrian," said Lachlan after a time. "Can't he go to Canberra on a diplomatic mission? Or just tour our Parliament buildings? Alone." Lachlan had been to Canberra once, an uninspiring place where he had dutifully toured the seat of Australian government and emerged into rain.

"I think she thought he'd be a prop," said Jo into a vacuum.

"Did she?" said Lachlan sadly.

"It is tricky for him, Lach. He didn't ask for this situation." Jo bit her lip, ashamed of her blunder. "I'm sorry."

"We need to be strong," Lachlan replied. "That means working for Robbie. Not competing for the affection of a fourteen-year-old boy, who may or may not recover. Perhaps you could convey that message to her." He was about to touch Jo's black hair hanging over the pale face held in little hands. But he thought better of it, and left the room.

Back in the unit, Robbie was asleep. Activity was focused on the admission Lachlan had previously witnessed. He saw an old man rubbing his glasses with a green paper towel. Lachlan nodded at him, but the man's gaze was vacant.

Lachlan touched his son's forehead. It was cooler now, but his face was still pale.

"You're getting there, Robs," he said in a voice louder than he'd intended. There was no reply. Outside sunshine was holding sway. In a house across the street, hands reached up and opened dull curtains. The odd car crawled past. Lachlan walked back to the bedside and put his head on the sheet by Robbie's knee.

He had a rude awakening. Kathy stood over him, on the other side of the bed. Bossy fingers drummed a faded magazine.

"I spoke to the doctors," she said, firmly. "They have agreed. Providing Robbie keeps up this level of progress…"

Her tone had taken on the North American twang they both used to mock.

"…providing he keeps it up, we're taking both boys back to Canada."

360

CHAPTER TWENTY NINE

When Merrick walked back into the unit he looked forlorn and white. Eyes steady on his brother, he crossed the floor with trepidation, hesitating at the red line. His gaze shifted to Lachlan, who nodded, and the younger boy reached the bedside. Robbie's eyes were closed. Merrick put the flat of his hand on Robbie's forehead, throwing into relief a battered nose.

"He's lost his tooth," said a small voice.

"Talk to him, mate."

Merrick was uncertain. He moved his hand on to Robbie's hair.

"You've lost your tooth, Robs."

The eyelids parted; the patient attempted to smile. Seeing the two profiles in front of him Lachlan was struck by the difference between them. Merrick's chin jutted forward; Robbie's frown had returned. But his younger brother did not seem perturbed by the silence.

"Can I sit on the bed, Dad?"

Lachlan looked round. "I should think so." Gingerly, the boy edged himself on to the bed.

"He's sweating."

Lachlan passed him a paper towel, which was applied to Robbie's forehead. The frown deepened, then eased. Unsure what to do with the towel, Merrick passed it back to his father. A nurse moved over to close the blind; the midday sun was strong.

Jo entered the unit, looking smart and Lachlan felt a sudden relief.

"I think Kathy might be coming to sit with Robs for a while. Would you like some lunch?"

Lachlan nodded. "You happy to stay till Mum arrives?" he asked Merrick, who assented. Jo and Lachlan left the unit.

Outside the sun had fled, but he felt a sense of release as he sat, silent, in Jo's car. It was an ordinary day for the rest of the world, albeit mild for mid-winter. Minutes later he sat on the Newcombes' deck, less tense than he'd been since landing back. Jo was busy inside, Dave at the surgery, Harry and Emily elsewhere. Then he caught sight of Kathy's bag in the hallway.

"You know what she wants?" he fired at Jo the moment she emerged with a plate of sandwiches.

Jo nodded.

"I'm not sure I feel strong for negotiation."

Jo remained silent. A car eased down the road. "Robbie needs to recover first," she said eventually. "He looked better just now." The word 'better' again. It was Lachlan's turn to be silent. "I think Kathy's guilt is turning somersaults."

Lachlan eyed her. And nodded. "Why did she bring him?"

Jo held out a plate of food. "We all act irrationally. Especially in a crisis." Lachlan's eyes remained on her. "I think Adrian's going to head for Canberra."

He could not resist a smile. "Government business, I have no doubt. Good."

"Is it good?"

Lachlan looked at her sharply. "Could she take both boys?"

Jo paused, about to crunch her sandwich. "In theory."

"Legally?"

"I think the boys can make up their own minds."

He nodded. The weight of decisions was heavy. "I hadn't thought beyond the trip to England."

"I know. But you've made plans for The Tinderbox. You said so."

It was the first time he'd thought of the theatre. He needed to ring Brodie. But not now.

Reading his thoughts, she told him there'd been a message from Brodie the night before. Having been told of the accident, she rang, offering him support. The Dixons had rung, too, as had Lynch, the carpenter. And Norman. Lachlan assimilated the information. Tragedy was the time a friend's love came out best. It wasn't easy to phone, dread welling up when the ringing sounded on the other end, part of the caller praying they'd be out, yet the idea of leaving a message not right. But they'd all rung. "And someone called Kieren. I don't know him."

"He's a lad from school," said Lachlan. "A medic."

"I think he wanted to come to the hospital, but wasn't going to intrude."

"I'd like him to come. Bit of medical support."

"The number's there." She handed over a list of the callers. "Why not ring him now?"

"I'll ring him a bit later. Is there another sandwich?"

"You must be feeling better." And she disappeared into the hall.

He had dozed off on the deck; his cup of tea was cold and there was a fly on the sandwich. Jo was inside, about to go to work.

"Back around four," she breezed, emerging into the daylight. "Borrow Dave's car to go back to the hospital. He cycled to the surgery this morning."

"Any idea how long Kathy's going to be there? The doctors said no confrontation in Intensive Care."

"You could try communication," came the reply, and Jo was away down the steps.

"I could try," he murmured. "But not in the unit." Perhaps in that clinical waiting-room awash with paper handkerchiefs. Maybe they'd supply a map of Vancouver so he could see exactly where she wanted to take the boys?

Back at the hospital Kathy had left. But Robbie was more alert. His eyes followed Lachlan across the room, and there was the faint hint of a smile as his father put his hand on the boy's forehead.

The same nurse who'd explained how to read the machines came over and took down more data. She seemed relaxed, and for the first time Robbie watched her, though he spoke no words. Lachlan was hoping she would utter something encouraging, but she remained almost silent, humming to herself as the figures were transferred on to Robbie's records. The clipboard rattled as she administered a full stop, then she looked at Lachlan.

"Is he.. .?"

"So far, so good at the moment. We just have to keep up the progress, inching our way forwards, out of the wood..."

"Can I do anything?" The words were inane.

"No." The answer was not a rebuff.

At that moment she was summoned away. Lachlan hovered by the bed.

"Where's.. .Rebecc?" The words caught him off guard.

"She's back in England, Robs. Well, actually, no; she's gone on holiday to Spain. Remember?"

"Oh yes." His eyes did not move. "I'm a bit confused, Dad."

"Bound to be." Lachlan was concentrating too hard. Robbie closed his eyes. In Lachlan's head there was frenetic activity; part of him wanted to plan targets for the boy, another part was urging caution. How often had Lachlan felt this tug-of-war before; he longed to think passion defeated reason, but now he needed all the grist from past mills to help him steady a heart that leaped out of reach. Just as suddenly, the anguish stilled; he had faint pins and needles, he was aware of his breathing, trying to transfer that breathing to the inert form in front of him.

"I'm tired, Dad." The eyelids bounced apart. Robbie would speak when he wished.

Lachlan was deep in thought, when he felt a figure standing near him. "Kieren?"

The student pursed his lips. "I heard about the accident from Johnno." There was a pause. "He sends his best." The student was not ill-at-ease. After a minute, he walked around the bed looking down at Robbie. "Any signs of progress?"

Lachlan saw the medic. in him. "I think so. It's so hard..."

"... to tell!" Kieren finished the sentence.

"Have you done I.C.U. study yet?"

Kieren shook his head. "I think that comes later. During our clinical. I'm only a second year medic., remember. What's that American name for a second year...Softmore? Odd word."

They smiled as Kieren went for a chair; he brought it opposite Lachlan. And said nothing.

Robbie opened his eyes again.

"Who's this, Dad?"

"This is Kieren - you saw him at the beach that day."

"Hi, Kieren." But the face was blank.

"I hear you're coming on well now. It's good to know."

"Am I?" The boy was uncertain. "No one's said that to me." There was a faint spark in the eye. "Tell me, then."

Lachlan and Kieren looked at each other.

"You're sleeping less," said the medic. "That must be good. It means your brain is settling down. You've knocked it around a bit. Does your head hurt?"

"A little." He paused. "I'm no doubt on a lot of drugs?"

"Regular junkie."

The boy's eyes moved to Lachlan.

"Has Merrick been?"

"Yes. Don't you-? Not all that long ago."

"Can he come again? I'd like to see him." The eyes moved away. "And maybe register that he's here."

"I'll ring Jo." Lachlan stood up. "Are you happy to stay,

365

Kieren?"

"Sure. Good practice."

Lachlan left them together.

But it was Kathy who picked up the phone.

"Is Jo there?"

"No. Just me. And Merrick. Can't I help?"

Lachlan paused. "Robs wants to see Merrick again."

"I'll bring him in."Kathy had not hung up. "We need..."

"... to avoid confrontation. That means talking outside the hospital."

"Here, then." Her voice was sharp.

"Or a café somewhere."

"Whatever suits. But soon. I have to be back in Canada."

"When?"

"As soon as I can."

"And Robs?"

"With him. With both of them."

He had run out of rage. "I'm not sure that's such a great idea."

"For you, maybe not. For them it's essential. I'll bring Merrick in." The line died.

If he and Kathy were to talk now, it would leave Robbie alone. He couldn't expect Kieren to stay. But when he returned to the bedside his former student was in no hurry to leave.

"What are your plans for the day?" asked Lachlan.

"Not a lot. I've got a reading week. For once, no lectures or lab. work."

"You couldn't stay here with Merrick when he comes? And Robbie, of course. His mother's come over from Vancouver and we need to speak away from here."

"That's fine."

When Kathy arrived with a quiet Merrick, she was introduced to Kieren and greeted him with warmth. Lachlan felt a stab. Then she and Lachlan left the unit. She had not enquired how the boy was. Outside the waiting-room Lachlan hesitated.

"Bit public isn't it?" said Kathy.

"I didn't realise we could be choosy."

"Look, Lachlan. I haven't time for quibbles. Just find a room."

She hadn't changed, imperious and unrelenting. A woman doctor brushed past.

"Excuse me," said Lachlan. "Do you have a room that's less –"

"Public." Kathy's adjective was propelled by a false smile.

"There's a consultation room that's free at the moment, I think. Down the corridor, turn left, second on the right. It should be private." Her smile was far from false and she watched for a second as the silent couple moved away.

The room was deserted. Kathy entered and stood facing her erstwhile husband like an ancient warrior. "Well?"

He was taken aback, but shouldn't have been: her tactics were planned.

"Aren't you being just a touch premature? Robbie's still in I.C.U. and you speak of taking him out of the country. Do you realise how seriously he's been injured?"

"You're still hot on melodrama. Remind me to book a ticket for your latest play. "

"They're sold out, luckily. I'm sure you've a good theatre in Vancouver." Kathy gave him a smile that died at once. She was a consummate lawyer; he was on sticky ground.

"Jo says you want them both."

"Did she?" There was a glitter in the question.

"You know she did."

"Jo's a good friend."

"To both of us. Back to the boys, if you don't mind. Do you know how old Merrick is?"

"Funnily enough I do. Old enough to make up his own mind."

367

Lachlan thought of the temptations in the wilderness as he wrestled to keep hold of his reason. He tried to avoid the idea of a mind being poisoned.

"Can I say that now is perhaps not the best time to make such a big decision, never mind act on it?"

"I think now is an ideal time. Both boys are in trauma; they need a stable environment. Adrian and I can give them that. And a good standard of living in Vancouver. As good as here. With two parents."

Lachlan bit his lip. It was not inconceivable that Adrian would be away from home on occasions, furthering his political career. He was surprised Kathy wasn't flagging that career up for him already. Adrian was not without ambition. Nor 'without the illness should attend it'.

"You're so busy at the theatre. I understand it's not a nine-to-five job, just as teaching wasn't. In fact, you probably had more time as a teacher."

'Teacher' had always struck Lachlan as degrading; Kathy used it all the time. 'Schoolmaster' was too English, too dignified for her. And she would claim they were the same thing.

"Who's that student you've left my children with by the way? I'm not sure that was a wise idea."

"Then go back and see. You called the conference. We shouldn't be away from the unit at the same time."

"You give me three good reasons why the boys'll be better off with you." She said 'bedder' in her lazy American drawl.

"Three?"

In his panic, he couldn't think of one. He'd not been to Vancouver, though people compared it with Sydney and Cape Town. And Melbourne had recently been voted the world's most liveable city. But that was ammunition for travel agents, not sparring parents deciding the fate of two sons.

"Not even one?" The lawyer was in full stride. And she

knew it. Years ago Lachlan had taken two Grade 13 students keen to study Law to witness a murder trial, where they'd heard two brilliant combative speeches from defence and prosecution. Sampras and Agassi with words. But here he was not returning a single serve.

"They're used to me. They're in good schools. They know where they're going."

"Nul points, Lachlan. After a matter of weeks in Canada those claims will be annulled by Adrian and I."

"Adrian and me."

"By both of us." She waited. Lachlan saw her practised eye flick to an imaginary judge.

"No further questions," he snarled.

"In that case," she stood up quickly, "I request an adjournment."

When he walked back into the unit and saw her at the bedside, her posture was more assertive than before. The nurse was behaving obsequiously, nodding in response to questions, suddenly discovering an ally. Was it Lachlan's imagination or did the nurse react in a cursory, almost indignant manner to his return to the bedside?

"I have to go," said the actress, grabbing Merrick by the hand. "My little son needs some rest."

Lachlan thought it the best audition piece he had seen for a long time. He'd forgotten Kieren was still there; the boy had withdrawn on Kathy's return, his easy manner now threatened. The two stared at Robbie, who had fallen asleep again. Deeply, it seemed.

Kieren moved his chair and they sat on the same side of the bed in silence.

"You'll see a lot of this, I expect. In the years to come." The phrase stuck in Lachlan's throat. 'The years to come' was the penultimate line in a World War One poem by Yeats. 'An Irish Airman Foresees His Death'. Lachlan swallowed. His discomfort was noticed by Kieren, but the student

369

couldn't connect the phrase. The 'years to come' for him were laced with promise, immortality, even in a medical student.

"You have to believe he'll pull through, Lachlan."

"But there's no guarantee."

Teacher and taught had suddenly swapped rôles. Lachlan was in no hurry to change back. He waited for Kieren to speak.

"I've not seen many accidents. Not serious ones. But I know enough to realise a lot depends on the faith of the parents..." he stopped. "Parent."

Lachlan waited. "But surely all parents will their child to survive. It's only natural. Isn't it?"

Kieren looked Lachlan in the face. "That's not the same as believing they will pull through. Believe me. Robbie will make it."

The boy stirred at this. Lachlan leaned over him, but he fell back to sleep.

Another silence. Questions were superfluous, though in Lachlan's head they mounted all the time. He wanted to take advantage of a medic.'s time.

Kieren said, "I'm only a student, remember."

"'Only a student'." No one's that in my book. There was a pause. Machines bleeped around them. "I suspect my head's a tad full," said Lachlan, into space.

Kieren nodded. "Whose wouldn't be? Hang in there, 'sir'."

Lachlan swung round to find a cheeky smile confronting him.

Two minutes later Kieren was gone, leaving Lachlan alone with his son, who slept still. Instead of fighting the urge to sleep himself, Lachlan gave way to it.

When he came to, Robbie was awake, expecting conversation.

"Don't talk about Mum, Lachie."

His father nodded. This was an improvement.

"So what's the story with me?"

"Hard to say right now."

"Cut the crud, Dad."

"Right. You're doing better. We just have to believe it."

"I believe it."

"Have you been listening to Kieren?"

The brow furrowed again. But there was no question. Father and son understood one another. He should have given that as one of his three reasons for staying together. But it would have been countered.

"The story, Dad. Tell me the story."

Lachlan was suddenly lost for words. He knew what he felt, but couldn't at this moment ballast it with medical opinion.

"We're getting there, it seems, son. Wherever 'there' is."

"Does it matter?"

"Maybe not. Maybe that's part of the adventure."

"I'd not thought of it as an adventure. More like a trial."

"Well, perhaps we should."

There was a pause. Lachlan was unsure how much Robbie was taking in. "We've got to take it a day at a time. A step at a time."

"Sounds like that game you once told us of in Scotland. Grandmother's Footsteps. Bit of a wuss game if you ask me."

"Depends how you play it, mate."

"Mate." The moment swirled. Robbie sighed. That should have been my second point, realised Lachlan. We're mates. "What do I have to do, Dad?"

"Keep fighting."

"I am. I'm not sure if I can fight harder."

"You're doing well. Just don't let up."

"I want to play tennis better. I want to see your plays. I want to understand more."

"Don't we all?" concurred Lachlan under his breath.

The female doctor who'd shown Lachlan and Kathy to their consultation stepped over the red line.

"That conversation sounds healthy."

Lachlan winked at Robbie. The wink was returned.

For the first time Lachlan felt he could leave Robbie for a night's sleep. Driving Dave's car back to Hawthorn, he saw an ample moon over Burwood. The thought of Kathy on the Newcombes' veranda dulled his excitement, but soon after he'd walked up the steps he realised she was not there.

"Kathy's taken an early crash," said Dave.

The relief was unspoken.

"Coffee, Lach? Or would you rather a glass of red?"

Minutes later Dave and Lachlan were staring at the fullness of the moon. There was no mention of Kathy.

The fly-door slammed and Jo appeared, clutching a glass.

"Remember that evening here when we played 'Therapy'?" said Lachlan.

They nodded.

"I hadn't realised what a good game it was."

Jo nodded. Dave stared at his glass. But it was no prelude to serious discussion. An hour later they were still there. As was the arrant moon.

When Brodie rang early next morning she was hesitant, like everyone else. Lachlan told her Robbie was holding his own at present, but he himself needed to come back to work to take his mind off the hospital. The difficult thing was where to start: he'd been in England three weeks and back in Melbourne for nearly another one. The show was going on; he just didn't know which one.

"It's the end of 'The Government Inspector', and we're into final rehearsals of 'Death of a Salesman'."

Lachlan winced. If there was one play in the repertoire he'd have prayed not to be staging at this moment, this was it, perhaps the best twentieth century tragedy of all. Arthur

Miller inspired him, both as teacher and director; the precision of his stage directions, the range and timbre of emotions he depicted, the craftsmanship his plays embodied. Perhaps his favourite was 'All My Sons'; he'd seen an outdoor performance that stayed with him, young actors doing Miller credit. 'Death of a Salesman' told of the fall of Willy Loman, the father of two sons, who never rose above his position of a salesman, dragging his family with him, though the wife, Linda, was a support he did not deserve.

Brodie did not pick up his drift, thinking it was the work-load that baulked. "We're into final rehearsals, Lach," she asserted. "The spadework's done."

The problem, he realised, was that there might not be enough for him to do. Brodie had clearly coped, with the help of the company. 'People rally round,' his mother used to say.

"What day is it?"

"With me it's Tuesday." Brodie immediately regretted her attempt to be flippant.

"Any rehearsals today or tomorrow?"

"They're called at six tonight. And all day tomorrow."

"I'll come tomorrow."

He hung up without chit-chat. Looking at the clock he saw it was eight a.m. Time for the hospital.

He'd assumed Robbie would be sitting up in bed. He was not. But he was conscious, eyes furrowed. Lachlan felt again the burning need to know what was going on inside his son's head. Someone must be able to explain to him. And logic prepared him for the answer: 'Every case is different, Mr. Stacey. There's no fixed plot'. The irony did not elude him. Plots were unreal, the fulcrum of fiction or crime. Yet 'lost the plot' was understood to mean losing touch with reality, not fiction.

"What're you thinking, Dad?"

"Not a lot. Or rather, yes, quite a lot. Needn't worry you, though."

"Go on, Dad. Worry me. Give me something else to think about."

Lachlan looked at him hard.

"I'm thinking about us."

Robbie waited. "...and?"

"Just how things will end up. For all of us. Your mother. That sort of thing."

"Important stuff then?"

"The most important. Getting you back to normal."

"Whatever that is," said Robbie, echoing the words Lachlan had started to mouth.

"Getting you better."

"Fixing me up, as the Yanks say. What a crass expression."

It was the first sign of humour the boy had shown. Lachlan laughed, unrealistically long.

"Not that funny, Dad."

"That sounds like your brother talking."

"It sounds like me talking. Haven't done it for a while. No wonder you're confused."

"Maybe you should try it more often."

The boy's features darkened. "Am I going to recover, Dad?"

"Yes. We just need time."

Robbie nodded. And went back to sleep.

"Mr. Stacey?" The nurse came up behind him. "There's a message for you. A Mrs. Alice McBride." Lachlan did not recognise the name. "She was in the car that Robbie hit."

"What did she want?"

"Just to see how the boys were."

Lachlan noticed the plural. "Kind of her."

Lachlan thought of Mrs Alice McBride. Driving her children home one ordinary Saturday when suddenly a meteor hits her in the back, propels itself into space and lands in the path of an oncoming tram. The woman would have been traumatised.

"Did she leave a number?"

"She did."

"I'll just thank her. Kind of her," he muttered and with a look at the sleeping patient went out to make the phone call.

Alice McBride was not at home, so Lachlan left a message. He'd far rather have spoken with her, and found himself wondering what sort of woman she was. Kids at private school, husband in the city, living in Hawthorn, approaching forty. A churchgoer. He was amazed at his conventional thinking. She could have been a fit widow of thirty-two in need of enlivening. He felt the urge to ring her back. And say what? I'm sorry you were involved in my son's desperate accident. Would you care to come out to dinner in recompense? He let his imagination roam; it had been locked in transit and would need to function when he went back to The Tinderbox.

And there was no harm in conjecture. Alice McBride. He liked the name. She must have worried about the boys, enough to ring up and ask for information. Lachlan wasn't sure how she knew which hospital, but this was the main one. And how much less worried was she now? What had she been told? She was not a close relative.

His reverie was interrupted by the arrival of a trolley at speed. Its incumbent was shouting abuse, and as he was pushed past Robbie towards a vacant bay, Lachlan saw his upper body was covered in tattoos. There was no uncoloured skin on the torso. His language was foul and it took time to sedate him. Presumably the doctors were anxious not to mix drugs when the man was already 'high'.

Robbie was alarmed by the shouting.

"It's all right, son." His words were lost in a tirade of invective.

The boy's forehead clenched and he reached for

Lachlan's arm. Still the new arrival raged, making conversation impossible. Lachlan held Robbie first by the hand, then the shoulder. Robbie's eyes darted all ways at once. There was a furious climax to the man's ravings and he fell back on the bed. Lachlan was surprised no curtains had been hurriedly swished. One doctor moved away from the bay and raised his eyes at Lachlan as he sped away. A nurse came to the boy's bed, took more readings, and replaced the liquid still dripping into his veins. Lachlan had not noticed it was empty.

Nor had he consulted the monitor.

Alice McBride.

He stood up and watched the green flickering on the T.V. set that never went off. He was compelled to speak to the woman who'd showed concern for his sons. He'd ring from the Newcombes, when she would be in, he hoped.

Robbie had drifted back to sleep, so Lachlan brought out his copy of 'Death of a Salesman' and started to read it. He began with Act Two and was almost at the Epilogue when Kathy strode in, her mask of concern beautifully fitted. Lachlan gave up the chair to her and walked from the unit.

Alice McBride...

"Why don't you go away for a day or so?"

Kathy flashed the question across Jo' s kitchen. Lachlan saw Jo's shoulders contract slightly as she kept her back to her guests.

"You're joking, of course."

"Never been more serious."

"And let you have free rein with the boys."

A torpedo of scorn shot across the kitchen, sinking into its target and stayed there, trembling.

Lachlan left the kitchen. But she was on his tail.

"You're exhausted. You're tense. You're not sleeping. You're crumbling in front of our eyes. You're-"

"Any other charges? There'd be something wrong if I

wasn't. I'm sorry if it's uncomfortable to watch. It's actually quite difficult being in my skin at the moment."

"All the more reason for a break. I said a day, not a permanent exit from the stage you love so much."

Beyond her irony there was a nuance of concern, which made him hesitate. Lawyer's trick? He had to admire her skill.

Jo stood in the doorway, hands fingering the doorframe. She did not speak.

"And let you have free rein with the boys?" he repeated.

Kathy shrugged. "Intensive Care is not exactly free rein." Again she slurred the 'not exactly' in her lazy, infuriating drawl. "You need –"

"Space!" The word shot out before he'd registered it. Jo sidled away into the darkness of the hall.

"Go down the coast. It needn't be far. Have a good night's sleep, some sea air and you'll be refreshed."

Lachlan was staring at a fridge magnet, a tiny bottle of wine with 'Chateau Talbot' inscribed across it. A brief respite would be welcome, but he could not leave Robbie in hospital.

It was Dave who convinced him late that evening. He'd be on the end of a phone; Robbie would not lack visitors; Lachlan needed the break. Dave stalled him before he could protest that he was putting on the Newcombes again.

"We're just providing a bit of green in No Man's Land..."

"... and trying to silence two artilleries," completed Lachlan.

"Just one night, Lachie. That's all."

Lachlan raised his head. "Perhaps I should sleep on it." There was the hint of a smile, as he bade Dave goodnight.

But he lay awake, confused as to where he might go. The Ocean Road was not ideal with its memories of their holiday at Easter. Sydney was too hectic. Adelaide too far for one night. He didn't fancy driving. That meant a short flight, which put Sydney back into the reckoning. He could see Kerryn. He could taste the sun. And the Emerald City was only an hour away. In the first hours of another day's angst the gremlins of sleep lowered their portcullis.

He rang Alice McBride; again she was not at home. Again he left a message. But he was disappointed, having rehearsed his opening gambit.

"I'm the father of the lad who hit your car." On reflection that made it sound as though Robbie was on a charge of assault. Again Lachlan was struggling with words.

He drummed his fingers on the table. Then rang the airport and booked a seat for Sydney.

He was unsure whether to tell Robbie, but one look at the lad's anxious face when he walked into the unit told him that he must, though not straight away.

Kieren had looked in again, the nurse informed him. The girl had become part of their team. Lowering his voice, he told her of his planned temporary escape, expecting a reaction, thinking it would help. The nurse looked calm and nodded, turning back to her charge, whose eyes remained closed.

Lachlan was saying a prayer, its words reeling in the air, out of order, frantic, when Robbie opened his eyes.

"Still here, Dad?"

"I'm always here." The sentence stung. "But tomorrow..."

"Yes?"

"I have to miss coming tomorrow. In the daytime. Can you survive?" Fatuous enquiry.

The boy looked puzzled. He did not answer.

Lachlan sat with him for a couple of hours. There were no encouraging signs. As he got up to leave, Robbie was in a deep sleep. Lachlan looked towards the nurse, aware that he appeared guilty. The man with tattoos was shrouded by curtains. Everything was familiar now. Lachlan picked up his bag and went downstairs quickly. All that way to return to the same spot. Jumping into a taxi, his breathing was hard. He would have to stay calm, but Sydney would clear his befuddled brain. Spots of rain landed on the windscreen as he made a decision. He would climb the Harbour Bridge.

CHAPTER THIRTY

"I've taken the boys. Both of them."

It was as if the voice came from behind him. Lachlan resisted the temptation to turn round. The plane had levelled out, but he could still see orange ground far beneath him. It worried him that he had found no mention on the news of the previous day's accident.

The man next to him had 'The Daily Telegraph'. Lachlan found himself staring, willing the man to fold his paper away so he could ask to read it. The accident would be mentioned in the paper. Its owner had long fingers curled over the tabloid, and glasses that made him resemble Clark Kent. He became aware of Lachlan's gaze.

"Want to read about the Swans?" he asked in a deeper voice than Lachlan had imagined.

"Not the Swans." He paused. "I wouldn't mind seeing your paper when you've finished, though."

"Have it now."

Lachlan tried to leaf through the bulky paper with nonchalance; he failed.

"You got shares mate?"

"Not exactly. No. Just –" the sentence hung. As did the other passenger's gaze. He took off his glasses.

Lachlan was breathing fast. "I need to see if there's a piece on something I saw yesterday."

"A show? Or a game?"

"An accident."

The man folded his glasses in his long hands. Lachlan was tense, thinking the man would ask more questions. He thumbed through the paper, but could find no reference to the event. Far from being calmed, he was more anxious, handing back the newspaper with a vapid smile.

"No joy?"

The two words sunk deep. His eyes filled and he looked away, fumbling with shoes that he had taken off, as usual when flying.

"No joy," he said quietly to himself, aware that his fellow traveller still surveyed him. His eyes closed.

At the airport his luggage was a long time reaching the conveyor belt. The foolishness of disappearing for twenty-four hours was strident in him, and Kathy would have taken full advantage. But she could not have made off with both the boys.

He took a taxi and was annoyed to find the driver was a friendly Greek with plenty of questions.

"Had a good trip?" he asked cheerily.

Lachlan nodded.

"Where were you? Brissy? Adelaide?"

"Sydney."

"Smart city. You've been before, of course?"

Lachlan did not reply, but looked out of the window. It was a squally Melbourne day, rain splatting across the glass, then blown away.

"Better weather in Sydney, I bet."

Lachlan felt his rage climbing.

"It's usually five degrees warmer in Sydney. Or so they say. I've never been." The last statement was accompanied by a chortle that cut itself off. "No, Never been."

Ahead of them, traffic slowed. Lachlan's heart shifted downwards. Three lines of vehicles were easing to a stand-still, for no obvious reason. He looked at his watch. It was 1.49. He was due at The Tinderbox for four, which left little time for Robbie. More space for Kathy to act.

He knew the full confrontation had to come, but his

381

absence, instead of sharpening him for the fight, had done the opposite, so he was fearful now. He thought back to the woman's accident he'd seen from the bridge and his picture of toys stood up by unseen hands. Impatient, he leaned forward to see if the traffic was moving. It was not. The driver of the car behind had climbed out to peer through the murk. He could see little and lit a cigarette, catching Lachlan's eye as he flicked his match into the air. The man looked like Adrian, same build, same belligerent stance.

"Happens all the time these days," said the taxi-driver. "Makes you wish you'd put your bike in the boot."

At the mention of bikes, Lachlan jumped out of the taxi, slamming the door, and stood facing the way they'd come, drumming his fingers on the wet sides of the vehicle.

When the taxi started to inch forward, he was engrossed in thought. There was a hasty beep, and he jumped in.

"Something on your mind?" said the taxi-driver.

Lachlan bit back the retort. He stared out of the window all the way to the hospital.

Once there, he ran through well-known corridors, springing round the banisters and upstairs like a boy. Steadying himself at the door of Intensive Care, he affected calm and walked in, his breathing betraying haste.

Robbie had gone. In his place was the man covered with tattoos, who threw an expletive at Lachlan, then spat something from his gnarled lip. There were three nurses in the unit, none of whom Lachlan had seen before.

"Excuse me," he said. Two nurses turned round, one putting her forefinger onto her mouth.

"I know, I know," he thought aloud. "I've been living here for the past six days and nights."

"Do you know where my son's been moved to? Robbie Stacey?"

Visions of her response assailed him: "Discharged. He's gone to Canada. I thought you knew. You're his f –"

The nurse went to the central station and returned

promptly, though not before more foul words had been hurled at him from the tattoos.

"He's been moved to Springfield. Turn right, down the stairs, along –"

Muffling his thanks, Lachlan was gone. But once down the stairs he suddenly forgot the name of the ward. He scanned the signs, but none looked hopeful. Then he saw a makeshift piece of cardboard with 'Springfield' scrawled on it and an arrow pointing to a corridor where renovations were underway. He cursed, and ran down the narrowed space, his bag bumping behind.

Robbie was sitting up in bed, three or four away from the entrance. Lachlan saw a pair of woman's shoes crossed over beside him, but a screen covered the visitor from view.

"Hi, Robs," he exuded and leant to hug the lad, fearful of letting him go. Still with one arm on Robbie's shoulder, he half-turned to the visitor.

"Hetty!"

He pulled himself upright, relieved. Then held her to him. Hetty looked less strained and he noticed two books lying next to a Borders' bag.

"Some decent reading, Robs?"

The boy's eyes showed a mock rebuke, then he smiled.

"You could do with a good book yourself, Lachie."

It was the first sign of the old Robbie that Lachlan had seen. He was giving himself up to the realisation when he caught Hetty's agitation.

"What is it?"

The woman seemed paler now. So did the boy. Lachlan stood up from the bed, trying to capture them both in his gaze.

"Kathy's due any minute," said Hetty, her face, no longer bright.

Lachlan looked at his son. What he saw gave no clue. Then footsteps sounded behind him; he did not turn round. Kathy ignored him at first, kissing Robbie on both cheeks.

To Hetty she was cool.

"We're meeting at five," she levelled at her husband. "Our plane leaves tomorrow at twelve. Robbie will join us in a few weeks, God willing."

She had used many tactics, but never blasphemy, keeping it up her sleeve till needed. The master tactician. It was futile to mention he was due at the theatre.

"And the way Robbie's going, it will be a very few weeks," she triumphed, running her hand through his hair. "We'll be ready for him then."

Lachlan refused to look at Robbie; he dreaded any indication that Kathy was going to win this tug-of-war.

In the silence, Hetty twitched. Lachlan thought he could see Robbie looking into the near-distance, but he was not sure. The clock on the wall said 3.05. Silence hung. He noticed Kathy's necklace, coloured stones of different shapes run through a thin stick of liquorice. Old habits had been cast off. Her neck was slightly tanned, but he was struck more by the absence of perspiration. She was infuriatingly cool.

Hetty bent down to pick up her bag.

"I need time with Robbie," Kathy said, in a matter-of-fact tone.

Expectation grew. No one moved. Robbie had closed his eyes. A galaxy of conflict stirred in the small space containing the four of them. Hetty took a step away from the chair. Kathy lifted a cold hand to the necklace, another notch on the shield of victory she would polish later. Lachlan bent down for his battered bag, muttered a farewell to Robbie and followed Hetty out of the ward. Behind him, he thought he heard a faint voice saying thank you for the books.

There was no one in at the Newcombes. It was coming up to four p.m. He dreaded the chime of their clock, normally so welcoming, and walked onto the verandah, turning a biscuit over in his hand.

When the phone rang he was skewered by dread. He heard Dave's voice on the answer-phone and stood poised to move away if Kathy's strident voice followed the short bleep, barking instructions.

"I'm sorry to trouble you again. But I was hoping to speak to Lachlan Stacey. My name is Alice McB –"

Lachlan ran to the phone, picked it up and pressed the button on the answer-machine. On the other end the voice stuttered.

"This is Lachlan Stacey." His voice bit back at him.

"Hello?"

"Hi! Can you hear me?"

There was a brief pause of relief, Lachlan was not sure on which end of the line.

"Mr Stacey, I've been trying to reach you…"

"I know, I –"

"– to say how sorry I am about the accident."

"But it wasn't your fault."

"I'm not sure it was anyone's fault." Her voice held gentle assurance. Already she was calming him. "Might I ask how Robert it? It is Robert, the one who…landed on the tram tracks?"

"Robbie. Yes. It's him. Thank you for inquiring. And for ringing…more than once." He paused, suddenly aware that he'd had no medical comment on the boy for two days.

Alice must be presuming the worst. "He's out of I.C.U." Lachlan's voice returned. "Came out yesterday."

"I'm so relieved."

"Me too."

"It's a desperate time, I know. I just felt guilty." She went on to describe her part in the event, innocuous as it was. The wrong place at the wrong time, like every other accident. Lachlan thought back to the Bridge. He was no longer listening to the calm voice.

He was jolted back to it by the harsh swing on the fire-door, and Kathy's strident bootsteps in the hall. She was motioning to her watch, like a parent telling off her child for being too long on the phone.

The calm voice picked up his silence. "This is probably a bad time. I didn't expect you to be there in the afternoon. But I had to keep trying. I needed to speak to you. Thank you."

"No, thank you. For the call." He was thinking there was only one way of ending the conversation and its moment was close. But he wanted to ask her out to dinner, to offer free tickets to the theatre for her and her husband...

"Do I have your number?"

"I'm not sure you'd need it now we've spoken."

"But Robbie may want to speak with you when he's better."

He sensed her smile. "I don't expect so. He probably wants the whole episode forgotten as soon as possible. I would. We're in the phone book, in the unlikely event. Do give Robbie my best wishes. And your other son. I feel better for speaking with you. Goodbye."

"But I –" The line was dead. Between that quiet unknown voice and the panther prowling in the kitchen, Lachlan could not imagine a wider rift. He turned to the door, wanting to have a walk, clear his head before the pitched battle to come. It was 4.09. Kathy was alone in the house, putting final touches to her tightly packed argument.

He stopped and retraced his steps. She was making a cup of coffee, gazing into the garden. He strode in.

"Right, Mrs. Stacey," he launched. "Would you like to take the stand?"

She was not surprised. Futile to have thought otherwise, he realised at once. She finished making her coffee and licked her forefinger with its garish nail varnish, a habit she knew he abhorred. She was impressively controlled.

"Not here," she said. "It's not fair on the children. Merrick could walk in at any moment."

"You're so considerate...when it suits."

386

Kathy reached for her coat, slipping into it with ease; tension eschewed her. "We need to be in the open."

"In both senses."

Her look conveyed he'd had no need to highlight her pun. Lachlan saw three suitcases as he passed through the hall. Reaching for his car keys, his hand knocked against her mug of coffee, spilling a little. She stared at the splodges of brown liquid.

"Aren't you going to mop that up?"

He threw her a look of disdain, and made for the front steps, the fly-door slamming, hopefully in her face.

She had her keys, too, but Lachlan made for his car, unlocking the passenger side. After a moment's hesitation, she demurred, eyes fixed on him. When their difficulties began, she had asserted control by driving the family everywhere, something he didn't realise at the time. Easing out of the Newcombes' suburban calm, he headed for the freeway into the city. Already a stream of cars was escaping in the opposite direction. Once he was moving at high speed, he risked a glance. She was staring straight ahead. Many of their early rows had been in the car, not having to look at each other.

"Where are you driving to?"

He ignored her, desperate to call the tune in some way to prevent her being totally in charge.

In fact, he did not know. The M.C.G. flashed by, its lights already on. Trains thundered past, hurling occupants to their few hours' Sunday evening respite before the morning's drudgery began again.

The traffic lights stopped him on Richmond Bridge. Below them, the Yarra slunk into gathering darkness. This time yesterday he'd been changing out of his Bridge-climb kit, a moment both an aeon and a nanosecond away. On impulse he now swung right off the main road, along the towpath towards the boathouses. An 'eight' was carried across in front of them, its cox holding up his hand in thanks. He parked the car beside a red Scotch College minibus and moved towards the brown mass of water. Kathy followed in her own time. He turned round once, then headed for a bench, where he sat down.

It was the setting for a duel, mist lying low over the river, few people about. Joggers ploughed along the towpath, rugged up against the August night. Kathy stared into the river, adding to its coldness. Lachlan was not going to open the batting. She spoke at last, still not looking at him.

"You'll try to resist me, of course. There'd be something wrong if you didn't. But you'll lose."

Then she glanced at him, waiting.

"Kathy…" So many words had crammed his head; he'd rehearsed every combination. Now they had fled.

She was still looking at him. Two more joggers flicked past, their breath visible for a moment, before they overtook and devoured it.

"I can't let you have them both. Even when Robbie's better. It wouldn't be…"

"Yes?"

"Right. Just. Fair!" he screamed, already aware he'd lost the first round with his outburst, and that she would remain cool. Argue with an iceberg.

"Merrick needs the attention of us both." She was too polished to state the obvious, but Lachlan was partnerless; the accusation hung.

"That may not always be the case," he said.

"Irrelevant. It is now. He's been with friends for over two weeks. Good as they are, he's not with a parent. He lacks parental love…"

"They are our kids' godparents," he burst.

"It's hardly the same. They have their own kids, who could do with a bit of attention if you ask me."

Lachlan's anger brimmed. Clearly no one was to escape her scorn.

"He's only with them for the moment. When Robbie's

better…"

"When Robbie's better you'll be back at the theatre, and we'll be back at square zero."

She shifted on the bench, crossing her legs. Even now her legs were attractive. Lachlan blocked out invading memories; everything about her was calculated, there was nothing natural. She should be a politician, he thought sharply, and saw she was watching him, knowing his thoughts.

There was no point in fabrication. With its hours his job was impossible. That was not going to change. Ironically, teaching would be marginally better.

Lachlan suddenly found himself smiling.

"What is it?"

"I've seen the headlines in your Canadian papers. POLITICIAN ADOPTS ABANDONED BROTHERS. ACT OF ALTRUISM INTERRUPTS POLITICAL AGENDA. This will be wonderful for Adrian's career." Sounding the man's name induced bile in his stomach. "You're going to marry Adrian, I suppose?"

"Nothing to do with you."

"It's everything to do with me. If my kids are involved –"

"Our kids. Yes, I am going to marry Adrian."

"When, may I ask."

"Whenever suits –"

"His agenda. I'm sure it can be cannily rescheduled in the interests of two homeless Aussie boys."

Lachlan swallowed. Would they call Adrian, 'Dad'? Would he be impatient with them? Their questions? Their curiosity?

"It will be so much better for them," she said, quietly. "And they are the most important, you'll agree?"

She had always been a master of rhetoric.

"You see everything so keenly," he said. "In such a clear-cut, legalistic way. It's not like that." He paused, on the edge of a tirade against modern justice. Instead he said lamely,

"Of course they're the most important."

There was silence. No joggers passed. Nothing moved on the river. The greyness deepened into torpor.

Lachlan looked down at his feet. His nights without sleep were pulling at him, darting like barbs into areas of his mind where there might, for a second, have been space. Numbness seeped into crevasses of air, sealing them spitefully like elves at the end of a mission.

"I've booked three tickets to Vancouver tomorrow. Single."

"Three?" His temple beat hard in his head.

"Merrick, me, Adrian. I'll come back for Robbie in a few weeks' time. When we're ready for him."

"When you've got wheelchair access for him you mean? And twenty-four-hour carers so as not to hamper Adrian's political progress?"

"That was unworthy. Even of you."

His hand lashed out in the darkness that was trapping him, sealing him into an inescapable fate.

"And physical violence? Well."

He looked at her, anguish moulding his features. For a second he was outside himself, looking at a face that on stage he'd take hours to get right in someone else. Demons were tickling his brain; at any minute they would invade.

A lone sculler floated towards him, moving slowly, hunched over the blades with exhaustion. His shirt was sodden with sweat. Lachlan saw himself in the fragile craft, unable to move on, to make progress in any direction. His tense breathing had returned.

Kathy started gathering up her bag to leave. She remained polished, imperturbable, searingly cool. This was a boxing match with no need for the referee. She stood up, exulting in victory.

"If you could help Merrick pack I'd be grateful. Any little things you might have that he'll need. Jo and I can do the clothes. We've started already, of course."

"Of course."

"If you can do that immediately. Adrian and I are meeting friends for supper, so you'll have some space. Which is what you were about to ask for, I suspect."

"It wasn't actually. Almost the opposite."

Her eyes danced at him, sprites on ice, in aspic, relishing the extent of his defeat. A cyclist with no lights swerved as a dog ran across his path, then breezed on, his bike wafer-light between steady hands. Kathy lifted her eyes to the city. She was waiting to deliver the final blow.

Lachlan did not wait for it. He rose, swiftly from the bench, trousers sticking for a second to its cold slats, and reeled away. When he was sure to be out of sight, and earshot, he sank to his knees, and wept.

He came to himself some time later. It was pitch dark now, headlights scorching as cars raced from the city. Lachlan felt cold. He was preparing to walk back to the Newcombes, forgetting Kathy would have taken a taxi, so the sight of his vehicle was a surprise. He put his key into the ignition, then pitched forward onto the cold steering wheel. Driving back to the Newcombes was futile. Then he remembered Kathy was going out; with luck, Dave and Jo would be alone. He urged himself upright; the car crawled away from the river.

He had failed to make the rehearsal, and dreaded explaining why, even to Brodie. On reaching his friends' haven he hauled himself up the steps just as the clock chimed seven.

The next day he was back at work, dazed but determined. If he kept his mind on the play, all thoughts of Kathy's departure with Merrick would be kept at bay. He was glad the company was working on a tragedy: comedy would have been more facile than ever. Brodie sensed his anguish and said little, watching acutely when Lachlan showed Willy Loman how he might tackle the last desperate speech before he took his own life. The actor sensed he was being afforded unusual stimulus: he, too, watched Lachlan hard. By the end of the rehearsal all three of them were exhausted, so Brodie's suggestion of a quick drink at Southgate was welcome. But Lachlan said little. Then he sped off to visit Robbie.

Arriving back after two hours at the hospital, he found only Dave, reading in the lounge. For the first time since the accident, Lachlan made no attempt at courage. The suit-cases had gone.

"Tell me," he said gravely, refusing Dave's offer of a glass of red.

"They left about ten, I gather. Jo drove them all to Tulla. And they were due to take off on time."

That was it. Lachlan stared at the carpet. He'd not intended to say a painful goodbye to Merrick, but his insides felt stretched, and his eyes seemed curtailed by their sockets. Blood beat insistently in his ears.

Dave was reluctant to go back to his book, though Lachlan wished he would. The house was still. Suddenly Lachlan looked up at his friend.

"I don't know about the red, but have you a shot of whisky?"

It was November 5th, Melbourne Cup Day, and scorching hot. Robbie had been out of hospital for ten days after his three months there, and Hetty was staying with them to assist. David and Jo had gone to Queensland for the week-end. There had been no communication from Canada for several days, but the morning's post brought Robbie a letter from Rebecca, awash with stamps. Vibrant colours assailed the eye as robin, greenfinch, merlin, kingfisher and golden oriole blazed from the envelope. Robbie smiled as Lachlan put the letter into his hand. He steadied his wheelchair and rubbed a calloused thumb over the stamps.

"Robins fight to the death you know, Dad." He waited for Lachlan to reply. His father was watching him, a vision of red breasts spilling blood on an English snow scene.

"Not always, son. Not always."

Robbie reached for a knife to open the letters; it jumped from his hand and landed on the floor. Too quickly Lachlan dived to retrieve it.

"I could have reached it, Dad. In the end."

Lachlan resisted his urge to open the letter for him, and handed Robbie the knife. Tortuous minutes later, the boy had extricated Rebecca's blue notepaper from its temporary prison.

My dear Robbie,

Saul and I are thinking about you a lot at the moment, and hoping very much that your recovery continues. It was grand to hear you are now out of hospital, apart from your check-ups. We imagine you getting stronger every day, so it will not be long, God willing, before you can walk again and abandon the wheelchair you call your 'pram'. Dad says you've become quite a competent driver lately, which does not surprise us; you're not a lad for sitting around twiddling thumbs.

Saul is going to America next week, on business, a place called Louisville in Kentucky. They have good racehorses there, I gather, and he is hoping to see something of them while he is there. It must be around the time for your Melbourne Cup, which, I seem to remember, is the first Tuesday in November. I wonder if there'll be a winner like Phar Lap, who survived a kidnap attempt on the way to Flemington racecourse. I saw the film with Dad, many years ago now, and enjoyed it greatly.

Iain rang the other evening and seemed in quite good form mentally. I think Dad's visit jolted him, which is perhaps no bad thing. I worry what he'll do when he comes out of prison, but there's a bit of time before that happens, is

393

there not?

Excuse more. It's cold and dark here now, with Hallowe'en tomorrow, so must collect my broomstick. Take care, and look after Dad. You're both in our thoughts and prayers, (as if that needed saying).

Keep up the recovery; we're with you all the way. No need to reply to this, unless you fancy a quick phone call.

God Bless You, Robs.

Lots of love, always
Rebecc.

P.S. If this arrives in time, put five dollars on number 10 in The Cup. We'll pay you back out of the winnings.

Robbie thought for a second, then passed the letter to Lachlan. "Where is Kentucky?"

"Not sure exactly. My geography's not up to much as you know."

The boy's eyes registered mention of a school subject on which he was missing out, but he said nothing. Hetty came in with a bag of shopping, complained about the heat, and went into the kitchen.

"What is number 10 in The Cup, Dad?"

His father walked to the table and pulled the day's racing supplement from 'The Age'. There was lots of coverage given over to the big race, where this year the favourite was a horse shipped over from England that had run second in the Caulfield Cup, always a pointer to the more famous Melbourne Cup.

"Number 10…Toll Bell."

"Don't fancy it myself," said Robbie. "Let me see the field."

While he perused the runners, Lachlan went into the kitchen. Hetty was waiting for the kettle to boil. The phone rang and Lachlan picked up, a faint image of Alice McBride in his mind. It was Brodie, with a rehearsal schedule for tomorrow. The next play was a comedy by Peter Shaffer: 'Lettice and Lovage' about the guide at a stately home who embellished the true facts of the place unashamedly. It was crisply written, and was proving fun to direct.

"I'll be there all day," he said, casting a glance at Hetty, who nodded. "Got a horse for The Cup?" His co-director did not. He hung up.

"I'm taking Robs for some air. Probably the Botanical Gardens. Should be quiet today," he told Hetty.

"On a public holiday?"

"We'll risk it. Back in a couple of hours or so." He grabbed a couple of chocolate biscuits, and a baseball cap for Robbie.

Pushing Robbie's wheelchair down to the café in the Botanical Gardens, Lachlan was assailed by the sun. He leant forward to see it was not too fierce in the boy's eyes.

"Don't worry, Dad. I can stand it."

The voice was more like it used to be, but Lachlan felt angry there was no animation in his son's shrunken frame.

They sat outside, Lachlan with a coffee, Robbie a coke. It was busy, patrons in holiday mood.

"I wonder what Merrick's doing." The words seemed hollow, the voice flat. "It's his birthday tomorrow."

"Still in bed, mate. They're a long way behind us, remember."

"In time."

"In lots of ways," said Lachlan. He was suddenly tense, not wanting the boy to be in control, drumming his empty coffee beaker on the wooden table.

"Relax, Dad."

"I am relaxed."

"Really? We have to talk about it sometime. Why not now?"

Beads of sweat dripped from Lachlan's eyebrows, stinging his eyes with salt. He clenched them shut.

"It would be easier for you if I went," said Robbie. "Wouldn't it?"

Lachlan exploded, then stopped in mid-sentence. Robbie was looking away, embarrassed.

"I'm sorry, son. No, it would not be easier."

"You won't admit it. It's so hard with your job. And there being just you."

"Hetty's with us, isn't she?"

"But not for ever. There's really just us."

Lachlan was looking out over the lake, trembling. Canada geese strutted on the furthest bank. Adrian and his Parliamentary cohorts. Lachlan was helpless.

"I can't be a burden, Dad. Not to you, when you've so much else."

"I've nothing else." The words slipped out like brigands. He risked a glance at his son, who was looking in the other direction.

"I think about it all the time," said Robbie after a pause. "And I miss Merrick."

"Do you miss your mother?"

No answer. Lachlan wanted to say the boy was still traumatised, still hurting, on the recovery trail. Platitudes. Neither of them spoke. Eventually a frail voice issued from the wheelchair.

"But I'd rather stay here, Dad. If that's…"

Lachlan nodded. His shoulders gave way and he lurched forward, sobbing silently. The boy tried to reach him with an arm, but the wheelchair was too far away. To move it would be melodrama. When Lachlan finally sat back, he saw his son looking at him hard.

"Isn't there a race on that we need to watch? Your sister has a fortune running on it."

His father nodded, stood up and moved behind the wheelchair, releasing the brake. Two geese streamed overhead with a sudden din. The beating of wings was startling. Lachlan looked up, where the sun cut into his gaze. Ahead of them three youths, ignoring manicured pleas to the contrary, threw a 'footy' ball on hallowed grass. The tallest of them watched Robbie's wheelchair pass by, then pulled a face for his mates. One laughed, one did not. The thieves crucified on either side of Christ.

Scores of people were now walking in the direction of the city, some in black tie, ignoring the sun, others strode out in tails. Girls in skimpy cocktail dresses and high heels broke into a trot to keep up with their men. Several held glasses in their hand. A man stopped just in front of the wheelchair to replenish his girl's empty flute. Staring at her, not the glass, he spilt the champagne on Robbie's leg.

"Watch what you're doing," said Lachlan. The man took no notice; his girl pranced away. Lachlan put the brake on the wheelchair and came round so he could see Robbie, squatting down into the sun. The boy turned his head; his shoulder shook, once.

"Next year, I'll take you to The Cup," he said, putting a hand on the boy's knee. Robbie looked at him, but he said nothing.

"We'll go early and make a day of it. I'll ask the Newcombes along for a picnic. We can fill the hamper and –"

"Mum's taken the hamper."

Lachlan paused. Since Kathy's departure he had not done an inventory.

"Well, we'll buy another."

The boy looked at him, trying to smile. His facial muscles were still slack from the accident. Lachlan felt impatient. For a moment father and son were in limbo.

"Let's have another drink." Lachlan pushed him towards a kiosk. "What will I get you?"

"Just a lemonade, Dad. Thanks."

When Lachlan returned, the boy had tried to move his chariot out of the sun. Like Bucephalus. Lachlan waited for a couple to move away from a nearby bench; they made no

397

attempt to clear their detritus. They left a newspaper rippling in a squall of breeze.

"We can make our final selections, if we're quick." Lachlan turned the paper inside out.

Round the corner came a jester; his hired motley was too big for him, so he resembled a teletubby in his graceless movement. Robbie smiled to himself. Then a couple of vicars ran by, followed by a tramp, holding out his top hat as he passed. Lachlan dropped his coffee cup in to it. The group was completed by a hooded figure in black, with a white skeleton emblazoned on his chest. There was no sign of the scythe.

"Who's he supposed to be, Dad?"

"I think he's The Grim Reaper."

"Who's The Grim Reaper?"

Lachlan leaned across and told him. Sitting back after an unconvincing explanation, his eye fell on the newspaper.

"What's your horse then, Robs?"

The boy was trying to feign interest. But his dark eyes swam.

"I'm not sure I can see them, Dad."

"I'll read them to you."

Lachlan did so, after which there was a pause.

"Rebecca's on Toll Bell. I'll go for Born to Dream. What about you?"

"The favourite. Border Farmer. Even if it is English. They have to win sometimes."

"You're on."

Lachlan ran behind the wheelchair, scattering pigeons into a bush. The sun seemed hotter still. He thought he heard Robbie laugh, and bent the chair back on two wheels. The boy looked quizzical upside down.

"Speed up, Lachie. We might miss the race."

They lurched away, past a prim lady with her golden retriever and a gardener working on a flower-bed as delicately as a doctor. Unusual on a Public Holiday, thought

Lachlan. Slowing for a moment through the gate, they gathered momentum on the cinder track.

"Not fast enough!" shouted Robbie. A twig snapped under the wheel. Ahead of them a tram squealed. The air was tight around him, but Lachlan pushed on. Sweat hovered over his eyebrows, but he shook his head, avoiding the sting. There was quite a gradient coming up. They neared the obelisk where once he'd walked with Brodie to settle a theatrical dispute. A dog barked. He saw a little girl holding a kite, craving the breeze. He saw the birds on the envelope sent by Rebecca. He thought of the coming novelty, directing a real comedy, to make his audience laugh.

"To the wire!" roared Robbie, waving his arms with renewed glee. "You can do it, Dad. Sprint!"

Lachlan slowed for a second, then hurled himself on, meeting the gradient, riding the wave, breasting the rise, out of the chasm. Out of the tunnel. Into the future. Hope against hope...